THE BLACK SPRING CRIME SERIES – CURATED BY EDITOR LUCA VESTE

Praised and endorsed by some of the biggest names in Crime Fiction…

'Time to strap yourself in.' **– IAN RANKIN**

'I love, love, love great new crime fiction. How do I find it? Usually I ask my friend Luca Veste. I owe him hundreds of hours of great reading. Now he's doing it for real, not just for me - he's working with Black Spring Press, which means they're going to have a crime list that everyone will get excited about - and everyone will buy. Luca Veste is our genre's best talent spotter - Black Spring Press will be one to watch.' **– LEE CHILD**

'Crime fiction is going through a new Golden Age, finding readers looking for strong stories that explore the world around us and the problems we face. An independent publisher like Black Spring is the perfect fit for these fresh new voices and ways of seeing - and in Luca Veste they have a crime editor who knows the terrain like a skilled tracker. A great writer himself, he has an eye for the brightest and best. It's going to be an exciting and enriching journey for readers. Time to strap yourself in.' **– IAN RANKIN**

'I know nobody with their finger more acutely on the pulse of crime fiction. I value his recommendations; they show a great eye for what's worth my reading time.' **– VAL MCDERMID**

JASPER'S BROOD

JASPER'S BROOD

JK NOTTINGHAM

it takes a killer,
to raise a killer,
to raise a killer.

This edition published in 2023
By The Black Spring Crime Series
An imprint of Eyewear Publishing Ltd.
The Black Spring Press Group
London, United Kingdom

Cover design by Magali Nishimura Nottingham
Typeset by Subash Raghu

ISBN 978-1-915406-63-7

Black Spring Crime Series Curated by Luca Veste

www.blackspringpressgroup.com

for Magalita, Tobi, and Oscar. You make every day joyful xxx

One

Saturday, 5 January

The man who killed my family

Dear Gulliver,

On the night my family died, I'd run away from the beach house, and they feared I had drowned.

I wanted that.

I was eight years old.

I hid among the dunes for hours, slinking from one patch of wispy grass to another, watching the coastguard desperately running up and down the shoreline shouting my name. As if my parents had not already spent two hours doing the same thing.

And my brother, Craig, was there too.

He was ten.

He didn't shout my name as though he believed I would really answer. He lolloped along the shoreline where the others ran with every ounce of energy they could muster. Craig looked tired anyway; tired from fending off all the competition from the other Under-Tens Champion tennis players. Tired from all the attention he had to endure at the party my parents had thrown in his honour.

Was I jealous?

Of course, I was jealous.

It was never supposed to happen like this. Craig was good at everything, I'd made my peace with that, but he never made it to the absolute top of anything. Someone older or more experienced always knocked him out.

However far he got, he always had to lose eventually – but there I'd be, looking up to him anyway.

Not this time.

This time he didn't need me at all. I was eight years old and redundant.

I was also frozen.

When I started this little game, I hadn't banked on taking it so far. The sun was still out – low in the sky and inspiring the onset of a warm wind, but still definitely t-shirt and shorts temperature. The wind turned hostile very quickly, and by the time the beach was beginning to attract 'helpers' who actually just wanted to know what the fuss was about, I was feeling as sorry for myself as I thought I would if I really had been washed out to sea in the dark. I was so cold I began to believe I really was lost – and I began to think that perhaps, as I must seem quite believably pathetic here in the cold, if I could just manage to slip past the zombie beach combers and into the water, I might be able to roll out of the breakers convincingly enough to fool them that my imagined ordeal had been real.

But Craig knew.

Dragging his heels.

Perhaps he even knew I was hiding up in the dunes.

He never looked my way, but he stayed close and there was never any chance I could break past him to hit the fierce, rolling black waves. Silently I wished he would just go away, I wished Craig would stop casting a shadow over everything I did, and

I retreated a little over the land side of the dunes. Silently, I wished Craig had died before I was born, and I started to trip along the bottom edge staying in shadow, mindful that folk in their beachfront houses might see me if the light caught me well enough.

I wished I was the first child my parents had had, and then I started stomping my feet in petulant aggression. I imagined I was a giant, and with every step my parents grew smaller, and my brother faded.

Then, to my horror I realised I wasn't alone on this side of the dune. A man was there beside me a few paces down, striding in the same direction. His stride was massive, purposeful. He clearly didn't think I was anybody to concern himself with, so my fears were quelled. This was not my father, this was not the coastguard, this was not my father's friend Jerry or the local snooker hall proprietor or his customers. They were all still combing the beach, shouting at the waves, hoping for a miracle.

Hoping to be heroes.

There would be no miracles on the beach that night. I sighed with relief and carried on acting out my gigantic fantasy, but I kept one eye on the man.

He was the tallest man I had ever seen.

I was eight.

Since then, of course I've seen taller men.

I've killed taller men.

He was wearing a bright yellow t-shirt with a tuxedo over the top, buttoned once at the front and sticking out at the back, riding the crest of his buttocks because the tux was too small. He wore a baseball style cap with a cartoon on the front and that was why I was looking at him, there was writing on it I wanted to see. I continued my striding leaps in tune with the tall stranger, straining for a glance at his cap.

Then, I stamped down hard onto a broken bottle.

The pain was respectful enough to linger in the wings, awaiting such a time as seemed reasonable to launch itself into a spinning pirouette towards me. That time turned out to be well over thirty seconds; enough time for my slight vocal cords to muster a shriek, and my muscles to throw me violently backwards. I lay for a brief moment with my eyes shut tight, clutching my foot, and dreading the sound of approaching people called by my shriek, but there was only the whistle of that hostile wind, so I forced open my eyes and picked up my right heel to examine the deceptively clean looking glass-wrought gash. These were the final few seconds before pain took its cue, and I spent it curiously sliding my nail underneath the flap of skin, and lifting it upwards as far is it would go. Sand, and ooze came out, green glass specks glinted there too. Green against the deepest red, like pistachios on raspberry sauce, and the white of the bone flashed impossibly far from the surface of my heel.

The tall man was off in the distance. His rhythm hadn't faltered, and a few strides later, seconds only, he'd been enveloped by fingers of mist lying low in the gully.

The pain in my heel suddenly just splintered over my head like a hurled porcelain teacup.

Focused, vicious.

My blood was pumping onto the sand – the white dunes streaked with red, me still holding my heel, torn between squeezing it tight to make the pain retreat a little, or standing up and running to… where?

I was stranded.

And my breath was betraying me. Trust me, you find out what it is to really cry from physical pain when your breath won't leave your lungs without riding on the back of a pathetic kind of whimpering, nevertheless loud enough to carry upon the wind, whipped away into the night seeking the nearest willing ears.

Being alone and renegade wasn't fun anymore. T-shirt and shorts flapped in the bitter wind, just to demonstrate how thin they were and how inadequate to maintain my life throughout the freezing night to come. I pictured them finding my body, with the trail of blood stiff and jutting from my heel like someone skewered me with a raspberry ice pop. It seemed like a real enough conclusion to my ordeal. A two-headed silhouette, briefly outlined atop the dune, pausing there to look out to sea.

The last time I saw my parents.

Scanning their surroundings for any tiny sign of me even though it was too dark to see anything that wasn't clearly outlined against the sky.

Then Craig, head bobbing as he ran to join them, his silhouette then subsumed into their bodies.

Together.

I hollered to them. I shouted. I screamed.

But the cruel wind snatched away my words, and threw them back in my face un-heard.

I cried as the heads of my parents gradually became one with the dunes.

Back to their beach-side cottage.

Did they cry for me there?

What was the plan?

My mother to stay and look after Craig?

My father to tool up like Rambo?

Search through the night?

Scoop me up in his arms and carry me to safety?

It was a long time to be alone.

I curled into a ball drawing my knees up inside my t-shirt. I grabbed my wounded heel with my hand, so my palm sank painfully into stickiness, and every time I moved even a millimetre the grains of sand and specks of black stuff between my hand and the gash worked their way deeper inside and scratched their way further towards their new home hollowing out little caverns inside my flesh, forever.

To move my foot, excruciating.

To attempt to walk or even crawl, unthinkable.

Of course, I never heard the shots.

But I know exactly what they sounded like; I've heard the same more than a hundred times since. A click and a swish instead of a bang. A dull thud instead of a loud crash.

A coroner's report told me years later, that my mother had taken the longest to die. Her throat was pierced in an awkward manner that stopped the blood flowing out quickly. Her death was even more physically painful than it was supposed to be, but still silent, wordless. She would have had to watch my father and my brother both bleed to death on the kitchen floor in front of her, while she wondered whether she would actually die, or not.

She died.

With my father and my brother. She died. And while I lay shivering, quaking from head to foot and believing I was bleeding to death, almost fainting from the pain, my parents and my brother were, actually, bleeding to death.

Life is funny, isn't it, Gulliver?

And in my delirium, when strong arms scooped me up and I could smell that this was not my father, I reasoned it must be the coastguard.

I thought somebody from the houses with their lights on had spotted me huddled into a sand recess that I'd dug out with none of the skill a dog possesses to do the same.

Worse than a dog, me.

People can't survive in the wild – not comfy people.

Spoilt children.

Bundled between the folds of a coarse blanket and swung along like a rubbish sack on its way to landfill. I was scooped up without explanation. Even curled up in sand the slightest movement had been overwhelmingly painful so now, my raw wound scraping against rough woollen, sand filled weave, I simply screamed, and writhed, and clutched my foot desperately trying to hold it away, and tried in vain to make somebody hear.

And breathlessly, I shouted,

No. Stop. Please. No. Stop.

It was when I was slung onto a spongy surface and heard car doors slamming next to my ear that I was able to fling away my cocoon, and found myself on the back seat of a very cold car with shiny leather seats.

I sat there with my fingernails digging deep around my wound, and panted.

Tears streaming.

At the wheel was the tux-wearing tall man.

I whimpered but couldn't get words to form.

He just crunched the car into gear and started driving. I managed a stuttered syllable.

Wha, wha, wha...

And the tall man said,

Jasper, if you don't want to be dead as well as kidnapped, shut up.

His name was Foster.

Two

Sunday, 6 January

How I Killed Your Parents

Last night I slept on my plinth in the Crypt for the first time in weeks.

I dreamed of our past glories, but I woke up screaming, and probably scared the children.

All because yesterday I took delivery of your blood-soaked herald, Gulliver, and I couldn't face a night alone in the caravan.

I thought you loved that dog?

I shuddered to imagine your thin lopsided grin as you prepared it, and that one pointy tooth that always protruded. To me you were always a little absurd.

Goofy, even.

I hope a part of everyone can see a monster in such light.

Well, thirteen years I've longed to see you again, so come back and finish me off, if you feel you must, Gulliver.

Don't misunderstand; I'll fight you even though the idea breaks my heart.

Pitting your youth against my broken body with middle age only a rear-view memory, only a fool would throw their chips behind me.

In case I don't prevail, I'm going to tell you everything.

It is not my intention, Gulliver, to bring back bad memories. Foster neglected my needs on many different levels whatever his motivations toward my welfare. I want to tell you about your parents, to bring you out of darkness, not from any misjudged idea that you might stop hunting me if I enlighten you; I'm unburdening myself just as much.

This might be hard to learn, Gulliver. Even before your mother met your father, your mother was working for businessmen; hotels during lunch breaks, brief liaisons early in the morning, late night after drinks, sending them on their way ready to go to war with each other.

Ready to rule the world.

However it happened, whatever she charged, that was your mother, Gulliver, and before they were married, your father was her client.

The man who paid me to kill your mother had collected an obsessive amount of data. He'd been waiting, plucking up the courage to engage my service.

It's never the right thing to do. But I'll do it. Don't smoke, don't eat fast food, don't ride without your helmet, don't drink beer instead of water for three days straight when you've run out. Never the right thing to do, but someone, somewhere, benefits.

He waited so long that your mother married your father and had you.

He waited out the years, dreaming of your mother's demise.

All because he spent the night with her.

Just once.

But once was enough.

Your mother saw an easy opportunity.

Extort a handsome sum from the guilt-filled family man.

Cash for silence.
But he didn't bite.
He called her bluff.
No bluff.
Now his wife and children live in Florida.

Your father messed it all up for himself by arriving home too early.

How could I know he'd lever you out of school in record time that day?

Why did you have to pick that particular day to be extra compliant in putting on your coat, your scarf, your gloves?

All my research confirmed you were consistently a nightmare – giving him the run around for at least twenty minutes; hiding in cupboards, launching missiles from the stairwell, sneaking all manner of contraband into your pockets.

Unwrapped sweets.

Other kids' asthma inhalers.

The hamster.

Not that day.

I'm not saying it's your fault.

Seduction came so naturally to your mother; why shouldn't she use her natural gifts to save her life at the crucial moment?

I'm not proud of myself, Gulliver.

Your mother's attention was intoxicating.

Perhaps I let my guard down.

Difficult to say, though.

You know those times when you feel you'll let this play out as far as you safely can, see how far it might go before you end it?

Because you *can* end it.

Any time you want.

It's a power thing, right? I know you've played those games, Gulliver. Heck of a self-esteem booster in the moment.

But in truth, if it wasn't for your father...

Well, I'm sure I would have regained control of the situation before...

But anyway.

There he was.

A moment to absorb the scene.

A howl of rage that I instinctively assumed was aimed towards me, and then he was lunging at her, his thumbs bound for her neck.

Curious, isn't it, Gulliver?

What causes a man to crack...

I had to make a split-second decision: which one of them gets to see the other die? I figured I'd be merciful to your father. From the look in his eyes it seemed he wanted her dead as much as my client did.

So, I obliged.

Seconds later he was with her on the bed, their blood pooling together in the centre of the mattress.

Gulliver. I am sorry.

If I'd known you were outside the door – I would have protected you.

Are you more like your father?

Or your mother?

Gulliver?

Well, you looked more like your father as you launched yourself around the door frame with your little fingernails clawing at the air between us.

To stay eight would be wonderful.

Eight is a perfect age, you're old enough to appreciate that life is good, intelligent enough to make your own fun and choose your friends with discernment, while also secure in the knowledge that anything as scary as a meaningful exam is still years away, nobody is expecting you to work for them, nobody is expecting you to feed them, nobody expects you to do anything except be eight years old.

I tried to preserve that for you, Gulliver.

Even when you filed your teeth into little points and burnt off all your hair so it would never grow back – I still told myself I could preserve your innocence.

Of course, I was aware of the similarities between taking you home with me, and Foster scooping me up fourteen years previously.

But it was a different thing altogether.

For a start, you knew right from the beginning it was me who killed your parents. You knew because you saw us there, you saw their blood and you could only draw that conclusion.

Hang on. It's not what it looks like, son.

I wouldn't have insulted your intelligence.

Do you know how long I had to live with Foster before the truth was revealed? The truth that I wasn't just kidnapped and crippled, but I was kidnapped, crippled, and orphaned? Almost six months, Gulliver. Six months of hoping for the wrong thing, not just that I would be returned to my parents and my brother, not just that things might go back to how they were before, but that I would be able to ask them to forgive me. Do you understand how utterly devastating it was for me to find out that I could never be forgiven? I could never say sorry to my brother – my brother who always looked out for me, who put his neck on the line for me again and again, made sacrifices and took beatings in his role as the eldest, my brother who I couldn't allow to enjoy a moment of glory that didn't involve me in some capacity. The acid churning in my gut, of my risible selfishness from the day they died, has never left me.

I live with it.

Gulliver, don't you see? I was never supposed to kill you.

I didn't spare you.

Foster spared me.

He spared me when he first saw me beyond the dunes, and when I fell on the bottle, and when he passed me on his way back to his car.

Gulliver, for whatever reason, this man, this killer, decided that he wouldn't kill this child, this eight-year-old boy, even though he was contracted to do so.

I wasn't saving you from anything except growing past eight without a strong parental figure in your life. I was destined to remain Foster's prisoner because I could otherwise become his downfall. But you, you hadn't even seen my face – there was nothing about self-preservation in what I did – it was selfless, and I'll stand up for that statement before the Crown, before my Creator, before my mother's headstone. My intentions were pure. I wanted to make something right from all that wrong.

I know you didn't appreciate the black plastic bag or the sock I stuffed in your mouth.

Please understand, it was the fastest way out of there, to get you as far away from the bloodbath as possible, but I know it never really left you, and you know what? Me too.

In times of moral quandary, I can still smell your mother's perfume.

Three

Monday, 7 January

Jack, in a box

Foster said very little in the few days after he kidnapped me – on his kitchen floor he silently laid out my camping mattress and sleeping bag.

Threadbare carpet.

Cigarette-smoke stained walls.

The flat was three rooms – a bathroom with no bath or shower, just a purple, yes purple, toilet with a matching sink, and one of those carpets that moves when you stand on it because it was just laid across old, pitted lino rather than fixed in place. Then there was a bedroom, which was Foster's domain – I was only allowed in there on very special occasions, like when he was excited about showing off a new rifle, lining me up as quarry through the sight. Foster's bedroom was quite large, especially compared to the kitchen, but it only had a small, wire-framed single bed in it, with no wardrobes, only clothes on hangers hooked over the picture rail.

There was one picture, the only picture in the entire flat. It was difficult to get a good look at it because whenever I was in Foster's bedroom I was there for a reason, I had to concentrate on what he was telling me, but my glances over time told me it was a picture of a little boy who would have been about my age when I arrived there. He was standing in a field wearing Middlesbrough FC kit and grinning. The picture was tiny – lost within the stippled light pink wall, slipped down slightly within its stylish frame covered in an intricately pattered fabric of burnt umber.

Yes, Gulliver, *that* frame.

Then there was the kitchen, where I slept. I say kitchen, it doubled as a living room I suppose because there was an armchair in the corner that was so old you could hear the padding crunching beneath you as it turned to dust inside the covers. The fridge, oven, and sink all sat next to each other along one wall. No lino or tiles denoted that this was the kitchen area – the threadbare carpet continued, and the fridge and cooker sat on top of it, with a sink crudely screwed onto the wall above – a plastic waste pipe tacked to the wall and running out of the house by the shortest route with no attempt at concealment.

Of course, I noticed very little of this when I was eight – back then it was just a place – I took it all for granted, but you don't sleep on the floor in a room that isn't really yours, for ten years, without noticing a lot of details.

The first time Foster called me Martin, I hardly noticed. In the course of ten years it only happened another four times, but two of those were in the first year.

That first time, as always, it was when his guard was down because he allowed himself to get exasperated. I would learn quickly that the low rumbling sound I could hear when I was exasperating Foster, was his teeth grinding against each other. A glance at his face, and there was the vein – raised from his jaw to his temple.

I have told you already, Gulliver, that Foster was a tall man. Even after living on his floor like a dog for two days, I still only had an impression of him as a tall man. I knew his voice was unexpectedly high, but I only knew that because of the warning he'd given me on the back seat of the Allegro. He hadn't actually spoken to me since. I hadn't attempted to talk to him either – I was stiffly, clammily, terrified, so I lay there in my sleeping bag tensing all my muscles.

I was still bleeding copiously from my heel – I could feel the slight wetness, but it went numb after a few hours, so I resolved to forget about the gash.

That was a mistake.

I've borne the resultant pain for the rest of my life, but at the time I felt like I had no option.

By the second day I seriously needed to pee. I was writhing in my sleeping bag, Foster sighed, and broke his silence.

Toilet.

He said, standing over me and gesticulating over his shoulder with his thumb. I looked up gratefully, into his unblinking eyes, and I felt relief when I couldn't see malice behind them. I leapt up hastily, only partly from the urge to pee; mostly from wanting to do Foster's bidding, to make him feel I was on his side. But as soon as I leapt up, I knew something was wrong. My right foot was sluggish – and it felt wet again.

I looked down and saw why.

The sleeping bag had become fused with the bloody mess of my heel – creating the illusion that the material was actually a part of the flesh. In standing up so quickly, I'd ripped open the wound and it was pumping my blood out onto the threadbare kitchen carpet.

I hesitated, and looked up at Foster feeling a horrible mixture of pain, and fear.

His face a picture of exasperation.

Just go pee, Martin!

As I say – I hardly noticed what he'd said. I plopped off to the little bathroom as quickly as I could, leaving a bloody trail behind, terrified that Foster would lay into me for ruining his carpet. But when I'd finished peeing, he was cleaning up the blood as best as he could, and he used a towel to cover the stains where I had to sleep.

We both had to wash blood off our hands, and he helped me step up to the sink on an upturned bucket.

In retrospect, Foster should have put alcohol on the wound, or something.

It was the start of the most physically painful time in my life.

Beach debris trapped deep inside – sand for the most part, but splinters of driftwood too, glass of course, and little bits of black stuff I couldn't identify. It was impossible to coax it all out, though believe me, Foster tried his absolute best using tweezers, sandpaper, even pliers. Lots of stuff came out, but there was always more, and the last fragments were embedded so deeply that they looked like an integral part of flesh; the raw flesh inside, behind the skin, that you're never supposed to set eyes upon. Foster scraped those excruciating depths, to no avail.

All of which was painful, certainly, but nothing compared to the agony I went through once Foster had given up, then the infection set in. The entire sole of my foot puffed up like a balloon. The wound gradually started to close, though it wept green mucus perpetually. For a few weeks I couldn't walk at all. But more than the physical pain, I found myself missing Foster's attention, and I began to realise that the intimacy we'd shared as he tried to clean my wound, was a very rare thing indeed.

I felt, abandoned.

Foster didn't leave the apartment once during that time – he'd stocked up on dried food and tins of soup. I understand that – I do it too. Not that anyone would ever find the Crypt, but I wouldn't want to be seen shopping or pushing myself to the fore in the days following a hit.

You just cannot be too careful.

After three weeks, the pain in my foot settled into something I felt less as a hostile attack, and more as the invasive leeching of an unwelcome presence. I don't know – does the mind simply find a way to by-pass the pain, or did my flesh manage to stave off the growth for a few years? Many years later I came to realise that my bones were playing host to a marine fungus, basically a mushroom. Maybe my pretty meagre diet kept it at bay? Maybe familiarity took over; in the end, if constant pain becomes the new normal then you can't be sure it's still there, can you?

Whatever the cause, I was grateful for the relief.

The result was total numbness, like that feeling you have after sitting on your leg for a long time, before it wakes up and the interminable 'pins and needles' begin. I stumbled around a lot, but you soon learn to trust that something is hitting the floor to support you, even if you can't feel it at all.

I wasn't invisible; the local kids knew Foster had a kid they didn't see much.

A kid they hadn't seen for a while…

Eventually, almost a year into my time with Foster, after I'd proven my myself, he started taking me outside in the street to kick a ball around with him in the failing light.

And the local kids would join in, uninvited, but unchallenged.

You been with your Mam?

None of your business!

Foster would spit.

That was that.

I guess he was concerned for my health, and these times were extremely rare treats. The local kids began calling me Jack, because sometimes when I landed on my foot awkwardly, a stinging pang would shoot through my sole and I would either leap in the air or buckle into a ball.

So, I was Jack – like Jack in a box.

Nobody thought I was Jasper.

Missing Jasper.

Four

Friday, 11 January

Fairfax

Did you ever consider Michael to be your equal?

Not professionally, of course.

He had other talents.

Anyway, Gulliver, I couldn't compare you to any of the others professionally.

I cannot help the slivers of pride I feel for my part in what you've become, though mostly I feel that the world would be a better place without you, then guilt comes and I have to remind myself that none of my other children have grown so expertly impassive.

No, I mean to ask whether, in all those years spent together with Michael, did you consider him your brother?

I should feel like I had achieved a little good if so. Come home in peace, Gulliver. Michael is gone, so there's no jealous brother left here to resent you, but I'll happily kill something fat in your honour.

I know you resented the choice I pressed on you during the Fairfax job. Did you regret the decision you made, Gulliver? It is true that if you had made the counter decision, I may never have rescued another child, and then you and Michael would have been the only ones.

If the rescued cannot become the rescuer in the same context from which they themselves were rescued, then what is the point of the rescue? That was my philosophy then. Nowadays I don't know what to think. I have heard reports of course, that you have no such conscience these days, and I shudder to think what that means for your victims.

Sorry, your *marks*.

Fairfax may not have been your first hit after taking my Zippo to your hair, and filing your teeth down to sharp little points, but the way you held yourself and embraced your new look that night does stick in my head as the first time I felt we were partners.

Not yet equals, but something close.

I also consciously chose, that night, not to be overly concerned about your mental state. It might seem silly, but when you torched your scalp and revealed your spiky werewolf grin in the days after that very first hit, I did worry that I'd got something wrong. I think this is natural – I imagine it's the same feeling as when a teenager decides to get a tattoo.

How much do you worry?

How much you do support the self-expression?

But looking at your confidence and actual enthusiasm on the night of the Fairfax job, I decided; this kid is going to be ok.
One of the nicest things about contract killing is the gratitude. The ones who help you, hire you, who knew the deceased and want to show how thankful they are to be living in a world free from them.

Indirect, of course.

Messages passed on.

Invitations extended through a Pigeon.

Yes, I've been to the funerals.

There were no messages of gratitude after Fairfax.

I approached Fairfax with a fair degree of apprehension because I knew about the children. You know, don't you, Gulliver, how rare it is to be asked to remove both father and mother? That is why there might be years between the need for a rescue. It's not our place to question why a client would want to orphan a child. I cannot ask to pick and choose the twists and turns once the road is chosen. And yet, the rationale behind Fairfax was clear, I believe.

Clear, but so cold.

One only has to look at the unbelievable wealth of the Fairfax shareholders today to see what impact the death of the family has had upon their lives. There is no point in being respected, well established, reliable, if new blood in your chosen field is picking off your customers. One old man holding back the company out of pride for his brand tradition, while their main rival in toy car manufacture is branching out into batteries, even computer games; certainly motivation enough for a strong-arming into slightly early temporal retirement.

But what of his wife and son, and his son's wife and their children? I know you don't care for the whys and wherefores, but to me they are important. It was more than the destruction of a dynasty. Oliver Fairfax would have toed the shareholders' line. He'd no interest in the integrity of his father's business. No, we were hired that night, Gulliver, to create a story worthy of mass public outrage and sympathy. We were hired to provide a new enemy for the people of tabloid England – those no-good punk kids – the ones who set the fire. Those no-good, disaffected, television watching, computer game playing, punk kids who callously and knowingly burned an entire family.

A decent, respected, good old-fashioned toy car manufacturing family, callously burn to their deaths in a locked death trap of a mansion.

Sympathy sells.

Outrage sells.

Righteous indignation sells.

Do you know something, Gulliver? We may even have been responsible for the diversion of actual children from becoming real no-good punk kids. The few sacrificed for the many. They're not the ideals I would choose if I was first into the ideals shop and rifling through the racks at the dawn of time, but these are the ones I found left on sale after the crush, and they fit me well enough, so I make them work for me.

You see – nothing is so clear-cut as one would like to believe. One can be good and bad all at the same time, and an action taken that you always wonder about can always be justified. By the same standards it can always be condemned.

I hate fires.

Thank goodness for Foster and everything he taught me. I may be the last person on Earth who should be allowed to possess a moralistic threshold; but I do, and it's burning a person alive. There are perfectly good ways to burn a person without anybody knowing they were dead before the fire began.

Smoke inhalation.

Clear lungs.

Signs of struggle.

It's all get around-able – but it does take a long time to plan.

Remember, Gulliver?

I couldn't have done it without you, even though you were just eleven.

I've had other fire gigs since, but not on that scale with little people to rescue, to boot.

Not part of the plan.

It leaves me cold now to think of how easily you agreed to dig those bullets out of their mangled necks.

I was grateful.

Little fingers.

Precious minutes.

We were laughing.

I think it was because of the slapstick nature of the 'frying pan behind the neck' trick. Good one though, no bullet holes in walls. No splatter. That was a Foster trick - I often think he'd have made a great ballistics expert; a consultant in our field.

You were very sweet with Emily and Ricardo right from the off.

More attached to them, I think, than you ever were attached to Michael. And yet, they liked him more, I feel. You may deny it, Gulliver – I suspect they found you a little creepy.

Who could blame them?

Your blotched baldness and werewolf teeth. Little hands always slightly raised and your fingers twitching – you always looked like you were going to strangle something. In fact, that night on Fairfax when you went to pull Ricardo and Emily out from the flames, I did think you might have misinterpreted my intentions, I thought you were going to throttle the infants to make sure they didn't need to suffer being burned alive.

I'm not sure that you wouldn't do such a thing.

But whatever you might do in the same situation today, faced with my question, faced with the power to grant life or allow the black smoke of death to engulf them, that night you mustered enough compassion to pluck the children from their otherwise murky fate.

You were kind, Gulliver,

You were nice.

You were actually quite delicate with them once you'd clamped your hands over their mouths.

They were Emily four, and Ricardo six. Imagine the shock for the poor creatures, while the flames licked around their ankles they were spirited away by a phantom-esque child, with blood dripping from his fingers up to his wrists. Actually, that probably had a big impact on how they perceived you thereafter, Gulliver. You can't blame them for that. Their big trusting eyes, Ricardo clutching his teddy with one hand and his sister's hand in the other, those are the times when my conscience gives me one hell of a trip.

It was easier for them in the long term than it was for you and Michael, though. Adjusting to life in the Crypt, I mean. Because really, how much did they remember their parents? Or their grandparents?

I know they've seen themselves in magazines a couple of times at least.

They retain a certain celebrity status.

You don't.

You've been long forgotten by the fickle public, but Ricardo and Emily have legend.

The 'Fairfax Dynasty mystery children'.

Even now, a couple of decades on, they're still being used to sell die-cast model cars. It may not have been in the remit to swipe the kids, but by heck did they get more than their money's worth in the process.

Of course – I know even less about their movements these days than I do about yours, Gulliver. For all I know, they could reveal their existence to the world, emerging blinking from the darkness to claim their fortune and tell their story.

I'm almost certain they won't do that.

But I was almost certain you'd never turn against me.

So, what do I know?

Five

Saturday, 12 January

I must be a puppet

Sergeant Willows thinks he's caught a scent.

I've never really feared him succeeding in finding the Crypt, finding the children, finding me. I've always considered those things to be highly unlikely.

He's always just been annoying.

He's an annoying man.

But he was sitting on the bonnet of Martha's chunky Russian 4x4 today, waiting for me outside Tesco in the fading mid-afternoon January light. I really wanted to get home before dark, but he wouldn't budge - an uncharacteristically bold stance for Willows. And he fired some 'proper' questions at me that he must have dusted off from an old 'how to be a policeman' manual.

I've always thought he likes me, Sergeant Willows; always been sure he thinks I'm alright.

Do you remember when he used to lie in wait on Laromer Road? Sitting with his speed gun, pretending to do traffic duty when really he was just waiting for us to trundle along in the Allegro? Ha! Then you'd have to hide, and I'd end up taking him back to the Round-Table Terrace flat to drink tea.

He wouldn't even ask me questions.

I think he pitied me.

He knew about Foster, and about my family.

Guess at the very least he thought I was a basket case; a nut job haunted by my past.

A card I was delighted to play.

I always had you on my mind; curled up inside that compartment.

That wasn't ideal, but there was really no other way.

I still have nightmares about the time you came face to face with Willows, Gulliver.

That horrible ice cream van rolling around the corner playing the theme from M.A.S.H. Always the same tune — just to remind kids like you they were missing something good if they didn't get in on the action.

You - breaking cover - running outside.

The piercing wail cutting through the evening air.

Drowning out the plinkety plonk tune.

Willows's little car revving up, skidding to a halt in front of the line of kids.

The blue light left flashing.

Grabbing your shoulder.

Your scary little pointed teeth sinking into his hand. Despite your recklessness, that did make me proud, Gulliver.

But breaking cover was foolish.

Suddenly there I was.

Childhood abductee.

Crippled loner.

Day sleeper, night-time walker.

Outside with a pale-faced child nobody knew.

Do you know how many questions I had to field?

How many times I denied all knowledge of your existence?

Like Peter denying Christ, or maybe the other way around.

How do you convince an entire unit of officers that you didn't know the child who clearly ran out of your own flat? How do you convince them that all the dead peoples' details they stick in front of you have nothing to do with you?

The bloodied remains.

The charred remains.

The bruised remains.

The bloated remains.

Of course – all of that was old for me anyway – they'd squeezed me through that mangle before – but I couldn't be wrung out.

It was looking bad for you.

I thought you'd be carted off to some awful hostel, or kids' home. I should have known you wouldn't pull any punches in escaping. I was pretty surprised at your brutality – I mean, I know it was what I'd trained you for, but actually, Gulliver, there is only one person I've pushed off this mortal coil who wasn't a direct contract hit or collateral in the line of duty.

I never kill to get myself out of trouble.

But that's just me.

You're different, I know. You were only twelve though, Gulliver. But that was when you crossed over the threshold from extension of another's hand, to cold-blooded killer.

His name was Robbie Buchannan.

He had two brothers.

I hope they never come for you.

So, it seems Willows has changed tack after all these years, and he's yapping for my head on a plate.

If you don't get me then he might, I suppose. I'm not sure which I'd rather.

Willows' problem for the past twenty-five years has been short-sightedness: thinking Foster was the killer, and I simply the victim.

Even after, as part of my separation from Foster's orbit a few years before I met you, I told Willows face to face exactly what Foster did for a living.

And revealed myself as 'missing Jasper'.

Presumed dead.

Not dead.

Cue limelight.

I helped the police artist sketch Foster's laughable 'likeness', and I painted the picture for Willows: You won't find him, he's too good, like a shadow; gone to ground to escape underworld wolves and sharks after a contract hit went off-piste.

That was where they found me.

Wading through the gruesome aftermath.

Dragging behind me an understandable trauma convenient in restricting my openness.

Willows slotted together the jigsaw pieces he possessed, and he fashioned into existence the ones he didn't have.

He did a good job – they fit very neatly.

But they're bullshit.

And so I believe he has always since suspected that Foster controls me still, hidden in some windowless lair.

I imagine the scenario was completed nicely for Willows once my few days in the limelight had passed, and I used my handy benefit cheque bolstered by incapacity allowance to pay rent on Foster's recently vacated flat on Round-Table Terrace as soon as it was no longer deemed a crime scene.

Why would I want to live in my 'prison' of over a decade? With so many terrible memories?

I must be a puppet, and Foster my master.

If it wasn't so convenient, I might take more umbrage at his assumption that I can't really operate without Foster's guidance.

It's hard to take one's adversaries seriously when they couldn't even keep you still long enough to take a meaningful photograph.

After you flew the coop they were left with no evidence to hold me, just the enduring memory of a ghoulish child with animal teeth and no hair.

Still, Foster's old place had to go, after your little escapade. Good cover for solitary me, bad idea once I had responsibilities.

Anyway, that was well over two decades ago, but Willows has always clearly been niggled by me; why else would he so frequently abandon the big city lights and sojourn to little Penshaw? There must be myriad other demands on his time. On one level I'm sure he thinks I'm the key to filling the last shelf in his trophy cabinet. But I've come to realise it's deeper than that, there's a stalemate between us; I may also be his 'tell-tale heart', beating, beating, beating beneath the polished precarious pedestal his shiny career stands upon. Delightfully, Willows is scared of me for the things he thinks I may know, or might have seen when he was a young officer and I was an abducted child.

But I'm getting ahead of myself.

If only I knew what I'm supposed to know.

From time to time I'll find Willows watching me make my way around Tesco; he'll pass by the end of my aisle too often and too slowly for coincidence - his trolley never gaining more items. And I try not to buy too much food all at once, but really and truly, what if he does see me filling up Martha's car with enough food for ten people for two weeks?

Maybe he'll arrest me for gluttony.

Perhaps for having enough money to buy food when it appears I don't work or collect my benefits any longer?

He actually came by the caravan a few weeks ago, pretending to care about my well-being, promoting trauma counselling.

Still, good to shoot the breeze with an adult sometimes, even a dim one.

On that occasion he was only too glad to come in for a cup of tea – he had a good old poke around; I saw him clock the fact that there were boxes of food stacked up around the edges.

I asked him. Am I a marked man?

He just laughed nervously.

He clocked the cat food and asked me outright.

Do you have a cat?

No. I said.

And I looked at him as though he was the crazy one.

That was funny.

But today outside Tesco, sitting on the car, he narrowed his eyes at me in a way I didn't like at all. It was quite hurtful; he's had some kind of a revelation, and after all these years I think he truly suspects me of more than association.

Something's got him excited about your mum and dad, and he keeps dropping in little references to the Famous Fairfax mystery. *Nobody would blame you, Jasper, if you found yourself more than a little preoccupied with cases similar to your own. Obsessed, even.*

He said.

And I asked him.

Don't you have real criminals to track down in the city? Much more satisfying than getting yourself lost in the deep forest of my troubled mind, Sergeant Willows.

He could only muster another nervous laugh, and he did that pointy thing where you touch your fingertips to your eyes then at the person you want to feel surveilled.

I think he's frightened enough to back off.

For now.

Is it you, Gulliver?

Did you tip off the Fuzz?

Surely not…

You wouldn't abandon me to the unsubtle ministrations of local law enforcement.

Would you?

Six

Sunday, 13 January

Horror Night 1: Stacker and Ballsy

I'm glad I didn't know the Harrington job would be our last together, Gulliver.

Declarations of finality are meaningless.

Who can know?

Hiatus, is a much better approach.

I was sweaty palms nervous because there were children involved, and my dreams the night before were haunted by visions of your brutality from the hit on Lucrezia's foster home. There's a necessity, of course, to approach darkness somewhat in our line of work, but at some point you overtook me – I would even go so far as to say that I have started to slide more towards the light.

One changes as one gets older, you see.

I don't regret taking on Harrington. We gained so much from it after all. But there's no denying the seismic 'before and after' effect it had.

A chasm between you and Michael.

You and I, torn apart.

I suspect you've come to regret your treatment of Michael afterward. Even if he did make a mistake, you must know he didn't wish you any ill.

It must have been hard for Michael when you and I would barrel into the Crypt on a post-hit high, congratulating one another, and re-telling the glory moments from multiple angles. After the only time I took Michael with me, after seven hours sitting in piss and shit, he spent almost as long scrubbing himself clean.

I pledged to keep him in the light.

There's a fragility in Michael that made me want to save him in a different way. In the early days I think you did too. Did you realise, you were his constant? I saw you protect him in subtle ways – I saw you step between him and Lucrezia when she was hell-bent on destroying his confidence with her sharp tongue.

I saw you place a firm hand on Ricardo's shoulder when he was ready to square up to Michael for taking an extra blanket. I saw that you left your own blanket on his plinth when he wasn't looking.

Say hello to your brighter side from time to time, won't you?

If I never taught you this, I'm sorry.

Remember the Grey Horse?

To drink and laugh and throw caution to the wind, that was a masterstroke. In that dark nook on a drizzle coated Thursday afternoon, even your white domed head and spiky grin couldn't bring us unwanted attention. I have never advocated Dutch courage, but the Pigeon's notes made it clear our mark would himself be soaking up the Scotch from sundown. I limited us both to three straight drams, and it certainly took the edge off my pre-job anxiety.

We were a jerkily advancing skeleton army as we marched upon Paulie Harrington's faux Tudor pile, hidden only by the drizzle and half-light of late evening. The trees lining the gravel approach waving at us like oppressed peasants welcoming their liberators. Did I bow in their honour? I remember my face near the gravel. And your spasmodic moves to the rapid-fire beat of whatever Day-Glo TV show pulsated through the twins' bedroom window.

With the touchpaper lit, it's down to the unknown factors inherent in each hit to decide whether it's a slightly damp squib that you're forced to coax through the motions, limp, and empty, culminating with a pop, not a bang. Or whether instead the whole thing bursts forward crackling and spitting through an erratic, exhilarating flight.

Often the difference depends on the age and vivacity of the target. Too often the target is an old man, and the motive is revenge for fraud, or covering up their own fraud.

It boils down to greed.

Conduct your work for the joy of it, even if you only find a little joy in your work. Focus on that joy or else you'll go crazy and become consumed with greed; the only carrot dangling will be money. You know how unimportant the money side of things is to me don't you, Gulliver? Would I choose to divide my income between so many dependants if I wanted to be a rich man? Part of the reason I survive in this profession is that most of our contemporaries, once enough wealth is amassed, skip the country to live out their days in some pointless existence cultivating more and more flesh to render leathery beneath the sun.

Lazy, greedy, miserable.

I digress.

Little joy is to be found in arranging the demise of an old man jealously guarding golden eggs, or one sitting upon a lifetime of bitterness – though the satisfaction may be claimed in considering them mercy killings - there is little challenge.

No thrill in the chase.

No equality.

Paulie Harrington was one of the good ones.

Paulie was always going to put up a fight.

Perhaps on a different night, we might have dispatched him from afar, a rifle shot unseen and clean as he passed a window. Instead, we knew tonight Paulie would be shut up in a concrete bunker built into the foundations of his home.

Bunker… or, more accurately, gaming and home cinema room.

No girls allowed.

Last Friday of every month, Paulie's latest Mrs Harrington would up sticks and head out on the town with the girls; Paulie's mum and their housekeeper, along for the ride. Paulie was left babysitting the twins.

The reality was the ritual of 'Horror Night',

Paulie and his heavies, Stacker and Ballsy, vegetated in the bunker watching a horror film from Paulie's VHS collection, chosen at random on his roulette wheel. Scotch on the rocks flowed. A video child monitor set up beside the widescreen TV to keep an eye on six-year-olds Georgie and Anthony, who themselves were allowed to watch DVDs and drink Dr. Pepper into the small hours.

Any renegade child issues, Stacker and Ballsy took turns stomping upstairs and yelling the riot act.

Uncle Paulie never had to leave his giraffe skin armchair, and Horror night remained undisturbed.

So, we decided on Horror Night.

No point in a long distance hit when you're also planning a double mercy kidnapping.

Uncle Paulie was a man who could have been targeted for the chop by any one of a hundred ill-wishers; a rare and dangerous brand of mobster combining razor edge intelligence with raw muscle, and a spirit of indiscriminate ruthlessness.

I have never found proof of my client's identity, and that's as it should be (nothing worse than a leaky Pigeon), but the delightful level of detail available concerning Paulie's habits leads me to strongly suspect this was a family matter. Although Paulie's business dealings and many alleged grievous bodily maimings had been widely reported and speculated upon, there was one aspect of his life the popular press failed to cover.

Paulie's brother, Clark Harrington, who lived a decidedly poorer part of town, was not intelligent, neither was he brawny. Assuming my hunch is correct, I guess he was somewhat of a coward, too. I can only guess that his motive was revenge for Paulie having coaxed his pregnant wife away from him, six years earlier, since when he'd been left at arm's length in a bedsit surrounded by similar dwellings inhabited by Paulie's henchmen.

'Protecting' him.

My speculation goes further to imagine that Clark was eyeing Paulie's ill-gotten material gain. If that's the case, then I don't know whether I'm sorry for Clark. He probably didn't deserve for Paulie's accountants to vanish with the bulk of the cash, but he really should have seen it coming. My theory is further bolstered because I never saw a penny from that hit, Gulliver, not a penny. I was to be paid after the hit – the client begged the Pigeon, and the Pigeon begged me via several muffled phone box conversations - to take the job for cash on completion.

The begging was unnerving… but I'm a sucker for a sob story, even if it's one I've fabricated myself.

We did get little Georgie and Anthony out of it – they proved a great boon on so many occasions.

Everybody leaves.

I was looking forward to being on heavy duty that night, rather than trigger. I know you were relishing being let loose with my beautiful L96, too. I know, you had unfinished business with that gun, Gulliver, but I might have thought twice about letting you borrow it if I'd known it would be a thirteen-year loan.

I'm a gun man. But I can't deny there was something incredibly satisfying about the weight of my (t)rusty Victorian iron lamppost ladder-bar nestling in my palm. The jagged piece of decaying detritus I'd torn from the ground many years before, it's a much cruder instrument than Sgt. Willows' foam covered truncheon. Complete with big knobbly bits either end, one can take comfort in the fact that however thick your target's skull, a heavy piece of Victorian street furniture will likely crack it like eggshell.

The soundproof bunker made it difficult to get face to face with our mark, but it made breaking and entering his home an absolute dream. The exaggerated urgency of the twins' cartoony soundtrack gave us mandate to channel Dick Dastardly and Muttley as we diverted off the driveway to avoid breaking the motion sensor for the front door camera. Lightly, we made our way along the side of the house, and jimmied open the ground floor hallway window. Shadow like, we poured ourselves through into the house, and assumed our pre-arranged positions; you with your back against the front door, encased in the shadows from the coat stand, and me at the other end of the hallway outside the door to the bunker staircase, concealed only within the element of surprise.

Easing open the door to the stairwell, I peered down to the second door, that led directly into Paulie's bunker. Only then could we hear the film Paulie and his heavies were watching.

When I was 7, and Craig was 9, he was allowed to have some friends round to sleep in his room, and because my room connected to his, it was easy for me to make myself an annoying addition to their party. They might have ratted me out, except that one of his friends had brought a stash of his older brother's magazines.

Instant cred.

They were certainly not something Craig wanted my parents knowing about, so I was allowed to stay lest I do some ratting out of my own.

There were naked women in the magazine.

Lots of them.

Looking back, I have to laugh at myself in awe of these boys two years older; a flock of pigeons discovering a discarded rubber chicken.

But their greatest excitement came from the pages near the end, where movies were reviewed, and especially a full-page feature about the forthcoming release of *The Texas Chainsaw Massacre*. None of us knew what a massacre was, but the page was dominated by a woman in front of a car, screaming and covered in blood – the rest of the page was spattered in blood, with red fingerprints, a gun, a noose, and of course, a bloody chainsaw. This was much more our level of illicit behaviour. Blood, violence, screaming – they weren't things any of us particularly enjoyed, but we could describe them in the playground next day.

I had nightmares for weeks. I could hear that woman screaming, and her desperate eyes would materialise into any dream I had, to dominate, obliterate, and terrify me until I woke up sweating, and whimpering.

I have never seen a horror film.

That feature about *The Texas Chainsaw Massacre* was my only experience, but I felt I'd seen enough to know what horror films were all about. I figured as soon as I opened that door, we would hear screaming, and chainsaw noises, and gunshots, and a shrill orchestral soundtrack.

Instead, I had to strain to hear anything at all. There was talking, and I thought Paulie and the boys were just shooting the shit together. A minute more, and I detected American twang, and if I leaned in further, from time to time there were other sounds – blustery wind noises, owls hooting, a car passing by but not stopping, and eventually, the creaking of an opening door, then a change as a bubbling of more voices was added, their words lost within the hum of a small space.

I know you must have been grinding your teeth waiting, Gulliver.

But we had agreed I'd pick the moment, and whatever the three men were actually seeing up on Paulie's widescreen, I was formulating my own version, driven by nothing more than the suspense I felt in the lengthy silences. It was clear something make or break must be happening to the American men. They'd come inside from the night, and there were lots more people with them now, but soon after they arrived all the new voices had gone quiet. Just one or two spoke from time to time, and the tone was distinctly British and didn't seem welcoming. The American twang would rise in response to the more guttural tones of the newer voices, and increasingly, the Americans seemed to be protesting. I guessed, their only wish, was not to have to go outside again.

But another few minutes, and outside was exactly where they were again because the owls were back hooting, heralding the palpable dread of discovering some terrible unknown.

So, that was the moment.

I gave you the signal, and you slipped out of the door onto the front porch, immediately triggering the security camera above you in the corner.

Don't show your face.

Head down.

I know you enjoyed banging on the front door; you did it with gusto only just short of rattling the stained-glass triangles out from the top of the door frame.

It would take something spectacular for Paulie to leave his favourite easy chair.

Having to answer the front door during Horror Night was tedious, but hardly spectacular. The current Mrs. Harrington had a fondness for overseas mail order catalogues. Still, my heart was in my mouth as we waited. That top-down camera would show off your shaved bowling ball of a head, and though I'd begged you to wear a cap befitting a delivery man, you had been quite forceful in your refusal.

The sweet spot, we'd agreed, was ten seconds banging.

Then five waiting.

And another five banging.

And there we were at the crux; the whole plan rested on the right man coming upstairs to deal with the front door situation.

Could be Stacker, could be Ballsy.

Must not be both of them.

Must not be Paulie.

The top door shut now, I strained to listen. And sure enough, a slight creak as the bottom door opened, and the slow stomp of a heavy man on the stairs.

Just one man.

It was disconcerting to see you impotently waiting; a fractured shadow on the other side of the front door – unable even to hear what I could. Unable to know if your knocking had been successful.

Or too successful?

As he neared the top, I could hear the laboured breathing of a very large man indeed.

I tightened my hand around the rusty iron ladder bar.

The door swung open, obscuring my view.

Dense footsteps made their way towards you, their owner barely visible through the frosted glass panels.

I had to be sure.

Silently, I pushed the door shut, and exhaled gratefully as my eyes adjusted to the stocky rear of a man way too short to be Paulie.

According to our Pigeon's notes, this must be Ballsy - a fist shaped man, kind of a human wrecking ball.

I lunged forward with my iron bar raised, knowing he'd hear me and turn. I feel better thwacking a man facing me. Ballsy was short enough that I had a really good swing at him from above. I thwacked Ballsy's shiny bonce with the heavy metal knob on the end of my ladder bar, and with a rasp he deflated onto the terracotta floor tiles.

You were there immediately, pulling him out onto the porch, rolling him forward on his stomach like Mr. Wobbly Man from the Noddy's Toy Town, and holding up our pre-prepared scribbled note.

LOCKED OUT!!

More banging. This time from me on the inside.

I channelled Ballsy. How would he bang on the door if he'd really locked himself out?

Maybe it had happened before? What if Stacker and Paulie were tuned to recognise his specific knock?

Would he beat on it like Fred Flintstone?

Or rattle and bellow like the big bad wolf?

In the end, I decided if he was holding up the note with one hand, he'd most likely just grip the handle with other, and shake the door in its frame so Stacker and Paulie might really believe he'd manage to break the lock if he wasn't rescued first.

Seemed like a Ballsy move to me.

Looking back now, isn't it funny to think we'd pegged this as the riskiest part of the whole plan? The genuine possibility that such suspicious activity might bring Paulie upstairs instead of Stacker.

I crept back to my station by the upper basement door, and listened.

The pause button had not been deployed when Ballsy left the bunker, and I could hear the distant wails and moans of an American man facing something terrible. Suddenly, the sounds intensified, and I clenched my fist in silent celebration. The lower door had opened, and if Paulie had been on the stairs, he would surely first have stopped the film.

Much lighter footsteps than Ballsy's were creaking up the steps accompanied to begin with by the echoing sounds of the unfortunate American and the growls and exaggerated snarling of his attacker. Just before the lower door must have swung shut behind Stacker, a guttural howl clawed its way upstairs, then, there were only the footsteps, right on the other side of the door.

Again, the door opened, and again, my view was obscured as the footsteps headed towards you and limp Ballsy behind the front door. I pushed the door shut, and smiled as a slightly hunched beanpole of a man was revealed swaying somewhat unsteadily away from me.

Raising my iron bar like a premature trophy, my arm was suddenly wrenched backwards at an agonising angle.

Stacker! Stacker! Stacker!

Trilled two quick-fire little voices harmonising behind me.

Stacker spun around confused and vacant in a Scotch drowned stupor, sliding on the terracotta in his socks like the scarecrow from Wizard of Oz.

Oh my.

The munchkins had me pinned.

Stacker was lurching towards me, clearly unarmed, my iron in his bleary sights. With one twin pulling on each of my arms with all their might, I was temporarily unable to recover my balance (let's say it was temporary, I'm sure I'd have gotten the better of them in another ten seconds). Stalk-like fingers grabbed my rusty iron bar and lifted it up. I screwed my eyes shut braced myself for the crack on my skull. Then came the sickening thwack of cold hard metal on flesh and bone.

But no pain.

I opened an eye, in time to see Stacker's eyes roll up in his head as he bent double and flattened against the floor like a reed in a whirlwind.

And you. Behind him, lifting my L96 back up to your shoulder, wiping the barrel on your trousers to get rid of any little bits of Stacker's scalp.

Thanks, Gulliver.

Now, little Anthony and little Georgie were screaming. They weren't the screams of terror one might expect from a normal child at the prospect of being beaten to death by a stranger with a sniper rifle. They were more like the whoops and hollers you might expect from a couple of kids playing cowboys and Indians. And they were still holding tightly onto my arms.

So, you actually held your barrel to little Georgie's temple.

I can't condone that, Gulliver.

The recollection still makes me queasy.

Both of them did, of course, immediately relinquish their grip, and a heart-breaking note of fear crept into their screams, along with the worrying added shouts of Uncle Paulie! Uncle Paulie!

Ten seconds more and they were locked in the cupboard under the stairs, within which they proceeded to thrash scream and scrabble with their eight limbs like a huge trapped spider wearing clogs in an upturned glass, with a drum kit.

You've got to love the brain. Hard wired to generate its greatest moments of inspiration right in the middle of the most desperate circumstances. I cradled my brain in my hands while I tried to think past Anthony and Georgie's cacophony, and yes, Gulliver, I was more than aware that your own default solution would be to barrel down the stairs with your sniper blazing.

We know now, that wouldn't have ended well.

Those screams and hollers were winning, taking over my thought process, and I gave in. I clawed at my forehead and joined them, screaming, screeching, bellowing. It was raw, and cathartic, and honestly without intention. But as soon as I'd started, I realised it was genius. Wide eyed, I beckoned you to join in, and I started rattling my iron along banisters, drumming on tabletops, and all the while changing my screams and howls, with you in harmony, relishing the release. One second we were a snarling wolf pack, another second a choir of wailing banshees.

We wouldn't hear the lower door open this time, and our absurd chorus would drown out approaching footsteps. All we could do was watch the stairwell door – you, back by the front porch

where a single snipe shot could zip through Paulie's throat like Evil
Knievel through a ring of fire.

That was the plan.

Seven

Sunday, 13 January

Horror Night 2: Paulie & Woodward

This time when the top door was rammed open, it almost crashed into my nose. From the force he put behind the door, I guess Paulie was pretty pissed off to have Horror Night truncated. What I couldn't tell was whether he'd been suspicious enough to arm himself. Only you could see his empty hands and Muppet print silk pyjamas.

I continued my banshee wails as the door swung into my face.

I could only imagine what Paulie went through in those moments; emerging into the hallway confronted by a soup of noise, his Scotch-blurred vision attempting to understand what he saw at the end of the hall.

Somebody? Or some-*thing*?

Perhaps he thought the figure with domed head and fangs was Nosferatu levelling a sniper rifle at him.

In that moment, poor Paulie would have known, there was nothing he could do.

I knew the clean click-whizz of your shot was coming.

The end of this hit.

Not exactly how we planned it, but, job done.

But, no.

Instead, with the door still in my face, a different sound, and my heart nose-dived to drown in my stomach acid.

An impotent clank.

No whizz.

Perhaps Paulie's head cleared somewhat; he chuckled, and expelled a long breath as an almost inaudible whistle, as if his front teeth were set apart a little.

Immediately I pushed the door and revealed the man in all his colossal glory; wide as Ballsy, high as Stacker; a power station cooling tower in human form. You and I were obscured from each other by his mass, disconnected, and clueless what course of action the other would choose.

I lunged forward with my rusty lump of iron raised, certain I had the element of surprise.

I did.

It didn't matter.

The bulbous end of the iron was a ping pong ball to Paulie's armoured tortoise shell.

At first glance, Paulie was an over-inflated version of Ballsy; the Tweedledum and Tweedledee of North East England's Mob scene. But everything about Ballsy had been lovely and squishy, even his scalp had yielded to my iron like a firm but flexible pie crust.

Paulie was the least flexible man on Earth.

As he swung round to face me with a roar, he flexed his considerable muscle mass and his chest rippled like oily water in the wind. His arms were too built to swing effectively, but if his grasping fingers found purchase on any part of you, you could say goodbye to that part. He was lunging for my iron bar, but shuddered to a halt as you grabbed both his arms from behind, and it looked like you discovered that bending Paulie's arms backwards was a bit like trying to bend a brick.

His strength overwhelmed you and you fell to the floor with a sickening whine as the wind was squeezed from your lungs. Seeing you fall was enough of a shock for me that I let my guard down, and Paulie took his chance to pluck my rusty iron rod from my hand.

I grabbed at the front of his pyjamas, the only loose bit of him I could find.

I was vaguely aware that you were back on your feet launching yourself at him too, and a brief game of bucking bronco ensued with both of us simply scrabbling to find purchase while Paulie flailed with the rusty iron, trying to catch one of us wide enough to strike. As long as we stayed central, we could avoid the lethal outer edge.

Briefly, because seconds later we were joined by Woodward.
Deaf.

Almost blind.

Arthritic in one leg that dragged and bumped around behind him.

But bigger than some ponies, still powerful, and powerfully motivated by the distress whistle of his Master.

That damned whistle I'd clocked from Paulie and dismissed as a goofy tick.

Perhaps the only sound that mutt could hear.

But now we were facing down the slavering jaws and whitened eyes of an angry Hell Hound.

I'm a cat person.

Can't really blame the Pigeon.

Who would have factored in the blind, lame, deaf, perpetually sleeping family dog in his winter years? But the moment Woodward's slavering jaws sank into my wrist, I was cursing the Pigeon with gusto as you may recall. Thirteen years later and that line of little puncture scars is still very apparent across my wrist. Thankfully nothing in Woodward's stinking saliva was able to bury itself in my bone and set up camp to multiply like the fungus did in my leg.

You abandoned me.

Suddenly I was there alone, and my banshee wails turned to actual screams of agony as Woodward simply ground his jaws around my wrist, lacerating skin and breaking through cartilage with sickening little pops. With the tide turned, Paulie started enjoying himself shouting *good boy good boy!* Laughing maniacally as he thrashed my iron, still unable to catch me as long as I stayed close to his body. Woodward growled low in annoyance as one might trying to chew through gristle, and I knew I had to make a move if I didn't want to be a one-handed hit man as well as a one legged one.

Paulie had reached critical velocity, a deadly flywheel still wielding my iron bar. I grabbed Woodward's collar and pulled him close as he peered at me through cloudy eyes, trying to locate my jugular. The iron whistled past my ear more than once per second, a spiralling deadly double helix, but I shut my eyes and ground my teeth against the pain in my wrist, and I nodded my head in time to Paulie's undulating rhythm, I counted, one, two, three – then I dropped Woodward's collar catching the mutt momentarily off guard so he fell backwards dragging me with him by my wrist, and as we both rolled off Paulie's curved concrete torso, I reached up with my good hand and managed to close it around my iron rod, which tore through my palm with its raised rusty notches, ploughing furrows like an invading alien warship crash-landing on a golf course. But I held on, and pulled my entire weight away from Paulie so he could get to me with his free hand. Paulie let out that breathy whistle again, and mercifully Woodward relinquished his grip… only to lunge at my other arm, fastening his teeth into my shoulder, letting his whole dead weight hang there as I yelled and thrashed my head around against the pain. Ironically though, Woodward bought me time – his weight actually helping me to pull against Paulie as a counterweight, so the big red angry man could only pull and pull on the iron rod trying to shake me loose. Delirious, I knew I was losing blood from my wrist and I could feel it pumping out of my shoulder around Woodward's deepening bite. I screamed to keep from passing out, but I felt myself rising above the pain and effort – it was all getting easier, yet still, I knew I couldn't let go, I had to hold on or I would immediately be thrashed to bits at Paulie's iron wielding hand. We eyeballed each other as I faded, and I watched his lip curl into a sneer, not of victory, but utter contempt. He never doubted he would win. The last rusty shards of the iron rod sliced through my palm as I crumpled to the floor. Paulie raised it above his head with a sick glint in his eye, and licked his lips. He froze in that position; a sadistic cat revelling in supremacy over a trapped mouse whose back is already broken.

I tried to muster the last bit of fight within me, but found myself hopelessly grounded by the dead weight of Woodward still fastened on my shoulder.

I screwed up my eyes and waited for the whistle of iron cutting through air, but it never came.

I peeked out, and there he was, in the exact same position, but the glint in his eye had vanished.

Supremacy turned to fear.

A distant click.

Paulie shut his eyes tight and howled before the vast wasteland between his eyes erupted into crimson streams, and his dead mass toppled forward.

Revealing, you.

Clutching Paulie's own smoking pistol.

Woozily I stared down its barrel – you held it still, and for a brief, brief moment, I thought you might pull the trigger on me too.

Then I realised – the dog.

My shoulder.

But my shoulder had lost its intense pain. I reached up and found only blood and drool.

Thus far Woodward had been a dutifully ruthless tool of his master, but something primal had stirred inside him. His master was dead, a new beast crept into my fuzzy vision – hackles raised, advancing on you with his master's pistol trained between his clouded eyes.

And I became aware of a low, deep scraping sound – his growl of grief.

I expected a second bullet any second, but this was an evening for embracing the unexpected, and I was beyond being surprised when you lowered the pistol, and placed it on the ground between you – eyeballing Woodward every moment.

From the basement, through the doors you'd left ajar when you swiped Paulie's pistol, the movie still played, and a bloodcurdling howl sliced through the air.

Perhaps you expected it?

You didn't flinch.

Woodward flinched – it must have seemed a distant echo from a primal ancestor. Perhaps he thought it was you. He lifted his head to the chandelier and let out a howl of anguish shot through with deadly intent. The stalemate broken, the snarling beast leapt for your throat with reckless blind Samsonesque vengeance.

If it were me, I confess I would have fled, but you stood your ground.

Blue light from the stained glass played on your bald head as you faced the beast, curling your lip above your pointy teeth.

Glowing, otherworldly, vicious.

Howls from Woodward, howls from the bowels of the building, and you joined them to complete a dreadful three-part howl-mony. A pressure cooker bursting deep in your chest, and Gulliver: Slavering Fire-Eyed Hound of Legend, was born before my eyes, which, granted, pulsed painfully from my plummeting blood pressure.

Poor Woodward.

His grief still an open wound, he found himself facing off against a virile alpha-dog / vampire hybrid whose terrifying teeth gnashed towards his jugular spraying spittle into his face like a fire hose. His howl had returned to that menacing low growl, and he still looked dangerous to me – if I had to put my money on a jugular at that moment, I was still firmly betting on Woodward's half-inch fangs still spotted with my own blood, to find purchase on your white neck and tear your throat away in a single motion.

I couldn't see your own little vampire needles doing much more than inflict a surface wound and get hair stuck between them.

Would you actually have attacked the mutt?

Would you have sunk your teeth into his neck?

I believe you would have.

I heard the moment Woodward wavered.

That growl was joined by a whine of confusion as his primal subconscious conceded to fear of the unknown. There was no DNA rulebook for this fight.

No new tricks.

He dropped his cloudy eyes to the floor and allowed the whine to escape fully in place of his growl, and as he swayed his head mournfully over his dead master's mountainous body, I truly believe we heard the poor beast cry.

You lowered your own howl to a growl too, and I thought you were going to pounce on him.

I managed to muster the words.

Let's leave.

But you were still advancing on Woodward.

Arm outstretched.

When I realised you were offering him comfort – I couldn't help but feel a little neglected, Gulliver. I was, after all, lying in agony on the floor soaking in a sizable pool of my own blood and fighting hard to remain semi-conscious.

I also still thought it likely Woodward would claw back his mojo and take your arm off. But no, he let you slowly place your hand on the back of his neck, and massage his raised hackles while your growl became a low comforting hum.

And a beautiful friendship was formed.

The blessed flood of Oxytocin after childbirth gives new mothers such a rush of pure love as they meet their baby, that it keeps them from passing out from the pain and dropping the baby on the floor.

Nature's provision.

I really think something similar was keeping me conscious, something paternal. I couldn't hear the twins hammering and hollering any longer, and I was worried for them, especially considering we still had the shocking fact of their uncle's untimely demise to break to them.

At least we were on the same page at that point, Gulliver. Your re-appropriation of Woodward's collar as a makeshift tourniquet for my shoulder was certainly welcome. Although, as you yanked it tight, I did crave Michael's gentler ministrations.

Patched up, we approached the cupboard door with trepidation, released the latch, and stepped back a little expecting a pent-up release of dust and fury to fly out like an Acme limbs tornado.

Instead, nothing.

And you said.

Secret tunnel.

With a grin.

I almost, almost, threw my arms up in the air in a petulant show of defeat, before I remembered how painful that would be.

But you were wrong.

The cutest little giggle emerged from the darkness, and further exploration revealed the truth. Two little boys, exhausted, fast asleep on top of one another, dreaming of the cartoons they'd stayed up late to watch that Horror Night.

I don't know, Gulliver.

Had you always planned to leave the Crypt soon after Harrington? Or did you feel driven to it? Woodward was a bit much in the space, but we could have made it work, I think.

But blaming Michael for the gun jamming...

Even if he did neglect something, I can't believe it was intentional.

More and more, I think you'd planned to leave.

Maybe it happened more quickly than you thought.

As we rode home slowly in the Allegro, Woodward on the back seat sitting upright like Scooby Doo between the sleeping twins, we left behind much more than a dead mobster and two unconscious henchmen.

<u>Eight</u>

Monday, 14 January

Little Hye

Hye-Kyoung Yang was clad in voluptuous furs from some rare species, dotted all over with diamonds and emeralds. Unusual within a small tea-room populated by elderly English people eating scones.

Living in the North East of England in semi-exile from her Korean mafia boss father, HKY had burrowed out a niche for herself as a cosmetics agent slash arms dealer, to whom every person living in the North East of England in need of a good clean, untraceable firearm must pay a visit. And when I say untraceable, I don't mean some steel Smarties tube passed along through a chain of twenty members of the North East's criminal underbelly, the serial number hacked off with an iron file, and the mechanism so playful it might be mistaken for a child's plastic Lone Ranger pistol. A once worthy rival of mine had his entire arm wrenched so far back when his dodgy pistol backfired, that his tendons ripped clean off his shoulder and elbow.

Hye-Kyoung smelt like a perfume counter.

Actually, scratch 'counter', substitute 'department'. Hye-Kyoung smelt like she might be the bulging package containing one of these entire departments in flat-pack.

And of course, her favourite trick, the best and only joke she knew, was to say,

What can I do for you today?

Then pretend that she didn't know you were not there to buy perfume or make-up, but rather to obtain a brand-new weapon, and some high quality, untraceable ammunition.

I'd seen Foster grit his teeth and play shop with her ten times or more.

He always updated his arsenal through Hye-Kyoung, and he always took me along for the ride in the back of the Allegro, and I was allowed out in broad daylight during the exchange, presumably because a man in a café with his eight-year-old son looks less likely to be buying guns than a man without.

Like Wordsworth in his little boat, I gained an increasingly revealing respect for this woman and her talents as I grew bigger and drew back. Foster always came away with bath-salts or something.

We didn't have a bath.

But when I started operating on my own, keeping my own kit current through Hye-Kyoung, then I began to understand.

She was like a guns and perfume Avon lady.

That last time I checked out with Hye-Kyoung's firepower supermarket, I bounced the Allegro over the un-surfaced car park at the cafe, and right away I spotted her car, a powder blue Range Rover four-by-four. Grimacing at the monstrosity, I clambered out of my old faithful and pulled twenty bob from my pocket. The windows of the car were all blacked out – but I went over and pressed my head against one of them. I don't know what I wanted to hear, but I heard nothing at all.

I shrugged and walked into the little eatery – a wood clad, lakeside shack catering mostly for retired folk giving themselves a treat after pulling their dog around the footpath.

This time I pre-empted Hye-Kyoung. I told her right off as I walked up to her table. I'm here to buy bullets and a rifle. Nothing else.

She said,

Your poor wife.

I haven't got one,

I said. Like she didn't know.

I mean your future wife,

She replied, then she said,

Let's all hope there never is one.

Have you heard this rumour, Gulliver? That she added a precious stone to her furs for every man her daddy offed for rejecting her?

Who cares when you're connected, right?

The best part of meeting Hye-Kyoung was that nobody was looking at me. Nobody was thinking 'weirdo' today, and speculating about my reclusive life. When you meet Hye-Kyoung, all the furtive looks are cast in her direction amid much whispering.

I was certain the elderly Northerners had lots of opinions about Hye-Kyoung.

I digress.

I desired the contents of the lower tier of her immense perfume box. I coveted the little boxes of round tipped 7mm bullets, and beyond everything, I was slavering over the brand new, modified Daewoo K2 rifle, tweaked for sniper precision by their military labs. I knew she had it hidden down there somewhere.

Hye-Kyoung's enigmatic father is the unofficial filter between factory and armed forces – he weeds out the pieces that fail his quality control – he's a great patriot, you see, he would never let a potentially dangerous weapon get into the hands of a good Korean soldier. And the weapons he filters out, he makes sure they are very carefully 'disposed of' via an incredibly intricate 'procedure' within his own factory.

I suppose all this means he would be very disappointed to find his daughter using her pretty perfume box as a front for hawking untraceable, fully refurbished Korean army surplus rifles modified for extra distance work.

My tongue might be firmly in my cheek, but I'm being unfair to Hye-Kyoung's perfume box, actually, really and truly, it wasn't just a front. She seriously wanted to talk scents and concealing creams.

Every time.

And that day, even though I'd told her,

No perfume, I'm all scented up, thanks.

Right there, she began un-packing her perfume case, laying the little glass bottles out on the table in the café – turning the default smell of the air from sweet chocolate to heady rose-garden.

Always this ritual – the perfume, the make-up – the firm but jovial refusal, and the hurt look spreading across her face. She just doesn't get a kick out of selling ammunition and firearms.

Being an arms dealer was never what she imagined for herself.

Parental pressure.

But the game, the refusal, the banter, now that really is all an act. I'm acting, acting for my life because those are the keys that unlock the bottom tier. Because everyone knows, when you buy your arms from Hye-Kyoung Yang, you always buy some perfume.

The trick is to make it seem real – it's not just as simple as walking up to her and saying, yeah I'll have two bottles of CK-One and a grenade launcher please, love.

Keep the change.

No, Hye-Kyoung thinks she's a saleswoman, and her job satisfaction stems from believing she's selling you something you didn't previously think you needed.

Every one of Hye-Kyoung's customers knows this.

Every one of Hye-Kyoung's living customers knows this.

Today would be the last time I bought firearms from Hye-Kyoung Yang, today would be the last time I ever had to bring home a little boutique bag tied with a ribbon along with my carry-all of precision weaponry. I hoped at the time, that it would not be my last time purchasing the tools of my trade from the Yangs.

But thus far, I have been forced to make do with the equipment I acquired that day.

I was bothered by the smallness of the café we were sitting inside. I'd met Hye-Kyoung in several different locations previously. Most of the places we used to frequent with Foster had been closed down, and Hye-Kyoung liked her traditions so she would seek out the meeting place, usually buried somewhere within one of the small, outlying villages peppered around the North East of England. Something like McDonalds would have been less conspicuous – but no – always a different quaint little café. There were only four other customers - two elderly couples sipping Earl-Grey at the other tables.

Do you enjoy being noticed?

I asked.

Yes. Now shut up and give me some money,

She said.

Yellowing net curtains were bunched up at the sides of the long-curved window – pointless for any sort of concealment, and way past their useful decorative life. Everything that could be was painted dark blue, including the windowpanes and all the light fittings.

After the obligatory lipstick and mascara exchange, it was brass tacks time.

Leaning forward as much as her folds of fur would allow, Hye-Kyoung pushed her face into mine and said,

You had better be good for this my friend, the grapevine has been leaking tales of unhappy customers.

What could she be referring to?

I told her,

I'm good for it, don't worry, I have a low-rent place.

And she said, quick as a flash,

But how many mouths to feed?

Mafia. They just know.

None of your concern.

She held up her palms and she sat back on her creaking wooden chair.

Not my concerns, you're right, Mr. Jasper. My father's concerns.

If only she knew.

I think your father has other concerns besides my track record, I told her,

Me and your father, we're like that.

And I crossed my trigger and middle fingers, sticking them up at her then lowering them flat like a gun.

Bang,

I said quietly,

Now, are you going to show me some toys?

She laughed and threw back her head as far as the viciously protruding combs and clips in her hair would allow.

I like you Mr. Jasper,

She said.

There was no getting away from she shrillness of her laugh; the old couples sitting on the back wall watched their tea ripple from the centre.

Like that! She repeated. And she attempted my gesture but only managed to make her heavily ring clad fingers knock together like little armoured gladiators.

The banter had gone on long enough. You have to drink the milk before it turns sour.

I'm looking for a Daewoo K2 modified as DMR.

She raised her eyebrows.

I know you're not good for that, Mr. Jasper.

I'm branching out,

I told her.

Into what?

She said,

The fur trade?

Maybe.

She sighed. Look. I don't care what you want it for, I don't carry K2s.

Not usually. Today you have one, and it's a gift from your father to me.

And before she could begin laughing again, for fear that the porcelain cups might gave up the fight and shatter, I recited loudly,

Hark! the death-note of the year
Sounded by the castle-clock!

From her sunk eyes a stagnant tear
Stole forth, unsettled by the shock…

There followed a pregnant pause.

Then, one of the elderly ladies clapped her hands, while the other couple shook their hung heads, muttering and reaching for their coats. But my eyes were fixed on Hye-Kyoung's. She was wrong-footed. Slowly, without dropping her gaze from mine, she unbuttoned the top of her fur coat, and reached into the endless folds beneath, extracting a small, folded piece of paper. Unfolding it she finally dropped her gaze and her olive eyes darted over the words written there.

Looking up she nodded,

Well, Mr. Jasper. It appears I'm your Santa Claus.

I opened the passenger door of Hye-Kyoung's powder blue Range Rover four-by-four monstrosity. The interior was also powder blue – mostly dyed leather, off-set with cream piping. A little disorienting – like staring at the sky while lying on a hot beach. There was no denying she needed a car this size though; behind the two front seats was a glittering wall of jewel handled drawers and mirror fronted cabinets. Even with the modified seat pushed as far back as possible, squeezing in the undulations of HKY's decorated furs and velvet skirts was a complex contortion requiring a dexterity I hadn't appreciated she possessed.

There was a little girl sitting on the passenger seat regarding me with suspicion.

She said something to HKY in Korean, still looking at me.

I raised my eyebrows.

She says she saw you put your ear on the window earlier on.

Oh. Sorry about that.

Hye-Kyoung fired off a string of Korean in response. She turned to me and said,

I told her you're a weirdo, and can't be trusted.

I nodded.

Does she speak English?

I asked.

Hye-Kyoung narrowed her eyes so much she created little fault lines in her thick foundation. Listen to me Mr. Jasper,

She hissed,

As far as you're concerned, she doesn't even exist.

I raised my palms.

Ok, ok,

I said,

It's just... I'll need to fully check my investment, there's no room in here and I don't want little hands getting all grabby... any accidents...

Hye-Kyoung sighed impatiently,

Take it to your car then!

I don't have blacked windows; call me paranoid but...

What do you suggest, Mr. Jasper?

She snapped.

Let her play in my car while we do check out; it's right there look. We'll be able to see her.

And I asked the little girl,

Do you want to play in a real car?

Shut up!

Spat Hye-Kyoung,

She can't understand you.

She barked an instruction to the little girl, who clambered towards me,

Don't think I won't have you covered, Mr. Jasper.
I lifted my hand with my fingers crossed again.
Like that
I said,
Remember?

On the back seat of the Allegro was the old teddy of Michael's – you know the one, Gulliver, the one you'd shot in the stomach when Michael ate your yoghurt that time. I'd been meaning to sew up the exit wound, but it was all I had for her.

Play with teddy. I told her. He's been shot, so you might want to comfort him a bit. She just stared at me with big dark eyes and retained that suspicious expression. She reached out for teddy though, and by the time I was sitting back beside Hye-Kyoung, teddy and the little girl looked like firm friends.

The K2 was in Hye-Kyoung's lap.

Long, elegant, polished steel at one end. Chunkily militaristic at the other. Stark, and silent.

A gun to die for.

Hye-Kyoung's heavily ornamented fingers were ill equipped to hold onto it as I reached out and gently slid it from her.

Bullets?

Silently, sullenly, she handed over a box full, I picked one out and rolled it between my fingers. No numbers, no codes.

I cracked open the chamber, and Hye-Kyoung jumped at the sound.

Not here.

I have to check it's all in working order. This is where your blacked out windows will seem like a really good investment,
I told her.

I ran my finger around inside the chamber, checking for powder residue.

I knew I wouldn't find any.

A virgin gun. There is a certain thrill to being the first – but you have to take your time. In the wrong hands it could be explosive in all the wrong ways. An untested gun, brand new mechanisms cocked and ready, loading such a machine you put your trust in the people who made each tiny part and assembled it. One less than precise rivet, ratchet, pin, or lever, and it's goodbye hands. Goodbye face.

So, I stopped breathing, and ever so carefully, my fingers steady as a brain-surgeon's, I placed the tip of the shining bullet into the top of the waiting chamber. I paused, and I looked up at Hye-Kyoung. She was mesmerised, holding her breath along with me. Our eyes met and she nodded almost imperceptibly – still with my eyes on hers I pushed the bullet into the chamber, it slid into place beautifully, and registered a satisfying click.

We breathed.

I looked down and from this angle I could see the high contrast colours of her face, reflected in the top of the bullet.

Now,

I told her,

Don't move.

Meanwhile, back in the Allegro, Hye-Kyoung's little girl had been pulling teddy's head off. And his arms, and his legs. In fact, there wasn't much left of teddy.

I didn't tell Michael – he probably still thinks teddy's in the bear hospital waiting to be mended.

The little girl was smiling though, and when I landed in the driver's seat, she scrambled through to sit beside me in the passenger seat, and presented me with teddy's severed head.

Well done sweetheart,

I told her.

You'll go far.

And to think, I was supposed to wipe her out along with her Mum!

They picked the wrong assassin – poor Hye-Kyoung, she probably recommended me herself.

I stashed the K2 under the back seat, we hit the road and left the powder blue spam can on wheels as a fitting sepulchre for the fresh meat slumped inside.

Mummy kissed the wrong man, and you came along,

I told Little Hye,

So, Mummy had to be sacrificed to preserve Grandpa's honour.

With a bit of luck, you'll never have to meet Grandpa.

And hopefully, neither will I.

<u>Nine</u>

Tuesday, 15 January

Escape

'Oh Saints of the Mediocre, do not chastise the completeness of my actions; the mind is apathetic, but the spirit is surprisingly diligent.'

After six months imprisoned with Foster, I escaped for the first time.

There was a time when I believed that to carry out every little task and daily chore to the very best of one's ability was not enough, and that instead one must strive for a level of achievement at which experts in the field, even if the field were simply washing up a teacup, would marvel. This is straight from Foster, though he did not himself practice such discipline.

Not any longer.

Foster was a man of very few words.

His actions really did speak louder.

The difference behind an apple thrown and an apple rolled.

Leaving out the superior blanket for me when it was an especially cold night.

Refusing a hit if he considered I needed to study more.

The bulk of Foster's educational tactics revolved around feeding me textbooks that he made clear I was expected to read and complete. They were out of date course-books from years, sometimes decades, ago, but the only real difference was in political history – all those idiots shifting boundaries by a few miles at massive cost and a huge death toll. The leaders of the world, Gulliver.

Those people have no respect for human life.

Despite all Foster's careful nurturing, firearms provision, and exciting excursions, I could never forget, after it had been revealed, that this man, upon whom I was reliant for food and shelter, for knowledge and even entertainment and encouragement, character building, and social development, had murdered my family.

Which was difficult, because had it not been for the fact that Foster was responsible for orphaning me, crippling me, and robbing me of any opportunity for a normal childhood, if it were not for all this, I could have grown content in my life with him.

I separated the conflicting emotions in my head into sections, like slicing up a birthday cake. I found that after a while, I was able to choose precisely which of the slices I wanted to taste, and which ones I wanted to put in the deep freeze until they might need to be moved out and thawed to make room for other emotions. Among the first of the frozen emotions was 'I hate Foster because he killed my family'. That emotion was just one slice of a very large and ornately decorated cake.

The slice I liked to taste the most, the one I made last the longest and enjoyed the best, was the one that said, 'This is a much more exciting life than your old one.'

It was partially subliminal, this slice of cake.

Of course, to begin with Foster was a monster.

If there was no reason to say anything, Foster stayed silent, and with just the two of us knocking around the flat day after day, conversation was sparse. Even today, I much prefer silence to music, conversation, birdsong, rippling water, whistling breeze – some of it is admittedly quite pleasant, but second rate to silence.

As a normal eight-year-old boy, before my family were murdered and I was kidnapped and crippled, I had been an expert time filler via myriad plastic figures and mechanical gadgets designed to blow a small boy's mind. My parents could afford the best of them in those days, and when I tired of those there was always TV. Living with Foster without so much as a digital watch did not cause me to descend into unbearable boredom. I was occupied – through textbooks and drawing. But sometimes Foster and I were occupied together, united by a fondness for board games. I hope, though I'm sure you would deny it even if it is so, that you have gained something of the same passion from living in the Crypt. Monopoly was always a favourite, but Scrabble was the clear winner. I loved to cultivate those words in the rack – staring at them for hours on end – I'm not exaggerating, it could be hours. It didn't matter – what did we have to do that would take the place of getting the best possible result from each move? One particular game lasted the best part of seven months, and finally Foster triumphed using 'quantums' on a triple word score. After seven months of suspense, I did not take this defeat in my stride, at all; I descended into melancholy for a week. It did inspire me to crack on with the decoration and alteration of the Crypt, which at that point I had been neglecting.

He wouldn't allow me to sulk though – he had me back playing a new game of Trivial Pursuit within a couple of weeks.

What amphibian did Pliny the Elder suggest be tied to the jaw to make teeth firmer?

And in his self-established role as my educator, those questions were pitched like an exam.

What is the minimum number of masts on a schooner?

It was fun, but fun with a great deal of pressure attached.

What did the first Spanish dog to be fitted with contact lenses not see the day after the fitting?

Frog

2

The car that killed him.

I did protest. There is no way to prove the dog didn't see the car.

When I said something smart like that, that Foster liked, he always sat back in his chair and raised the collar on his dinner jacket – happy to concede in this instance.

He always wore that dinner jacket – too short in the sleeve – he had a collection of brightly coloured t-shirts from charity shops, one of which he'd wear under his dinner jacket every day.

It was his look.

But it also made him look like a slacker.

Nothing could have been further from the truth.

Foster was extremely active – it was just that his action came all at once over several days. After he spoke to the Pigeon and started preparation for a job, he didn't sleep at all.

Poring over maps.

Plotting routes.

Reciting co-ordinates under his breath.

Training his sight eye by throwing marbles at flies on the wall - with about a 1/3 hit rate.

Through gentle manipulation of my ideals, Foster shaped my desires.

Reject the mediocre.

Embrace the perfect.

He did allow me to get things wrong – careless answers in my academic work, a wet spoon in the sugar – but that was ok; the training ground is the place to make mistakes.

Foster was focused on the result.

The flawless hit.

Nevertheless, there were times when obsession crept into daily life. He once discovered that, over time, over years, my tea mug had become stained light brown on the inside edge, and to Foster it became the embodiment of my failing attitude to detail and diligence, a picture of gradually accumulating ineffectiveness.

I stayed up all night scrubbing it, and all the other mugs, and the cutlery.

He hadn't asked me to.

I got blisters.

And yes, that was even after I 'discovered' the truth about my family.

In a way, that terrible revelation liberated me from the incessant gnawing hope stopping my life in its tracks. Painful. Yes. But pain either buggers off, or it stays, and you learn to live with it. You find, after experiencing lots of pain, that you stop realising which of those options has happened.

At every stage in your life, you think you're at the peak of wisdom. You can look back to a time that now, with hindsight, shows you to have been naïve. But not now. Now, whenever now is, is the culmination of everything learned from all your previous silly mistakes.

Even at aged nearly nine, we succumb to this fallacy. I fancied after six months of finding my place within Foster's realm, that I knew the score. I felt I'd probably done enough to cement Foster's trust in me.

And so, as I planned my escape, I dreamt of pirate adventures and car chases, never questioning that I was the Captain, the Driver. My world had flipped so suddenly out of all recognition, like an adventure tale, and I'd read enough adventure stories to recognise that the hero has to endure some pretty uncomfortable moments; otherwise, what kind of hero would they be? Escaping nothing?

So, I decided I would escape like the hero, and one of the last scenes in the film of my story, would be Foster's wistful smile as he read my note, and a sparkle in his eye that said,

'I'm proud of him, I taught him well, but now, although it hurts, I must let him go.'

Dreams can be treacherous, especially recurring ones. They can make you believe that reality will follow the same course. And so, almost exactly six months after my capture, with the white early morning light peeking through the edges of the grubby blinds, when I knew we had at least an hour before Foster emerged for breakfast, I wedged a door-stop under Foster's bedroom door, stuck a chopping knife in my coat pocket, and limped out of the kitchen door, effortlessly ignoring the pain in my foot as liberation beckoned.

It was easy.

I suppose Foster might have locked the kitchen door if there had been a key. But I think I was wrong about that; I've never felt the need for keys myself as you know.

So, it was easy to get outside of his flat into the stairwell.

And then, actually, outside.

Six months of being indoors made the sunlight sting my eyes like shampoo, and my eyelids felt swollen as I tried to move forwards. The air around me, that I thought would feel open and vast, was closing in on me, stabbing at me, trying to push me back inside. Choked, and with aches in every muscle, I half stumbled, half rolled forward, step by step moving so slowly into this so-called freedom I'd imagined so differently. You know when you run at full pelt on a hot day, and you stop with your hands on your knees panting, and you can see your heartbeat pulsing through your vision as though the world is just out of reach through a slightly cloudy pulsating membrane? That was my view of the world out-side Foster's flat.

Completely blindsided.

But still, I struggled down the road, gaining a greater field of vision with each step, and thankfully feeling the clawing atmo-sphere gradually loosen its grip until I'd regained my sense of pur-pose, and began to breathe more easily.

Once I'd reached the end of Round-Table Terrace, the corner with the greasy little place selling a pizza and chips for £1.99 at lunchtime, I almost felt confident enough to stop there and eat, as if that journey along the road represented a long enough flight away from captivity. I realise looking back, that it's odd I didn't have the urge to enter the shop and blurt out my story, who I was, why I was running. Seek sanctuary. I was so close. But I remained outside simply because I had no money.

My main mistake, apart from being so foolish at all, was the doorstop. The noise of it must have woken him up, and did I really believe it would hold him in his room?

Yes, I really did.

As I lingered at the end of the road, a tall dark figure emerged around the corner, and stood with his arms crossed over his chest. Foster, had run along the back passage, and added a bit of theatricality to my re-capture.

Though he was clearly really pissed off.

He took me roughly by the shoulder, and marched me back down the road without a word.

In the film of my life, I whipped out the concealed chopping knife, and stuck it in his thigh, racing off down the road while he doubled up in pain.

That was in the film of my life that played out in my head at night.

The reality was that if Foster's hand hadn't been on my shoulder, I couldn't have walked straight because of the tears in my eyes. Tears not for my lost freedom, but for the broken trust I'd inflicted.

Perhaps we simply all need somebody to be proud of us.

This was my new normal, then.

And my punishment, was the truth.

A newspaper told me the truth.

Not that newspapers are reliable sources of the truth – but this one asked the right question.

Missing massacre boy kidnapped by killer?

It was the day after my attempted great escape.

The evening, the night, spent in agonising silence, not only bereft of words but of any kind of noise of the soul.

I must have slept, and during the night Foster had left a newspaper on the kitchen work surface – he'd never made such a mistake before - he never did again. Even within the relative stupor of his life between obsessing over hits, there were things Foster conducted methodically, like carefully controlling what I was exposed to.

It wasn't unusual for Foster to sleep the morning through, but this morning the strip of light beneath his door flickered in unusual ways. Although my stomach was still knotted with something like guilt, I had a raging thirst, and my gut told me Foster wouldn't be joining me for breakfast.

I got up off my floor for water, and discovered the newspaper.

That headline.

From four months ago.

A picture of me.

In my school uniform.

And there were pictures of my mum and dad, and Craig.

Jasper's family – massacred.

I had only a vague idea of what a massacre was.

Now my tears felt warm and right, they flowed from a completely different place and they didn't stop. For hours they were a comfort in themselves, and the light still flickered and shifted beneath Foster's door.

Later, once I'd recovered enough to decide to stop crying, I allowed Foster to discover the newspaper next to me on the kitchen floor. He removed it while I pretended to sleep.

We never spoke about it.

I do wish I had that newspaper. I wish I'd squirrelled it away; it wouldn't have been difficult. Maybe it could have been a totem for my grief, a focus, a window to the past.

I have no pictures.

Who knows if my memory of them is even partly correct after the twists and turns of time? I imagine not. Back then, I cried a lot at night – the kind of crying that wells up at the slightest catalyst of a thought.

A happy memory.

A funny story.

A regret…

But as weeks passed, I found nighttime weeping punctuated by periods of dry insomnia, sitting, staring at a point on the wall, unfocused, unthinking – and beneath my sleeping bag my fingers were at work on my foot, in some state between conscious and unconscious, I would press my finger down onto my tender, swollen, damaged foot, and gradually build pressure until I could feel something.

And continue until I could feel pain.

And continue until I could feel matter give way.

And continue.

Ten

Wednesday, 16 January

Greenleaf

The year after you left, Georgie and Anthony turned seven, and they loved war games like fat kids love cake. A priceless deadly double act.

I don't know how much of Georgie and Anthony's initiation into the Crypt you were aware of in the days after Paulie Harrington's Horror Night? I'd hoped Woodward's presence would sweeten the pill, you know?

Here's the deal boys – we killed your Uncle Paulie, you live with us now in a big stone coffin in the woods.

And we don't have TV.

But hey, your dog's here.

Except, he wasn't. Woodward was off with you, God knows where.

And soon after, you crept off into the night with my car and my favourite gun.

And your dog.

So maybe you weren't aware, but Georgie and Anthony swallowed their bitter pills pretty easily – no sugar required. I told them straight – somebody paid me to kill your Uncle.

They smiled at each other.

Mob kids.

Guess Uncle Paulie might not have been the greatest parent or guardian in mob-land.

They started on the job a couple of years after you left, then accompanied me on almost every job for the next seven years.

They weren't always terrific, but they were competent. I could rely on them not to freak out or scream. I couldn't rely on them to stick to the script, and they'd insist on playing out their little action sequences, but hey, we all have to separate ourselves from reality in some way, don't we, Gulliver?

The Greenleaf job was political.

You know the type; shady, patchy intelligence, Land Rover with blacked out windows, smart hard-eyed woman in business suit, thick white envelope. They could save a lot of money doing it all through a Pigeon, but Governments are very cautious. Lots to keep covered.

A week previously, there had been no valid requirement for Ricardo Fairfax to attempt a Tarzan-esque swing across the old barn we were staking out, only the need to escape boredom. His instinct told him correctly that the rope was sound. The beams were not rotten.

A graceful leap into the void.

His nimble fingers effortlessly connecting with the rope.

Then there were wings.

Flappy, cold, stinging wings of leathery flesh.

Ric's instinct had missed the bats.

Flitting around his head only briefly but enough to make him claw at his face.

With both hands.

Three broken toes.

He was lucky.

To Ric's enduring credit, we finished that hit without a hitch, but afterwards, he curled up on his ledge, and I could hear him gritting his teeth against tears. I went over and I wanted to hold him like I would have even just a couple of years before, but there's a big difference between 13 and 15... This boy who used to fall asleep in my arms when he had toothache, violently shook me off the instant he felt my hand on his shoulder.

I don't know.

It angered me.

Why should he be allowed to play at being a man, and I had to accept that? I was still his authority figure and he, actually, was the one who'd messed up mid hit due to boredom.

I stiffened my arm against his shoulder enough to keep him where he was, and hissed in his ear,

You want me to treat you like a man? Act like a man.

And I shoved him, just a little bit, and walked off.

I've never told anybody about that before.

It was never quite the same after that.

Ric and Emily both left a couple of years later, after a lot of whispering in the shadows, and furtive looks over shoulders.

So, anyway, Ric was out for the Greenleaf job, and Emily too, by extension.

So, Anthony and Georgie volunteered and initially I refused; I wasn't happy for Greenleaf to be their first real hit; the mix of State spooks in the shadows, and excitable novice assistants fresh from training... I wanted Little Hye, and I told them so. She doesn't just hide in the shadows. I told them. She becomes them. Plus, whichever way I put this particular puzzle together, I can't be the trigger guy; there's ivy to climb, and I can't do the Spiderman stuff with my peg leg.

All of which made them more determined than ever to show me they were ready.

Stealthy as Hye.

Just as steady on the trigger end.

They just begged and begged until I told them,

Fine, but if you compromise the job, you'll forfeit crème brulee for a month.

Anyway, best to keep Hye under wraps as much as possible, I thought, especially with government spooks sniffing around... The Greenleaf house was superficially walled; pretensions of fortification, easily scalable via leg ups and scrabbling. But once we were inside the parameter - I knew I had to be on the ball - I couldn't just sit around watching for a target to appear at a window. I was in the bushes, and I told Anthony and Georgie,

You're second unit, get around the other side, together, and stay on the walkie-talkies.

They loved all this, all wrapped up in their winter coats and gloves, each with a long-range rifle slung round their necks via coloured shoelaces. I don't think they were even listening, so perhaps my main mistake was giving them so much to do.

As soon as they started running off from me across the grounds, I was groaning. They were barrel-rolling immediately, perhaps they thought they were taking the job seriously, but from where I was standing they looked like reckless fools - and tonight of all nights; infiltrating a family household terminally infected by spooks.

Wraiths in the shadows; I felt their night vision goggles on me, and I felt like an idiot.

My professional status, my reputation, eaten away with every barrel-roll from those nitwits.

They were playing ninjas – they'd been training each other as bloody ninjas all week – bouncing off the Crypt plinths and padding down the tunnels of blackness. Leaping out at one another and scaring me half to death. My only hope was that the spooks might be fooled into believing I really had trained a team of tiny ninjas to carry out my bidding.

Or their bidding.

Objective: Dispatch Greenleafs (Greenleaves?)

Discredit them by leaving the scene to look like a family blowout.

Their time was up.

Sometimes these things can surprise you. I thought the Greenleafs were pretty normal people.

Normal for people who lived in a Baroque mansion with an ornamental lake populated by albino flamingos, and a miniature railway running the length and breadth of the thousand-acre grounds, with real steam locomotives to pull it along, and carriages made entirely from glass to provide the greatest possible view of their collection of sports cars from motion picture history.

But, not for public consumption.

Though the private parties are legendary in certain circles.

Really and truly, if Anthony and Georgie wanted to be real ninjas, they should have done some grappling next to the Pontiac from Knight Rider, on proud display on a ramp in front of a fake waterfall. Actually, I'm glad they didn't because it was all lit up – not very stealthy. But apart from all these over the top, just for the hell of it, pseudo-cool, attempts to buy an identity beyond the mundane, the Greenleafs were pretty normal people.

Or so I thought.

Perhaps all that crap in their garden – the house and the water features, the 'Faux'bergé eggs on gateposts, and the tropical beach with wave machine, perhaps all of that was actually a distraction for how they were making their money.

Greenleaf Enterprises made the best pencils in Europe, right? Well maybe, but who knew they were also the brains behind the biggest, well actually, the only, organ harvesting outfit in Britain?

Not me.

Not anybody.

I guess there just wasn't enough lead in those pencils to feed those flamingos. What does a family of three need a mansion with sixteen bedrooms for? Why does a pencil magnate, with large pencil factories around Europe, have a steady stream of large delivery vans trundling in and out of his personal grounds?

Of course, at the time, when I was watching Georgie and Anthony silently perform rapid running scissor-kicks over the head of an inquisitive black cat with one white ear, who had wandered over from the lit pantry window, sending it one way then the other without touching a hair on its little head, I had no idea of the reason the government wanted the Greenleafs out of the picture.

I just trusted that they had a good one.

I'm a very trusting person.

So here were the boys, bouncing over a cat when they should have been skulking.

To skulk is to survive.

They knew what they should have been doing, so all I could do was train my rifle on their little heads and hope one or other noticed the laser sight and got the message. The best and most ruthless spooks in the UK were there somewhere too, I was certain of it.

Anthony got the message.

He landed on his toes, noticed the laser sight playing across Georgie's forehead, and lunged forward knocking Georgie off his feet. They both landed with an audible 'whoomph'. By the time they got up they both realised it was my sight, they glanced my way before getting down to good skulking, with the cat following them on its belly. I had no orders to kill the cat, but it wasn't looking good, and if scratch came to shove, I resolved to consider it a card-carrying Greenleaf.

They were back on track now, my boys, but my heart was still in my mouth as I watched the little figures give each other a leg up onto the ivy. This is where you just cannot underestimate the role of small children as part of a professional hit squad. That ivy would have had a very difficult time hanging onto the brickwork under my weight. And my prosthetic leg would never have found purchase in the cracks.

Then they were gone.

Sitting in the bushes waiting for the walkie-talkie crackle, I shuffled nervously and tried to decide where the spooks might be hiding, watching. Just like me, the cat decided there was no point continuing to stare up at the point where the boys had vanished, so it wandered lazily in my direction. I kept my eyes on the task in hand, but I could see its one white ear out of the corner of my eye, skulking towards me. Clearly my concealment was not particularly effective, but cats are happy enough to defect to anyone's side as long as they get a little affection, and I took its presence as a compliment.

I found rubbing it behind the ears therapeutic.

I still do.

Had Georgie or Anthony pulled a trigger before coming to live with me? Mob children get initiated fast, and it seemed like the necessity of death was already in their blood.

The cat stiffened about twenty seconds before the gunshots.

Nothing resounding, of course, the slightest little 'phfft phfft', that my ears could pick up because they'd heard it so many times before. You're not a fan of such subtleties, Gulliver – but I like to attach a certain finesse to my work, even if I am hopefully never credited with it beyond the confines of the Crypt. Yes, the cat knew, every muscle in its scrawny body went as stiff as a carrot, its ears pricked up and it stared right at the house. Then when the sound came, it relaxed, and looked at me, accusatively, I fancy, and hissed with its eyes glaring like streaking red comets. Then it turned tail and tore off across the garden, vanishing into the night.

Drama queen.

Then the walkie crackled.

The geese are grounded,

An urgent little whisper; I'd let them choose their own code language.

Copy that,

I said,

Let's get the gosling.

Now it was up to me, the artist.

You know me, Gulliver, I would have found a way into the house if I had to, but those boys were so nimble, so light footed, so eager.

Even with my prosthetic, I'm not exactly cat-like.

They'd padded through the rooms, located the right one, and in the dark, without a sound, they'd conducted the job without bother.

The senior Greenleafs wouldn't have known anything was happening. Perhaps their dreams were invaded by a couple of mischievous sprites, then catapulted into the ever after.

Anthony let me in through the front door, and I gave them the replacement bed sheets.

If you aimed well enough, there will be no chance ballistics will guess it wasn't him.

My end of the bargain.

The little girl.

It did cross my mind that the kindest thing to do in this case, might just be to put this little girl out of her misery.

These days I suppose this sounds sexist, but I do sometimes feel like the life I'm able to provide for a little girl isn't the life she would have chosen for herself. However well they take to the job, like Little Hye, or badly, cough, Lucrezia… I just feel more peace about training boys.

Silly, I know.

Sarah Greenleaf's bedroom was only a few doors away from her parents'.

It was pink, and it said 'Sarah: officially an angel' on the door.

That killed me.

And I went in.

She was, sitting up in bed with the sheets around her knees, waiting, listening.

The expression on her face was the same as the cat.

She knew.

If she'd have been asleep – my goodness, I still don't think I could have done it, Gulliver. To this day, I've never killed a child under the age of sixteen. A trophy; it's not easy to be so compassionate in the face of such personal risk.

I risk the lives of all of us by failing to fully complete orders.

Jeremy Greenleaf: up through the jaw.

I wish I hadn't looked inside the rooms on the floor below. There are some things you should never witness lest the images become burned on your retinas.

Mangled corpses – lined up side by side. Slashed open here, a cube cut out there.

Eyeless all of them, heartless for the most part.

Empty remains.

Harvested.

Bertha Greenleaf: directly through the forehead.

They were on the roof you know? The spooks. I didn't get a proper look at them, but I turned around and saw them as we skulked back over the garden.

Shadows flowed down the sides of the building – those were real ninjas.

Clean-up ninjas.

There would never be any trace of the horrors below. I understood afterwards – the government was staying one step ahead of the media. Someone must have squealed to someone who knew someone who could get the word out.

We skirted the lake, we followed the narrow little train tracks, and we headed for the far wall.

Me struggling underneath my heavy bundle, my leaden synthetic foot and leg sinking a little further into the mud with each step. Anthony saw it first – the cat – only the tiny streak from its one white ear, tearing towards us,.

He's going in the lake. Whined Anthony,

Never mind the cat!

I hissed.

But those boys, they couldn't help but stand and watch.

The little fur ball realised just in time that the lake was in the way of getting to us, or rather, to my precious bundle. It skidded to a halt, and screeched as it got its paws wet, rippling the water. Then it was off again, streaking round the lake to meet us. And as Georgie scooped it up, his gloves and coat scratched to pieces, we vaulted the wall with a hundred pure white flamingos like gigantic snowflakes, rising overhead from the disturbed lake.

Jeremy killed Bertha, then Jeremy killed himself.

Respected pencil magnate buckles under pressure of recent stationary slump. And their little girl, Sarah? Well, she ran away didn't she? Keep your eyes peeled, you might find her walking the streets, begging for food.

Lost and confused.

That was the story, that was what happened.

To everyone that mattered.

That was what happened.

The blood-stained bedsheets stored at the very furthest end of the longest tunnel in the Crypt tell a different story, of course, but nobody's ever going to find them, because nobody's ever going to find the Crypt.

Are they, Gulliver?

And Seaburn, the cat, never got a mention.

Eleven

Thursday, 17 January

Charles, under the bridge

The first time Foster took me outside on his own terms, running for freedom didn't even cross my mind. I guess after eight months on his kitchen floor I instinctively knew that the world I'd known aged eight and a bit had already vanished; who in the world expected I was still alive?

The mystery of little Jasper was forgotten as soon as another more interesting story broke.

Internet fraudsters steal Mussolini's brain.

Jasper who?

My family.

The feeling in my right foot.

My hope of rescue.

My desire for rescue…

Gone.

Two months since my first inept escape attempt, and as I limped along a deserted canal towpath beside Foster, the Allegro falling further into the distance, I hated myself for feeling a thrill at the clarity of the evening; no oppressive atmosphere squeezing my lungs or stabbing rays of light to blind me.

Not this time.

Trust Foster to know when the time was right.

My breath became solid in the air, and I remembered the day on the dunes. This day was colder, this day was in mid-winter when the sun only briefly raises its head above the sheets, before it tucks itself back in for a long spell.

The water in the canal was glass-like, but sometimes you'd see the faintest ripple; maybe a fish, maybe an escaping gas bubble. It looked like the water desperately wanted to turn into ice, but couldn't quite manage.

As we walked silently along the towpath, passing nobody because it wasn't somewhere you'd like to be found after the sun goes down in winter, I gritted my teeth against the treachery of that thrill, and pictured my Mother's face. Immediately I was engulfed by an overwhelming desire for her arms around me, and I couldn't quite stifle a sob.

I did a good job of turning it into a cough.

As we walked my eyes flitted from Foster's stiff white hand, with his long fingers and cracked dry skin, and the smooth dark water, thick and slowly undulating. I genuinely couldn't decide between launching myself into the all-consuming soup on one side, within which I fancied I might be as lost to Foster - and to myself - as I already seemed I was to the rest of the world, or else drawing myself to Foster's side, committing myself to dependence upon him for every aspect of my existence.

And then, Foster took my hand.

Firmly, without looking at me.

Perhaps - together we could fight against a world that we both found it difficult to fit into. It wasn't at all a bad feeling, but as an act in isolation, it didn't give me what I needed – it was simply better, right at that moment, than plunging into the unknown.

Of course, at that moment, there was no way for me to know where we were heading. I didn't know what was inside the long leather-bound case Foster was clutching just as firmly in his other hand. We just walked, and it grew steadily darker until I had no choice but to trust that Foster knew every step and footfall, because I certainly couldn't see the ground beneath my feet. There is something extremely sinister about knowing that right next to you there is a channel full of stagnant viscous water that you cannot see. Now that darkness had fully fallen, I wondered about what I would have done if I really had jumped into the canal – would I actually have been delivered into another reality, one beyond the confines of my mind? Or would I have become a very wet, very cold, very dirty child – a bane for Foster rather than an assistant.

Oh, because that's what he was bringing me along for, by the way, to assist him in his work.

Help him to meet his terms.

We stopped at a bridge.

It was virtually countryside, there were so many untended weeds and tall grasses by the side of the path, and yet I knew we were not out of the town, because on the other side of the canal there lay the blank, silent walls of concrete, rising out of the water – the toilet brush factory. Graffiti covered the kerbstones and the walls, none of it executed with anything like an imagination. Lots of the messages were completely illegible – though the tags were usually rendered with more care – here there were messages courtesy of Ripp, Ghrhyme, Mugz, and Bittah – and the smell; stale urine and shit.

And then, the bridge - black, iron, high.

It mercifully allowed traffic to bypass not only the canal, but a whole part of the town, within which nobody would want to loiter – even at a traffic light.

But then there was the underside of the bridge.

The design meant that underneath the bridge, there were huge struts rammed deep into the ground and secured with tons of concrete, and around the struts, were large, wide, concrete pits where, if one was creative enough, a shelter could be made. This is how more people than you would ever consider possible within a medium sized town in the North East of England, live their lives for one reason or another. During the day, you hardly notice them at all – if they're out and about they blend in perfectly with other rag tag citizens of the corporatocracy - some asking for money, some earning it, some losing it, some stealing it, some promoting Jesus. Perhaps some even stay in their little shelters beneath bridges like this one, curled up in a torn sleeping bag, glad to be out of the wind.

As we approached the dark hulk of the bridge and I had no idea yet to what it played host, I could see there was something more than initially met the eye. There was an orange glow, a flicker from deep down at the far ends of the struts, and as we came closer and peered down from the edge, about fifteen people stiffened and eyed us wearily, warming their hands at their open fire – sitting in their concrete bucket and waiting for the morning. Foster told them he was supposed to be meeting a man named Charles – as soon as he said it, the concrete bucket resounded with laughter.

Nobody sees Charles.

He told them,

I wasn't asking your permission. Now show me where he is or get him to come to me here, or I'll personally make sure the survivors never stop talking about this incident.

Still holding Foster's hand, I was glad to be with him rather than being one of those people sitting in their concrete windshield looking up at us with a mixture of hatred and fear. I couldn't elect to join them in reality, but in my head I made a clear choice between their situation and mine.

To my shame?

Charles, it seemed, was determined to remain elusive, but Foster wasn't fazed — he looked cold and bored, but he always looked bored, so really, to me, he just looked cold. I could tell he was ready to go home as much as I was, and Foster decided to speed things up a bit by undoing his leather-bound case. There, complete inside, without any need for assemblage, was a gun. It was a rifle, a German built, Korean imported IG-Sauer SSG 3000 (I know this now, I did not then) In one fluid movement it was out of the case, nestled against Foster's chin and shoulder.

This story is quite exciting Gulliver, so I'm going to slip into the present tense, for dramatic effect.

Humour me.

So, who wants to tell me where Charles is?

Says Foster, and he allows the laser sight to play across the forehead of the smallest child in the concrete bucket. The child's mother yelps and picks him up, but Foster's laser sight stays right on the little boy like a helicopter tracking a stolen car using a heat sensor.

There's the click of Foster's gun being cocked, and now the mother is frozen to the spot — she's terrified, and I'm glad her baby is asleep. But the little red dot still dances across the baby's head. Just tell me where Charles is. Says Foster. It's very simple.

But nobody's saying anything – the only sound is the sobbing woman holding the baby, and the occasional crack from firewood.

Nobody except Foster is breathing – Foster's breath comes hot and thick like a dog's, visible in the air, becoming one with the smoke from the fire.

Even I'm not breathing, I believe Foster is capable of putting a bullet in a baby.

Suddenly, an almighty clanging sound, and the entire bridge reverberates like a giant tuning fork. Everyone looks up instantly, everybody except Foster – he keeps that laser sight right on the baby's forehead.

But, I look up.

There, nestled into the black criss-crossed girders of the bridge, is a collection of torn blankets and, incredibly, a fridge freezer just visible in the shadows – its little red light showing clearly through the darkness like a mirror of Foster's laser sight. And there's a man – a man whose face hasn't seen a razor in months, dressed in baggy grey sweats, and holding a yellow snooker ball, which as we watch, he smashes down onto the girder.

Clang.

Then, barely registering that the man has made any kind of movement, I find myself flying backwards to land on my bottom in a freezing puddle. The hood of my sweater has come down and feels heavy – I reach behind inside it and retrieve the yellow snooker ball.

Impressive, Gulliver. By the time I've clambered to my feet the man in the girders has reloaded his fist with another snooker ball.

A green one.

The grubby folk of the concrete basins are settling into a spectator role, but Foster still has his sight trained on the baby's forehead.

This one's for you skeleton face!

Growls the man in the girders, and I can only deduce he's talking to Foster.

Take your gun off the baby and I might only break you.

Foster doesn't look up, doesn't move at all. The girder man's fingers tighten on the hard green sphere, and his muscles tense.

I wait. My eyes screwed up, for Foster to fly backwards with a large dent in his skull.

Waiting.

Silence.

Nothing.

Then, a bang that resounds deafeningly through the metal structure – my eyes on the girder man - and with the bang his snooker ball vanishes. I look at Foster and there he is, his lightly smoking gun re-trained upon the man. Shards of green snooker ball hit the thick dark water beneath the bridge, cutting it open like the top of a yoghurt, and vanishing beneath.

Minutes beforehand I might have envied those shards.

I'm making myself feel a little inferior.

Here I am writing to you, Gulliver – a better shot than me, on a good day – about a duel between two men who I've no doubt could each have shot a single ladybird off a snowdrop from twenty yards away, with a slingshot and a lentil.

Without disturbing a petal.

I don't mean to be gushing, but that split-second birthed a sudden giddy rush for Foster's world, bound up in an instant gut punch of self-loathing. Even today I can't enjoy the adrenaline shot of an exciting hit for more than a few seconds without the self-loathing chaser.

You and I tick in different directions, Gulliver, you probably get a rush from self-loathing. Anyhow, that moment sowed a whole garden of bittersweet seeds in my fertile little boy mind. And those shards of hard green snooker ball were the shards of my broken former life, buried as far as possible to a depth where I could probably never find them again if I tried.

But what of the rest of that night? Back to the drama.

Until now, despite all the clues in the form of weapons and dead family, I'm blocking my mind from deciding that Foster might be here to off someone – though someone getting killed is seeming increasingly likely.

Enough. No more denial.

The proud moment has arrived, when Foster puts his faith in me.

Hold this. He says. Thrusting the rifle towards me, always keeping his eye on the laser sight so it never budges a millimetre from the centre of the girder man's forehead.

I am not expecting this.

I am nearly nine years old.

I take the gun – I wrap my little finger around the trigger and I'm proud to say the sight only drifts across girder man's forehead about an inch.

Foster leaps straight into the air and grabs the nearest overhead girder, his sinewy arms lifting him high into the structure, he swings forwards and lands on top of a girder like a gangly tail-less lemur, just a few metres from my target.

Charles,

Says Foster,

This is really nothing personal.

Then he starts talking too quietly for me to hear, we strain, all of us on the ground, but Foster's words are not carried to our level.

After a little while Charles snarls something back – all the while his eyes on me, and my rifle.

His life in my hands.

And Foster pauses, then he lifts himself along the blanket clad bars, and prods the matrix of knotted textile stretched out across the frame – like trying cold water with his toe. He decides to take the chance, commits his weight to the creaking construct. It holds, and he bounces along, heading for the fridge with its little red light – and now that I focus on it I see a wire heading way up into the top of the bridge, tapping power from streetlamps. The least of Charles's crimes, I imagine.

Eye to eye. The space between us petrifies.

He's going to lunge. I just know it.

It's a split second, but I feel we're connected through the thin red beam between us. I sense his molecules tense.

Slow heart beats. Deafening.

You know the feeling Gulliver – we all know the feeling.

But I'm nine years old. And I allow myself to be distracted by my frozen fingertips, and my right foot, which this evening is tingling inside as though a procession of ants is marching across the inside of my sole. I mention all of this to justify my shot you see Gulliver. When Charles lunges at Foster, Foster with his head in the fridge, the internal light illuminating the scene is like a porta-loo at an outdoor rock concert.

I don't quite get him in the forehead.

I get him in the throat.

Foster doesn't move away, he finishes rummaging in the fridge, then he stands up, bounces back across the blanket matrix stepping over the gurgling, draining, form of Charles, and swings himself back down to the ground. By the time he takes the rifle back off me, there's a thin thread of blood running down from the centre of the blanket nest – pooling on the cold concrete floor.

Steaming in the night air.

My first kill.

Had I saved his life? Foster did not thank me.

But he wasn't disappointed.

It would be years before I killed a man again.

What he was whispering to Charles, I never found out – but he took a parcel from the fridge, and before we headed home, we made a little delivery to the back entrance of Penshaw police station. We cut the lights on the Allegro and cut the engine down the street. We rolled up outside and I barrelled out with the parcel – it was thick plastic, taped around the middle and both ends. Whatever was inside was squishy – it reminded me of the one inevitably dull parcel at Christmas; that I knew from the feel of it contained a home knitted jumper from my Granny.

I wondered if she would knit one for me this year.

I scooted the parcel up to the door and rapped on it – it was about 8pm and they'd already shut up shop. I limped back to the Allegro, and Foster just backed it into the shadows at the side of the road.

I looked at him, questioning.

Foster put his finger to his lips.

As though I would dare to speak.

The door opened a crack and light streamed into the cold night air – Officer Willows peered out into the street, I swear he looked right at us, then looked down at his feet and toe-kicked the parcel into the station.

Slamming the door.

Go get. Said Foster

Go get what?

Silence.

I went.

At the foot of the door in darkness, a thick envelope with nothing written on it. I scooped it up and ran back to the Allegro.

Foster pocketed it and we drove home.

He made spaghetti hoops on toast, for both of us, and he fried an egg on top of it.

I basked in that glow.

Twelve

Friday, 18 January

Chickens become chicken

Even if you do destroy me, know that I love you.

You may sneer, but, Gulliver, I always gave of myself for you, in the early days at least, everything I did, I did for you. Perhaps you were too young to remember – trips and treats in the normal world. Outside this stone bubble world I've created to protect us. Adventures in the open air, caution thrown to the wind.

You were enthralled by the mundane.

Your greatest wish was to visit the high multi-storey car park at the Metro Centre. You'd seen it from below when you came along in the Allegro for one of our covert black uniform stock replenishing trips, a treat in itself, I might add.

We parked near the gates of course.

But that concrete parking tower with its helter-skelter exit ramp was stuck in your mind; it kept slipping into your chatter on a daily basis. So, I took you there after dark one autumn evening when the rain reflected a hundred colours back at us like fairground lights, and we sped up and down the ramp. You laughed with abandon, and on the way home you fell asleep on my arm with your Big Mac and fries unfinished in your lap.

I often remember you from that night, a highlight from the years before.

Before you burned your hair.

Before you filed your teeth.

Before you killed anybody.

In those days it was almost as though our life was like everybody else's.

I was only 21 but I was devoted.

Do you remember?

I have learned how to regret very little.

The key principle in this is to imagine the inevitable alternatives to all the things that, on the face of it, seem repulsive things to have done.

Have you worked this out yet?

I wouldn't want you to be more miserable than you deserve. And on some level I do know that we deserve to be miserable, Gulliver. But regret looks backwards, misery is for the present and anticipates the future. I believe that misery in moderation, if given a clean and spacious outlet, can motivate, inspire, even sharpen the mind and enhance the senses.

Even so, if I hadn't taken you along on the Anderson hit, perhaps you'd still be here with me now.

The first for my first.

Everything else follows, like water leaping over rocks. Natural, smooth, but subtly destructive.

It may mean nothing to you – but allowing you to come that night opened up a door – so every subsequent member of my brood would join me in the field.

Except Michael, of course.

Do you remember the night before?

The last night when you and Michael could pretend to be equals? And we played Monopoly in front of the fire in the Crypt, and Michael beat us with cold calculation.

We urged him to spend his money, have fun and build his world. And he shook his head.

Resolute, he wrote,

I will win.

The game was still fresh with every potential move and counter move un-played.

And he had never played before.

So, we laughed at him.

He only bought three properties.

The utility empire; he took those two squares from us early, spending little. Then he stopped.

So, we coveted them, and tried to take them from him, and we destroyed each other doing so.

And all the while, it was his third property that won the day – the one he just 'happened' across.

Trafalgar Square... the slow and steady earner.

Even though you were only ten and I was 22, I felt that night I was ready to cast off my loneliness. Do you understand what I'm telling you, Gulliver? I took you along on the Anderson job because of that feeling – because I was a sore loser, and Michael had beaten us both so easily.

Gulliver, I set you on that path because I felt that together, you and I, we had similar wounds, similar scars.

Michael's scars... didn't match mine.

My research for the Anderson job was painful – I was repulsed by what I saw them doing to those poor birds. A job's a job – but it's so much easier if you believe in what you're doing. Sometimes, you have to force yourself to believe. Phillip and Naomi Anderson were not my usual kind of job. Usually it's the rich, sometimes even the famous. The Andersons were neither. They were just about managing, I suppose. Their little plot was an odd place, a neglected farmhouse almost completely hemmed in by modern houses.

I assume that either Phillip or his father had sold most their land for development decades ago for a pretty penny, but then (I speculate), pissed it all away.

So instead of fields, their farmhouse was set inside an almost comically narrow 'moat' of scrubland – then rotten board, and razor wire.

Only on one side was the house afforded a little breathing room – thank god, because that was our in. There, the woods at the edge of the town had escaped clearance, not for any environmental reason, but because that land had been sold to a telecommunications firm, the trees dwarfed by a towering radio mast.

Lack of space and capital, I assume, led them to their unorthodox method of intense poultry production. If it wasn't so repulsive, I might be drawn to applaud their ingenuity. Still, they must have put in an astounding amount of work for very little financial return… So, another assumption I feel justified to make is that they were also just a bit rotten inside.

Each giant chicken had to be hand plucked before it was cut up.

The things were supposed to dead before the plucking commenced, but they killed those birds under a big wooden door.

Unhinged.

OK, so they weren't really giant.

They were just about twice as big as a usual chicken. But that was what kept the Andersons in business; big wings, big thighs, big breasts.

Plenty of demand, no legitimate supply.

Monstrosities like that required a healthy dose of a very specific steroid.

Once commonplace, now contraband.

With the chickens just locked in what used to be the Anderson's ample hallway. This was not a clinical operation, or an exact science. With no way out of the corridor Phillip Anderson would simply drop the heavy wooden door on top of about fifty squawkers at a time, and then he'd shuffle around on top until he considered it likely most be dead.

Dead is pretty loose in this context.

Naomi could deal with a few giant heaving breasts, just so long as they were too far gone to attempt escape. I watched that woman pluck and dismember more living, wriggling chickens than words on this page, and I was only keeping tabs three hours a day.

Wriggling, squawking, bleeding, dead meat.

Chickens became chicken.

Free range, yes.

Humane, no.

That night was the greatest adventure of your life so far. Your little face all flushed, not its latter-day perpetual paleness, and it was sunken beneath your Parka's furry pit. I like to remember you this way, Gulliver – before you burned all your hair off.

A clear, freezing cold night.

I was excited too, watching your breath drift out in ribbons illuminated by moonlight. Perfect. Do you know what it reminded me of? It reminded me of when my parents used to take me and my brother to the biggest firework display for miles around for Guy Fawkes night. Anonymous cars chugging over the grass and mud, beckoned forward by men in neon vests standing like lighthouses in the midst of the fog and mud, not because they were being paid, but because they thought it was a nice thing to do. Those kinds of people are the real heroes.

Well anyway – those nights I could see even my Father was happy that we were happy, my brother Craig and me.

There were rickety fairground style rides strewn throughout the field, one was just a man taking twenty pence pieces then hand-cranking a circular wooden platform so it spun around slower than walking pace. But there was something about being in the middle of a field in the dark that made you feel like you were in the world of grownups. There was always the same fantastic smell from the hog-roast baguette stand where a hundred other versions of my father stood in line. And it always tasted so much worse than the smell promised – but with the hog roast sandwich in hand, spinning on the wooden platform in the dark, slow enough to see that your parents were smiling, laughing even, and they were holding hands, you felt like the world was a pretty good place to be.

I never found out what my father and mother had done to warrant their deaths.

I know they weren't like the Andersons for instance.

Fraud, I expect.

My father worked in financial services.

Looking after the pennies, was bollocks,

He said.

Forget the pennies. You can spend your life chasing pennies.

He said.

I held your hand that night.

The Allegro rocked along over the grass between the trees just like the cars at the bonfire. And you in your parka, with your wellington boots on, smiling.

I felt then, that you trusted me completely.

With hindsight, I'm not so certain.

After you burned off your hair and sharpened your teeth – when you started to hunch your shoulders when you walked and adopted that constant hunted look - I would look at you and see staring back at me a character that you had created, but for which I must take some responsibility.

The wood bordering the Anderson farmhouse, complete with its wind whistling radio mast, that's where I'd been laying, watching for weeks. Phillip and Naomi, they never did anything together. They never left the house together, never arrived back home together. And yet, they operated like a well-oiled machine. They may have loathed each other – but God they were made for each other.

He reared them, dosed them, and killed them, the chickens. That was his job. His part of the deal.

She plucked them and chopped them up.

To begin with I couldn't work out where she went every day. Phillip left early – to drive the carrier bags of yesterday's pre-pared meat, to rendezvous in a variety of lay-bys, car parks, and back streets where men in vans would drive off with the flesh, off down the road to legitimacy and barcodes.

He'd buy chicken feed, collet packages from a PO Box, and make bank deposits.

And he was good at losing a few hours in the pub.

But Naomi – she would wait an hour or so after he left the house, and then she'd skulk out. No need to skulk like she did – there was nobody to care where she was going.

Her house, her time.

But I had to know, so I followed her.

She always met the same friend, a woman, a bit younger than Naomi perhaps, a bit better dressed, at the same park bench, where they'd feed bread to the ducks.

I figured Naomi was pretty normal really; I was suddenly glad it was only Phillip I'd been employed to dispatch.

There was a deathly stillness over the house that night, the sort of stillness that means every rustle magnifies ten-fold.

Where were the noises of the night?

The odd plane perhaps? Maybe an owl?

There was nothing.

So, every time you whispered, I put a gloved hand over your mouth.

So began your education.

We scrambled through the trees at the edge of the farmhouse, stoked by raw anticipation, me with my long black case, and you with your gloves stretched out in front like railway engine buffers. You said happily,

I'm glad Michael isn't here.

And I told you,

That's not nice.

Michael had his place that night, he was at the Crypt, filing the serial numbers off bullets.

Of course, I did give Michael his day too.

But he dragged his feet and languished, dreading what we were going to find. To be fair to Michael, it was a miserable job. Sitting in the dark in unrelenting drizzle for seven hours with a puddle of diluted piss rising slowly round our ankles until we were sitting in it. Not just one person's piss, hundreds of peoples' piss.

And bits of shit.

But Michael was useless on that job – he just froze up. I could see he was gagging from the putrid air.

He was ten too, like you were.

He nearly ruined the hit clinging to my leg.

I didn't tell him he was useless.

I didn't say anything at all.

But I couldn't risk taking him again.

I digress – we're talking about your first time.

I have to say, Gulliver, you weren't initially a lot of help on the Anderson job. You whispered a lot, and every time you broke a twig under your clumsy feet you'd say, 'excuse me!' out loud as if to make things worse on purpose.

I winced at each crack and crunch, because upstairs in the farm-house, now within spitting distance, three whole rooms were crammed with over three hundred chickens each, divided between rooms according to their stage in the life cycle, sitting in the dark with their bobbity heads stuffed under their wings.

Waiting to be crushed, plucked, torn, and bagged.

But if one of them got spooked, the whole lot would be set off, hitting the ceiling, flapping and squawking. The perfect early warning system for something approaching the house, and Phillip knew anything coming his way was likely something he wanted to turn around immediately, or else silence for good.

No happy visits.

I guessed it was an animal rights group engaging my services.

Extreme action.

Commitment to their cause.

Or something.

I was wrong, as it turned out.

But it doesn't matter if you're wrong, only that you believe the excuse you've come up with to make you feel better about blowing someone's brains out.

Someone you don't know.

Anyway, that treehouse was charming.

That was a perfect place to settle down for the long haul. The sadness of its existence was not lost on me, but with you by my side, it felt suddenly bright and warm, as though the walls once lovingly constructed from the desire to make a child happy, were embracing us, thanking us, for fulfilling their purpose if only for a few hours.

It couldn't have been further from poor Michael's acrid latrine nightmare. There were even some damp cushions, the faint comforting smell of wood stain, and a mattress.

We waited, belly first on the mattress, taking turns to squint through the rifle's telescopic sight.

Line up the crosshairs.

Shut one eye, line it up, then swap to the other eye. How can you ever be sure of what you're seeing when each eye sees things so differently? Most of the time, all we're seeing is a compromise between the two, so how is a man like me supposed to trust his peepers to tell him when his shot's lined up?

That's where intuition comes in.

That's when it stops being something learned, and starts being something you were born to do.

Naomi Anderson gave me the shivers beyond even the clear cold night. We had the bedroom in view through the window, there they lay side by side, but she just lay there, unnaturally motionless, I thought.

As we messed around, looking through that telescopic sight like we were on a beach pier, her eyes opened as she lay beside our target. Unmoving - white orbs glinting in the cold moonlight, then her head turned just slightly, and she was looking directly down the barrel of my gun for several seconds, almost inviting me to finish her too.

Actually, when I still believed our client was an animal rights protester group, the thought had crossed my mind to do Naomi for them too.

Off one, off one free. Oooof...

But I'm a professional.

No free rides or everyone would want one.

And now I'm certain she was wide awake the entire time.

It should have been obvious.

Her duck feeding friend, the younger, more smartly dressed woman in the park? Beatrice Marshall, a giant in the legitimate giant poultry world, with a strangle-hold on giant honking, giant gobbling, giant cooing, even giant quacking... but not giant clucking, because in the North East of England, Naomi and Phillip had had giant clucking in the bag for decades. Massively undercutting the competition.

Beatrice. All she needed them to do was to go away, I suppose.

Who approached whom, I do not know.

But a call was made to someone, who made a call to someone else, who made a call... to me.

So now, I realise, Naomi knew I was there, lurking in the tree-house, and I'm certain she nodded at me. It was almost imperceptible – just a movement in the scattered moonbeams reflected in her eyes through the double glazing.

As soon as I saw it, I told you it was time.

Perhaps I shouldn't have given you such a risk-filled first job, but of course you were excited, and so was I. Still lying belly down on the mattress, blissed-out by the sense of occasion, you grabbed the eyepiece and thought you were perfectly aligned.

Look with your other eye. I said. But you just ignored me and mashed the trigger with your thin little fingers poking out of your mittens, tilting the whole set-up by at least an inch. And your first ever shot, where did it go? Directly into the butt of their Staffordshire Bull Terrier, asleep on the edge of the bed.

Their baby replacement pet, I fancy.

Their marriage placed upon his back.

A burden he had been unable to support.

Then, uproar.

I would never have guessed then that you'd turn out to be such a perfect shot.

There was the click of the trigger, then the suction sound of the silencer, the sound of broken glass as the window gave way – then the agonising yelp.

The dog flew around the room snarling and barking blue murder, desperately snapping at his own bleeding buttock, then writhing yapping, running full pelt trying to escape the pain.

Phillip Anderson was supposed to die quietly – perhaps not instantly, but quietly. My signature shot – middle of the throat – that was the set-up. However much they scream, nothing will come out but gurgling and a whole lot of blood. I've been told it's less painful than a head shot, which is often much less instanta-neous than movies would have us believe. I also feel it allows the victim a little time to gather their thoughts – not long, granted, but as they drain out and fade away, it's my hope that on some level, they're able to make peace with what's happening.

It preserves the face for an open casket too.

And it's really quiet.

But Phillip Anderson's throat was not pierced by that bullet. All Michael's hours of scraping, scraping, scraping. Oh, I expect that bullet would be dug out of that poor mutt's butt, but thanks to Michael it would never be traced.

Poor bullet. It never reached its potential – condemned to an embarrassing retirement in an evidence room filled with other more fortunate specimens who hit their intended targets.

Exhibit 'A's and him, only an investigation's sideshow.

So, Phillip Anderson's throat was never touched.

But his forehead was drilled.

Gulliver, that was when I knew you were one of the few. Stone cold talent under pressure; quick as a flash you whipped back your parka hood for a better look, rectified the shot, and almost as soon as he sat up in surprise, watching the dog barrel around the room in agony for few seconds, zip! Instead of a slow demise bleeding copiously onto the sheets beside his wife as she pretended to sleep, the wretched chicken crusher splattered her with bits of brain. He slumped over onto her, and she couldn't keep up the pretence, leaping up, flinging open the sash window, shouting obscenities at us.

Already we were sliding down the wooden ladder, our palms taking on a hundred splinters. But I saw her, she glared out at me, and her white eyes shone with fury.

Whatever she was shouting was drowned out by the dog, who by that time was tearing through the whole of the upstairs, leaping among the hundreds of squawking birds each almost the same size as him, we could hear them smashing around the house, trying to get away from him, and as we scaled the fencing to get back to the Allegro, giant bloodied chickens were dropping from the window around Naomi, feathers flying under the moonlight, backing up behind her, following each other blindly, pecking, tearing, clawing at her back until she lost purchase on the window frame and fell heavily into the scrub-land below, the dog following behind, tearing into her back with his teeth and claws; just wild and mad with the pain.

And we were ready to slip away.

Like phantoms.

Well, I was. I was covered up.

But you, I suddenly realised, were fully on display - your red face glowing with accomplishment, still clutching my rifle.

Your body shaking, with laughter.

Cover your face!

But... you'd decided to throw me a complete curveball, my words fell on deaf ears, and there you were, heading back towards the house. To my horror, you were lining up your shot, and in the time it took me to reach you, you'd taken it.

You got your throat shot after all.

The dog gurgled, spasmed, and went limp, trapping the wailing Naomi underneath, scrabbling to get up from within a sea of blood and feathers.

Was it a mercy kill, Gulliver?

Or something else?

I want you to understand, Gulliver, I had to scold you as well as praise you after that. I couldn't let your recklessness go unchecked.

Ignoring my instructions before taking that first shot, going back and taking that second shot, exposing your face!

Perhaps I laboured that last point too much.

It was easy to forget you were only ten.

And it wasn't lost on me that your botched and bloody scorching of your poor scalp came in the days to follow.

I hope my praise took root as deeply as my scolding.

Talent like yours has to be managed lest it become tyranny.

I failed.

Thirteen

Monday, 21 January

Fat Angel

Before you, before Michael, before Little Hye, and even before I fully embraced this calling, there was the Crypt. And I must thank Foster.

Funny to thank Foster...

Perhaps you still think it's your home.

I hope so.

Although, of course, the inscription above the door makes it clear that we are only the present occupiers – where others have carved out bolder claims in the past.

It read:

Herein they rest. The Saints of the mediocre.

With 'mediocre' in skewed letters carved painstakingly over the originals. Whatever word was there before – someone had devoted a considerable amount of time and effort to get rid of it.

Foster was too tall to be a really classic killer. He was always poking above things and being seen.

He lacked long-term vision, too – and the Crypt is a case in point. Foster knew about the Crypt, but he disregarded it because he'd forgotten what it was like to have a sense of wonder.

Foster found the Crypt through pure chance — he'd done a reccy of the hit we'd be preparing for over the past few weeks, and been delighted to stumble across a piece of perfectly flat forest floor upon which to lie on his belly and angle his shot out from the forest, directly into the bedroom window of his mark's cottage, a quarter mile away.

These days. The forest has grown so dense, the cottage is impossible to glimpse through the trees.

On the day of the hit itself, I'm actually quite bored. I've been with Foster for three years, and this hit is pretty routine. I'm on look out and clear up duty waiting outside the cottage itself.

Foster settles into his snipe spot, and waits, and while he waits, he starts thinking about this perfectly flat piece of forest floor.

A bit odd.

He clears some of the foliage and moss, and finds flat stone beneath.

A sort of, lid.

But there appears to be no way inside.

In a rare moment of openness, Foster later admits to me that he left his gun and went rooting around in the undergrowth trying to find an entrance.

He literally stumbled across it; fell right down a set of stone steps completely obscured by thorny foliage.

He didn't admit to me that he fell down them, but when I joined him up there later — his jacket was covered in burrs, there was a rip in his slacks, and he had a fresh graze below his eye.

The thick oak wood door was locked shut with a rusty padlock.

Foster hardly ever used a silencer.

He thought it was cheating.

But this was a silencer moment.

Five shots. Tougher than a throat.

A sunny Summer early Saturday morning, on the hill above his hit, and Foster's there shooting at the lock like it's target practice.

Pfft, Pfft, Pfft...

So I'm waiting down below, I hear the shots and I know, that's Foster, but that's not my signal. And I realise I'd be upset if someone killed Foster.

I'm down by the cottage, supposed to be a look-out for Foster up in the forest on the hill, but I'm playing – sitting cross legged on the edge of the driveway, I'm playing with the smooth round stones I find there, subconsciously arranging them into little piles that represent a mum and dad, and my brother, but with little heads, big fat bodies.

And with the fingernail on the tip of my index finger, I flick each one of their heads as far as it can possibly go – my father's head soars into the air and lands smack in among all the other stones on the drive. lost. I put more forward pressure onto my mother's head, and she flies across the courtyard, hitting the target's red Range-Rover on its driver side door. It leaves a little glint that you can see, but nothing for anybody to worry about.

I flick Craig's head with all my might, and it goes flying towards a window of the house. It hits the glass with a noise much louder than such a small stone has a right to make, and I see the pane crack before the stone falls to the ground. I'm frozen, petrified that the occupants will have heard, but the worst isn't over. The crack creeps further up towards to the top of the window, and sub-cracks veer off at crazy angles. The integrity of the glass is weakening before my eyes – and I leap forward instinctively, intending to… what? Catch the glass as it falls? Hold it into the frame forever? Gently remove each piece and lay it on the ground?

I'm too late anyway.

Four separate pieces drop outwards from the window frame like falling icicles, they hit the windowsill with a clatter, then shatter among the stones below.

It's the loudest noise anything has made. Ever.

A stout man in his mid-fifties races out of his house.

He wears a white bathrobe, and his black hair streaked with grey, long, down to his shoulders, is scraped backwards off his head. This guy has just been having a shower, and now he's running barefoot across his garden.

A fat angry angel.

Waving a rifle.

I realise he must think someone threw something at his window from the garden. He hasn't even seen me squatting awkwardly next to the window.

Just as he's about to turn around and definitely see me, he halts jerkily in his tracks, and sinks to his knees.

Foster.

From afar.

With mighty accuracy, and no time to remove the silencer.

From his knees the fat angel rolls to his side in one fluid motion.

A scream comes from the broken widow, and out from the cottage runs a girl in her mid-twenties, with wet hair and a loose blue bath robe.

She spots me right away, sitting there against the side of the cottage, with the headless corpses of my family separating us. This girl, her wet hair is long and really dark, and the bits of her skin showing look like toffee yoghurt. She strides over and grabs my wrist, but I'm quick and slippery so she has to grab my other wrist too. I'm struggling, and slowly, with no way to fix it, her dressing gown drifts open to reveal more and different shades of brown. I'm hanging by my wrists, staring at her breasts. She just smirks, I'm an eleven-year-old boy – she isn't going to let go.

So I swing forward on her wrists, and bite her nipple. I'm not holding back, I really grind my teeth together – and there's a sound like when you bite down on gristle in a bad steak, and you know you're not going to break it down however much you chew – you have to spit it out. She screeches and lets go of me but we both fall to the ground together, her with her hands on her breast, doubled up, and spitting murder. Me, I land on my knees then scrabble to my feet and hobble off across the lawn. She starts after me, but another 'pfft', and a bunch of the stones on the drive in front of her fly up into the air, shattered and raining around her.

Foster, with a warning.

For a moment wide eyed, she stops shouting, then buries her head in her arms.

I shout that I'm sorry. Then I pass the bleeding body of the target and I skid to a halt. I go back to the body, give it a little kick to make sure, and then I get on my knees and take his bath robe in both hands. Yanking it violently I manage to roll him over and there it is – among the spattered pink and splinters of white – sitting in a little pool of red – the bullet.

A useless mission, but I gave it my best.

When I reached Foster after digging the bullet out of our angelic target, he had already vanished through the door with the newly blasted lock. The rotten timbers surrounding it had splintered a little way revealing a multitude of woody colours, from black and slushy, through damply orange, and ending in the dry hard core of dark brown oak, harder than the rusty iron shackle ripped apart by Foster's bullet. As I swung myself into the stairwell cavity before the door, just as I was about to follow Foster's trail through the unknown gloom on the other side, I realised the old wooden door deserved a closer look. There were, or there had been, relief carvings on the surface, although they were now quite swollen and black from the relentless streams of drizzle coming off the forest floor above. There were four panels in all, and the bottom two were so deformed from also sucking moisture from below, that I couldn't start to hope to decipher their original message. But the top two panels were in better condition, I could see that the left-hand panel bore a message, and the right-hand panel bore an intricately carved picture of something.

The text of the message was written so that the words filled the entire panel of the door, stretched out so that there was more space taken by the words themselves, and the letters were discernible only by the gaps in between.

Easily missed. But ever since my encounter with Charles the snooker ball guy, I had found myself looking upwards in new situations.

A useful habit.

The door itself was over seven feet high, and my eyes were level with the very bottoms of the top panels; I had to strain my head backwards quite painfully to take them all in, squinting at the shadows, but line by line the message was revealed:
An eternal home
 for the dead,
 And sweet rest
 for the living.

You helped Michael to re-touch it in bright rainbow colours once, and later Ricardo and Emily with night sky, stars, and gold leaf. But when I first saw that message, it struck me very powerfully, and I knew it was more than chance that Foster and I had been led there. And the picture? The next panel? Oh yes, you know it well too, Gulliver, I know – two figures lying side by side, a man and a woman, him - gaunt with eyes shut tight, her - hearty and whole, with eyes wide and watching, staring out into the forest forever, a guardian angel for the dark places at her back. These too, these two, have often times been repainted and even re-imagined by little hands – and sometimes I did wonder about the less than perfect results of their makeover, the goggle eyes, the lolling tongues, the Halloween skeleton rendering. I would silently offer up a prayer of repentance to the Saints of the Mediocre.

Oh Saints, may our mediocrity be marvellous in your eyes.

One, two, three, four more steps beyond the door, five, six, then nothing – a rock wall in sheer, all engulfing darkness. Groping with my hands I only found rock, and then there was space in front of me, and I stepped forward into it.

My foot didn't find purchase.

With my arms flailing around my head, my knees gave way and my body slumped forwards into a dark void. Of course, there were more stairs – there wasn't always a light bulb on that staircase, Gulliver. I fell heavily, banging my head on several steps.

And I lay there on my back, on the cold stone floor, and although I didn't know it, although I couldn't see them, the dead were stacked all around about me in the dark recesses of their eternal resting places.

The dead in rotted wooden caskets.

The dead in stone chambers.

The dead with just their bones left lying on a plinth.

The dead, some of them, in remarkably preserved ceremonial dress holding staffs, crumbling books, medicine bottles, or small animals.

OK, the small animals is a slight exaggeration – only one had the skeleton of some creature or other lying in her arms – I think it was either a beloved pet dog forced to die with its doting owner, or a fox that got into the Crypt and ate whatever the dead woman had been holding.

I couldn't see any of them – I was still lying in the dark on my back when Foster stepped on my hand.

I shouted out in pain. He said,

Quiet, we're leaving.

And he climbed over me and walked up the stairs.

So, we left.

Fourteen

Tuesday, 22 January

The Sad Breakfast

By the time you came to live with me in the Crypt, I had been living there for two lonely years.

The confusion, then terror on your face as you took in the stone plinths and chiselled epitaphs for people long laid to rest, is carved into my memory. I could have handled the entirety of that day in better ways, but what's done is done.

I hope when I am gone the Crypt will live on as a home to more and more generations. I want my legacy to endure beyond flesh and bone.

When I was a child, and Craig was still my big brother, and we lived in a house with a bedroom each, I used to think every object in our house had consciousness. I even used to think that the parts of the house; the walls, the ceiling – they could feel something, that they were conscious. And because I was the only one in my family who could perceive those things, I thought the whole house, in a way, belonged to me, and to me only.

My reasoning went, that I couldn't imagine not feeling something, or being aware that I was a thing. I thought it must be true that a mug could see – that a mug could perceive something, even if it was just whiteness, or the smell of milk. This was something I attempted to explain to my Father, but probably should have kept to myself.

He just raised his eyebrows quizzically and said 'hmmm?'

After I was eight, I stopped believing in such fantasies. The three years following my first escape attempt I simply grounded myself in living on Foster's kitchen floor and trying to please him. But once we'd discovered the Crypt, I kept re-living my tumble down the stone steps.

The hidden door.

Allure, of such an exciting place.

When a hit came in, Foster stirred himself into meticulous planning mode, and everything went pretty much according to plan. But the route was peppered with tangents, stumbles, and Plan B's that hadn't been planned.

Sound familiar, Gulliver?

Of course it does.

But to Foster those things were little blights on an otherwise perfect plan, and he wanted me to join him up there on the precarious ledge of impossibly lofty expectation. But whenever Foster took a tumble from that ledge, his extended plunge into misery did little to sell this mind-set to me.

As he ground his teeth into rock-like stale bread rolls breathing hot air from his nostrils like a bull while staring out the window, or succumbed to bouts of self-loathing by suddenly stabbing the tabletop with a kitchen knife and snarling when he didn't hit his last mark precisely, I thought – fuck –that.

Unhealthy, impossible, stifling.

Shadows I lived beneath.

I understand a little more now.

The hole in Foster's heart was Martin-shaped.

Assuming the role of sidekick was not something I deftly slid into immediately following the hit on Charles the snooker ball guy, although Foster seemed to believe that I would. I've come to the conclusion over time, that a large part of Foster's success as an assassin was his simple mindedness. Not that he was unintelligent, but he was a great believer in two twos making four, whatever the situation, whatever their context – never mind if one of the twos had been put through a woodchipper. It was still a two, right?

And so, I was a little boy.

Foster's experience of little boys, I believe, was greater than most, in that he had raised, or at least part raised, one before.

I'm certain Foster simply treated me the same way he did Martin. Feed it, exercise it, show it cool stuff.

Boys like cool stuff.

He wasn't wrong.

Foster's world, post Charles the snooker ball guy, became my world too.

Whether Martin was Foster's actual little boy, whether he had been there by his own free will or not. On some level he'd achieved what I had failed.

Escape.

Escape became increasingly important, because of guilt. The guilt was building like interest on a bank account, and my debt was to my family – I owed them more than settling for Foster's world that was daily losing its oppressive darkness, even guiding me towards appealing, exciting, slivers of light. I owed them the drive, determination, and anguish they'd surely expect.

I owed them escape, but this time, it would be a different kind, and the beginning of a slow journey towards paying off the guilt debt in full.

After the first year sleeping on Foster's floor, my nights became fractured with sudden pain and cold sweats. Partly because, after a year of incubating a cocktail of glass fragments and grime, my foot had simply become numb. The wound wasn't pretty, but my foot still looked like a foot. The black fungus that I now know was taking root beneath the surface wasn't yet visible. But during the night, a searing pain would often wrench me from my sleep; a red-hot poker to my flesh. The first several times it happened, I screamed openly, loudly, and lengthily, until Foster bloody well came and assessed the situation. The first time, he kind of 'tutted', and wandered over to the back of the kitchen, stood on a stool, and retrieved a jar.

Gobstoppers. Huge ones.

A hidden trove.

Bite it. He told me.

And he pulled me up to sit against the cupboards.

Then he took a pint glass, placed my foot on his thigh, and rolled the glass over the swollen part, massaging the scar until the pain subsided, and I fell asleep. In all honesty, I don't remember him going back to bed the first time.

The next time, after ten minutes, he handed me the glass. And the time after that, he just came and put the gobstoppers, and the pint glass, on the floor, and retreated back to bed.

I still have the pint glass.

I've never been able to find gobstoppers so big.

So, foot pain, was one reason I woke constantly.

But there was something else. I could literally set my watch by the sound of the train passing by a whole storey beneath, not so much a rousing rumble, as a feeling that the building itself was quaking in its foundations terrified of actually collapsing. But Foster, once asleep, never stirred from that particular noise. At least, I never saw the tell-tale shadows shift beneath his door.

So, by the time I was eleven after three years ingesting Foster's idiosyncrasies, and two years into my painfully fractured nights, the passage of time allowed me to naively consider that there had actually been only one flaw in my previous escape plan aged eight and a bit.

Timing.

Me aged eight would never have entertained the possibility of escaping at night. In the unknown darkness.

Eleven-year-old me had been on enough night-time excursions to know that darkness itself is nothing to be afraid of, but rather the ignorance of what exactly lies within it.

Now, I surmised, at nighttime the likelihood of Foster hearing me carefully release the door latch, half hop, half slide down the stairs avoiding known creakers (a particular triumph, I thought, considering my foot), and slipping out into the night, was minimal.

Plus. I tried to convince myself I didn't care any longer.

That's what acts of rebellion are built on, I thought:

Not giving a shit.

Foster's flat was just off the south-east side of the city centre, part of a dingy row of 1940s terraces that would have benefited greatly from being pulled down and replaced by soulless tower blocks. At least that would have saved them from subsidence. The entire row of houses crammed together on Round-Table Terrace had been slowly but relentlessly drifting forwards, at an alarming rate of seven millimetres per year, ever since the Metro light rail system was installed in the deep cutting outside the front doors. I did wonder how much the sleeping Foster was contributing to those millimetres per year purely through adding his weight at the top of the house.

I could see the cracks in our abode widening daily; it was alarming even to me, but a perfect excuse to reccy a new hide-out.

Just one I had no intention of sharing with Foster.

The posters on the Metro light rail system listed the names of all the wayward losers who'd been caught riding it without a ticket. They were named and shamed, or perhaps named and famed. In truth, I would have loved to see my name up on any poster.

Getting on a Metro train without a ticket is easy for an eleven-year-old boy. Under sixteen you don't need to pay, but you must be accompanied. The trick is to stay out of sight and refrain from entering the station until you find a suitably respectable looking man entering. Walking close to his heels, and even looking up at him occasionally.

Worked every time.

I looked respectable enough beside the respectable gentlemen that could be my father; Foster brought me clothes from charity shop piles whenever he remembered. I never had to ask.

He must have spent a bit of time picking them.

In the small hours, any respectable man boarding the Metro was probably a businessman en route to Newcastle Airport.

Casual-ish clothes.

Suit bag over one arm.

Cabin bag trundling behind.

The first time I slunk onto a Metro light rail train behind a fake father dragging a cabin bag, him wearing a checked shirt with a brown suit jacket and washed-out jeans, I was in my corduroys with a sweatshirt to go with it.

Oh, and the sweatshirt said 'an apple a day, makes you want oranges'.

Too cute to be profound.

Looking back now I realise most of my clothes were childish for the age I was. The kids around the street would probably have properly laughed at me if they hadn't been terrified of Foster.

I tried, Gulliver, to get you age-appropriate clothing. You might not have realised, but I did try not to underestimate the importance of that kind of responsibility.

I took the Metro to the little village station of Penshaw, only a ten-minute ride. In time, it became habit, and I'd climb from the village, up into the forest. The first time I alighted at Penshaw, I came face to face with my first love, a girl on a billboard, advertising shampoo.

I didn't pay her much attention that first time; just enough to feel her big eyes on me and feel unnerved.

Hers were the only eyes I'd felt on me thus far on my little adventure.

I passed from her sight.

And she passed from my mind.

That night, anyway.

The faux Greek columns of the folly above Penshaw are lit up at night so it can be seen for miles around. It's all most people really know about Penshaw; defined by something useless someone built for no good reason. It sits there like a party hat on a confused granddad at Christmas. There are so many more interesting stories in the village – the church dates back to 1748, I know you've haunted the churchyard from time to time – we all have peace of mind to search for, I know. Did you ever notice that the flaking church walls bear an uncanny resemblance to the walls of our Crypt? I can only imagine how many other secret stone spaces lie in our forest waiting to be stumbled upon, and networks of tunnels whose existence and purpose have long ago been forgotten.

Only one, very tiny, almost not there at all path leads up to our Crypt. Even the rabbits whose ancestors made the path seem not to be able to find it, because I never saw a rabbit around the Crypt, did you Gulliver?

I have to believe that only those predestined to find it will do so.

And so, Gulliver, we are honoured.

And yet, we should still fear the forest.

When I first re-visited the Crypt, I neglected to bring anything with me at all, most importantly I forgot that the place would be in darkness.

And my God, it was creepy.

Have you been there alone in the dark? Silent but for slight creaking?

That night, I didn't venture inside.

I spent hours trying to pluck up the courage, but they passed like minutes as in a trance, and by the time I'd made up my fuzzy mind that it might not be so bad and that anything lurking inside could just as well appear at the door and pounce on me from there, the first vestiges of sunlight were beginning to crawl through the leaves. A beautiful sight, the Crypt laid out before me, only mine, with all my ideals of what it could become.

Sunlight meant I was late.

Late enough to make sure Foster was awake.

To make sure I couldn't sneak back inside.

Because I'd decided, this act of rebellion was going to bring change.

I was much closer to enacting the movie version of my plan that time, Gulliver. But in that version I saw myself strolling nonchalantly back through the door.

Yeah, I went out.

Now I'm back.

Deal with it.

Turned out, I gave a shit.

And I couldn't hide it from myself.

It actually knocked the wind out of my lungs; a genuinely unforeseen panic at what I'd done.

Again.

The twin guilts knotted together and strangled my stomach to nausea. I tore back through the thick forest towards the train, lacerating my arms and legs, my leaden foot letting me down every few metres. I kept dragging myself up using branches and cable-esque thorn tentacles that left barbs in my palms. Biting my lip against the pain, I made it out into the open daytime, playing punishment scenarios over in my head, but already planning my return.

That's why the forest let me go.

It knew I'd return.

In the couple of minutes I had to wait for the return Metro train early that morning, the shampoo billboard girl stared across the tracks at me from the opposite platform, and I was able to take in more of her. Her eyes said,

You don't understand, our souls are fused.

Her hair was being kissed by unknown lips.

If you use this shampoo, you too will fall in love.

She seemed unbearably lonely.

And worn. Her skin was cracked and faded. Her edges ripped, corners dog-eared.

A sad irony was, then, that she had endured in that place because she sold too few bottles of shampoo.

Too few eyes on her.

And not the right kind.

Our silent communication across the rails would become a source of great peace and comfort to me.

In time.

That first night, her steady gaze only stoked my panic, and the arrival of the train, blocking her from view, was a great relief.

The train was almost empty, but I couldn't sit still — strutting, fretting, biting my nails.

It was only as I dragged my foot upstairs, soaked with sweat, and pocked with undergrowth lash marks, I managed to breathe more slowly and regained a little of my earlier sense of triumph.

Rebellion.

When I quietly let myself in through the upper door, the beast had indeed awoken. Foster had his breakfast laid out in front of him, and he was unnervingly calm. The kitchen had none of the warmth or smell of activity, the toaster was cool, the kettle was still, and Foster's breakfast looked like plastic toys.

Rubbery toast.

Tea that had stopped steaming some time ago.

Without making eye contact, he poured me a bowl of Ricicles and splashed them with just the right amount of milk. Then he picked up his tea, reached inside the rim, and extracted a thin skin from the top between his thumb and forefinger, laying it on the side of his plate beside his sad toast.

We ate without saying a word, and I was acutely aware of each deafening Ricicle crunch.

It would take me a long time to understand that breakfast, Gulliver. Not until I'd experienced the fear of losing my own children.

Fifteen

Thursday, 24 January

The Desecration of the Saints

The next time I braved a night-time escapade, I was more excited than the first.

Almost a full month had passed.

A respectful period of time.

I kidded myself, I actually believed, that I was keeping Foster on tenterhooks wondering whether I might break camp again.

When?

And that was probably true… but the real reason it took a month, was to fully regain Foster's trust.

To show him what was true.

I'm in this for the long haul.

Now.

The man I sat next to on the Metro light railway could definitely have passed for my father, just the older end. He had my thick dark hair, thicker round the ears and nape of his neck – and coming out of his ear holes.

He was in his early sixties, but he was wearing a basketball jacket like I was, and a matching cap that made his ears fold down a little at the tops.

He was different from the travelling businessmen.

I wished he was there every night.

This time I had a rucksack full of goodies. A torch, some paint and brushes, a small rolled-up rug, a small toolbox with the essentials, several changes of clothes.

Some of the stuff Foster had, but didn't know he had.

This was my project.

According to all maps and plans that I've been able to find, our Crypt is simply not there. I didn't linger at the top of the steps this time. The forest opened before me as I made my way there, but it felt like the trees and undergrowth closed pretty quickly behind me as though trying to erase my trodden path. So the Crypt itself felt inviting, warm even. I eased myself down the damp steps mindful of my previous less than dignified descent, and happily shut the door behind me, leaving the indignant forest to sit at the door and wait for morning.

I skulked around the place with my torch, illuminating human remains in their little niches like the macabre goods of a secret shop of horrors. It was difficult to scope out a full impression of the place by torch light.

I was three visits away from a wonderful discovery.

Electricity.

I've probably let you think I installed the electricity supply in our Crypt. But the truth is that the thick black wire running out from the stairwell and punctuating the forest floor, emerging over half a mile later to discretely connect with cables running to the pylons at the side of the mud track…

That was tapped.

Illegally.

Expertly.

But not by me.

I did notice the light fittings.

Not the first time they flashed into my limited field of vision. Funny what you take in your stride when there's no herald to announce the off kilter. But once my brain had caught up with my eyes, I scanned the ceiling in more detail, and couldn't stop smiling. I paid no heed to the anger of the forest as I made my way back to the station when dawn arrived. And I was still thinking about those light fittings when I joined Foster for another joyless breakfast.

Joyless for him.

Over my next couple of visits, I searched the place from top to bottom by torchlight, trying to find the path to the light!

I searched methodically, but not without many a cause to scream my frustration and thump the stone floor with my little fist. And one day it hit me, the one place I hadn't looked was beneath the dead. I began to lift the crumbling remains from their stone shelves – gagging at having to breathe in the clouds of disturbed dry skin even with a T-shirt wrapped around my mouth. I felt around in the stone underneath, and in the wall opposite, trying to find a switch, or a panel of some kind. To begin with I attempted to arrange the remains back how I'd found them, but whoever had arranged those bodies before me, they were skilled beyond words.

I don't mean the fresh bodies, oh no.

I mean the crumbled ones.

Those were the bodies that went into the Crypt. I know this because of what I discovered, the crudely constructed power switch beneath Stephen Horchester, 1791. One of a few Horchesters, along with some Goldings, a couple of Renworths, and a Gill.

I committed all of their remains to the wind.

I would never be so hasty in doing so now, but then, aged eleven, I thought very little of it. I required their space, and they were dead. But they've haunted my dreams, Gulliver, especially Stephen Horchester. He scolds me for ruining a work of great effort and magnitude, and he tells me that one day I will pay for my crimes.

I sleep on his vacated plinth when I'm resident within the Crypt.

I am there now writing this, and currently I am the only one awake. I can see little chests rising and falling, lying on mattressed plinths where once lay the bones and skin cells, rags and brittle hair, of the dead.

We know a little more now of course.

We know who tapped the electric link.

Who carefully arranged the dead I so callously dispatched.

I'm not sure she'll ever fully forgive me.

Her name is Martha.

That she is not happy with me, has not excluded us from one another's company. Martha has become very dear to me, and even though there are grey aspects of her past, present, and future that scare me even more than the prospect of facing you again,

Gulliver, I have been very open with her regarding who I am, and she has not yet condemned nor forsaken me.

Martha is an incredibly attractive woman.
    Not externally.

But she does possess an exquisite elegance, a wonderful inner peace, and the complete inability to give a shit about whether something pleases me or not.
    I like that.
    The 'discarded human remains' issue remains an extremely sore point. She calls it the Desecration of the Saints (picture me, Gulliver, I'm rolling my eyes).

Her pact with the dead.
    Precisely thirty years.
    In all that time she would seek no news.
    Great restraint.
    Upon her return she found the dead replaced by the living, by young life, and she thought the cosmos had listened to her.
    I felt myself compelled to reveal the truth.
    In time she may come to see how she actually did have a part in breathing new life into old bones.

I cannot claim the Crypt as my own entirely any longer. Martha is as much a part of it as you ever were.

Bittersweet attachment.
    If not for Martha, I believe Michael would still be here. I don't consider his silence a disability but, well, there are labels in the

world outside just waiting for people like Michael. Anyway, his emotional vulnerability meant I'd just never considered he would venture away from us, alone into the great unknown. How can he make a purposeful living? He doesn't have your skills.

So Michael Granton, missing to the world since the age of nine, presumed dead, is now truly missing. But my greatest fear, though it would break my heart, is not that Michael is dead.

My greatest fear for Michael is being subsumed into normality; welfare payments and speech therapists, state sponsored housing and pretending to give a shit about paint colour charts.

Better to die striving for something, anything.

Complete the story.

Become a celebrated memory.

In her grubby buckram robes Martha brought absurd cosmic ideas into our home, and they swirled around too tender ears and wheedled their way into the unconscious to cause restlessness.

Michael would never have thought of such things by himself.

His note said simply;

I'm going to find myself.

Sixteen

Saturday, 26 January

The Toddler Twins

Vinnie and Jason were only three years old apiece when they joined us; even in the old days, I would have been mad to take them on. I may have taken the job, but I would have left the toddler twins behind. Sometimes you have to admit that leaving a child to take their chances with Social Services is a better lottery ticket than bringing them home to live in a stone crypt and train as an assassin.

But I am truly much more cut out to be fatherly now in my forties, than I was with you in my twenties. I feel now that I run a very stable, happy crypt, and they all bring me joy. With Martha often by my side, they're proving themselves to be well-rounded and mentally stable.

Gulliver, see how I try to make amends?

I tried to be a strong masculine role model for you, and now I have found you a strong feminine one, too.

There are only cycles of life ending in death and life beginning again. Look at Martha's mummies, thrown to the wind and here, in their place is new flesh, vibrant and learning every day. I have learned from my mistakes with you, my mistakes with Michael too.

I believe my protégés these days are happy with their lives – and I know about death and life now, Gulliver – I can tell them about the cycles of death to life to death to life to death. The old replaced by new. Your mother, your father, they're not gone either, a little of them lives in me, lives in you.

Nothing ends, only regenerates.

My brood. I would challenge anybody to find a set of children with more abundant life skills.

Only Little Hye remains from your era. She and I are still sometimes able to communicate imperceptibly, but more and more the openness and warmth she had for me when she was a child, is being replaced by a kind of mutual respect that seems just a little aloof to me.

If I dwell on it for long, that might break my heart.

Georgie and Anthony flew the coop six years ago. I miss them terribly, just as I miss Ricardo and Emily.

And for Michael and for you, Gulliver - the loss I feel is a physical wrench.

But I have enjoyed the new beginnings.

I can hardly believe Sarah Greenleaf is seventeen this year.

Purely elegant, whether she's flipping a Spanish omelette or raising a rifle to her shoulder.

Control.

Sarah can teach the others as well.

She's a credit to me.

I don't say that lightly, Gulliver. But I honestly believe I've got a few things right with Sarah – she was the sweet spot between having absolutely no clue what I was doing when you were my charge, and these days where I feel little Arthur and sweet Lynette suffer from my advancing years and inability to keep track of their social development.

It doesn't matter, though, you see, because of Martha.

Martha may have given Sarah a little polish around the edges, certainly, but Vinnie and Jason's surefooted confidence and deft people skills, I credit wholeheartedly to her.

Martha appears and vanishes as she pleases with no advance warning of either.

I had thought she was angry with me, which is often the case, and often well justified. But I've stopped assuming her every sudden disappearance is due to some wrong I've inflicted on her or another; it's good to curb one's self-scrutiny when it becomes habit. So, we had been existing with reasonably harmonious indifference towards one another, at times inhabiting the same space and enjoying tea from the same pot, and other times unsure of where the other was for days or weeks at a time. I had last seen Martha two weeks previously, and as I say, I was certain then of her anger towards me, but upon reflection, I hadn't fully understood my wrong.

I don't think it was so much that she was angry to find me still considering taking the hit on Vinnie and Jason's parents, it was that I'd asked her opinion.

Then ignored it.

I think.

In truth, I hadn't expected her to be so resolutely against the idea of the hit on Vinnie and Jason's parents. I'd thought I had her pegged; it wasn't for me she was returning more frequently to the crypt. Her visits increased dramatically and became longer within a fortnight of Emily and Ricardo saying their goodbyes and ending an era.

Even my weak male perception twigged that she had been hovering, ready to fill a void once the older more responsible kids had flown our nest. The cynic inside me would notice the hushed conversations between Emily and Martha, always just out of earshot, and never continued once I appeared. I can't help but grimace at the thought that she may have helped them to leave, but at the same time I know that whatever path she set them on, it would be better for them than any other scenario I could conjure up in my mind.

Including the one where they reclaim their lost fortune.

Whatever her part in Ricardo and Emily's departure, it was clear that Martha's end game was pure; she wanted to ensure the younger ones were properly looked after.

Well fed.

Well rested.

Appropriately clothed,

And not overworked at my hand.

These things are all open to interpretation of course. Is a well-rested child one who is forced to wake at 5am to sit with Martha in silent meditation for twenty minutes before breakfast-time? Is a well-fed child one who is given only a kind of seaweed soup with tofu when that breakfast-time finally arrives?

Apparently, the answer to all of the above, is yes.

It wasn't so much Hye and Sarah that surprised me, I watched them with mild amusement as they grumbled through the first few days, ignoring Martha's timetables, and turning a deaf ear to her little cymbals on a string. But then, first Hye then Sarah the next day, yielded to her insistence. They were young women; Martha was the closest they had to a lifestyle magazine, so I figured they'd treat her like a fad diet, and normality would resume within a month.

Not so.

Martha's real coup was to bring Anthony and Georgie under her spell too. I watched, astounded, from afar. They openly scoffed at the girls and their incense and controlled breathing, and tried to break their concentration by flicking cornflakes across the room at the Zen-like trio. I did see Sarah open one eye, and for a moment, I thought she would leap across the Crypt and wring Georgie's neck. But instead she breathed deeply, closed her eye, and smiled.

A victory.

A deadly team when they want to be, but competitive way beyond simple sibling rivalry when the right challenge came along, Martha neatly clocked where Georgie and Anthony's weakness lay, and bided her time until one early evening in March, a couple of weeks into her mediations with the girls. Georgie and Anthony were using the last vestiges of sunlight to fire your biro and nail darts at tree trunks with the help of a thick industrial elastic band I'd found near the station and brought back as a treat.

Actually that day I'd had a strange encounter while sitting on the almost deserted Metro train, fixing my gaze on the window beside me, I saw a man, in anguish, muttering to himself and twisting a thick black rubber band between his fingers in an intricate pattern while listening to headphones. He was about my age. And I thought he was reflected in the window, so I looked instinctively over to the opposite aisle where I thought he should be, only to find him absent – an empty seat. I looked between him and the empty seat several times in bewilderment before he slid along from out of my sight and I only then realised, he was in a different train altogether, on a parallel track, going in the opposite direction. Even if I'd wanted to talk with him, I couldn't. It was pre-forbidden. He was still muttering and crying, then he was gone.

It was after that, directly, that I stepped out of the station and found beneath my feet the thick black rubber band.

From another dimension?

In a way.

Can you imagine your nail and biro darts given propulsion, Gulliver? Stay, away! Especially when Anthony and Georgie moved on from being playful, to being competitive, then seamlessly into intense battle mode.

Evidently, Anthony was losing.

He sharply, bitterly, vocalised his frustration – howling into the trees.

We all went out to see, encountering a rage that might have seemed funny if it wasn't for the accompanying murderous look on his face.

I'd seen it before, of course, these two will probably actually do each other in, eventually. I've heard tell that their business in the real world is a hotbed for hotheads, and I wouldn't be at all surprised to read something incredibly sad in the newspaper one day.

About what one of them, has done to the other.

And regretted.

Forever.

And Martha played her trump card.

Firstly, she stood beside Anthony, and made disappointed noises whenever he threw a dart and missed the target. She kept it up for five throws, standing by him as an apparent support, but offering only disappointment and subtly vocalising a mild contempt that led poor Anthony to a silent rage that had him tearing up the forest floor with his fingertips.

And after five such attempts at a perfect throw, she left poor Anthony to wallow in his failure, and stood behind Georgie as he hit the mark one, two, three times in a row. Then she leaned forwards and told him.

You're focused, you've got control of your inner eye. You understand these things, I can tell. It's only your foolish boyhood bravado stopping you from fully achieving your potential. If you're ready to explore the fullness of what you can be, then join us tomorrow when we meditate, and you'll introduce yourself to the parts of you you're missing.

She aligned herself with Georgie. The victor,

Not with Anthony, the underdog.

That was calculated, cold possibly, but genius.

Within a week, both boys had become diligent early risers, joining in the meditation without a hint of insincerity. I was astounded, but I understood the trick Martha had pulled. It worked because deep down, Anthony's frustration stemmed from the genuine (justified) belief that he was as good as his brother at pretty much anything. I marvelled at Martha's perception and manipulation of that fact.

The same thing would never have worked for you and Michael. But Martha would have known that.

She could have tamed you, Gulliver.

Made a man out of Michael?

So she filled a void, and in doing so filled a void within herself.
That was me exercising my perception, see? She was lonely, she
never had her own children (I mean, I'm pretty sure not), and here
she was giving my dear brood a Mother. That's why I asked her
advice before taking the Vinnie and Jason hit; I'd decided she'd
simply be grateful, jump at the chance to play Mummy to sweet
three-year-old twin boys in need of some genuine care and a
Mother's love.

The hit on Vinnie and Jason's parents was supposed to be a hit
on Vinnie and Jason too. If I didn't take the hit, somebody else
might do who would complete the full To Do list.

An easy sell, I thought.

But she hit the roof.

And I didn't understand.

I still don't.

I wish I could remember her exact words, but the gist was all
to do with codes of ethics and wondering if I had any...

OK so just writing that down, I suppose it's possible she wasn't
angry at the possibility I'd take the hit, but maybe that I'd included
her in the decision at all. Maybe she didn't want to form any part of
a justification for another person's death?

Yes, that might be it now I come to think it through. She was
asking me to lean on my own code of ethics, not borrow from
hers. Huh.

Seventeen

Saturday, 26 January

The Saviour Machine

Actually going ahead with the hit on Vinnie and Jason's parents may stand in itself as the most bullish thing I've ever done. I knew I would need her to look after them for me, and I didn't have her blessing. It was pure stubbornness – after being told off like a little boy, I wanted to force her path, feel in control of her.

And she wouldn't abandon two little boys.

I've already told you how Sarah Greenleaf's hit went down, complete with the novice ninja team of Georgie and Anthony on their first hit aged ten.

They were with me for the hit on Vinnie and Jason's parents, too.

Older, wiser, competent.

I only thought I needed them to bundle the twins away anyway – temporary nannies to wrap them in snuggly blankets and coo soothing words at them on the back seat until we got home.

That was the plan.

You would have loved the setting, Gulliver. There was an actual stage for your theatrics. The Royal Theatre in Newcastle was simply nothing special. There was nothing wrong with it, and the place had enjoyed success through the 1920s and 30s, even escaping through Word War Two virtually unscathed and continuing sold out runs through the 1940s. It was built by Henry Royal in 1909, history does not record whether or not Royal was his real name, but he was a rare example of entrepreneurial pluck mixed with creative flair; he produced every play at the Royal over three decades, with a keen eye for what put bottoms on seats, and a talent for securing sponsorship deals. A master of self-promotion, Henry was often front-page news with some hitherto unseen physical wonder or irresistible gimmick.

Most ever live camels on stage (three).

A real aeroplane (hung from the rafters and dangled perilously close to the audience's heads).

One hundred violinists playing at once (who claim they were never paid).

The Royal Theatre was always cramped, hot, and ugly inside and out, but Henry made it work, and then, he died in 1949.

Fast forward through five decades of bad decisions and complete lack of either business nous or creative flair under two generations, and we find Sonny Royal, Henry's grandson and his wife Penelope, co-owners of the Royal Theatre, now in their early forties, penniless, living at the theatre, and struggling to cope with three-year-old twins Vinnie and Jason.

Now, to give him credit, Sonny did love the theatre. He tried to recapture his grandfather's past glories, where his own father had been content just to employ a manger and watch the place tick over.

There are always enough dreamers to keep a theatre hired out for short run debut plays and vanity projects most months. Pay the hire fee – who cares if they play to empty seats?

Sonny cared.

He spent every penny he had on new lavish original productions, and watched each one fail spectacularly.

No eye for good gimmick.

What he did gain, was a reputation for being the guy to go to if an aspiring actor was looking for a big part on a small stage. Even after all these decades, the Royal name still had a little clout on a CV, and the heritage was undeniable.

And so, with his head in his hands and the wolves at his door, Sonny found his lifeline in the form of young actress Penelope Papadakis. She came from Greece, she was hungry for celebrity; she studied acting at Newcastle University. That's where Sonny caught her eye, and when she told him that her folks were minted, his eyes must have lit up and he offered her a stint at his theatre, as the lead.

And she said,

I want to be a famous actress, I want to tread the boards and be adored, I want to be on television, I want to work with famous directors, like you.

What else could he do? He smiled and said,

I'll see what I can do.

I expect that's how it panned out anyway.

Whatever the details, Penelope's folks ended up agreeing to put up money to fund the show, and then, when it became apparent Sonny was about to lose the Royal completely, they put up the cash to save the place – on the understanding Penelope become co-owner.

Seemed like a good deal at the time.

Several failed shows at the Royal later, coupled with a very broken Greek economy, and Penelope's folks were buried in poverty.

She couldn't even afford to visit their graves.

Why did faithful Penelope stay with Sonny Royal?

My guess, he was the only person who believed in her talents, and continually told her she was a star.

Maybe that's all anybody really wants.

Do you know how difficult it is to get entry to an old theatre if all the doors are locked and bolted? Public buildings are like fortresses, especially those built closer to the start, than the end, of the 20th century. It makes you realise how ridiculously easy it is to break into a normal residential home.

I won't bore you with the details, Gulliver, but suffice to say, by the time I was inside and looking to get the job done as quickly as possible, I was already worn out, cheesed off, and sweaty. I suppose too, the gnawing guilt of having gone against Martha's wishes was weighing heavily. I just wasn't into it – I wanted to go home.

So, the plan, had been, you know, pretty classic. Materialise from the edges of their dreams into reality by simply waking them up, then shoot them as soon as they have a moment to sit up, but before they can fully process the dread of your presence.

I had come through the Stage Door, and made my way up the steps and across the stage, which was dominated by the skeleton of a huge, mirrored silver ball, mostly cut away with oval apertures top to floor all the way around, revealing inside a dizzying array of buttons and switches. On top was a giant lightning bolt. There was no way around the ball, only through – so I stepped inside and looked outwards. The main curtain was halfway to falling completely, so I could glimpse the cavern of the auditorium beyond, where bed sheets and towels were draped across the backs of the seats to dry, like ghost costumes sitting alongside the real ghosts of audiences from decades past. I stopped there inside the sphere for a good while allowing my composure to return. It's a funny thing, the stage; standing there you can't help but conjure up images of the myriad folk who've strutted and fretted their hour there, giving themselves to characters in front of a hundred watching folk or more, with no second chance if something should go wrong. I can quite see why Sonny would feel compelled to dedicate his life to saving the place.

I thought there was an aeroplane passing, then I realised I could feel the boards rumble beneath my feet, and it wasn't stopping. I passed over to the other side of the stage and into the corridor set through with dressing room doors. The whine and rumble grew, and I grinned. It was a washing machine. Perfect cover for my footsteps, I could tap dance my prosthetic up to their bedroom door if I wished.

I was only halfway up to the end of the corridor, when the final door opened, and out stepped Sonny.

Trimmed dyed black beard.

Long brown waxed coat.

Bare feet.

And a gun.

Stop right there,

He said, channelling Dick Turpin and forcing each word above the noise of the washing machine,

Now, turn around, slowly.

I have a gun too,

I called out.

Sonny took a moment to process this fact then leapt back through the door. He emerged almost immediately, clutching a bleary eyed three-year old Jason, in Thomas the Tank Engine pyjamas. A woman's stream of protestation followed him, and he motioned through the door for Penelope to stay put.

Turn around, slowly,

I sighed, and turned around.

Walk,

There was only one route, back the way I'd come, back onto the stage.

Keep going. Into the machine.

The machine? I realised he meant the mirrored sphere. I stepped inside, and faced him.

Do you like it?

Asked Sonny.

I shrugged.

You stood inside it for quite a while. It's wired up, see, pressure pad. Turns on a light backstage. I built it myself. During the production it'll tell a stagehand when to PUSH THE BUTTON!

He shrieked the last three words with his eyes wide and nostrils flared. There was an awkward silence, then I felt something move under my feet. Suddenly, the board I was standing on gave way and I dropped through the floor.

I dropped, just far enough that I was looking at Sonny's bare shins instead of his face.

Damn!

He shouted. And he stamped petulantly.

Damn, damn, damn!

He leaned down towards my protruding head,

Obviously by first night we'll have ironed out the glitches.

I was worried for Jason more than myself. Sonny was waving his pistol around right next to the poor kid's ear. If it went off he'd deafen him.

I couldn't train a deaf assassin.

First night - of what?

My sliver of interest was everything Sonny dreamed off at night. He gazed through me, and turned to look out at the empty seats.

It's going to be amazing,

He said,

What you're standing in. That's the saviour machine.

Saviour machine?

From the Bowie song!
He snapped.

I told him I didn't think I'd heard that one, which immediately set Sonny's top lip into a derisive curl, and his grip tightened on both the gun and Jason.

It doesn't matter!
He spat.
You'll pretend it was always your favourite song once this production hits the West End!

Ha!
It was Penelope. She stepped up behind Sonny with Vinnie in front, slow clapping patronisingly.

Consequently Sonny jumped, and looked over his shoulder, and lifted his gun just enough that I could plainly see PROP written under the handle in white correction fluid.

Penelope looked tired, she wore an oversize striped shirt and grey jogging bottoms stained with bits of the twins' last few meals. Vinnie strained forwards to see me, held back by his mother. His pyjamas had those little green aliens from Toy Story on them.

Why are you standing there shooting the shit?

She demanded,
> He's got a gun! Call the fucking police!

I cleared my throat.
> A real gun, no less. One more than your husband has.

Shit,
> Said Penelope.

Sonny threw the prop gun to the back of the stage and dropped to his knees, grasping Jason's shoulders with both hands, holding him in front of his face.

Use Vinnie as a shield!
> He shouted at Penelope,
> He won't shoot the kids.

She pulled poor Vinnie back towards her but stopped short of covering her face with him.

It was all a bit baffling, Gulliver. Penelope was shaking like a clockwork monkey, but I could tell she was partly just inhabiting a role.

> Actually, the children are crucial to the hit,
> I said,
> like in Richard the Third.

Immediately, out in the gloom of the auditorium, the sound of two rifles engaging, and Sonny and Penelope's foreheads each gained a little red laser dot.

Georgie and Anthony. Richard the Third; they'd chosen the trigger word after much debate.

Sonny and Penelope looked at each other from behind their children, with the first real dread I'd seen in their eyes.

Much more satisfying.

You're not a debt collector?

Whispered Sonny.

Fucking, Rosemary?

Spat Penelope,

I shrugged again, and I told them I don't know who. I just do it. But I don't kill children. If it can possibly be avoided.

Suddenly they launched into a desperate appeal, tag-teaming bits of information meant to stay my hand, mistaking the hooded executioner for a for a high court judge.

It's his cousin, Rosemary…

Began Penelope.

Sonny peeked out from behind Jason,

She was livid when we had the twins; it was checkmate for inheriting this place!

His eyes imploring me to understand.

Now, we're all Macduff's to her,

Swooned Penelope.

She's - evil!

Pleaded Sonny.

I laid my gun on the ground, and hoisted myself out from the saviour machine. I picked up my gun again, and felt fully justified to look down with disgust on Sonny trembling behind his toddler shield.

Penelope's grip on Vinnie was tight, but at least she wasn't hiding her face behind him.

I bent down low. She was shaking uncontrollably, and I could see the hair on the nape of her neck standing on end. I whispered in her ear.

Three outcomes. Try to escape - my associates will pick off all four of you in a split second. None of us wants that. Keep hiding behind the boys – my associates will simply wrench them from your grasp with everybody kicking and screaming, very traumatic. Or, you can tell the boys to come with us – and tell them everything is going to be all right. Which it will be, I promise.

Throughout my whispering, Sonny strained to hear, firing expletives and pleas to be let in on the secret. His fight had gone, deflated, he was wails and whimpers now.

I was glad Penelope was clutching Vinnie rather than Jason. Her grip on his forearms must have been excruciating. Jason would have broken down crying, I'm certain, but Vinnie suddenly yelped and tried violently to twist free. He couldn't, and Penelope kept her grip, with her head buried in his back. I was worried I'd broken her completely, and the wrenching would need to commence.

I moved over to Sonny, knelt down beside him, and barely took a breath before Penelope was on her feet, clapping sharply three times with such an impressive display of renewed control that even I felt compelled to stand to attention. No longer in Penelope's grip, Vinnie rubbed his forearms with his little hands, and sidled up to Jason to hold his hand.

Sonny let out a long breath like he was slowly deflating, and fell back on his heels, looking up at his wife expectantly.

She crouched down to address the twins directly,
You're such good boys. We're rehearsing for a new play Mummy and Daddy are writing. And we want you to be in it.

Jason looked at Vinnie suspiciously. But Vinnie was hanging on his mother's every word, and I could see his eyes flashed with excitement.

In a minute,
    She continued,
    the men with the guns are going to pick you up and carry you off the stage. It might seem a bit scary, but can you try to be brave?
    She paused,
    And… try not to cry?
    Her voice cracked, just a little, and I could see all the toes on her right foot furiously clenching and unclenching as she fought to maintain her poise.

Her watery eyes searched her sons' eyes for an answer. Slowly, Vinnie nodded. And Jason, of course, followed suit.

Now,

She said,

It's such a very sad scene, so Mummy and Daddy are going to cry. But here's the exciting bit for you: You're going to have lines.

She bent down to the two little boys standing in front of their crumpled father, and whispered in their ears, first Vinnie, then Jason.

Then she leant towards Sonny.

I'm not saying that!

Spat Sonny.

Then, you'll think of something else,

Murmured Penelope.

Are we ready?

Again, Vinnie nodding, his eyes excited, the fear gone, and Jason happily pursing his lips; eager to say the line his mother had given to him. To make his Daddy proud.

And I gave the nod.

From the stage it looked as though shadows undulated down the side aisles. Those red laser sights flickered on Sonny and Penelope's foreheads, but never left their marks for a moment. As they climbed up the steps either side of the stage, both my boys lowered their rifles to their side, and I settled in with mine – trained on Sonny, but able to pivot my attention to Penelope immediately should she try anything.

As Anthony approached Jason, and Georgie knelt down in front of Vinnie, of course my mind flashed to that painful evening infiltrating Paulie Harrington's Horror Night, and the bundle of sleepy boys we found exhausted under the stairs. If I'd had any doubts about this job, they were extinguished as I watched Georgie and Anthony confidently and calmly inhabiting their roles in this hit. They were so gentle with each of the twins as they scooped them up and wrapped them in snuggly blankets against the cold outside, even allowing Penelope to tuck in the last corner, and stroke each boys' face.

My darlings, I love you more than life itself. Never forget me.
    She said.

Sonny stepped up for his final performance,
    I love you both too. Remember the good times, boys.

And Vinnie said,
    We love you to the moon and back.

And Jason,
    Yes, we've loved you since forever.

There was no hiding the tears streaming down Penelope's face, now. She fixed eyes with each of her boys, and clapped, and smiled. Then, she let go, and wailed. Sonny embraced her, and they stood as one, shaking and heaving in their grief as Anthony and Georgie carried the twins through the Saviour Machine and exited quickly stage right.

And I was free to do what I do best. Their grief did not last for long.

You can't tell me I didn't do a good thing.

The twins are loved, and they're a credit to Martha.

They filled that void for her.

They made her whole.

I did that.

Eighteen

Sunday, 27 January 13

Losing My Coat

Do you remember being fifteen, Gulliver?

A shorter mental journey for you than for me, and if you don't remember, I'll happily enlighten you. I actually think you went through a lot of the same feelings and frustrations that I remember from my own adolescence, and we share context – we both became men, physically first, and mentally later, living in the Crypt.

I mean.

Technically I was still living with Foster, but increasingly my heart remained within my personal stone sanctuary.

It was 1982, and Foster had given me one of the best presents of our years together, a huge, quilted overcoat.

To wear it was to become one with it.

Sheathed.

Shielding me from the cold, yes, but more importantly from anybody knowing what I was doing beneath its unruffable exterior. I could be dancing a salsa inside that coat while walking along the street, remaining a tank-like quilted shell, rigidly borne along by my grubby trainer-clad little feet.

It gave me blinkers, too.

Sure, in the field, as Foster's eyes and ears, I was a 360-degree sense station.

Alert.

Poised.

But on my trips to the sanctuary of the Crypt, I enjoyed the forcibly forward focus the coat allowed.

People sitting beside me on the Metro. Not there.

Homeless people with their pleas on cardboard signs. Not there.

The whipping barbs of the forest's tentacles; the gauntlet through which I must pass to reach and leave the Crypt.

Not there.

Thanks coat.

I lost the coat.

This is the story of how.

It was cold out.

It was always cold out by the time I was on the Metro zipping towards Penshaw. A hot Summer's day in the North East of England can be glorious, and don't let anybody tell you a balmy evening isn't possible. But also don't be fooled into thinking you could fall asleep beneath the stars; the small hours will still freeze your bollocks off. So, on a Bank Holiday Monday night in late August, after everybody else had been enjoying unbroken sunshine over the long weekend, I was back inside my impenetrable overcoat, revelling in its warmth as I stepped off the train onto Penshaw station platform. The first thing my tunnel vision allowed me to see was a girl, her arms wrapped around her body, upon which was hanging the briefest spaghetti strap top. I'd seen plenty of similarly clad women walking down Round-Table Terrace from my vantage point reading at the kitchen window over the past two days. It was completely appropriate in the heat, but unfortunate if you found yourself outside at this time.

My first impulse was smugness, and to turn my limited field of vision towards the shampoo billboard girl who I'd made it my custom to converse with a little each time I alighted there.

But immediately my fifteen-year-old instincts bade me turn to look again. Her arms were wrapped tightly around the bottom of her chest, so the fabric of her vest top bridged the void between her breasts tautly like a drum skin. however frozen she might be, I could imagine that small space beneath and between, would be warmer than my coat cocoon.

The thought excited me enormously.

But something was wrong.

I whipped my head back around to my shampoo billboard girl, only to have my fears confirmed; she'd been replaced by the embracing shadows of an elderly couple.

Life insurance.

I couldn't have predicted how deeply her absence would affect me. Anger. And something akin to grief.

Stupid, I know.

Raging hormones when you're that age, though.

That's how I rationalise it now, anyway.

I went up to the billboard, right up close, and found exactly what I thought I might. She was still there, pasted over.

They'd buried her.

I could see the thick glossy paper layers at the edge, and I started teasing away a small portion of the top layer. It was therapeutic, like when you peel the top layer off your toenails.

An achievement, even.

I wanted a memento.

I would have continued uncovering her mangled skin until daylight until I was arrested.

Excuse me.

It was a soft, warm voice.

I turned, and she slotted into my vision like the next slide in a carousel. Shivering vest top girl. Her hand was on my shoulder.

Do you have a light?

She didn't have a cigarette as far as I could see. But my ego swelled pleasantly at the implication of equality; she was pretty.

Sorry,

I said.

What are you doing?

She asked between chattering teeth. She seemed genuinely curious – not incredulous. So I told her,

There's a beautiful girl under there. They covered her up. It made me sad.

The shampoo girl?

Somehow, I had always thought nobody else could see her. Or that nobody else would notice her because she was so worn. I don't know, Gulliver, maybe lots of people had secret internal conversations with shampoo girl on that platform, but in that moment I chose to believe that the girl standing in front of me, was the only other human being ever to notice her.

So are you trying to uncover her?

I don't think so,

I said.

I might take a piece. But it has to be, the right piece.

Cutting her up? That's kind of creepy...

She didn't look like she thought creepy was bad.

I am a bit creepy.
How so?

I was out of my depth, Gulliver. I've played the moment over in my head a hundred times, and I've decided that the ideal response at that particular moment, in the film of my life, would have been:
The kind of creepy that doesn't offer a freezing girl his coat, but unzips it instead and offers her refuge inside against his warm chest.

I did not say that.
I had no tools for this situation, so I decided to try out the truth and see where it got me.
I'm an assassin's apprentice,
I said.
He killed my family and kidnapped me. I'm on my way to my secret Crypt in the forest, it's where I go to escape him for a while.

She smiled slowly from ear to ear.
Is it warm in your secret crypt?
Yes,
I said.
It's got a heater.
Can I see?

I grinned and I must have looked like a toddler getting his first ice cream. But I hesitated. I just kind of froze.

So she continued. I share a room with a girl who brings her boy-friend home, and they fuck while they think I'm asleep. I don't care how gross your place is.

OK,
I said.

I didn't have to say much. She started talking openly about her crappy situation. She'd come from Romania, working in a bar until late at night, sending most of the money home and spending as little as possible.

I do have a coat, though, you know,
She said,
It was just so hot today, and I wasn't supposed to do the late shift too.
I know, Gulliver. I left the girl freezing her butt off and I just walked along beside her in a fog – I wasn't focused on her at all, I was obsessing about the whole situation:
What if my wildest dreams actually come true?
The Crypt didn't have running water or a toilet.
I was sure sex was messy.

We arrived at the forest edge, and she was no longer at my side. I looked back and she was rooted, finally silent, staring into the dark swaying mass in front of us.
Really?
She said.
It's a secret place,
I said, by way of blunt explanation.

Only then did I clock the need for some gentlemanly behaviour.

There are some really sharp bits on the way.

I took off my coat, and she eagerly wrapped herself inside it; just the way she did it made me feel I'd entered a new world of sensuality – it was a perfect fluid movement resulting in the coat draped over her, the sleeves hanging empty; her hands clutching the lapels as she squirmed happily into the sheer mass of the thing that engulfed me, and looked as it had eaten her up in one gulp.

I thought that would seal the deal.

She'd follow me into the undergrowth revelling in the excitement of an adventure with a fascinating oddball.

I started towards the briars.

She hung back.

Still.

I held out my hand, and she took it, not to be led, but to lead.

Come on assassin's apprentice.

Coy. Inviting.

She tugged at my hand. And I tightened my grip.

There was no question about who was stronger, and immediately I saw myself dragging her through the undergrowth, not actually physically hurting her because of the total encasement of the coat. Like roughly manoeuvring a flat-pack wardrobe up narrow stairs safe in the knowledge the contents are packed in enough polystyrene to survive being pushed off a cliff.

I let go, because I was angry with myself, and I thought she might be scared.

Wrong.

She was the angry one.

A slender middle finger emerged through the lapel buttonhole.

She didn't run. She bobbed along as she made her way confidently down the hill, the moonlight picking her out for a moment, falling on the roundness of her padded shell.

Like a Pac-Man ghost.

Then, she was gone.

I guess she had me pegged, Gulliver.

She knew I was weak.

She was angry.

And I was left, scared of myself.

Nineteen

Friday, 1 February

London

Dusty cornflakes.

Just one of the few downsides of living in a crypt.

A concoction of dust types swirling together. The first that always comes to mind of course is the remains of the remains – the last vestiges of our dearly departed ancient friends, whose eternal resting place we have occupied.

On that, I was thinking the other day, if it's really an eternal resting place for their souls, then our stay here will be a tiny blip in time and space, hardly worth a mention.

I can't compete with eternity.

But I doubt much ancient bodily matter really ends up in my breakfast. Mostly it's the kind of dust made from dried sweat.

A little blood.

A few tears.

All our DNA just mingled together, drifting around, settling down, getting disturbed, and floating into half full cereal bowls.

But there's another type of dust, the kind that takes a relatively direct flightpath down from the ceiling of the Crypt. It bears a reddish hue, there isn't lots of it, but it seems there's always more there to be dislodged from the ceiling whenever there are feet running around above.

Where the void of the crypt pushes deep into the hillside towards the forest edge, there must be a good distance between the Crypt's stone ceiling, and the mossy ground of the forest above, but my guess is that all the tree roots above us form an intricate network above the stone ceiling. That reddish brown dust is partly stone from the crypt, but mingled with roots and earth, and falling down between the stone slabs lining the void we live inside.

The morning before the hit on Lucrezia's Foster parents, Little Hye was up early practising her long jumps with Ricardo right at the forest edge. Their exuberance disturbed an unusually large deposit of reddish-brown dust, which sprinkled itself liberally in and around my breakfast.

I smiled, though.

Because I knew it wasn't Ric pushing Little Hye harder than usual, I could bet it was actually Hye herself getting him to set her target further, and further.

You know, Gulliver, that I would never have dreamed of suggesting she join us on the hit that night if I hadn't known without doubt, that she was already prepared, physically, mentally, for the task.

She was.

But Little Hye wasn't leaving anything to chance.

Studying and re-studying the layout we'd been given.

Practicing her particular role with the focus and poise of a state-sponsored Olympic gymnast.

Still. Landing like that and dislodging a load of earth, wouldn't do at all. There's such a thing as over preparing, and I decided I'd better go outside and relieve poor Ric.

Sure enough, as I popped my head out into the wan light of the early Summer morning, Hye was there coiled like a spring, eyes shut, just about to silently leap into the air, aiming for Ric standing with a mattress.

To an outsider, an impossibly long distance.

Not impossible.

Hye had been building up her distance for weeks. A little at a time until here she was, an unknown record breaker dedicating her skills to the job we often love, and always take seriously.

It wouldn't have been right to break her concentration. I watched silently, and still, she remained coiled there, motionless.

The trees waved and whistled a little in the breeze.

Distracted, I looked up.

The slightest movement in the corner of my eye.

And when I looked down again, Hye was on top of the mattress, pinning Ric beneath.

I clapped.

I know you are there,

She huffed.

I should hope so,

I said.

But that's enough practice. Conserve your energy and come to it fresh.

You know well enough, Gulliver, the sullen look that little girl could conjure.

Ric pushed up the mattress, de-stabilising Hye enough to make her lose balance and slide gracelessly onto the moss. As she picked herself up I could tell she was on the brink of tears, and I had to remind myself; this child is only six years old!

I beckoned her over, and I went some way to meet her in the middle. What remained of my leg was really twisting its daggers that damp morning and I winced as she hugged me.

Enjoy today.

You're well prepared for tonight.

I have complete faith in you.

From the few little drops I've collected from the grapevine, I know you're not operating within the same guidelines as me, Gulliver. But I have always considered it a rule not to encroach upon the already established territory of another within the profession.

Lucrezia's hit was an exception, and we travelled beyond our boundaries knowing full well that we may find ourselves hunted by greater foes than local law enforcement.

I feel I did everything correctly though, Gulliver. Did I not reach out to our counterparts offering a joint venture?

Their silence, I surmised, was strategic.

But I couldn't help feel it ominous as we made our trip.

My reasons were well considered, I feel.

I must protect my client in this case. But I will tell you, Gulliver, that I was deeply moved by his heartfelt petition on behalf of those poor souls who had been part of our targets' home in the past, and in protection of those who may be in the future.

We must not blame him for Lucrezia, Gulliver. He knew nothing about the poor child thrown into their care at that point in time.

Only that there was always one.

And would be others.

And why did he seek out my service particularly?

It wasn't because he thought I might take any current residents under my wing.

He couldn't have known about my brood.

My ego told me he knew something of my work, giving him confidence in my abilities, in my trustworthiness.

Qualities elevating me above a more local outfit.

Stupid ego.

Of course I should have heeded that red flag of silence from the local outfit…

You kill and learn.

I enjoy a more remote playing field as you know, so to face the challenges not only of a city hit, but an unknown city to boot, made the prospect of Lucrezia's foster home a particularly daunting prospect. Though I believe your eyes glinted more than usual at the idea. Perhaps I should have left you and Little Hye to tackle it together.

Maybe I'm the glue, though.

I like to think I play fast and loose with the rules.

Scooping up all the complimentary mints in a hotel.

Exploiting loopholes in cereal box coupon offers.

Dodging library tickets.

Just for the thrill.

So I kind of admire people who find ways to screw the system. Providing it doesn't hurt anybody.

If I was being charitable, I might say Lucrezia's foster parents were victims themselves.

Foster some kids with learning difficulties.

Feed them entirely on budget instant noodles.

Use government cash towards gambling addiction.

But I'm not being charitable.

I'm being truthful.

Simple neglect might have seen malnourished waifs with horrific skin problems and an aversion to sunlight.

Only callous cruelty could allow untreated burns.

Broken toes.

Padlocks.

So screw their desperation - they were cold-hearted, self-serving, child haters.

Calculated, too.

The learning difficulties were the key.

Not many takers for the broken ones, see?

And who'll listen to them?

I suppose I'm a Northerner.

That's a reluctant admission, because I wasn't one of those people who'll tell you how London is a wanker magnet. That's not fair, is it, when you've never even been there.

Turns out, it's true, though.

Maybe the overnight drive contributed to the bitterness. Maybe it was having to park the Allegro in Stevenage and hire a different car for the actual hit.

Maybe it was the stress of hiding you and Hye from sight. I'm not blaming you, Gulliver, but I took that burden on my shoulders alone. No wonder I was exhausted when we finally arrived.

Still. Necessary.

I felt like a sausage in a sherry trifle anyway. I certainly couldn't have pulled off normality with you two in tow to boot.

I never would have accepted the hit if I'd known how hard it would be to park.

It's all very well changing the plates, but if every dark alleyway is playing host to some kind of human activity whether it be curious eyes peeking from under a dirty blanket, or drunk canoodlers fumbling on a wall in the small hours, my research had not prepared me for the 'literally nowhere to hide' scenario.

Sometimes, hiding in plain sight is the best answer.

This time, we had no choice.

A cheap hooded sweatshirt for each of us, then two hours, actually quite pleasant, nestled into a cosy corner in a McDonalds, avoiding the security cameras until darkness fell.

Tell me you weren't just as happy as Little Hye, Gulliver? You might not have worn her grin, but the speed with which you chomped through your food told a different story. What a treat!

Even so, you were focused.

As it turned out, more focused than I was.

And Little Hye, tightly coiled.

Both of you, staring across the road at our target's house, Little Hye tap tap tapping her toes, rolling a French fry between her finger and thumb until the two ends flicked themselves across the restaurant.

A scowl from you.

A quick, frightened glance at me.

We all prepared in our individual ways.

And it was time.

<u>Twenty</u>

Friday, 1 February

A Leg To Stand On

London has a lot of lovely, solid, Victorian homes. They knew how to build things to last, the Victorians. Street furniture is solid metal, cast with the dates it was made and richly ornamented:

This is not fleeting.

We believe in the future.

We are proud.

But there are also the hastily glued together identi-bland boxes, and that's the kind of house we were headed to.

At least it was easy to break in.

Nothing particularly solid about any part of that house, was there?

Lots of creaking too, unavoidable.

I've never worried too much about that though – rhythmic creaking is the thing you really need to avoid; most brains are hard-wired to interpret rhythmic creaking as something approaching, retreating, or getting it on.

All things that can inspire a 999 call before you're halfway up the stairs. The way to avoid it is through randomness – a couple of steps, a pause, and few more – a quick pause – a slow scrape. Scary noises. But probably just the house settling, or the foundations sinking a little. Right?

How likely is it to be a monster? Really?

Or three?

Multiple hits are not rare.

What would you say, Gulliver? Somewhere between thirty and forty per cent?

A husband and wife.

Business partners.

A spouse and their lover.

Multiple reasons for multiple hits.

But usually, you don't expect there to be much fight in them. It's not like a movie. Nobody's lying awake with a knife in their sock. Nobody gets to look you in the eye and say wistfully.

I've been expecting you.

No.

But this pair was different.

I didn't tell you at the time, because I didn't want to scare you, Gulliver, but I had less information about Lucrezia's foster parents than any other hit I can think of. Sure, we had location maps, I knew we had a windowless inner room to factor in. I knew how many steps we had to navigate, and through which walls the neighbours would be able to hear a shot.

I didn't know how old they were.

That was disarming.

And I didn't know, that as I entered the windowless inner room via a flick of the wrist to the handle, a drop to the floor, and a roll across the carpet, that I would not be swishing almost silently into the shadows of a bedroom wherein two people gently snored, but instead into a brightly lit home-office space, with two very awake, elderly people tapping away at computer keyboards.

They did both stop tapping when I rolled across the floor.

You were off opening surprising doors of your own.
I wonder how you would have reacted.
They were surprised.
But God help me, they were not frightened.

The way they looked at each other.
Have you ever seen Ricardo and Emily exchange an enigmatic look, which you know has just brought them onto the same page together? And if you're arguing from a different chapter of whatever manual they're operating from, then you're out-numbered, out-argued, out of luck.
That's how this elderly couple looked at each other as soon as they saw me roll across their floor.
Raised eyebrows, a short exhaling of breath.
Here we go again.
I understood, right then; our local counterparts had not been snubbed in favour of our superior services.
They'd been defeated.

I'm sure I don't need to remind you, Gulliver, how frail they were.
How materially defenceless.
Anyway, we've discussed that too much in the years since.
I know.

Strange, isn't it, that what seem like our low points when they occur, lose their power without much time passing. It's the unguarded mildew of neglect, procrastination, and denial that congeal into the really deeply held low points.

But perhaps allowing such regret to bubble up is to allow it power at all.

Suppression, that's the way to do it, Gulliver.

I thought I had hit a new low as rolled into the yellow light of the room, on full display to those elderly eyes. Farcical.

But there was no danger really – not physical danger. The old man had no weapon to hand, and sat still on his stool, while the old lady leapt to her feet positioning herself between me, and the man. She'd grabbed a plastic set-square from the desk. A vicious weapon in the right hands, but hers were shaking; and her grip was so tight she was more likely to draw blood from her papery palm than from me.

The man said,

And I suppose you're here to do us in, are you?

He was much calmer than the lady.

I didn't engage. But I sat up. To be completely honest, I hadn't got a clue what to do. This was off the menu, you know?

The man continued,

I imagine one of our former youngsters came to see you. That's what happened the last time. Wasn't it?

He turned to the lady. Her wild eyes looked away from me for the first time since my entrance. And she nodded.

But may I ask you a question?

I didn't engage. But it didn't matter.

Is there a reason why you'd believe that person's account?

I wanted to say. It doesn't matter. I'm hired. You're the target. It's that simple.

But I knew I shouldn't engage.

I stood up. The only thing moving, apart from me, was the lady's trembling outstretched hand.

Will you be shooting us?

Said the old man, motioning towards my rifle. And he paused, In a way, I understand.

He said,

But doesn't it bother you, that the lives you extinguish may be innocent?

And I wanted to say. Nobody is blameless. But I didn't engage. Instead, I cocked my rifle, and levelled it at the old lady's throat.

That's right,

Said the old man,

I don't want her to see me die. You will make it quick?

And I wanted so much, to nod. But I didn't engage. Instead, I repositioned to a crouch, and backed towards the door, with the butt still trained on the old lady – my eyes never left his for a moment.

It was the sobbing that got to me. When the old lady whimpered and sobbed, and he turned towards her, still perched on his stool, and held her in his arms, that was what made me feel myself a coward; one who usually hides in the shadows, snuffing out life without staying around to view the consequences.

A moment of weakness was all they needed.

From beneath her skirt the old man dextrously retrieved two little handguns – contemporary, quiet, vicious.

I hadn't engaged, but it didn't matter, he'd built himself a few split seconds; all it takes. I had actually braced myself, when both guns simply flew out of his hands.

They were surprised for longer than I was.

I may have momentarily succumbed to a slice of un-antici-pated stage-managed humanity. But I wasn't completely without a plan. That inner room was an unknown, and Little Hye was my catch-all solution – poised, coiled, silent in the darkness.

An unseen presence.

It's not the things that creak and groan that you should fear; it's the things that approach as spirit, that fill you with unease, and chill your spine without making a sound.

It was what she'd trained for over many weeks, and when her time came, she deployed perfectly, springing through the doorway to disarm our hosts with little more than a swish, and a dull thud.

The man still didn't move, but that swish as Little Hye passed them by, left the end of his right trouser leg swinging for a second – enough to make me understand why he hadn't moved from his stool.

His right leg was missing somewhere below his knee. In the low light of the room, the absence of a foot was an easy oversight. But that's no excuse.

My senses returned to me accompanied by a renewed sense of pro-tectiveness over the six-year-old girl who had just saved my life. Rising to my knees, I levelled my rifle at the man's throat, and said,

What do you mean, 'last time'?

I have in my years, had cause to marvel at the ability of the human face to remain virtually static and yet morph completely from one expression to another. As I watched, this man's pock-marked, wrinkled facial lines remained motionless, and the colour of his skin remained painted over by the yellow light bathing the room. But his expression as I finished my question, altered undeniably from frustrating calmness, to abject terror.

And for a moment, I thought the cause was me.

Then I realised he was looking over my shoulder.

At you.

He must have wondered how many more shadow dwelling phantoms would materialise. I did enjoy the power shift.

It would seem you're on the back foot.

I might have said, with a wry smile, if I was James Bond.

Instead, I held my shot steady, and shuffled backwards enough on my own stump, so I could glance to my side, and there you were, otherworldly in the doorway, your bald head illuminated by the cold clean light of the moon – positively spectral compared to the pulsating warmth of the bulb lighting their windowless den.

And behind you, the shadow of the girl you'd just liberated.

Lucrezia.

Another chance for you to throw a little theatricality into the mechanics of a hit along with your default enigmatic stoniness. Slowly you opened your thin grin, your sharpened teeth making their entrance like ballerinas, whiter than the moonlight. And from your side, you lifted a burden from your side, and swung it effortlessly into the room where it thudded onto the carpet.

Our hosts certainly recognised it before I, or Little Hye. But we were only a second behind.

A thigh, connected to a buttock. Frozen.

One of our own. In a way.

The horrible answer to my question.

The old man knew, the game was up.

I really don't want her to see me die,

He said. And he turned his head to look into her eyes. She looked back, horrified, and shook her head. I couldn't risk a meltdown, so I carried out his wishes. She was side on, so no throat shot possible – the whizz, zip, and a neat dot on her temple.

She crumpled, and the old man hung his head.

His grief was genuine. I know he'd fooled me once already, but I really think, whatever their crimes, they loved each other.

Lives just, go in the wrong direction sometimes.

But I suppose, you would never have forgiven yourself for letting such a golden opportunity pass, would you? All I knew, was that before I could level my rifle at the old man's waiting throat (and he was waiting, Gulliver, waiting to join his wife), you strode past me, swept up the frozen thigh and buttock in your sinewy little hands, and dealt the man a vicious blow to the side of the head, toppling him from his perch at last.

He landed in his wife's pooling blood, and I hope the last thing he saw was her face. But the last thing he heard, was certainly Lucrezia's thin laughter, as she clapped her hands in glee, spurring you on to straddle him and bring the buttock down heavily on his head.

Again and again.

Far beyond any remaining sliver of necessity.

He was dead by the second blow.

By the fifth, unrecognisable.

By the twentieth, pâté.

And Little Hye, was gone.

That you might have put Little Hye in danger by causing her to run away from your pointless little piece of performance art, made a kind of anger rise up inside me that I've since rarely felt. I never thought it possible for me to feel that way towards you, but I can't deny it, and I'm telling you now, because perhaps after all this time, you deserve to fully understand why we started to become distant.

Lucrezia had her part to play, yes; a convenient excuse, but not the full picture.

But in that moment, as you know, to my shame, I simply walked away.

Even if I'd been of a mind to speak with you, I don't believe you could have told me where Little Hye had gone. You, Lucrezia, and I were too engrossed, or horrified, in your display, to notice her slink out of the room. It was petulant of me, unprofessional, I know, but tunnel vision led me down the stairs and out to the car, hoping to find Hye waiting crouched next to it, and frankly I was ready to leave you and Lucrezia to find your own way home.

Lucky for you, she was nowhere to be seen.

And I was frightened.

That's when I put my fist through the window of the rental. Thank you for never mentioning that.

Modern car window glass isn't a very dramatic thing to punch through – it turns into little circles that don't cut you at all – but the impact hurt my knuckles enough to snap me out of tunnel vision, and I suddenly realised I could hear that thin gleeful laughter again.

Lucrezia, outside, in the street.

God knows how many people saw her pale, grubby pyjama-clad form laughing hysterically like a stir-crazy hyena escaped from captivity. But in truth, you were a more arresting sight; little were-poodle caught in the headlights.

Sad to say, but the one and only thing I have to thank Lucrezia for are the first words she ever spoke directly to me. As I pulled all three of us close to the building.

Your Chinese girl went up, not down!

Then more laughter. What was so funny, Gulliver?

I hopped towards the open door, and Lucrezia's surprisingly strong grasp fastened on my sleeve.

Wait! She's coming.

She said.

How do you know?

I didn't wait for an answer. I wrenched myself free and barked at you to take Lucrezia to the car (I know, you didn't like that.)

Stumbling up the stairs, I shouted for Hye without care for who heard. Blinded by anger, frustration, fear.

I heard a muffled voice above me. It said,

Don't move, I'm coming.

I reached the middle floor where the doorway to our night's work was still open. But the voice was still above me.

Nearly with you,

It said.

I peered upstairs to the top floor, no light up there, but by the wan light from the room behind me I could make out a small figure noiselessly stepping into view on the landing.

Little Hye. Both arms clasped around something half the size of her.

The voice came again, from within the room behind Hye,

Nearly there. Hang tight, John. John? Winnie?

The whites of Hye's eyes stared down at me, confused, questioning. I raised my hand to tell her, stay there. And suddenly it hit me.

That cunning bitch.

I stepped into the room behind me. If I had the skill, I'd paint that scene. The olive-green carpet-stained deep claret, crumpled lovers, thawing buttock. It could hang in the National Gallery.

I bent and raised the old woman's left hand, her right hand still clutched the set-square, but this one was balled up tight. I prised open her fingers. They cracked like chicken bones. And nestled in her palm, my suspicion confirmed.

Little red flashing light.

Panic button.

She's coming.

Lucrezia knew.

Hello? Hello?

From below now, clear not muffled. And I understood - the voice above was from a monitor.

She'd arrived. Some poor care worker, completely unaware that she may just have stepped over the threshold of her own eternal peace of mind.

I don't know how you run your own operations, Gulliver, but in my book, collateral damage is unacceptable.

I couldn't let her see the blood and buttock room.

She was puffing up the stairs, she sounded out of shape. I took a deep breath, and stepped out onto the landing pretending I hadn't heard her, and I closed the door behind me.

I called cheerily upstairs to Hye.

Let's go, darling.

Who's there?

A red-faced woman. Maybe early fifties. She was unzipping her peach-coloured anorak to cool down as she emerged from the bottom floor.

Who are you?

She demanded,

Where's John?

Little Hye reached the bottom of the stairs, still clutching what I could now see was a tall rucksack type bag, clearly heavy for her.

I scooped her up and she dutifully wrapped her arms around my neck. Children are great diffusers. Simply her presence softened the care worker's hackles.

Oh, hello sweetie.

It was time for some pretending.

I'm a friend of John's,

I said, feeling my way. I had only a half-formed idea at this point, Gulliver.

Jim Flannigan, he might have mentioned me?

I extended my hand, and she shook it slowly, cautiously.

No. No he never has.

We served together, 80s.

Ireland?

I just nodded. I looked at the ground.

We have a lot in common.

I said.

And she threw me a bone I wasn't expecting. I was all ready to lift up my trouser and show off my bloated black leg. But she said.

Oh. Of course, you're a foster carer too.

White Dad.

Asian child.

Assumptions made.

Yes,

I said.

I don't know you from the register though...

And Little Hye said,

We drive in our car.

From up North,

I explained.

Where are John and Winnie then?

She wasn't stupid, Gulliver. She was smarter than Willows, for instance.

Turns out they're not in,

I muttered, weakly.

You've come a long way, to miss them...

She looked at Hye's tall bag – she'd seen Hye struggle downstairs with it.

What've you got there, sweetie?

She asked.

Yes. What had she got there?

Hye's answer silenced both of us for a few seconds,

Jim's new leg.

Jim's new... what?

Hye looked at me.

A wordless understanding that sent a shiver up my spine.

Jim say it's a secret.

What is, dear? Enquired care worker, visibly stiffening.
Bless her. Bless Hye.

She'd given me everything I needed. I sighed,

It's embarrassing,

I said,

You know what one of these legs costs? You see,

I said, rolling up my trouser leg to reveal my spongy blackened
stump and bloated foot rammed into my tennis shoe, the dark edges
of invaded flesh curling over the edge like an overcooked muffin,

I did say John and I have a few things in common.

The care worker put her hand over her mouth.

They're making me have it lopped off – but NHS standard
issue peg legs... John got his fancy new one yesterday, and...

Oh bless him, he's giving you his old one.

He didn't want Winnie to know...

Whyever not?

Oh I understand really. You know, he and I saw... terrible
things together. We... did, terrible things together.

In service?

I nodded sagely, she'd already bought into it, her bottom lip
quivering,

John can get... well you know, the memories...

I trailed off.

Winnie thinks he shouldn't dwell on the past. She's probably right. So, he took her and their girl out while I snuck in for the leg.

Of course,

She extended a hand and squeezed my upper arm. Then she frowned,

But, why did you press the panic button?

Hye looked me in the eye again, and without breaking our gaze, she said,

Sorry, Jim.

I raised my eyebrows,

You pushed a button?

I said sternly.

She hung her head.

Oh child.

Smiled the care worker,

Don't you worry, a big red button like that, just calling out to pushed isn't it? Like a toy. And look at you clutching that leg – you're so sweet to carry it all the way down for your... well, for Jim!

That was it. I welled up, and I let a little tear roll down my cheek. There was nothing remotely made up about that.

I took the leg from Hye and slung it over my back, and I hugged her tightly.

Yes,

I said,

She went upstairs and found it for me all by herself. She's the sweetest, most thoughtful child I know.

And I'll never let her go.

Twenty-One

Saturday, 2 February

Smoke & Mirror

I had slipped into melancholy.

In the days and weeks that followed my brief encounter with the shivering girl on Penshaw station platform, I dwelt bitterly on my threefold loss.

Shampoo girl.

Shivering girl.

My coat.

Everything lost, I felt, except my virginity.

Which became a new obsession that Foster must surely have noticed, though at the time I strove to hide the pornographic magazines I stole from the convenience store outside the station (a feat rendered infinitely more difficult without the concealment of my all-encompassing coat).

It didn't help that we were tunnelling through a fallow period. Months since our last job, and nothing on the horizon.

Until, without any of the usual signs having given me warning, Foster hastily serviced his hardware one evening, and asked me to clean a second rifle, which I could only hope meant I was to be a second gun with a more interesting task than my usual scene-neutralising responsibilities following Foster's usual swift and stealthy short-range throat shot.

The kids were on holiday with their father.

Our client was a decent man. Foster told me. He had waited patiently to engage our services until it was school half-term, and he could take the children skiing without taking them off school.

Enjoying the Chamonix slopes.

Watertight (snowtight?) alibi.

Valuable distraction for the eight-year-old boy and six-year-old girl, to take the edge off the shock of learning their Mother had been shot dead (by her cocaine supplier, it would transpire).

Hence the second rifle.

There was to be some theatre to this hit.

A crime scene to create as well as a mark to dispatch.

But I didn't know any of that, until afterwards.

It was one of those charmless homes with some promise of character on the outside, but a disappointment on the inside.

All façade.

I might live inside a Crypt, Gulliver, but some houses are much more effective tombs for the living.

We were there to end a marriage.

Conclusively.

Foster was upbeat, with the almost playful air of someone tasked with keeping a surprise party secret from the guest of honour, but unable to keep a lid on their excitement.

In Foster's case that meant speaking to me a bit more than usual as we rumbled through the night in the Allegro.

Not conversation.

One way.

But more.
We're actors tonight,
He told me,
You're playing the lead.

This was surprising. But it made me feel strangely warm. I was being passed a torch.

I still had no idea what he meant. This was not how it usually unfolded.

No positions, no measurements.
No plan.
OK,
I said.

As with so many hits, the first thing we did, was wait. We were parked up on an adjacent corner within sight of the house, which again, was unusual. We weren't exactly on display, tucked around the corner, but still – we'd usually walk the last mile or so.

It was drizzling, cold.

So I appreciated the relative warmness of the car – especially having lost my big coat.

She was waiting.

Ready to take off and fly around the room.

Ready to forget, for a little while at least, about the precious things slipping through her fingers.

Too late for a last grasp.

But the gentleman caller she was expecting, would never arrive. The Pigeon had made sure of that.

Not difficult to pay off a drug dealer.

Instead, her caller would be Foster, accompanied by me, his dark minion.

It didn't feel like I was playing the lead, as I stood some paces behind Foster as he'd instructed, visible to her when she opened the door, only as a shadowy presence.

He rapped on the door with his knuckles, and as we waited he gave me the only instructions I'd need.

I'm un-armed,

He said,

Be prepared.

And I understood – I was indeed to play the lead role – stepping from the shadow.

My rifle.

My finger.

My mark.

Have you ever allowed yourself to revel in the kind of brief fantasy that swells inside the mind during a dizzy spell? I don't mean a sickness or fever, I mean the kind of rush of blood to the head you might feel after getting to your feet after a long spell sitting still.

Momentary.

Transporting.

Consuming.

I'll admit it to you now although it seems silly, but during such a head rush, I'll often roll my eyes up as far into the top of my skull as I can possibly manage, clench my fists, and tighten my stomach all in an attempt to remain longer inside that moment. If you experience them in the same way I do, you'll know that nothing tangible reveals itself, but I feel as though the edges of those swirling points of colour, simultaneously colourful and blackest black, are a glimpse of something other than this present world, allowed to us by something benevolent we cannot understand.

I'd been sitting on my good leg inside the Allegro for an hour before Foster slipped out of the car, and I had to follow, tottering along in an ungainly fashion, trying to wiggle feeling back into my good leg. As I reached her front door, and stood on the black and white tiled pathway, I found myself succumbing to a head rush episode.

Great beauty.

Tantalisingly close.

Tragically brief.

And when the present world swam back into view, the door was opening, and I felt maybe my fantasy was continuing, but coalescing into human form.

My mark.

She was there suddenly, inhabiting the doorframe like smoke drifting from an incense stick. A loose fitting thin black gown, black hair piled up, and a cigarette between her fingers. Today, I would see past her façade to the empty void beneath, but there and then with my fifteen-year-old hormones raging, she was easily the most alluring woman I'd set eyes upon.

Foster, was in no such thrall.

Gabrielle?

He enquired in a monotone.

Gabrielle rolled her eyes.

Let me guess. More papers to serve? More summons? It'll have to wait, I'm waiting for somebody important.

Foster raised his case.

No papers. I'm your somebody important.

It was as though a warm gust of air blew from behind her, she billowed forwards still graceful and fluid, and looked the street up and down before beckoning Foster inside, curling around him to block him from view as soon as he crossed the threshold. She only noticed me then - shuffling down the path.

She looked me up and down with something I fancied was appreciation. But she looked exasperated too – there wasn't enough of her to conceal both of us from prying eyes.

We're together,

Said Foster,

He can sit on the step, if you'd rather?

In answer she drifted to one side, and I lurched over the threshold. She immediately shut the night away, and her sense of relief was palpable.

When Foster let himself through into the living room with no regard for the light cream carpet, her eyes flashed angrily, but they sparkled when he wordlessly opened his case.

I had never seen a person take Class-A drugs, and I felt immediately sick as I realised I was going to have to stand there in my silent minion role, and watch her snort a line. It felt like being present at a stranger's medical examination; horribly intimate at a level you know you can't return from, like someone you barely know, asks you to wipe their ass.

I wondered what came first, the etched mirror coffee table or the cocaine.

Does one lead to another?

Which is worse?

Bent double filling her nostril, surrounded by the soulless adornments heralding wealth without taste, Gabrielle's allure had taken quite a hit.

Her eyes rolled up into the top of her skull, and she spread out backwards onto the sofa, a smile on her lips that despite my revulsion, made me desire the deep inner peace fuelling its existence.

It's about the money,

Said Foster.

Yes, yes,

She waved her hand vaguely in the direction of the kitchen,

It's in the Teapot, the ethnic one.

No,

Said Foster,

Your husband hired someone, to hire me, to kill you, tonight. And it's about the money. He wanted you to know that. If you hadn't been so greedy, you'd have been ok.

She sat up woozily, her smile losing form.

I'm not greedy!

She twisted to look at me, the only jury member. Her eyes were wide, not scared, yet,

I'm NOT greedy,

On the verge of tears.

Foster held up his hands,

Don't shoot the messenger,

He didn't crack a smile,

This is a very different job for us,

He continued,

Against my better judgement, you might say. But you get bored with the same old same old.

What she was feeling, albeit through a fog of altered consciousness, is something we've all felt at some point. It's that confusion you feel just after you laugh, but before you're fully certain the person speaking is serious.

It makes you feel a bit silly.

Her graceful movements abandoned her, and she twisted sharply to squint at me, then back to Foster, then back to me.

Agitated.

I hate it when I'm able to see the terror arrive in their eyes. It's only happened a handful of times.

We might be cowards on that front, Gulliver.

A shot from afar.

A precise execution in a darkened room.

Sometimes a flash of white eyeball illuminated by the moon on a clear night...

My sense of unease rose further to anger that Foster would plunge me into this situation. A brightly lit room, with the mark between us like a rabbit inside its own warren, trapped between two skittery foxes.

She understood.

Her next action rested on a knife edge, and I thought I'd called it correctly when her wide scared eyes left mine and her head bowed. I thought she would cry.

But she laughed.

Composed, still alluring.

A deep and knowing laugh, at herself; the punchline of a joke she didn't know she was in.

From that point onwards, she assumed an impressive level of control.

Funny things, drugs.

I'm curious to know how the chemical altering of my own mind would manifest itself. Badly, I think. That's why I've never done it. Chemically, everybody on Earth must be so different from each other, the slight differences in our surroundings, and the tiny differences in the things our mothers ate while carrying us. The different levels of pollution they were exposed to, toxins in the water supply wherever they were, and the adrenaline spikes from scares and thrills, highs and lows.

They all surely weave together to create in each of us such a unique chemical construction that nobody would ever be able to claim much in common in the way our minds operate.

Gabrielle had gained focus, and resolve.

She fixed me with an inviting stare, excluding Foster from the equation entirely in that moment.

Make your appeal to the man with the gun.

Hello,

She breathed herself towards me and I stepped back although she hadn't physically moved any closer.

Her full intention, her offer in the moment, was clear.

I felt more like a boy than ever before, this woman bathing my pitiful experience in her light. The little I'd learned and felt, laid stark as an embarrassing noon-day shadow.

I started to notice my body responding to Gabrielle in lots of ways I couldn't control, my mind recognising they'd happened a split second after the fact so it was too late, my tongue had already run across my lips, my eyes had already lingered on the line of her bra through her nightgown, and my arm had already dropped a few millimetres so my rifle no longer aimed directly at her throat, but traced an invisible trail downwards along her smooth neck and onto the soft flesh at the very top of her chest.

Quickly rectified.

Undoubtedly noted by my two companions in the room.

There's sport to be had,
    Foster told me.

I felt as a baby must feel when they're first given over to a strange person to be looked after.

Abandoned.

Without precedent.

Without a plan.

But where a baby is allowed and expected to openly cry and grasp at their parent as they plunge them into the unknown, I had to watch with as much composure as I could muster as Foster simply left the house. I tried to communicate with him through my eyes;

This, is not ok...

But the only person fixing my gaze was Gabrielle; I'm certain she could see the well of panic, deep and deepening, in my unblinking eyes.

Click.

The front door was shut.

Foster was gone.

Sport? That really made me angry, it went against everything he'd taught me.

I considered, maybe it's a test?

Or, a gift?

I was mostly angry at the thought that Foster considered I might actually be on board for such sport.

But my moral compass was clear.

He doesn't seem like much fun,

She started.

Shut up,

I told her,

I'm going to kill you now.

I adjusted my rifle at my shoulder.

She took a sharp intake of breath, and drew back. But she immediately recovered her composure and adopted a mock-wounded face, with big eyes drifting behind her lashes like a harvest moon through twisted branches.

Yes, I've re-imagined this scene a lot over the years.

What she didn't understand, was that keeping her calm and turning up the seductive heat in the same way she might with a more experienced man, was still unbearably intimidating for me; I guess I looked older, but I felt like the teenager I was, complete with a ragingly horny body eager to get on with fucking someone's brains out.

I may have jammed my finger tight around the trigger rather than suffer the embarrassment of being engulfed by confusion and nerves. Except, I noticed her foot.

Her foot was twitching crazily, like it was trying, and almost succeeding, in shaking itself free from her ankle.

She was terrified.

She was frightened.

Of me.

And now I knew, I was in real danger of succumbing to what was on offer. I felt myself grow powerful, and I allowed myself to imagine fucking her brains out before I shot her throat out.

As I grew in stature, I watched her begin to cower; just a slight shift in our positions. It wasn't about actual movement, more about subtle changes in our breathing patterns. But this, this dynamic, was an undeniable turn on, and my moral compass suddenly didn't seem so clear.

The right thing to do?

Was to kill her.

Without first taking advantage of her.

And what really made my blood boil, was that Foster would never know what choice I made.

I could tell him.

But there would be no evidence either way.

I could tell you, Gulliver.

But you would be under no obligation to believe me.

<u>Twenty-Two</u>

Tuesday, 5 February

Keith Granton's End

Ten years as the sole pupil in Foster's boot camp.

I kept myself sane.

I kept myself grounded and feeling human through intermittent nocturnal flits to the Crypt.

My Crypt.

To begin with I only visited, stayed there and used it as an escape, but slowly, I began to alter parts. I would add things when I found them, like chairs, and even bedding for the little plinths of the dead. Within time, I found enough stuff that it started to become a proper home to me. I made other things, and I had many surprising encounters there those ten years.

I imagined a post Foster life alone in the Crypt.

Reclusive weirdo by day, assassin by night.

Part penance. Part relief.

It could have worked that way. But there was enough room for you, and I realised I was excited to share my life with you, Gulliver.

You were eight years old, I was twenty.

But I was never formulating a plan to save other children.

I'm just not that much of a forward thinker. I'm very reactive; if I was to see an appeal for cancer research funding on a train, I can very easily ignore it, but if one of their bucket shakers was to appear at the caravan asking for charity money, I'm likely to give them anything that's in my pockets. In the same way if I see a small child looking sad because I've just shot their parents, then I'm likely to scoop them up and feed them and clothe them, and love them, for the rest of my life or until they leave me.

We all have our little quirks.

Foster never rescued other children.

He must have left others behind - or done them in like his task sheet told him to. That's one of the many ways Foster and I differed – for me, rules are there to be bent to breaking point.

Sometimes beyond.

Foster always followed the exact wishes of his clients, even if he thought they were silly wishes.

Michael was just, there.

He didn't mean to upset the balance in our home – he just needed a place to stay because he suddenly found himself without any parents or wider family.

I knew there was a child, but I didn't know how old he was. Usually a client omits the little details unless they're telling you about someone who might pose a threat.

Unusual hit.

The clients were a collective, sharing a common purpose.

Michael Granton's father had been killed just after Michael's birth, by a marauding circus freak-show troupe gone feral. This is the kind of thing a client will pass on to the Pigeon, just in case it's useful.

Sometimes it is.

Michael lived alone with his mother. Flora.

His mother, whose name and address I had on my sheet of paper.

Plus child.

They were all solo missions in those days.

I'm sure you would have had your own opinions about whether or not to bring little Michael home, but more than that, you could have held him in one room while I dispatched his mum in the next. A different child I probably would have tied up in another room, but Michael, I couldn't tie up Michael. Could even you? Gulliver?

Imagine the psychological damage.

I kept having to place him firmly outside the door, whereupon he would just open it and come back into the room before I had a chance to aim and shoot his Mum.

All the while said Mum was becoming more and more frantic, but pretending, for Michael, that everything was ok. Everybody pretends for Michael.

He wanted to be near to his Mum.

He wasn't worried that I might be a bad man.

I'm not a bad man.

I told her to talk to him about staying in the other room. Holding back her tears, Flora held him tight and whispered in Michael's ear. And, obediently, he trotted off to wait on the other side of the door.

She clutched her hand to her mouth, and her tears flowed as the door clicked shut.

I promised her I'd make sure he was well taken care of. I promised her I'd take care of him personally.

Then I shot her directly in her throat and listened to her gurgling; her eyes wide and growing glazed until, what always seems like about half an hour later but is actually only about twenty minutes, she was still. I think it's important to sometimes, not every time, but sometimes, watch them – just to fully appreciate the gravity of what you've done. However deserved the hit might be, this person is still dying, and it's us, Gulliver, who make the final decision about that. I'm not just stating the obvious here, I'm reminding you of a basic truth it's easy to forget or turn a blind eye towards. If they have to suffer in their death, there's no reason we shouldn't share that with them. I think it sweetens the pill, too, having someone there in their last few minutes.

Flora Granton was one of the most generous and genuinely caring women you could ever hope to meet or have the privilege of calling your friend.

That was what one of her friends said at her funeral, and that was the quote the papers chose to run. I had to laugh at that. But of course, she was a mistress of deception, she even seemed mild mannered and demure to me when I met her shortly before her demise, but the truth was that her gentle exterior concealed a stone-cold cruel streak. It is a fact widely acknowledged by all but the courts, that Flora Granton paid that feral circus freak-show to mutilate her husband. One can only surmise that she chose such a deranged band of misfits to conduct the killing because she knew they were unhinged enough to ensure an intensely painful, drawn-out death. Keith Granton was discovered tied to a tree, naked, in thick forest above Fort William in the Scottish Highlands. His penis had been sliced along the tip, so it bled copiously between his legs, pooling on the forest floor among the leaf mulch. The resultant smell of blood and urine mixing, inevitably, with faeces, soon attracted eager attention from swarms of hungry Scottish midges – Ceratopogonidae, the tiny blood sucking bane of tourists, hikers, climbers, the hopelessly lost, and Keith Granton's stricken member.

With his arms tied firmly above his head, looped round the boughs with a length of rusty circus tightrope cable, poor old Keith's face was painted up in the most expert manner, to look exactly like the face of the woman Flora had recently discovered he was screwing.

Those feral clowns had some serious artistic talent – when a bunch of Swedish hikers found the body three weeks after he'd been strung up, they reported discovering the mutilated body of a middle-aged woman.

I'd like an audience with those circus freaks – they brought an entirely new dimension to a job that can sometimes feel a little stale. I would be slightly worried about becoming obsolete if they continued to hire themselves out, but mostly I feel we could learn a great deal from one another. I keep my ear to the ground for news of other work that might bear their stamp, but so far the only one I came across that even slightly reminded me of Keith Granton's demise was the discovery of a woman whose outer body had been sliced with an industrial ham cutting machine. It had been set up to cut off another piece of her every time she struggled.

Ingenious, but more Blofeld than Big Top. I don't think it was them, but it's nice to know there are more than just a few people out there exercising an imagination in the field.

Keith's old chap had been used as an all you can eat buffet by swarms of ravenous midges, the repeated bites of which are usually enough to cause grown men to buckle at the knees slapping various parts of themselves and sobbing in desperation. Keith Granton had to watch as his wounded manhood was slowly peppered with tiny, excruciatingly painful red dots that only grew bigger and hurt more intensely. Keith must have been praying, begging, for the respite of death for hours upon hours before it came to him through a mixture of exhaustion and asphyxiation.

Well you know what they say about a woman scorned.

I was the long deliberated over tool of Keith's family.

Revenge.

Swift upon Flora's recent acquittal (lack of evidence). I was to put a bullet in her precious son's pretty face, right in front of her; fitting retaliation for Keith's mutilation.

But I rescued Michael instead.

Another failed hit?

Success and failure - I find it so difficult to judge between them.

Twenty-Three

Thursday, 7 February

Premier Lodge

Two nights after my rendezvous with Gabrielle, with my blood still boiling, and my hormones reckless in their seat of power over my body, I took a different direction off the Metro at Penshaw.

Away from the Crypt.

Away from the town.

Out towards the dual carriageway slip-road.

Behind a petrol station.

Premier Lodge.

It was my sixteenth birthday, and I picked the Premier Lodge because I genuinely thought it would be a classy place to take a woman.

Genuinely.

I figured, this time, I'd do it properly – no dark forest paths or talk of crypts and assassins. I'd bought flowers (from the petrol station, very convenient), and I was wearing my best clothes; a faded green flannel shirt tucked into black jeans, with a black overcoat that I figured looked sophisticated because it had lapels.

I'd set everything up perfectly. Armed with the cash I'd stolen from Gabrielle's house two nights ago, and a rifle strapped to my back under the coat, just in case the police turned up.

There were plenty of trimmed evergreen bushes lining groups of parking spaces, so I crouched down behind one of them, and waited for 'Connie' to appear.

The idea had presented itself pretty organically. The first time I ever went into a phone box with Foster and listened to the unintelligible babble coming through the receiver high above me, I soon lost interest and explored my small surroundings.

I was nine. And of course, there were cards, with fluorescent writing over flesh, so much flesh. Women in leather, women doing suggestive things with their fingers, women bending over, and women looking surprised.

Foster looked down and saw me scanning the photos, and I had to wait outside the phone box from then onwards, even in the rain.

There was a phone box almost halfway between Round Table Terrace and the Metro Light Rail station. I pretended I was making a call while I chose the right card.

I didn't like the look of the ones in maid and nurse uniforms. Would I have to adopt some kind of role too? Too much work.

And I didn't want to be dominated, so leather and black vinyl was out too.

I quite liked the surprised looking ones with big red lips, but I couldn't quite see what about me would make any woman so surprised...

So I was drawn ultimately to the bottom-lip biters. Demure and innocent, lingerie and stocking clad, with eyes fixed towards the corner of the card, biting her lip, trying to decide whether a naughty thought she's just had is a flame she should try to extinguish, or embrace and be damned.

Embrace me, and be damned. Take my call, meet me in the Premier Lodge outside Penshaw.

The main thing I remember about that call, is the voice. No way would the bottom lip biting woman on that card speak in that rough cracked rasp. I did have the presence of mind to ask.

You're... just a receptionist, right?

Something like that.

I want to meet the girl on the yellow card, the one with black hair, looking up. I want to meet her in the Premier Lodge at Penshaw.

Silence.

I can pay a bit more.

How much?

What does she usually cost?

Make me an offer, if it's stupid, I'll hang up.

Six Hundred.

More quiet on the line.

She'll meet you at your Premier Lodge tomorrow. What name is your room gonna be under?

Um. I looked around for inspiration.

Glass.

Well, Mr. Glass, bring cash.

Crouched behind the bush with my flowers, I took the yellow card from the phone box out of my pocket. Would I recognise her fully clothed?

I was sweating, and biting my nails.

Booking the room had been ridiculously nerve-wracking. I don't know why I cared that the girl behind reception might know what was going on. She didn't flicker when I told her my wife would be arriving later. She didn't even acknowledge it. I wanted her to ask where we were travelling from, where we were going. I would have told her my whole prepared back story: my wife on her way from home to the airport ready for our planned holiday, and me meeting her halfway after an unexpected trip north to sit by my father's deathbed.

I wanted her to care.

I wanted it to be more... elegant.

I wasn't used to the buzz of the bright strip lights.

The drone of a distant vacuum cleaner.

The hum of the vending machine.

Suffocating.

I had to get out into the fresh night air, so I mumbled something about meeting my wife outside, and stumbled out into the car park.

Who comes to a Premier Lodge on foot?

Me.

And, as it turns out, her.

After watching several tired families check themselves in, I realised even if Connie had changed her look since the card was made, I was going to recognise her.

A woman alone.

A young woman.

With no bags.

There was a brief deflating moment when a sturdy woman dragging one of those tartan shopping trolleys appeared from around the side of the building.

Alone.

She wiped her brow, and stood for a moment staring into the car park, seeking. Me?

Thankfully not – behind me an elderly red Nissan Micra rattled into the car park, and out popped a gentleman who matched the woman in virtually every way except that he had slightly more facial hair.

Relief.

She was tapping her watch and grumbling.

He was unloading some cases, and I watched the real version of the story I'd prepared for the receptionist, as they bickered their way through the glass door.

And when they'd vanished, I realised, there was a shadow at the door, straight out of a film noir, she was smoking with long, black-gloved fingers, a small feminine bag at her shoulder, a brimmed hat shading her face from the harsh strip light in the lobby, and a slender dark coat concealing what I could only assume was the perfect realisation of all my adolescent desires.

I caught myself working up the courage to approach her, before I remembered that she was supposed to meet me in the room.

So we waited.

I waited for her to move. And she stood there, smoking, slowly.

Right down to the ash.

And then I saw beneath the strip light, her fingertips. Shaking.

The butt end of her cigarette was flicked into the night, and she slipped both hands into deep pockets either side of her thighs, pulling out from one side a thin flat metal flask, and something else I couldn't see, clutched in her other palm.

Her lightly shaking fingers unscrewed the top of the flask, and she managed to tip it up to her lips without tilting her head at all.

Pure grace.

She drank for more than twenty seconds.

Then a quick movement with her other palm, and a hiss.

Mouth spray.

She would taste of something pleasant I supposed — but I felt sick — suddenly nauseated by myself as the cause of her distress. I was too young to understand the feeling in the moment, only to understand that I was the cause of a wrong. I took the yellow card from my pocket and looked at the woman pictured again.

Her eyes looking up to the corner had taken on an air of desperation; searching for a way to escape her rectangular box. And was she biting her lip coquettishly? Or to control her shaking?

I looked back to the woman at the lobby entrance.

Gone.

Inside.

It could have been her, Gulliver. I'll never know.

Putting the card back in my pocket, I brushed the rifle beneath my coat.

Compelled to take it out.

Crouching there beside the bushes, I understood that my given place in the universe with the specific talents Foster was helping me to nurture, was to be the solution, and never to be the problem, or the cause of distress.

Our line of work brings finality, Gulliver.

For somebody, it brings peace.

How many people can say that?

How many people spend their lives in process?

Oiling the cogs of distant distress?

The light came on at a bedroom window above reception looking out onto the car park. An elegant feminine figure appeared as a blurred silhouette behind the curtain.

I raised my rifle to my shoulder and lined up my perfect shot, and I said.

Bang, bang.

And I left.

Twenty-Four

Saturday, 9 February

Lucrezia

The time was fast approaching when you would have felt compelled to leave anyway, Gulliver, I know that, but I also know that Lucrezia acted as a very effective catalyst.

On this point you and I remain united.

Revolted.

Do you remember though, my excitement? Another little girl aged six, a companion for Little Hye? It seemed like fate smiling on us, and for Little Hye too – I think she was shy, but genuinely happy at the prospect of a sister her age.

Perhaps the warning signs were plainer than I like to admit.

Perhaps I'm trying to rationalise your horrific actions, Gulliver, but I have wondered if even the hit on Lucrezia's foster parents was cursed by her in some way; did you feel compelled? Or was it some honourable desire to see justice done – to see pain endured for pain delivered?

I don't know, it seems to me that altruistic motives for the severity of your actions are unlikely.

Martha believes some of your behaviour is concurrent with patterns of one enslaved to dark forces within the cosmos. I'm getting very fond of Martha, and I'm coming around to her belief in a supernatural realm and a spiritual element within all of us, so (without completely losing grasp on reality) I do wonder whether Lucrezia was encircled by some kind of negative force.

Poor child.

She was accustomed to foster parents anyway — I probably wouldn't have felt compelled to have her join our little brood if it hadn't been for your lamentable display.

She'd have been ok with that nice care worker.

So, I do appreciate that Lucrezia was partly responsible for your departure, but you must accept your part in her being with us in the first place.

Anyway. Hindsight.

You needn't have worried, really, because she was gone very shortly after your departure. Well, perhaps not gone completely...

I really find it hard to talk about Lucrezia.

Because of shame, Gulliver.

That you never made the slightest attempt to share that burden with me caused it to linger potently.

How was I supposed to respond to a child with serious psychiatric challenges? I took her in and looked after her with the best intentions, and I know there are myriad influences from within and without that conspired together to fill up the colossal blender of neuroses, absence of self-awareness, pure bloody minded self-obsession, infuriating refusal to acquiesce to anything, and straight up physical abuse of those weaker around her. Oh, and don't forget the bitter gall, the genius ingredient, yes, the fact that she did of course actually have plenty to gripe about.

Plenty of death.

Plenty of abandonment.

Plenty of abuse.

Plenty of pain.

But, Gulliver, couldn't we all say the same? And we all have our moments, but the malice I perceived inside Lucreczia was something else entirely.

That's what gave me sanction for our plan.

To cut her loose.

Oh, God.

You are going to share this burden with me.

Stomach some memories even you might want to forget.

Confessions that might just create some new nightmares.

You deserve them, Gulliver. And I deserve a little respite.

Lucrezia got deep inside your twisted little psyche, didn't she? Iron-clad though it usually is – you thought to begin with, maybe you'd found a suitable protégé for yourself?

A kindred spirit?

But she was playing you.

Controlling you, turning you against me, because she wanted me all to herself.

You, below me.

Little Hye, below you.

Remember the bog break on the way home from London? We were all a little shell-shocked, perhaps. But I felt as though spirits were on the mend, we'd enjoyed some 1980s radio hits on the M1

— Little Hye enjoying Spandau Ballet, hysterically shouting Gold! Just a few seconds too early. All the more when she saw it made you laugh.

But I noticed, Lucrezia glowered, and when the girls re-emerged through the turnstile after their comfort break, all the way back home, it was Lucrezia who sang, and Hye who glowered.

For a time I suppose you were blind-sided by Lucrezia's apparent respect? Me too.

And that was the proper way to be, right? A new girl from a difficult background, joining a new home, trying to fit in; of course we would welcome her, make time for her, even make some excuses for her. Those kindnesses only get you so far with someone like Lucrezia – I think if we'd been more perceptive, taken heed of the warning signs, and clamped down early, then we might not have had to deal with her so severely.

There's an amazing skill to the act of self-serving manipulation; you have to be someone who can very quickly spot a threat, and almost as quickly ascertain the weakness that allows that threat to be crushed.

Lucrezia quickly clocked that you and I were the decision makers, the givers and takers. And once she realised that we were both fond and protective of Little Hye, and although I was horribly oblivious to it at the time, Lucrezia clocked just how to get under Hye's skin.

I had a dog in one house once.

He thought he was a person.

You remind me of him.

Don't you mind them laughing at your voice?

You'd be pretty if you had normal eyes.

My naivety knew no bounds – I thought they'd swapped sleeping plinths by mutual agreement, but turns out Lucrezia suggested Hye would always be quite short, so she may as well take the smaller plinth.

All of this in plain sight.

My own flesh crawled when Lucrezia probed me with intimate questions about Michael.

Why doesn't he speak?

Does he look like his Mother?

Do you love him?

Imagine a stranger trying to extract your belly-button fluff with a fishhook, finding yourself too polite to protest until it's red raw, then you explode – and slash your assailant with the fishhook over and over…

Her masterstroke was strategic crying.

Jasper, I'm feeling down.

I'm having flashbacks.

I'm suffering from panic attacks.

I need somebody to talk with me.

Can I tell you a secret?

Can we sit down and talk?

Don't tell anybody I told you this but…

The crying, the stories of battling inner demons, tales of people who mistreated her (everybody), the self-pity, deaf ear to anybody actually offering solutions, that snide little flicker at the corner of her mouth that told you everything she said was calculated to allow her maximum attention, and everything you said would be used only as food to make her own ego continue to grow into something grotesque and glistening.

Vitriol, vitriol, vitriol.

Here is the most infuriating problem I've ever encountered, Gulliver. That vitriol comes not from her, but from me, even thinking about her.

A nine-year-old girl.

With an undeniably abusive past.

And learning difficulties.

Whom, I hate.

Have you tried, Gulliver, to describe to people exactly how Lucrezia could, alone, bring such misery into an entire formerly stable home environment? It's very difficult, isn't it? None of the single actions in isolation and without the accompanying feeling of creeping flesh can ever hope to impart quite what her sins actually were.

When I try to explain it, people look at me and think I'm exaggerating.

They think I'm a terrible person; I can see it in their eyes.

And I do tell people.

Postman. Cashier. Barmaid.

But face to face adult conversation opportunities are limited.

I don't know.

Sometimes I just need to test out what I'm feeling, or let off a safety valve. That's why I started calling the late-night radio shows.

I told them, I'm a part-time killer, and full-time father, with some skeletons in my closet.

They thought I was really funny.

I bet I was good for ratings.

Am I self-obsessed? Just a thought – maybe I am.

I started pouring out my heart to the late-night disc jockeys after you left, Gulliver. Raw anguish and real questions about how to raise children of healthy mind, body, and spirit, interspersed with high contrast flashes of my greatest 'hits'.

A thrill to some extent.

Ultimately unsatisfying.

Because nobody gives you any answers.

They can't tell you how to assuage the gnawing guilt inherent in feeling repulsed by somebody you want to simplify as evil, but know is more likely just rotten inside from years of abuse.

And ultimately I stopped calling late night disc jockeys and began writing to you instead, Gulliver, because there was so much I couldn't tell them, even incognito.

Like how we got rid of Lucrezia.

She was a jagged rusty nail in our home, gouging flesh wounds in everyone who brushed against her, and we left those untreated for too long. When infection takes root like that, there's no healing, only cutting away, and inevitably, some healthy flesh is going to get sacrificed.

By the time we decided on our final plan I had already lost you, and lost pieces of Little Hye that have never returned, riddled by insecurities that once embedded, never die.

Isolation.

It was the only way.

One knackered box trailer out of the classifieds – several rejected for lack of a skylight – I'm not a monster, Gulliver.

Here's irony.

Wanting to let something go free, but first having to imprison it for an extended period.

At the time, it felt like tough love, but it felt right. I convinced myself it was right. She was well fed, comfortable. She had toilet facilities and lots of room to roam. She just didn't know where she was, or who exactly was leaving her food.

But she did have a TV.

And an old Nintendo with a Star Wars game.

Eighteen months was the plan, then a tranquiliser, some gift-wrapping inside a big sheet, and deliver her like a big angry present onto the steps of social services in Middlesbrough in the wee small hours. I was certain she'd be unable by then to describe any of her 'captors' in any meaningful manner, and pretty disoriented all told – her stories, however jumbled, were sure to make her the centre of attention for a spell. We decided it would be exactly what she wanted.

Amazing what you can make yourself believe.

We picked eighteen months because it would ultimately mean Lucrezia had been in isolation just as long as she was with us causing havoc to the dynamics inside our crypt.

Comfortable.
Plugged into the world.
Entertained.
Out of sight.
Out of mind.

Well, maybe not out of mind...

Twenty-Five

Tuesday, 12 February

Purged

Yesterday, Gulliver, you missed the most incredible display.

You would have loved it, you would have had your part to play, I'm certain.

Although… would it have happened?

Considering the nature of the thing, and what was taken, and what was left behind, perhaps you would have been taken.

Forgive me, Gulliver, I don't revel in the idea. If you were taken away never to return, I would be distraught.

But I'm babbling, and I can almost visualise your frustration.

What is my fuss is about?

A fire.

Fire born from an argument.

Bemoaning, as she often feels the need to, the desecration of her Saints at my hand, Martha was whispering dark utterances, sitting on her haunches and rocking slightly while staring past our little open fire, into one of the tunnels.

I could tell she was restless, and she was frightening the children, so I asked her.

What will it take for you to settle down with a book?

And she said.

Settled I'll never be, settled I'll ever be. Settled I'll never be. Settled I'll ever be.

And she kept repeating it and staring into the tunnels.

I tried to ignore her, but after a while she stood up, and walked suddenly past the open fire, and into the tunnels. It really took me by surprise. You know as well as anybody what those tunnels house. Seaburn takes her chances, and the children hardly know, but I simply choose to forget. It took me a good few years, but I forgot about everything we brought home. It even extends to new jobs, I tuck some things away in one part of my brain, and I forget about it, neglect it, starve it.

I always imagined this starved and wretched part of my mind would eventually just die.

But when Martha hot-footed it down that tunnel, immediately I felt like she was stomping a path through my neurons towards a piece of my subconscious that suddenly seemed a lot closer to the surface than I'd given it credit for.

Immediate migraine.

The little dancing flames of the fire at the mouth of the tunnel, picked out the shadow of Martha's baggy vestments for few seconds, fading as she strode further. I really had to gather my courage, but I went after her, groping in the dark.

Is this revenge?

I asked her.

For your desecration of the Saints?

She asked.

And she said,

No.

But I didn't believe her.

I told her.

There are things in these tunnels that need to be left in peace. I know you're still upset about the remains I evacuated, and I understand they deserved peace too, but punish me directly, don't disturb these souls.

She was angry.

I've never seen her like that.

Her voice dropped into her throat like she had the flu, and she told me,

The world around you is not made from parts of you. What you have stored here, is not just a physical remnant of terrible things and people long gone, rather they are tortured living memories. Festering in your tunnels, rotting in your mind, even infecting the minds of the children.

She warned me,

In time, they will consume you, and destroy everything around you.

But I didn't listen.

I still thought she was being vindictive.

And I was angry that she had disturbed a nice restful evening.

And I really, really didn't want to clear out the tunnels.

Can you imagine that job, Gulliver?

So it became the trigger for all my frustrations.

I am really fond of Martha, but I prefer her when she's simply the embodiment of inner peace.

When she gets agitated, I find myself worrying I might lose control.

I shouted at her,

These tunnels are none of your business. You have no idea what Gulliver and I have been through to conceal all these unwanted mementos.

Bits and pieces.

Splinters and stains.

Evidence against us.

I was wrong. And that's why she got really angry with me. First of all she just tensed up, which for Martha is really something, she's a picture of serenity the vast majority of the time.

Grubby, dishevelled serenity.

It was like she stretched up above me. I could see her fists clenched, and she spoke in a hiss from between grinding teeth. She didn't really need to say anything, just seeing the change in her, Gulliver, I immediately knew I was in the wrong. When you're faced with the fact that your actions have twisted purity itself, then you know you're the one the universe is pressing shame upon.

She asked me,

Shall we talk about what is my business and what is not my business?

I cowered below her, silent. And her voice rose and rose.

We would be here for eternity I promise you. And you, you have pitched your tent in no-man's land, and yet you believe you have business in both the been, and the beyond? These passage-ways have seen the passing of greatness between realms, and ush-ered darkness into light. And what have you done? You think yourself a great man for managing to light up some sticks on the edge of existence? And you store up for yourself not simply stolen treasures, but pieces of those from which you stole it. Both lie here as testimony to your great shame. Things bought and things created, things loved and things hated!

Sorry,

I said.

My voice cracked a bit.

She softened into a kind smile.

I felt immediately that her face had returned to my level. She touched my face, and said,

Jasper.

We both cried, Gulliver. I only knew it when I tasted the salt in my mouth. Then I saw tears glinting between Martha's crow's feet and her nose.

I watched the wetness on her face, and she held my gaze.

Then, her focus shifted, subtly, almost imperceptibly, but she wasn't looking at me any longer, she was looking beyond me, beyond the stone walls.

To a distant place.

Light moves faster than sound or heat. To begin with I thought Martha's tears were dancing on her skin. Fingers of copper snaked along her face, and I didn't understand, until I felt my good ankle warm, and heard the distinctive crackle of flames consuming their fuel.

Martha, she was standing there wearing a fixed expression as though not tied to this realm.

You set fire to the tunnel?

You set fire to the tunnel!

No,

She murmured,

The tunnels will endure. My fire is consuming festering memories.

I just stared at her.

You'll kill us all! Put it out!

The children.

The sudden thought of them fending off the flames and smoke at the other end of the tunnel jolted me towards them as fast as my plastic foot allowed. I slumped back to the Crypt's main chamber.

The flames were behind Martha, rising up from deeper in the tunnels where our collected detritus lay. Glancing back I can only describe what I saw as a fireball, and Martha outlined against it.

I could feel the flame racing towards me, so I flung myself forwards with more force than I thought I possessed, and I emerged into the main chamber coughing, although I didn't need to cough, I just felt I should.

The children were certainly awake, wide-eyed all, watching the scene before them – flames licking out from the tunnel entrance, but that's where it stopped, it made no attempt to enter the chamber of the Crypt.

And Martha, still in there.

I couldn't get near, and I wanted to weep openly for Martha, but I was also so angry with her, for bringing this on herself, and us.

It just seemed so meaningless.

As the children and I stood gazing into the flame, there suddenly came the most obnoxious fumes – there was no denying the power of that stench; it was the flames finding real purchase on the hidden detritus of our profession. Entire eco-systems, perishing civilisations of tiny things feeding on death.

Along with possessions.

Things bought, and things created.

Things loved, and things hated.

Fumes from plastics, and damp wood.

Rubber seals, and ageing food.

It was a heady mix that found its way to our airways, Gulliver, and we succumbed, each one of us. I saw each of my brood droop and drop, and I could only watch because I was on my knees, my eyes streaming, shouting out with a silent scream as the crashing and crackling of destruction grew ever louder.

Then, black.

I awoke, Gulliver. We all awoke, laid on our plinths like the Saints.

The fumes, departed.

The tunnels, clear.

Martha, vanished.

But written in soot at the tunnel's entrance, a word:

Purged.

Twenty-Six

Wednesday, 13 February

Stumped

My father was a great believer in 'sink or swim' parenting. Not that he would personally throw Craig or I into the depth, but neither would he warn us if we teetered close to the edge. I suppose he thought he'd leap to the rescue if sink looked likely to triumph over swim in any given situation. More times than I can remember, I found myself lying on my back on the muddy bank of a dangerous situation, gasping after only just dragging myself out of danger.

Not swimming,

Not sinking.

Cuts and bruises were plentiful, and I'm really not complaining about being given free rein to do dangerous things. I just think my father drew the line in an odd place. For instance, it's just about acceptable to let two small boys under seven walk home from the shops alone as long as you set them off on a route you know they can't veer from.

Just about.

But telling them to use their initiative and work out the route alone without guidance, knowing that one distinct possibility is wandering onto the railway line with its deadly live third rail just lying there waiting to be stumbled onto palms first, not to mention, you know, actual trains...

Surely a few steps too far?

Credit to Craig. He told me not to touch the rail. He told me to stay really close to the wall as we went through the tunnel.

He knew those things.

He was swimming.

But he was still lost.

So he used his initiative.

A man in orange workman's overalls was happy to walk us home.

But my father told us off for talking with a stranger.

You should know better,

He told Craig.

Hey, Craig, wherever you are, I understand better now. You weren't really trying to beat me at everything. You were trying to please our father. And I don't believe you ever succeeded.

Not sinking.

Not swimming.

Bumps and bruises, cuts and scrapes, and Craig was the keeper of the plasters. However deep the cut, or wide the scrape, he would stem the flow with an arrangement of plasters placed together in the same way a small boy builds a Lego house: without a plan – but excited to see what emerges.

What about removal?

The times would come when those cushioned constructions needed to be removed, itchy and grubby, my skin around the edge sallow and leathery.

I knew how Craig would do it – a short scrabble at the edge with his fingernail, then a sharp tug, a fleeting sting, eyes screwed up, wincing.

Then, done.

I could never, ever, do it myself.

And so you stumbled upon me, Gulliver, just a few days after our London jaunt, sitting against a tree at the edge of the forest.

In only my underpants.

Idly passing the blade of a machete back and forth in the flame of a portable gas stove, and dejectedly regarding the dried sponge form of my useless foot, a tourniquet pulled tight around my calf.

I knew, this piece of flesh had already defeated me, the blade had been glowing red for God knows how long, but I was deluding myself that any moment I would jolt myself to act.

The truth is that the necessity of having to remove my foot had struck me very early on our drive home from London. Allowing Little Hye's thoughtful gift of the old man's prosthetic to go to waste wasn't something I could allow to happen.

I could see the little cogs spinning away in your head. You clocked it right away, and that thin little smile broke across your face. I'm certain I don't need to beg your forgiveness for my slight hesitation before handing the glowing machete over into your eager outstretched little claw...

And again with the theatrics.

But to delay the moment itself I was happy to play along as you beckoned me follow you to the flat stone roof of the Crypt, there to kneel before your will as both the worshipper and the condemned man must...

The tourniquet bit down hard around my veins as my knees protested on the hard stone surface. I could feel every heartbeat course through my calf desperately trying to burst the dam.

Close your eyes.

Hold your breath.

Count down from three.

I filled my lungs with air and held it, and in that moment every sense was channelled into my ears, a high-pitched whine inside my head, and the only external noise was your breath, Gulliver.

Excited, still.

One...

Suddenly fast and hot.

Two...

Sucked in hard and held. Silence

Three...

Wet at my knee.

But no pain.

The world flooded back, and I knew, my leg was still a part of me. I know; you don't want to remember it. It happened, Gulliver. We all have our weaknesses. I turned to face you just in time to see your ashen form turn limp, your knees buckled, and the machete clattered onto the stone. Then hands slipped under your armpits.

Catching you.

Lowering you to the ground.

Clean hands.

Michael's.

There was no smile on Michael's face as he took in the scene, then slowly picked up the machete. I looked down at my legs and realised the wetness I could feel was indeed my blood – surface damage, the tourniquet wreaking new damage on my mangled flesh, literally slicing through my skin, deep red oozing around its tightness..

Immediacy was required.

And Michael was there.

Of course he was. This wasn't a job that required brutality; it required a firm hand and a reassuring stare. How many times has Michael patched you up after a struggle with some broken window, or headbutting a splintered doorframe?

He hardly dropped his gaze from mine at all while he turned the gas stove back up to full heat and moved the machete blade backwards and forwards in the flame.

Just a few inches.

The blade burned bright.

He set it down, and took off his shirt.

Do you think of Michael as skinny?

I did.

But in the dipping sunlight I was surprised by the look of his white torso, statuesque and powerful in a wiry kind of way. All that bullet filing, all that barrel rodding, all that baby rocking.

He wrapped one end of his shirt around the tip of the blade, and grasped that end with one hand, and the wooden handle with the other.

It wasn't a marksman's job, Gulliver.

It was a surgeon's job.

I sat facing him, and I stretched out my blackened leg, that dried, spongy version of my foot still clinging to its previous identity via broad bean-esque toes and the odd remnants of yellow nails, where the form of life inhabiting it was thriving, the marine fungus I had unwittingly nurtured – its roots penetrating and gradually disintegrating my bone over decades.

I watched it, mercifully unable to feel connected, only joined. It twitched a little.

Waving goodbye.

Perhaps.

Michael's eyes fixed on mine, and he set the blade alongside the tourniquet. He rocked it back and forth a little, and I understood.

His eyes were questioning.

My answer was,

Yes.

I was so very ready to say goodbye to that part of myself and the pieces of history for which it had for so many years served as vessel.

Michael's arms tensed, and he dropped his gaze to the blade. His movement was swift, and he put his entire physical strength into the action. Both hands firmly pressed. He rocked the blade from side to side, and I felt sinew, bone, and cartilage splintering.

Yielding.

A horrific sensation.

But no pain.

Not in that moment.

The world grew suddenly rapid, like somebody pressed the fast-forward button, but smoother. I watched the sun dip behind the trees as quickly as a pebble passing through water.

I was vaguely aware of Michael moving, tending to me, heating the blade again, passing it over the wound.

Searing it shut.

Then the pain came – a two-pronged attack of the physical flesh trauma, and a sense of loss I'd never expected to be so immediate, so visceral.

Then, black.

Twenty-Seven

Monday, 18 February

Dancing on the edge of infinity

Once I'd realised that I was striving for some kind of unreachable perfection simply in order to please Foster, I was truly liberated.

My first kill – Charles the snooker ball guy, he liberated me to be able to live happily and contentedly with Foster, to live with a purpose and to know there was something in life that made me feel alive. But it couldn't be like that forever - Foster must have known it.

Why did I roam at night?

My growing habit of midnight excursion to the Crypt became my refuge from Foster's constant prodding towards some kind of fantasy horizon of perfection.

Saints of the mediocre.

I understood completely: strive for the best but yield to the fact that perfection is relative.

From the point of view of an all-powerful creator, the best we can manage is mediocre.

Don't worry about anything too much.

If you don't get it right first time, never mind.

Why consume myself with pointless things like guilt?

Meaningless.

A chasing after the wind.

An eternal home
    for the dead,
    And sweet rest
    for the living.

Sweet rest, Gulliver. I needed sweet rest.

With Foster, every little achievement was merely a step upward towards perfection, but where was the peak of perfection? Was there one? For years I believed there was, for years I strove for what Foster wanted me to become.

Sweet rest, no. Anxious rest, yes.

Do you see, Gulliver? How I just couldn't continue? Do you see the mental anguish Foster was putting me through, albeit unintentionally, with every job together. Oh, Gulliver, you had it good. You don't know you're born. To begin with, in the years after Charles the snooker ball man, I did enjoy those jobs with Foster – measuring out the shots, cleaning up spatter, digging bullets out of walls and throats. I did it all – I tell my little Brood today, as I told you and the older ones so often, I've done it all before – those little mundane jobs that you often think don't matter, or that get your fingers bloody – they're essential work on any hit, and I've been there too.

In those days I saw Foster as an expert, a master of his profession, and I aspired to be like him.

The Crypt altered that.

I took to spending more and more time in the Crypt, to cleaning it, working out how to power it, and evicting the former occupants (and let me remind you that the Saints of the Mediocre promise an 'eternal' home for the dead, so I cannot believe that those poor souls were actually removed by my hasty actions – I merely cleared away the scant remains of their earthly vessels).

From the age of eleven onwards I would sneak out of Foster's apartment maybe three times each month, and those were the only times I had to myself, here in the Crypt without the constant searching beams from Foster's critical eyes laying me bare.

Plugging in an electric heater was supposed to be the pinnacle of achievement in the Crypt. I thought if I could provide some heat in the place then I could really begin to see it as a home. But you know what? The electric heater looked so pathetic sitting on the hewn rock hundreds of years old, it looked so wrong, as though I'd forced together two children from different times, who couldn't understand one another and probably wouldn't even have been friends if they lived in the same time anyway. The demise of the open fireplace is just another example of mankind striving ever onwards in the desire to better what we already have, the desire to perfect, when we are already surrounded by perfection. It's the same way with cutlery – we think the invention of a fork makes us better, when in fact it takes us further from using the perfect eating implements we were born with.

I hope God laughs.

The electric heater made the Crypt feel horribly dry, but not much warmer, it was as though the unseen inhabitants of the space were sucking up the warmth and farting it back out as cold little draughts.

Well, I decided to make a real fire in the mouth of one of the tunnels. It wasn't quite as easy as you might think it would be with all that wealth of forest surrounding me Gulliver, perhaps you could have made shorter work of it, or perhaps Foster's influence still lay too thickly on me, but it took me weeks to collect enough sticks of the right consistency, the right level of dryness, and the right size and length to be burned. Worth it, though – when I finally blew it into flickering light, and the tunnel behind it sucked the air gently backwards like a bellow, I was happy in a primal kind of way.

It was a beautiful fire.

I felt the path of my future was missing something, even though I was enjoying my life and new vocation with Foster. Gradually, as I continually joined Foster on more and increasingly elaborate hits, he allowed me to play a bigger and more important role until, by the time I was twelve, it wasn't unusual for me to be the one pulling the trigger, cutting the rope, or throwing the knife. And for me, the climax of every single hit felt like standing on top of a cliff in a fierce gale, holding my arms out either side and closing my eyes – feeling the power, feeling I was on top of the universe, and if I were to take another step, or allow the wind to blow me forwards just a little, I would abandon myself to thin air – for good or for bad – who knows?

That was the feeling of having reached the very furthest point possible without hurling oneself into a very great unknown – reckless dancing on the edge of infinity. I am certain that's why so many seemingly happy, intelligent people decide to depart this earth by throwing themselves from great heights. They've reached the pinnacle of their own experience – it's time for something else – the next great adventure.

So, am I a coward?

I don't think I could ever take that next step. Not alone.

- Oh Saints, help me to accept my limitations, allow me to be grounded and yet content -

I managed to be content to enjoy that feeling of the powerful wind and my own achievement – for me, it was enough.

For me.

Those people who launch themselves prematurely into the great unknown, the beyond time and space, I came to realise that they shared Foster's way of thinking – they would never cease to strive for perfection, and yet, Foster was either a coward who could not take such a step, or he didn't fully understand his own desire – either way, he was tragically anchored to his own limitations and to the limitations of an imperfect world.

I knew I could help him to overcome this tragedy.

Foster was not content to allow me to just enjoy the post-kill cliff top. So many times in those first few years I thought,

This went so well, he'll definitely be happy.

And he wasn't unhappy, he was just, indifferent.

Beans on toast.

No egg.

Sitting by the Crypt fire with my arms wrapped around my knees, watching the shadows race up and down the tunnels. I would spend hours, rocking gently, turning ideas over and over in my head. Fantasy to begin with, but soon there was flesh on the bones, and then I became consumed with bringing my creation to life.

You see, sometimes you have to give people what they want - really try to make them proud, even if it's not what you want. Sometimes, this is a good thing to do for somebody you care about. I decided to push for the perfection I knew I couldn't attain. I resolved to strive for it even though I knew I couldn't have it.

Childhood years came and went.

Puberty arrived, and stuck around.

New energies filled me to bursting point with all kinds of frustration. I was acutely aware that I was becoming a man. I felt strong, I felt primal, and I relished the idea that I was different. I hadn't asked for it, but nobody else my age had this life or the anonymity to work out their plans free from society's expectations.

Six years in the making, Gulliver.

By the time I'd put everything in place, I was weeks from my nineteenth birthday.

Six years seemed reasonable, but after that, I resolved to be done with perfection.

So now, as well as creating a comfortable home from the Crypt when I sneaked out at night, I was also putting faces to names. By and large, names that did not want anybody knowing what their faces looked like.

On pain of death.

It was all a bit like throwing a surprise party.

Obviously, having absolutely no money, I had to fund it myself; I had to find just under four thousand pounds. Now, I'm not saying what I did to raise this money was right, but as robbery goes, surely to rob from somebody recently deceased, and when I say recently, I mean they had usually met their end about a minute beforehand, isn't that the kind of robbery where the victim is concerned with other matters?

Eternal matters.

You can't take it with you.

Foster only ever knew I took something from the scene of a hit if it was directly specified that we should do so by the client. You know the kind of hit, Gulliver: Make it look like a robbery.

Foster had taken such a huge quantity of valuable goods over the years, that he could have retired several times over.

It's not about the money.

The odd thing is, I have no idea where Foster stashed his potential millions. Mine cluttered the tunnels before the purging flames turned all but the jewels and precious metals to ash.

But Foster's?

Who knows? Maybe the local charity shops benefited, or maybe, I don't know if this is related or not, but the night I killed Charles the snooker ball man was only the first time Foster had me drop a package outside the police station.

Twenty-Eight

Monday, 25 February

Finding Emily

Gulliver, I want you to know something.

If you forced me to choose the time I've been happiest in my entire life, I would choose the couple of years after Little Hye came to join us. With you and Michael, Ricardo and Emily, Little Hye and me.

The good times.

I feel like it was a perfectly balanced and healthy home. And we cared for one another, didn't we, Gulliver? I mean, I know you never really bonded with Michael, but I think deep down, somewhere inside, you love him as much as you love the others. At any rate, you were my sidekick then – you were the oldest, and I know the little ones learned so much from you. They followed you around everywhere – climbing trees and killing squirrels - do you remember, Gulliver? And Little Hye, bless her, she was only three, but she would toddle off with you, Ric, and Emily, and you always waited for her, always took care of her like she was your own little sister. I'm not sure there are any other three-year-olds who've learned to climb trees like Little Hye did under your insistence. I should have told you more at the time, but I was so proud of you then.

It always amazes me how small children communicate without language. There she was, Little Hye, without a word of English, and still she laughed and played with Ric and Emily like they'd always been together.

Not many locals have ever set foot in the forest on our doorstep, because of its lore. Whether the wilder stories hold a grain of truth or not, it's true that we live on the edge of one of the most impressively dense forests in Europe. I've never seen so complete a canopy. Even in the very stillness, when no leaf rustles and no bird sings, the air appears to whisper all around, and the dimness seems composed of the flitting shadows of long-limbed creatures.

We have of course revealed some of the secrets and wonders of times long past and forgotten by all but those who wish to forget. And since the fungus addled remains of the thing I once called my foot and lower leg are planted there, presumably thriving, spreading, mingling with other fungi and feeding the trees – well, it pleases me to think that I am physically part of the living forest too; I am one of its secrets.

Funny.

I always thought Michael would be the first to know what I did with my leg.

You know why…

But turns out it's you first.

Again.

Seaburn has explored further than any of us, and always returns in great humour from her trips within the forest. But although the romanticism of exploration is an exploit I feel drawn towards,

I've always felt dread just stepping past the light green of the outer limits of the forest floor. The light quickly expires, and a conflicted feeling overwhelms as though to explore further would be a wonderful experience, but one from which I might never return. I don't know more than this – I don't know if it means I would lose myself in the darkness and be unable to find my way out, or whether I would keep walking until I emerged from the other side to live a different life, or perhaps that I would remain there happily, a forest dweller. Others have described similar feelings, not you, obviously. But since that day we almost lost Emily – I expressly forbid entry beyond where daylight penetrates, to anyone in my care.

It's easy to forget the hand wringing and brow beating that that took place in the three hours before we realised where she'd gone. Before you spied her cardigan discarded just inside the tree line.

Did you realise just how frantic I was?

Is that why you took her rescue upon yourself?

We were a team then, which is why you left me behind, bounding off into the forest without a word. I was mightily perplexed at the time, and I rationalised that I was still clumsy in my new synthetic leg, but now I fully understand; it wasn't my leg, but my fear that would have been your albatross. But the feeling of helplessness was more than I thought I could bear. I did have a role to play – Ricardo was clawing at the ground with his fingernails as I held him tight and forbade him from running after you to find his sister. Even with the limited vocabulary of a seven-year-old he managed to spit accusations at me.

Lack of compassion.

Cowardice.

Neglect.

I fully agreed with the last two.

Maybe one day you'll tell me what you saw there beyond the place where sunlight reaches. But the sense of relief I felt when faint rustling became the unmistakable sound of snapping twigs, and then, there you were, Emily up on your shoulders, her face pressed into your cheek, her knuckles white from clinging to your neck. When you set her down she looked up at me with her tear-stained cheeks, and it broke my heart to see there in her six-year-old eyes, the haunted look of an experience from which she had given up hope of return.

She hugged me tight, and whispered.

Sorry.

And she cried fresh tears.

After that you were Emily's hero, don't pretend you didn't know it. You gave her confidence, and I know you would reward her school efforts with your little shows – how many squirrels fell foul of your darts? I expect they never knew what skewered them. A squirrel is a very small target, especially when it's on a branch a hundred feet away and behind a thick curtain of foliage. Emily, your gun dog – faithfully running to collect your prey.

I know you'll smile when you read this, Gulliver – whatever your intentions towards me now, you can't help but think fondly on those times. I still have a box full of your biro/nail darts, but they're useless to me.

We don't eat so much squirrel these days.

Do you see then, Gulliver, how much I needed you? Don't you realise I wanted you to stay there with me and look after the children. They can't help but look up to you, imitate you, learn from you. Emily and Ricardo, Little Hye, even Lucrezia for a short while before you left – they were leaping ahead with their schoolwork, they were becoming as smart as any child with a normal school education. Smarter. But not just that, it was their training too – Emily became so accustomed to blood and the ruthless nature of the life we lived that when she was only eight I was able to take her along with me to carry out minor intricacies.

Spatter removal.

Minor distraction.

Trail erasure.

She was a natural. And Ricardo learned to shoot a target over his shoulder with his back turned – you taught him that, I know you did, and I can't say I was happy when he executed the move on his very first job aged ten and a half. But strike me down if he didn't get the guy right in the throat – straight as you like. Genius because that way there are no faces to torment his idle waking hours. I would that you had stayed around to teach all of our children in the same way, Gulliver. It's true that they could have done without copying your 'uniform' – I could just about bear to see them all shave off their eyebrows and all their hair to become your identikit minions, but you have to understand why I stopped you from filing their teeth into points – I couldn't bear to see them like that.

Anyway, you can see that my tutelage is mundane in comparison with yours – sure, I can show them how to set up a good shot, make sure they know how to lie in wait without getting cramp, I can educate them in the ways of clients and pigeons and how they might find us, I can advise them how to think about each job, how to maintain a clear mind and ignore crippling doubts, and I can give them the knowledge they need to make a clean getaway and cover their tracks. I can give them all these things, Gulliver, I gave them all to you, but only you can take a frightened child and truly change them.

For me they'll give what's asked.

For you, their all.

My cross is heavy; I am saviour, and captor.

Without you, though I love them, all, I was alone.

On the long nights when I was away on the job and I'd come home mentally exhausted, dirty and more than often dragging something bloody for concealment within a tunnel, you were there to help me stash it, bury it, burn it. I did appreciate those things, Gulliver.

Michael could run a hot bath.

He remained in a dim kind of light, while we, Gulliver, we immersed ourselves so completely within our work that I came to think that Michael was not even a part of the reality we lived.

What happened, Gulliver?

What made you want to leave?

In my heart I know the past can never disappear, but can't you pretend? Wouldn't it be so much happier?

Imagine, I had come through ten years of uncertainty and confusion with Foster, and those years I mourned for my family, for my parents and for Craig, I felt there was nobody lower than me.

Surviving, because I was hiding when they died.

And then to continue to survive, relatively comfortably, with the man who killed them.

Each day I woke up and I despised myself, Gulliver. I despised myself and I despised Foster.

And yet I loved us both as well.

Can you understand this?

But after Foster, I mean when we had well and truly parted ways, when I first moved into the Crypt for good – that was the beginning of happiness; the first rays of true contentment, where I was in control of my own destiny, ultimately unclear, and in all probability a path to eternal damnation... it was my decision Gulliver.

I began to find that some days, I forgot to despise myself at all.

But I was lonely.

And then there was you.

And by the time Little Hye joined us, I was enjoying myself. I think, in those days, I'd been on the job for just short of seven years.

I'd killed twenty-two people.

That's what my diary told me.

They didn't weigh heavily on my shoulders.

But I think, after you left, I started to keep more of a mental log – when you left it was thirty-nine, and the faces of each one, long filed into the depths of my psyche, they started to come out to knock on the doors of my worst memories when all they wanted to do was grow old in comfort and die alone. And those faces began to inhabit the vacant spaces in the forefront of my mind, to seek out the empty channels where no thoughts were, and there they would lay stagnating, jeering at my crumbling resolve.

This was a gradual process, Gulliver – but it definitely began when you left. That's just a fact. And by the time I'd clocked up fifty hits around the turn of the millennium, each face was a regular contributor to my anguish, and the only thing that could soften the prickly little tormentors was to immerse myself completely in another job.

Vicious.

Circle.

I have been dreaming about your mother, Gulliver. I think it's because I'm writing all this for you, it's dredged up such vivid memories.

There's nothing too weird about the dreams she's in – she's completely in context, knelt on the bed before, well...

But there's a bit of regret that creeps in where there wasn't before. I think it's because she's beautiful, it's my body that feels the regret for a missed opportunity.

Erotic regret.

Anyway, I've been thinking a lot about your Mother recently because Sgt Willows won't let me forget her. He's all excited, round here every other day. At the moment I daren't even go back to the Crypt lest he's waiting to follow me. Not that it would matter too much, one way or the other, it would be the last thing he ever did.

I could lead him up that particular garden path anyway. Yes, but the thing is I quite like Willows. He's not a bad man – well not these days anyway.

He's not a target.

I have nothing against him personally, I don't actually know enough about his Officer days to feel any righteous indignation on behalf of others.

I can guess, but I don't know…

He's a family man too.

So I'm living a lot of the time in the caravan at the moment — sitting in the cold and the damp, peering into the gloom in case Willows is there waiting for my move.

It's no kind of existence.

They've tracked down a few more of your mum's former clients. Amazing I know, but it's taken the police all these years, twenty-six to be precise, even to work out what your Mum did for a living. How excited they must have been when they found out the truth — how much fun they must have had tracking down all the guys. They've got a list, see, a list of all the employees from the five buildings in the business district where she worked, and they're going through each one of them in turn, asking, so I should imagine, did you ever screw a high-class call girl calling herself any of these names?

But eventually, I imagine, they got around to my client, the little man with the big guilty conscience. Willows has linked me to your mum and dad, Gulliver, so I surmise that my former client has cracked under pressure, and told them all he knows.

Except, all he knows is not a lot.

I've always been careful.

No names, no contacts. Just a problem solved.

But you were the first of my little mementos, and Willows is beginning to get some of the correct puzzle pieces next to each other.

I was walking the cat the other day, along the main track down to the road, and Willows rumbles up the lane in his pristine little squad car, flecking little bits of mud along the bottom sills. I told him when he stopped,

You should be careful – your white paintwork is getting muddy.

I've never seen him looking so smug – it was unsettling, and with Seaburn hissing and spitting behind me, leaping up trying to get a good look, I have to admit I was slightly flustered.

First time ever.

Have you ever stayed at the Alvis in York?

First question. Obviously, he must know that I have – but did he also know that the blood-soaked, bed sheets of Room 117 had been sitting in the hillside tunnels beneath his feet for 26 years, until being burned up in Martha's fury a few days ago?

He's sauntering along a frighteningly accurate path. I told him I'd stayed in other hotels in the sprawling metropolis of York too.

What of it?

He just smiled.

Have you ever engaged the services of a prostitute in York?

I said,

I'd much rather you fantasize about me being a pimp than a John. I'll be an underground brothel owner, you can bust me, let's role play.

He dropped his smile.

You know, Jasper, I think you're a very clever customer, and I know you think so too, but you may just have been a little careless in your youth.

I reminded him,

I spent my youth as prisoner to a serial killer responsible for murdering my family.

Willows' smile came back.

He said,

Yes, you did indeed, Jasper.

I matched his smile and replied,

He was an acquaintance of yours too… as I recall.

It's a card I haven't played before, but it was quite satisfying, and the right moment, I felt. We both let that hang for a moment, and Willows nodded and shut his eyes. Swallowed.

Then he said,

One last question. Who is Gulliver?

Twenty-Nine

Wednesday, 27 February

Tempest. + Transcendence

Why do I continue to put myself through pain?

Men of much less moral fibre than I dedicate their lives to themselves alone, and are celebrated for their past distinction. While I, finding myself attached emotionally to the ones who depend on me, attract only derision.

I am sorry, Gulliver, I shouldn't be infecting you with my own self-pity, but after what I've been through the past twenty-four hours, I am a fully squeezed teabag.

It's a troubling tale.

It revolves around Little Hye and her sudden desire to explore. I suppose I have kept Little Hye on an even shorter chain than the others.

Figuratively.

Nobody is more searched for in the world outside than Little Hye.

I feel it.

And in many ways, she has had more liberty than any.

Don't picture her as that little girl any longer, Gulliver. She's a woman now. I hardly noticed it happen, but there she stands, a head taller than me, stately. She has the closest thing anybody could call a bedroom here. Thank the Saints, again, for Martha. When Hye turned twelve, Martha brought her a blanket woven with intricate symbols and characters from (I think) medieval Eastern Europe.

Rows of saintly figures, intercut with rows of folk brandishing farming implements, and others who looked like helmeted soldiers wielding spears and crossbows. Martha used it to cordon off one corner of the Crypt; a thick curtain that served to brighten up the place as well as giving Hye a private space.

Sooner or later I would have realised the need for Little Hye to be private. Martha beat me to it; she made it her mission to make Little Hye comfortable.

That in itself has been pure joy to me, Gulliver.

Shadows of family life.

What a shame then, I believe, that of late Martha has been dripping the complex spirits of supposed liberty into Little Hye's receptive ear.

The fact is, and I can't deny it any longer now, that Little Hye and I have all but lost the connection we enjoyed when she was little, and we could communicate volumes with just a glance or a smile.

The other day, I saw that she was busily concentrated on something in her corner, and I watched from across the Crypt. After a while, I realised the repetitive action I could see, was sewing.

So I walked over to her and my heart skipped a beat. There was her teddy, I'd not seen him since she was a little girl. She'd carried his severed head around with her the first couple of years after the hit on her mother – then I'd assumed she lost him.

Here he was.

Wow. I said.

I bent down to pick him up. Hoping we could reminisce a little.

Big mistake, apparently.

Little Hye leapt up, and clutched him to her chest.

Don't touch him!

I didn't know what to do. I just walked off with tears in my eyes.

I'm fully aware that it's something everybody who watches their children become teenagers will face, and a cliché, but over the past few years I feel like Little Hye has been replaced by a completely different person. I look at her and I don't see that plucky child I drove home after shooting her mother. I see somebody who used to think I could answer everything, but for a long time now has given up asking me anything at all. I want her to find answers, but not ones that lead her away from me.

I couldn't bear to lose Hye too, Gulliver.

Well, two days ago, I thought she was gone forever.

By the time I realised she was missing, several hours had passed.

Beyond the curtain, she had left a note.

I'm exploring. Don't look for me.

It broke me to pieces, Gulliver.

Nearly losing Emily, the memory of the full horror of that, just fell on me like the roof caved in.

This time, there was no you to bound off into the forest and save the day.

I was newly crippled from the moment I found Little Hye's note. I couldn't face the search alone, and I couldn't face losing her, either. I roused them all, all the little ones. I became a barking dog, full of sound and fury. We could have been a much more effective search and rescue team had I been a true leader. Instead, they obeyed me partly from fear, and partly because they worried for their sister.

And what did I think I was doing?

I saw the look on Emily's face when you emerged with her from out of the gloom. You may have kept the details of your little adventure close to your chest, but there was no denying how tightly she clung to you. Her devotion to you in the years afterwards painted the missing pieces very clearly. The forest had swallowed her up, and to say that she was hopelessly lost until you arrived, would be no understatement.

I know you're nodding, Gulliver.

Because I'm no longer just speculating.

Now, I've experienced it myself first hand.

I led my trusting brood into waiting jaws. I told them each to take their biggest knife.

No guns.

Funny, but I was aware that all this was folly.

I was consciously aware of it, not simply a feeling, but I kept going. And as we crept between the trees in the last of the rapidly fading light, I was certain the creaks and rustles were the trees laughing at me, and my fear of them was so real at that point that I felt myself glad my prosthetic leg was not wooden.

But I take full responsibility for blazing my own trail. I led them, piper like, into the abyss. The boys found the will to take each new step through sheer dumb bravado – laughing and pushing each other, racing between the trees - but all beneath a thick cloak of dread.

They always lapped up any the rich lore of the forest they could find.

Legends of sacrificial lambs.

Sometimes of late in the dusk half-light, Vinnie, in the spirit of developing the devil-may-care recklessness I've already mentioned, and of which he is increasingly proud and seeks to nurture, gathers the younger children with the pretence of playing catch, only to treat them as gun dogs. Hurling a dart (yes, one of yours, Gulliver) to which he's attached a red cotton thread, into the forest as far as possible, inevitably its path halted abruptly by a tree trunk. There it would lie, its whereabouts concealed by that thick but oddly shifting darkness the forest is drowned within during the changing of the guard from sun to moon. And on the ground, that tantalising thread running off into the unknown.

At my insistence, no child of the Crypt would usually dare to venture even a few feet into the forest at this time, but Vinnie's game allowed them to dip their little toes into danger, clinging to daylight by a thread.

Literally.

He never makes Lynette chase the dart. And I'd like to see him try making Sarah do it.

But last night, all caution to wind, there were no red threads behind us as we ploughed blindly through the trees. Lynette stuck to my heels like a Spaniel. Sarah's eyes flashed with anger, and worse, with hurt at my reckless demands. She, more than anybody, holds those tales up, perhaps not as literal truth, but as a warning, and there was no disguising the fear behind her creased brow.

Silly masks that we all wore.

None sillier than my own.

That's why the forest laughed.

Almost as soon as we stepped beyond the treeline, the Crypt seemed far far away. At least we should all be together. But my all-encompassing fear as we cracked our way steadily through the forest without direction, became the possibility that we might be condemned to walk through this mocking forest in post twilight dimness without finding Little Hye, until we expired.

It's an inevitable consideration whenever one walks a dark path that becomes longer than one expected.

What if the end of me, comes before the end of the path?

We'd been walking for over two hours, when it began to rain. It was sudden, and torrential. The streams were almost painful in their force on my skin, and little Lynette semi-buckled beneath it, so I scooped her up. A renewed anger took me over, and I determined to become you, Gulliver. To simply fight, and refuse to give in to the forest.

The boys were losing their bravado, though, bedraggled, exhausted, Vinnie looked at me with fire in his eyes, and his brother Jason dragged his feet, only spurred on from time to time by Stephen beckoning to him from slightly further on.

It was Sarah who knew what to do – herself exhausted, she seemed to take heart from my renewed vigour. She smiled, and wordlessly lifted up little Arthur. The effect was golden, his face was a picture of sheer indignation. As if he, a man, would need Sarah, a girl, to carry him as I was carrying Lynette. Such a thing could never be allowed to pass. He struggled and broke free, and the boys marched on, each of them keen to avoid being singled out as weakest.

Sarah winked at me.

She might have been winking at Lynette.

It felt like victory as we fought on, and the forest had stopped laughing, pouring its energy into the rain instead. But something else was different, the way did not appear so uniform as before, there was variation, and I felt we were actually going somewhere with hope of an end.

Any end.

But another hour passed, and I found myself beset with tricks on mind and vision. I'm sure you experienced the same when you searched for Emily; cruel glimpses of colour among the undergrowth, the fleeting ghost of movement, yielding nothing. I began to wallow in darker and more absurd scenarios wherein the masterstroke of eternal damnation is to eternally kindle new hope.

A cycle broken by a most welcome sight.

A foreboding figure in her sodden buckram drapes, she appeared before me, barefoot.

Martha.

My first thought was of greater despair, because I understood she'd come to seek us realising my folly, and I thought that she too had been foolish enough to condemn herself never to...

- - -

Gulliver, I truncated mid-sentence above because

Martha's hand landed on my shoulder – I don't know how long she had been standing watching me write. Perhaps she's watched me write to you before and never made herself known.

I'll continue where I left off but, well, I am more… at peace, now.

I'll, fill you in after I finish telling you what happened inside the forest.

Well inside the first time…

I'm getting ahead of myself.

Where was I?

Ah, yes, after Martha appeared in the middle of the down-pour. I had written above that she appeared foreboding in her dark drapes. Foreboding is not the correct word if I am to be completely honest; her arrival was in truth a great relief, and she appeared resplendent, her attire actually seemed more like robes.

I put down little Lynette first, and I took some steps towards Martha, but she shook her head, put her finger to her lips, and beckoned us to follow her, and only minutes later, I could tell we had entered a part of the forest that we hadn't touched upon; I knew that for most of those three hours we'd been walking in cir-cles, exactly as I'd feared.

The rain continued unabated until that point, but then, off to the side, a way away through the dense trees, there came a sigh.

It was the strangest feeling, as though the air and darkness had lungs that drew breath, very lightly at first, like a little welcome breeze on an oppressive day. But as it progressed, a gentle caress became a mighty wind and we found ourselves compelled to draw back to the shadows, then cover our faces as a tempest raged.

I marvelled at Martha's perception of the elements.

Did you ever, before, well you know, before... Gulliver, did you ever pull the bottom of your coat up over your head and run into the wind trying to fill it like a sail, and take off? When you're little, it really feels as though that might actually work. You feel your little body become lighter, and you think,

This is it... I'm flying!

But you look at your friends doing the same thing and they have the same looks on their faces, but they're actually pathetically on the ground and you realise, so are you.

Still, at first it's a thrill.

At first, this wind felt the same. For about twenty seconds the wind provided that deliciously frightening feeling, and then, it wasn't fun anymore. Vicious little gusts actively slashing at any exposed flesh, like a wire wool car wash.

Like the moment when you begin to see through an intense darkness that initially appears impenetrable, so most of our senses adapt to their environment remarkably quickly. The last thing I saw before I was thrown to the ground and curled hedgehog-like in the leaf mulch, was Martha, somehow still upright while the gale and torrents beat her.

I thought my death would come through the gradual stripping of flesh down to bone at the whim of the mighty wind, but only minutes later, my body relinquished its total grip on my senses, and my mind reasoned with me.

It's bad. But it's not getting any worse. It said.

It might even, be getting better…

I raised my head and opened my eyes fully expecting my task would be to inspire courage in my brood to do the same. What I found instead stunned me – they were already on their feet, one and all. I was proud and mortified in equal measure.

But they hardly noticed me stand up and join them. They were agape at the scene before us. As the wind dipped, the density of the trees above relented a little and allowed fingers of white light to pierce the canopy, so we could see that before us behind Marta, there was a parting of the trees, an avenue if you will.

A wind tunnel.

And taking her last few steps along that avenue, sodden as Martha and every bit as elegant, regal, even, came Little Hye, blinking as the light shafts painted her face. She stood beside Martha, her dark hair lank and sodden, plastered to her shoulders.

None of the haunted desperation I'd perceived when you rescued Emily.

Little Hye was serene, like Martha.

And she said,

Didn't you get my note?

Do you remember that time you built a little birdhouse from twisted twigs and moss, and all the children thought it was such a wonder, mostly because it was you, Gulliver, and you did not do things like that.

No, you did not do things like that.

I knew, Gulliver, it was Michael's.

I'd seen him start the thing days before, just a square base and some of the sides, a frame only.

We have very little privacy or places to hide anything in the Crypt, but it is possible. A child's imagination is never short on inventive places to hide things. So there are only two possible reasons that you were able to find that birdhouse and, to give your dues, complete it. Either Michael had discarded it, or he never even remotely considered that anybody would take it and claim his work as their own.

I suppose you made it your own in the end; Michael would never have included the twine to fasten shut the little door.

The moss is gone, but the frame remains, hanging just beyond the forest's edge, and as we filed back through the trees behind Martha and Little Hye, with me bringing up the rear and dragging my heels somewhat, I saw it swinging there gently in the wind.

The door shut fast.

I don't know why I didn't call you out on that deception at the time. Looking back now, it must have been seriously galling for poor silent Michael to watch all the fawning over you from the younger ones. If ever Michael and I meet again, I owe him an apology for that.

I was feeling petulant as I passed by the swinging birdhouse and followed the others down the steps into the Crypt.

My Crypt, not Martha's.

I contorted my face behind their backs, a silent scream like a child who knows he's in the wrong, but needs to react against something anyway. No surprise that I found myself, soon after, writing you a cathartic letter, Gulliver.

But it was a huge surprise when Martha made her presence known. That hand on my shoulder was firm, and I was used to Martha being firm, but this time, it was something different too.

It was, I don't know, there was some tenderness there, softness to the way her fingertips gripped through my shirt. I would never have before considered doing so, but it felt right in that moment, so I raised my own hand and placed it over hers. Our fingers entwined, and she drew me out from the Crypt, back up into the wet dark night.

The smell of saturated bark and dense foliage after a long heavy rainfall was so comforting I didn't care about the rain still falling, soaking us both. I didn't even care that I was barefoot, and had only a thin shirt keeping me from the cold.

I didn't feel it.

I was focused on Martha leading me through the trees, her long dark matted hair glistening under beads of water infused with moonlight, running from the strands and onto her sodden buckram coverings. We'd gone perhaps a hundred paces into the forest, and turned and twisted just enough that I couldn't have told you the direction back towards the Crypt, and Martha stopped, still holding my hand. She stopped, completely, from doing anything. It was the eeriest feeling, Gulliver, because Martha exudes control.

She is always in control.

But in that moment I realised, it was consciously relinquished. To me.

It was my moment, and I was immediately compelled to place both of my hands on her shoulders, pushing her backwards against a trunk. It was exactly what I wanted to do, and yet, it felt unsatisfying, and I realised that she was inviting me to choose.

How much to dominate, and how much to share?

I took her hand, and extended her index finger, I slipped it under the top button of my shirt, forcing it upwards until the button popped off and landed on the forest floor. Martha wasted no time in wielding her newly regained power, grabbing the fabric either side of the buttons, and tearing them apart, each button falling among the twigs at our feet.

My bare torso is not what it used to be twenty years ago. More rolling hillside than rugged moorland. So there was plenty of flesh for Martha to grab hold of once my shirt was gone, and grab hold she did – laying her palm first on my chest, and digging in her perma-brown nails to draw her head forward – fixing me with a wicked sparkling stare, and fastening her teeth into the flesh around my nipple.

I cried out in genuine pain, and immediately it turned into laughter infused with the overwhelmingly base intention to complete the union. Martha blinked slowly and deliberately, and her eyes shook off their invitation to wicked mischief, instead urgently imploring me to allow my physicality free reign over her body.

There was a brief moment of complete silence while we both read and understood that look, that invitation in the other's eyes, and then we were pressed against one another, each seemingly attempting to force the air out from the other's lungs, while clawing at the remaining bits of cloth keeping us from becoming fully, desperately intimate with one another.

Even if I wanted to, I couldn't completely describe Martha's nakedness to you, Gulliver, because we were both focused on that visceral, vigorous feeling of, well, I can only describe it as trying to climb inside the torso of the other. Faces pressed closely against flesh, biting, sucking, laying trails of spit across each other's bodies. Grasping handfuls of each other, knowing and relishing the fact that the red marks would last for days. The forest, the trees, the moonlight, no longer anchored by above, or beneath.

Flashes of silver moonlight streaked across flesh we barely knew as our own or the other's, reflecting in huge raindrops barraging our bodies.

Branches scratched alongside raked fingernails, and moss and forest mulch felt warm and welcome invading the darkest most intimate parts of both of us, indistinguishable from firmly placed palms and probing, pinching fingertips.

For a long while my palm was placed firmly over her pubic mound while my fingers were overjoyed to find a lubricated welcome to their exploration at the entrance to her body, all the while though we still writhed and gripped and grunted. I was aware of the attention she was giving me too – I felt at times that my hardness had grown larger than the entire rest of me put together - as though it was most of me. For a long while we each engulfed the other with our mouths, with waterfalls of saliva mixing with sweat and with the juices of arousal. And when I finally entered her I felt that was exactly what was happening – I, fully every part of me, was pushing into that warm inviting place, and she was drawing me further and further inside, and she could engulf me to the point of suffocation if she wanted to, and I could invade her to the point of turning her inside out. But instead we revelled in the fullness of dominance, and vulnerability one for the other, and we stayed that way for longer than I can say because I don't believe time as we know it, had any place in the moment.

When we woke up, the moonlight was gone, and the pinkness of dawn was creeping through the trees. We both felt cold, so we came back to the Crypt and stoked the fire.

Thirty

Wednesday, 27 February

New shoots

Sometimes it's important to look at all the blessings in your life, especially with more years behind than in front. The facts are, I find myself seated in a place of respect within my professional field, and enjoying the company of a woman who doesn't consider me a monster.

But much more than either of those blessings, as I look around the Crypt at the rising and falling chests of each of my little ones, I feel like each of us has found some kind of true peace here. Little Hye and all those you have never met, Sarah of course, Arthur my pint-sized solider, sweet little Lynette, and the twins now aged ten - little hothead Vinnie who's my go-to snipe at the moment as long as he's stayed away from the Rola-Cola for 48 hours. And his much calmer twin, Jason — whose marksmanship I'm certain is going to surpass his brother once he's stepped out of his shadow.

Even Stephen, who joined us almost three years ago aged nearly ten, filled with a pre-set suspicion and aloof hostility for anything that tries to interact with him for the first time. Even Stephen, despite himself, finds peace on a day like this.

You and I possess a hard won sixth sense for when hostile eyes are fixed on us. A chill through the nape of the neck, hackles rising

- ready for a battle or pursuit of a spook. But recently, I've had to endure that feeling even in the most intimate setting of my home. Stephen, now a friend of the other children, especially Jason, and these days a dutiful student, even an amiable ally in the field, frequently stares at me from afar and believes I can't know.

I do know.

I understand more than he realises.

I used to watch Foster in much the same manner.

He's asking himself the big questions. How did I end up here? Am I a prisoner? Does feeling some kind of contentment here make me a bad person? Has Jasper remembered to buy cereal bars?

He'll work out some of the answers in time. I did. But I can't give him a recipe – everybody's different.

We were picking those purple mushrooms the other day, it was cold and breezy, but clear.

A pretty day.

Lynette suddenly asked me,

Jasper, if Jesus came back, do you think he would come back in a tube of cloud?

I had to laugh,

A tube of cloud? What's a tube of cloud, child?

There's a tube of cloud in the sky right now,

She said.

And there was.

Lynette is the antidote to Stephen's steady gaze. There's no wariness in her brightness. She reminds me so much of Little Hye, back when Little Hye was still little. Both plucked from the grasping claws of a stifling parent just, just, before that key moment in a child's life when the weight of their understanding becomes too much to ignore, and choices, decisions, have to be made that will have an effect forever.

No words can do justice to the delight with which I dispatched Lynette's gnarled guardian.

Clean hit.

Clean soul.

Lynette clearly feels no sense of loss at the deft removal of her tormentor. This is something I don't understand – one would think such sustained wrongs against even a person so new to the world would leave a residue of mental disturbance. But Lynette has simply accepted my patronage and embraced me as her new guardian with all her bright little heart.

I can only conclude, and this is important Gulliver, that there must be a weight of goodness to the doctrine she was raised beneath – a truth that passes my understanding, but that illuminates her spirit despite the best efforts of those who wielded it.

But I think we'd know if Jesus came back.

Then there's my latest – Arthur – he was a complete surprise, completely within the rules. I had no idea he existed. I know, I know – how is that possible?

Shoddy research.

I suppose you'd be right to think it – but truly, there was nothing to say this child existed anywhere. I almost missed him completely.

He was hiding. But he sneezed.

I'm pretty certain he'd been watching the whole thing through a crack in the door.

I guess that'll stay with him.

You never really know how these things will manifest.

He doesn't have the peace of Lynette – but his fear and gritted teeth are almost comical. When he found himself discovered, Arthur came at me with a pencil.

It's all about proving himself a man, and that, I respect.

He's smaller for his age, but particularly headstrong. He has to run twice as fast as the other boys just to keep them in sight.

Yesterday I watched with a worrisome anxiety I didn't know was in me, as Vinnie, taking any opportunity to nurture his own reck-lessness, beckoned Arthur and Lynette, and instigated a game of catch with them – right on the forest's edge in the fading twilight. They, of course, love the attention of the older lad, but I joined Jason in disapproval, on tenterhooks as they danced with the dark-ness, pushing their bravado out in front of them like cockerel's chests, flirting with a danger they couldn't hope to understand, much less master.

Stephen joined in too, slinking up awkwardly feigning nonchalance until Vinnie lobbed the ball his way. Vinnie's ten, Stephen's twelve now but Vinnie's already his height. Arthur and Lynette are both only eight. The look of terror on Arthur's face at being so close to the forest's edge made a mockery of his squared shoulders and pronouncedly purposeful stride.

They're a joy, Gulliver.

Even the difficult ones.

I wouldn't change anything.

All that's missing is you.

I miss Anthony and Georgie too, they simply outgrew us, that was only natural – no hard feelings.

As far as I know.

They're pursuing under-the-radar careers.

Operating in the shadows, untraceable men whom society can't recognise. I don't approve of all their pursuits; I have a moral issue with gambling.

It's not surprising.

You can take the boys out of the North East Mafia, but…

I do take pride in their independence.

They know I'll always keep an eye on them…

My uncle and aunt had two dogs, they were puppies a long time before Craig or I were born. When we were quite young, something like 5 and 7, both dogs died in the same month. They were brother and sister, the same age, they lived their lives together entirely; I don't think there would have been even one day when they were separated.

And they were obedient.

They picked up a command or task very quickly and would never forget once it was burned to their minds. But my aunt and uncle took great effort to make sure they were well trained, three times a week at doggie training school, sitting, fetching, staying, walking at heel, barking on command. I suppose it was some kind of practice for training children – my aunt and uncle had five of them.

Don't be insulted by the implication. I put effort into training you, but the raw material was explosive. Anyway, I'm not drawing this parallel to talk about you, Gulliver; I'm drawing it to talk about the little ones.

After their first dogs died, my aunt and uncle got two more, and they put in nothing like the effort they put into training the first two.

They were older, they had kids; they were tired.

And the new dogs, they loved my aunt and uncle, but they dug up the garden, they bowled over elderly folk, and they barked at the smallest provocation. They were smart dogs, but they remained unshaped putty, raw potential.

The un-carved block.

I'm tired, Gulliver.

Perhaps you'll find I've grown soft, too.

Things have changed, Gulliver. Ideology changes, doesn't it? This is the next generation; I'm established now, it's not about giving a home to the strays, it's about bringing them into a hallowed inner circle with every conscious expectation of what I want them to become.

You might say I've lost my way, diverted from my true calling, but just because I have mentored you to mastery in your true calling, one that nobody would deny you inhabit perfectly, it doesn't mean that same calling is mine.

For what purpose are we placed within this universe, Gulliver? Perhaps my purpose has more to do with those I mentor than what I mentor them to do. In which case, the artistry of the perfect hit, those skills I've honed and owned, are secondary to a greater call, and that is where my mark on the universe will remain, all else will fade to shadowy legend with no root for the curious to trace.

Will you tell my story as one whom I blessed, liberated, loved?

Sadly, your encroaching chill grips my heart with the answer. And if you cannot forgive me for my wrongs, at least promise me you won't blot out the future for these little ones.

My true legacy.

Thirty-One

Thursday, 28 February

Edinburgh

The hit came through Foster's usual pigeon.

She became my regular pigeon too, but not my only. I'm much more diverse. As far as I could tell virtually all of Foster's work was channelled via this one pigeon, and because of his limited supply line he missed out on all the government jobs – maybe that's how he liked it. It always worked the same with Foster – his telephone would ring, nobody ever called unless it was a job. Once, it was the phone company, but in ten years that was the only time I knew it was somebody other than the pigeon. So the pigeon would call, and Foster would talk – I mean – really talk. It was amazing, these were the times he said the most, ever. But it was all fake, he'd have an entire fake conversation about fake kids and fake school plays, fake shopping trips and fake trips to the cinema.

He'd talk about the news, and the weather.

And then, always two days later, we would go to a phone box.

Never the same one twice in a row, and rarely the same one twice at all. We'd make a day of it, pack up in the Allegro, usually at night, and off we'd go, more than often it would be over an hour drive - another town or village. I loved those trips – the car journey made for a great breath of fresh air outside the apartment, and as morning dawned I would drink in those rays and renew my energy. Hits happen mostly at night, and I always had to be back from the Crypt way before dawn in those days, so my pasty skin tingled deliciously when it was treated to those tastes of sunlight.

We would spend a fake day doing real stuff like sitting on a windswept beach with an ice cream, or looking around a museum of rare geological formations. I really believe you can't imagine how important those outings were to me, because I never kept you locked in an apartment. You never had to escape, you were always free to come and go, and I always took you out on trips. And I enjoyed them with you Gulliver, I really enjoyed them.

Spending time with you.

As I got older, our dynamic on those trips altered. I no longer played the little boy on a trip out with Daddy. Though it must have irked Foster, we had to play at being something like equals. Words were still seldom spoken, but we would take turns with the camera – I learned to be bold – to push the envelope, taking the camera from Foster, eyeballing him and knowing he would have to relinquish it or cause a scene. I'd walk as far as I dared away from him to take a picture I truly wanted to take, and walk back again.

There was film in the camera.

As time progressed I even walked a little in front of Foster and steered us towards the museums or exhibitions that interested me. Where we went mattered nothing to Foster. Having me lead, that worried him.

When I'd pushed things too far.

Fingers clicking at his hip.

He kept a very close watch on the time, and then, when we'd faked enough fun, he would feign nonchalance inside the phone box while I waited in the car. When I was smaller, I would sometimes have to wait in the hidden under-seat compartment that you know well enough yourself, Gulliver. Sometimes, if the job was simple, he'd be back with a scribbled scrap of paper within minutes, seconds even. But often, he'd be there the best chunk of an hour, and return flicking through his leather-bound note pad, already marking up measurements and intricacies.

Those were the times I knew he was going to need me to be on top form. Those were the times I worked myself up into an internal frenzy, blanking out everything but the desire to be the best version of myself on that hit.

This hit was no different.

Foster got the call, and talked through a range of boil-in-the-bag mundanity he must have researched solely for this purpose: did you see the latest episode of that TV show that humiliates people for laughs and they have to pretend they're not mortified, how unfair it is that more disabled spaces have taken over normal ones outside the shopping centre, the price of guacamole...

It was, as usual, flawlessly dull.

Two days later, we were on the road.

Now, the pattern I had noticed over the years was this; if the hit was to be a big one, a complicated one with lots of preparation, perhaps with more at stake and a greater necessity for, shall we say,

physical elaborations, then we went further away to find a telephone box Foster deemed suitable for the pigeon call. This time,
we started out at just gone four-thirty in the morning, stretching,
yawning, silently relishing the dim light from the moon and the
general absence of anyone.

We were still driving at 7 o'clock, and we'd been heading north
all the way, leaving the north east conurbation twinkling orange
behind us, we'd been trundling through grey stone villages and, after
the first hour and a half, we began to glimpse the sea over the windswept grass cliff tops. It was with no small degree of excitement that I
realised we likely weren't going to stop before hitting Scotland.

Hit it we did. And we carried on going, my inner little boy
broke out and my nose was pressed so hard against the window it
hurt. For me, Scotland was a mythical land wherein I might very
well find populations of flame-haired warriors, every one of them
clad in their specific tartan, armed not just with ancient weapons
able to inflict much cruelty, but armed with elaborate stories of
slaying monsters and liberating peasants from oppressive English
settlers. The feeling that any one of the people who lived within
the low roofed houses and farm buildings we were passing, might
prove hostile enough towards English folk to attempt to run us
off the road with a primitive catapult, or run us through with a
flint tipped spear, was such a thrill that I felt like leaping from the
Allegro and boldly knocking on the door of the nearest croft, or
homestead, or whatever these people called their houses.

I was eighteen years old.

My education of British history, courtesy of Foster, had thus far
not managed to extend beyond the late 1700s, but I fully recognise

there was also an element of romantic cherry picking to my mental construction of other countries and peoples.

It was, then, to Edinburgh we were bound. And there we spent the day – browsing through music shops on Prince's Street, sauntering through the gardens and taking photos of one another among daffodils. We visited the castle, and I tried to impress Foster with my knowledge, pre-empting some of the placards by spouting what I thought they'd say based on what Foster had taught me about Scotland. I felt that there must be some reason for visiting a place he knew had captured my imagination during our lessons.

Well done.

Foster said from time to time, at well-spaced intervals.

Our windy walk up Calton Hill, grabbing more fake holiday snaps in front of the monument on the top (which, Gulliver, I am proud to report, bears more than a passing resemblance to our very own little Penshaw folly), culminated outside a red phone box with a neglected flaked and dented exterior. Foster made me wait several feet away, but I could hear parts of what he said because every pane of glass in the box had been long ago kicked out.

What I heard gave me little goose bumps of joy.

The night drive home was wet and blustery.

The red lights of the cars in front transformed by the rain and slow swishing wipers, to look like those little targets you get on fairground shooting ranges. The Allegro was always a little damp, the rear window let in the rain – as far as I know, the bloody car was sold with that water feature as standard – along with the walnut drop down picnic tables and branded wine glasses.

How is she, Gulliver? My car? I miss her, you know? Martha's 4x4 looks like it's built to carry the bodies of front-line fodder troops back to base.

I would have bought you a car if you'd asked.

After Edinburgh, three days passed with Foster inhabiting his imminent hit state of focus. Eyes closed and nostrils flared as he repeated measurements back to himself, counted steps in his head, and calculated trajectories. Sometimes his eyes would snap open, and he'd shuffle around the flat, his fingers twitching restlessly over his arsenal.

On the fourth day, the Round-Table flat became a whirlwind of activity, as it always did in the few hours before a hit.

The day had arrived.

Funny way of working.

He could have spread all that activity over the previous three days alongside his subtle mental calculations.

Instead he crammed all the physical preparation into only a few hours before we left the flat, popping like a champagne cork.

Adrenaline thing.

I understand.

This time, he was packing up maps, and drawing diagrams on scraps of paper. That was another incredible thing about Foster – his memory. The pigeon must have given him a huge quantity of information on the phone in Edinburgh, three days ago. He just scribbled a few notes at the time, processing it all in his head.

Then on the day of the hit, it all came out in a geyser of figures, locations, names, co-ordinates, conditions, dos and don'ts, and directions. There appeared to be an awful lot to remember for this hit. Foster muttered and chuckled through those hours, sometimes his face looked like it was going to rupture from squeezing into such furrows, but other times he would relax into a full body recline, satisfied some aspect of the hit was sorted.

He was excited by this one; he was actually looking forward to it.

He couldn't contain it, and that was infectious.

Postscript: The Closing Net

Gulliver, I'm just back from the supermarket. And here is a chilling post-script to my letter above. Just as I was trying to remember if Sarah had asked for her yoghurt with crunchy chocolate hoops, or mandarin chunks in orange syrup, Willows sidles up to me. He says.

The net's closing in on you, Flint.

Of course, the first thing that struck me odd was that it's not usually a net, but rather the walls, that close in upon one, and a net is much more suited to catching, trapping, or confining. I'm left to decide which half of Willows' flawed statement I would rather turn out to be truth – would I rather be crushed? Or trapped? I see benefits in both.

However, I was struck, almost immediately, by the second odd thing in Willows' statement.

He called me Flint.

My stage name.

I told him.

I don't know what you're talking about, Sergeant Willows.

And Willows grinned with an unnerving confidence; he seemed taller. And he said,

I think you do Jasper. Jasper Flint. I think you know exactly what I'm talking about, and I think you're shit-scared right now, and you know what, Jasper Flint?

And then he waited, Gulliver. My goodness. How annoying – he actually had the upper hand, he actually held the strings! Of course I wanted to know what he was going to say – of course I knew it was likely to be - you should be - but what could I do? Just walk away? Maybe I should have, but instead, to save a little bit of face, rather than saying. What? I just raised my eyebrows.

I don't think I have ever felt more pathetic.

And he said,

You should be.

He swaggered off along the dairy aisle, enjoying applause from the assembled cheeses.

This sorry little episode raises some perplexing questions, and of the possible answers, there is no best option here; I can't even pick the least worst. I can only take a stab at the most probable, which, at a pinch, I would say is also the worst worst.

As I first began writing to you, when I began to brood on these things a few weeks ago, Gulliver, I told you I am almost certain you are coming for me. That - almost - is getting smaller, and I am now faced with the prospect that you are working with Willows to engineer my downfall. If not side-by-side, as I can hardly bring myself to imagine such a grotesque mutation of what used to be, then perhaps you are feeding him morsels of information.

For money?

Gulliver?

Spite?

Sick curiosity?

And I must face the fact that I may, inadvertently, have been the catalyst for your vitriol.

I feel now that you are extremely close by.

Today was the first time in two days I had left the Crypt to conduct anything remotely like normal activities. The children were going quite out of their minds, not from hunger, rather because I seem to have spoiled them somewhat – I am a little ashamed that my team of young assassins could be so crippled by a lack of individual tiramisu pots, or complain so bitterly when the piccalilli runs out. Some tightening up needs to occur I think – these things used to be treats rather than the norm. It isn't easy being responsible for the sensible upbringing of six young children you know, Gulliver.

Thank the Saints for Martha.

Back here in my caravan following my run-in with Willows, I felt alone.

The last thing I needed was to find a set of Austin Allegro Vanden Plas wine glasses set out on the Formica table.

Filled with blood.

My own yoghurt, with black cherry syrup in the corner, will remain in the fridge.

I chose the mandarin chunks for Sarah – default to the healthier option.

Do you fancy there is justification for a… vendetta?
    Did you formulate your plan over years?
    I understand.

    But, Gulliver, the police? Willows?

    You have me, Gulliver.
    I begin to panic.

Thirty-Two

Sunday, 3 March

Mr. Broad Shoulders

Just as magazine cartridges needed to be filled, batteries replaced in torches and laser sights, and guns cleaned and oiled, so I needed to be brought up to speed. Foster would never drip feed me the details over days or hours – he would simply arrive at the point in his planning where it was time to fully brief me, and expect me to absorb it all fully in one go.

This evening,
He told me,
We're heading to the edges of town, to a complex just a few years old; Tinrow Luxury Treatments Spa and Conference Centre.

I'd seen it. It looked like a motorway service-station on the outside. Foster had pictures of the inside, which ran a confused gauntlet between vague oriental influence culled from martial arts movies, and faux Art-Deco detailing cut from chipboard.
Nothing new these days is built with a legacy in mind, Gulliver.
Still, there was no shortage of wedding parties, business retreats, and retired couples who had no reason to look beyond the façade, for whom Tinrow Spa represented the very lap of luxury.

The target was a no-good punk kid known as Mutt Jenkins.

Mutt's story, according to the pigeon, was that he'd screwed the sixteen-year-old daughter of the headmaster of a local school. A good girl with a bright future ahead of her. Only now, she was knocked up with a no-good punk baby, and her future prospects seemed a little damaged. The story went, that Mutt Jenkins had taken advantage of her – that was her story – but the damn judge, after four months waiting, said there wasn't enough evidence to prosecute Mutt Jenkins. The headmaster went crazy in the court-room, he pointed to his daughter's swollen belly and screamed out.

What's that if not evidence?

Then he pointed at Mutt Jenkins and yelled.

You're gonna wish you were safely in jail!

That doesn't mean he ordered the hit.

Said Foster.

Sometimes his sense of humour would bleed through like that.

But I found this especially funny.

Foster told me this was to be more complicated than usual. Mutt Jenkins lived in university halls, yep, a no-good punk student. He was either faking the punk bit, or faking the student bit. University halls. Bustling. Right in the city centre. Fortress-like in their security. Mummies and Daddies pay over the odds to pro-tect their spawn when nest-fleeing time arrives.

A hit there, absolutely possible, an interesting challenge.

But unnecessarily messy.

Mutt Jenkins had a job.

Tinrow Spa, behind the bar.

He slept during the day, and took a bus to the Spa for evening shifts. I knew Foster was relishing the idea of offing Mutt Jenkins at the Spa. I know you understand too, Gulliver. A place like that, it's little world away from the world.

Airports, motorway service stations, motels, conference centres, theme parks, spas.

They all exist like we do, Gulliver, right on the edges of society, fantasy complexes built solely to serve a temporary purpose.

Not quite able to contain the law of the land.

Bridges to the beyond.

A visitor in any of these is taking time out from themselves, it's a taste of the beyond, of the possibility of a life path not travelled, even a life beyond this life. To remain within any of them beyond your prescribed time would be to make a statement against the life you've chosen.

Mutt Jenkins was further towards the cliff edge than most.

We were just assisting him in the final few steps.

The Spa, was perfect.

Foster told me,

Listen really carefully because I won't repeat any of it.

He always said that. This time though, the hit truly was a step above the usual.

For a start. Lots of people.

Only the downstairs bar would be open, but it would be filled with relaxed folk fresh from being massaged, coated in chocolate butter, and wrapped in cling film by vaguely exotic ladies of indeterminate age.

Tinrow fancied itself classier than the Hen Party clientele. Most guests stayed over a couple of nights. Wives of wealthy high-flyers, groups of businessmen pretending the Spa facilities were secondary to the conference suites, couples trying to re-kindle a lost flame.

But the night of the hit, all the guests were to be competition winners. A prize that came with something or other they'd forgotten they bought.

A day of pampering, an evening meal, late bar, and home.

Foster said this was the best day for the hit; they'd be rowdier lager-swilling riffraff, not quieter wine-sipping socialites.

Quiet is our enemy.

The biggest challenge, as it often is, would be physically getting in and out.

But the pigeon had given Foster a wealth of information.

I could tell Foster was really up for it, and that was infectious. By the time we left Round-Table Terrace I was nervous about forgetting some of the intricacies, but I couldn't deny I was more excited than I'd ever been for any other hit in the ten years I'd been living with Foster.

We walked to the Spa.

Just shy of six miles from Round-Table Terrace.

A slow amble at my pace due to the mushroom of many colours my foot had become by then. After ten years of denial about what horrors lurked beneath the surface, the horrors beneath were rising to the surface seeking recognition. Back then I thought of it as rotting – but rot is about deconstruction. Now I know my bone and flesh were being slowly replaced – usurped by fresh fungus, an invader from the deep ocean. I still ignored it though; it still looked vaguely like a foot. So I still wore a shoe on it.

No disguising the limp though.

I knew a walk like that would take its toll.

There would be pain to ignore later in the night.

There would be ooze.

I know Foster used the walking time to explore the maps in his mind. He walked with his lips pressed together, thinking. Holding his breath. Letting it out all at once then slowly sucking air back into his lungs over the course of a minute.

I imagined him wandering around the plans in his mind, shaking their struts, testing their integrity, searching for weak spots.

It worried me a little that he was still in this state of mind on the way to the hit.

Did he think there was a weak spot?

It was 8pm when we arrived in the field behind Tinrow Spa.

Hoods up.

Heads down.

All our lovely hardware concealed under thermals, and we both knew the drill.

We sat down in the shadow of a hedge, and waited while the sun sank behind us, and a drizzling winter evening became a full-on rainy winter night. Just after 9pm the lights in the upper levels of the complex were shut down. Only the bottom floor showed signs of life, the Spa was done for the day, and everybody had been funnelled down to the bar.

Mutt Jenkins in the thick of it.

Pulling pints, chopping limes, serving snacks.

Limp salad garnish.

Pale chips.

Without a word, we split.

The Spa was anything but secure. The kitchen was hot, so the rear entrance was propped open with a chair. Beyond this was a passage, with an arched opening leading off to the kitchen, and several other doors.

Staff toilets.

Service stairs.

Service elevator.

Storeroom.

I was the vulnerable one.

I was consigned to the shadows to rely upon the darkness at the end of the passage for concealment.

Foster slipped into the storeroom, shut the door, vanished.

Foster would tell you he was the vulnerable one, relying on my eyes to tell him when to act.

His life, in my hands.

But I felt vulnerable.

I pressed myself back into the shadows.

I pretended I was tiny as a fly stuck to the wall.

These things help a little don't they?

But when somebody broke out from the bustle of the kitchen through the archway, I felt naked, exposed.

Especially since my running days were over.

At least I had a balaclava. I looked the part. There's always some menace in a balaclava.

The guy in the passage was heading for the storeroom.

He paused, I fancied was turning.

I placed my hand on my gun.

For this hit Foster had seen fit to arm me with a pistol rather than a rifle – it meant he expected me to be somewhat pro-active, within the plan of course, rather than staking out one spot. That was concession to my burgeoning responsibility, and I have to admit, passing my fingers over it there by my side I felt a swell of pride.

Could he sense me?

I was just feet away. I felt huge. My breaths gale force gusts.

I gripped the gun, I slipped it upwards.

He carried on towards the storeroom.

Maybe he didn't even pause. I don't know.

He was tall, broad shouldered. His shirt was clean and ironed.

He was not Mutt Jenkins.

He opened the storeroom door. Inside, shelves of tiny condiment packets, spare glasses, boxes of crisps, tins of baked beans, dried chopped onion, hundreds of bottles – wines, beers, ciders, soda.

And Foster.

Silent. Motionless. Behind stacked crates.

A word from my lips stood between this young man and death.

We are powerful, Gulliver. We have great responsibility.

There is no place in our work for enacting a whim.

For unpredictability.

The broad-shouldered young man stepped closer to Foster than either of us had imagined. He lifted the top layer of crates away, filled with new glassware.

If he'd looked further, he might have seen a wisp of greying hair above the remaining crates.

Don't look too hard into the darkness.

You might find something obliged to kill you.

Foster's favourite short-range gun was a long-barrelled, custom drilled, paint chipped, German ex-service revolver, it was beautiful, and it never failed to deliver the goods to precisely the right spot. Of course, this had a lot to do with the fact Foster's aim was almost as good as yours, Gulliver, but the gun helped.

Short range, Foster swore by that gun.

The storeroom door was on a slow release closing spring. As the broad-shouldered guy turned and lugged his crate of glassware towards the kitchen, he faced me oblivious to my presence, oblivious to his place between two killers. Over his shoulder, the barrel of Foster's revolver glinted under the neon light in the passage. Or maybe it was the whites of his eyes, or a pint glass.

Something glinted.

Something watched me, and I felt that concern again, Foster's concern.

Where was the weak spot?

The door clicked shut.

Alone again in the shadows. Waiting.

The bustle of the kitchen, such a random, chaotic mass of shouted orders, bangs, scrapes, clinks, and whooshes. Random at first, but as I nestled into my shadow, the noise began to take on a strange order. I found I could predict when a bang would follow a whoosh, and how often shouted orders would pepper the other noises. A few minutes more, and order became rhythm, the slow song of the kitchen, an orchestra of pots and pans expertly played.

A funeral march.

I hadn't seen him enter the passage.

But suddenly I was aware of a figure, different to the broad-shouldered guy. This one shuffled, his shirt hung low at the back, creased. He did not exude urgency.

I had to be certain.

He was nearly at the storeroom, I took a few steps forwards. A little out of the shadows. I felt emboldened by the kitchen's rhythm. I was meant to be there, part of an intricate opera and I must play my part well.

He opened the storeroom door.

Immediately I said loudly,

Target.

Mutt Jenkins,

Said Foster. Stepping forwards.

Then, after a pause, I heard the faint click of the trigger being pressed on Foster's revolver.

A click. Nothing else.

Foster swore by that gun.

So much so, he hadn't brought a backup.

Mutt Jenkins screamed, and he slammed the door in Foster's face.

Now he'd lost his shuffle, and seemed to have gained a real sense of purpose. He was running back towards me as fast as he could go.

He must not make the kitchen.

Would you have taken aim right there and then, shooting from the shadow, Gulliver?

Did I doubt my aim?

Did I lack faith in my silly little gun?

I stepped briefly in front of the kitchen archway, blocking Mutt Jenkins, raising my gun towards him, and moving back to shadow lest I be seen.

Foster burst out of the storeroom.

With a yelp, Mutt Jenkins took the only route left open to him, up the service stairs to the next floor.

Foster leapt after him pointing his revolver with a steady aim, pumping the trigger again only to be rewarded with the same impotent click.

The same instant, my arms were wrenched backwards by muscles twice as powerful as my own.

Target! Shouted Foster in my direction.

But I was as useful to him as his silent trophy gun. Mr. Broad Shoulders had me in a powerful grip – he must have seen me that instant in the archway. He said,

What's going on here chaps?'

Ha ha. Chaps. Poor guy.

This was not part of the plan.

And at that point I knew Foster must be consumed with disappointment in me. I don't know what peeved him more – seeing Mutt Jenkins vanish up around the first bend in the stairs, or seeing me, stricken, pathetic, helpless to help myself.

Foster paused.

He could have gone on, focused on the target.

But he paused for me, Gulliver.

He was still halfway up the stairs and I saw his hand flick forward rapidly, just the slightest flick of his wrist and Foster's heavy metal pistol was flying through the air between us. It embedded itself into the forehead of Mr. Broad Shoulders.

The top edge of the barrel was ridged like a serrated bread knife, a legacy of ruthlessness that Foster had picked up in some part of France previously occupied by the Nazis. I don't know why, or when, Foster had been in France. Perhaps he went there specifically to purchase that gun.

He loved that gun.

Mr. Broad Shoulders with the revolver embedded between his eyes staggered backwards, and lifted both hands to the lump of metal. He winced horribly as he tried to pull it out, but then his eyeballs rolled upwards, and his entire body went limp – sagging to the floor like a ship's sail cut loose in a storm. A trickle of deep red blood ran from the wound. That pistol might have failed to fire, but it was still an effective killing machine in Foster's hands.

I wrenched the gun from his head, and slung it back to Foster. He caught it and leapt up the stairs without a word. The whole thing slowed him by about six seconds.

Precious seconds.

Pity the dead guy wasn't the target.

It was his time though, I felt it when he opened the storeroom and I almost shouted Target then.

And when I was listening to the funereal kitchen noises.

We all have our time.

My dragging of the body out of the back door was sound tracked by that rhythmic marching tune from the kitchen.

A cosmic Maestro bolstering my confidence.

And giving me an acute awareness of the people manning the kitchen.

Any of them could appear, at any second.

After a very fast burial beneath a tarpaulin, I wiped a spot of blood from the archway, and called the service elevator.

I had an appointment to keep.

Thirty-Three

Monday, 4 March

Mutt Jenkins

A spa is one of those things you really can enjoy more and more the richer you become. This is because you can go to ones where there are hardly any other members of the general public. Where's the fun in trying to escape to a fake version of South-East Asia if you can hear your next-door neighbour or the woman from the Post Office nattering to the masseuse in the next room?

Of course – if you are wealthy, you can book special rooms and special staff, just for yourself. If you're some kind of big cheese big shot, then you can book an entire floor and invite some friends.

Or if you're me, you can book the entire building.

For a week.

If not for my dead-weight foot, beginning to spot my sock with the dark ooze I by then fully expected to feel in such stressful circumstances, I would have sprung, gazelle like, up the stairs to reach our rendezvous, but my research told me the lift would suffice.

With the grace of a ballerina I arrived on the third floor out of six.

Spa Facilities. Announced a wooden style plaque behind a plastic pot plant in the lift.

For this week, they were my spa facilities.

You had to hand it to Mutt Jenkins – he was the most athletic punk I've ever met. All the way up the service stairs, never quite within Foster's reach. I knew their path and it played in my head: Through the top floor conference centre with its claustrophobia-inducing low ceiling. Down the carpeted guest stairway, crashing through the double doors into the buffet area – with Mutt Jenkins throwing chairs back at Foster as they went. On down the stairs to Floor Five – negotiating their slippery way around the tiny excuse for an indoor swimming pool, past the deep end, through the changing rooms and coming face to face with locked glass panelled double doors, Mutt Jenkins would crash right through them with his forehead, lacerating his face, and leaving Foster to hurl himself through the hole bordered with broken shards, scouring deep red lines into his arms and legs. They would emerge, bloody and gasping, into two long rows of bedroom doors, with Mutt desperately hurling pedestal pot plants along the corridor. Down to Floor Four back on the service stairs they would tumble, past yet more bedroom doors, and into the upstairs bar set about with tall mirrors each bearing a vintage logo for cola, tea, soap, toothpaste – all from slightly different eras. All produced in 1997.

And Mutt Jenkins would grab a thickly ornamented glass bottle of vodka from the bar.

I listened, straining my ears, I heard their thudding footfalls, then I heard the first mirror break beneath Mutt Jenkins' heavily wielded bottle.

Dealing with Mr. Broad Shoulders hadn't slowed my progress too much.

One smash, two smash, three smash, four. The heavy shards forming a carpet of pain beneath the thin, torn soles of Foster's favourite comfortable trainers.

And so, they sink to my level, leaping from mezzanine, to landing, to mezzanine, neither touching their feet upon the steps, simply launching from rocking wooden banisters, smearing blood and sweat along the art-deco style stripy wallpaper.

Red skid marks on the carpet.

I stepped back into the shadow of a potted monkey-puzzle tree – and counted under my breath as Mutt Jenkins began tearing along the corridor. Past the reception with its little oriental tea sets absurdly juxtaposed with Top Gear magazines, past the weights room, past the massage 'temple' until he was nearly on top of me and my tree. Five, four, - I counted, Mutt Jenkins turned on his heel – ninety degrees, facing a door.

Three.

Mutt wrenched open the door and flung himself inside.

Two.

A second later, Foster bundled through behind Mutt.

I stepped out from behind my tree, reached for the door, and gently pulled it towards me.

Click.

One.

Thank goodness for laziness – for the desire to have right now, and unrelentingly, what we could only previously have acquired following a prolonged wait, and then only for a limited time. All that palaver of heating up large rocks, or continually stoking a fire; who wants to be bothered with such tedium in the modern world? Certainly not the staff or patrons of the

Tinrow Luxury Treatments Spa and Conference Centre, that's for sure.

The modern steam room, the kind purchased, I imagine at great expense, by the owners of this convenient establishment, is powered by electricity in much the same way as an electric shower. I hate to think of the electricity bills involved in using such a set-up, when you consider that no waiting is involved; as soon as you enter the steam room, you can have steam. Think about how quickly modern kettles boil water – do you even remember how long it used to take for a kettle to boil, Gulliver? I'm not even talking about the ones you put on a gas stove – I'm talking about modern kettles from only fifteen years ago. Ones you would fill, and turn on, and then about three minutes later, a slight crackling sound would tell you that maybe, just maybe, something was happening. Impatience would, I must admit, often draw me to open the lid to watch the little bubbles collecting around the filament – because when that began to happen, you knew you were only going to have to wait another three or four minutes to get your cup of tea.

People don't stand for such waiting times these days. If you don't have a kettle that boils in thirty seconds or fewer, then you need a new kettle.

It's the same with modern steam rooms.

Like the one within which I had just locked Mutt Jenkins, and Foster.

In addition to the four thousand pounds it cost me to hire the entire facility for one whole week, I had to purchase a hefty padlock. The Tinrow Luxury Treatments Spa and Conference Centre know all about health and safety – they no doubt have a risk assessment solely related to use of the steam room. And I am certain that they have considered the dangers of having a lock upon the door.

So I installed one of my own.

I am an assassin.

Let's be clear about this.

My usual remit does not include torture.

I get my kicks from being out of sight, and getting the job done.

I know your own policy differs, Gulliver. I only provide this disclaimer because I know that you will, in all probability, revel in what I am about to describe and I want you to be clear that this was an incident in isolation – with good, hopefully evident, reasons attached.

Only Mutt Jenkins beat upon the door, only he shouted and screamed as the heat began to rise past bearable. He must have been confused – we had talked at length about the plan, and he had carried it out to the letter. But I knew this would be the case, because I had done my research. I knew that Mutt Jenkins had been a quite brilliant athlete before he fell in with the wrong crowd. I knew he would do anything for the kind of cash I was offering him, because I knew about his habit – developed over only eighteen months, but which consumed him and all his former brilliance until his light was virtually extinguished.

So sad.

He was everything I had been looking for.

I lied to him.

But I didn't kill him, Gulliver.

Foster killed him.

The truth is I neglected to tell Mutt Jenkins (whose real first name was Colin) that once the pigeon had spoken it didn't matter to Foster who the client might be. It was simply a hit. A job. A target. After a job was confirmed, Foster was a heat-seeking missile locked onto his target's flaming ass. It didn't matter that this hit came from me, and it didn't matter that when Foster was drinking in all those complicated instructions – plans of this building, names, descriptions, habits, and talents – when he was getting these details from the pigeon, standing in the phone box on Calton Hill in Edinburgh that gloriously exciting day, I was standing the other side knowing everything the pigeon told him.

Foster knew that now.

It wouldn't stop him from hitting the target he'd been given. Mutt, Colin Jenkins. He had a fighting chance there in the steam room. I didn't kill him. Foster killed him with his favourite gun. One second the door was shaking, rattling with the desperation of the young lad on the other side, and the corridors were full of his wails of injustice.

Then there was a sharp crack, and a muffled thud.

The malicious ridged butt of the German revolver was buried in the back of Colin Jenkins' head. I knew it to be the case even before I saw his body nearly two hours later.

Foster's last hit.

I was proud of him.

This was all about the research; starting with which wire to snip behind the control panel, to disable the pressure sensor that would alert the system to the presence of a person inside, thereby disallowing the searing heat of the steam cleaning function.

I snipped that wire the same night I installed the lock.

And obviously I couldn't lock Foster inside a weaponised steam room without knowing the tipping points. It was quite difficult to work out because there are so many variables.

For instance, you know that saying:

It made my skin crawl?

Well, the closest I can imagine to a literal embodiment of the phrase would be when, at a constant 150 degrees Fahrenheit, around the ninety-minute mark, the moisture in between the surface cells of your skin reaches boiling point and causes it to rupture. Slowly cracking and fizzing, opening up like a fault line in the desert until actual muscle tissue is on display, and all the fat deposits you hoped you didn't have start to ooze out and boil as well.

You know what boiling fat feels like on your skin.

The surface of your corneas will begin to sear and bubble after one hour forty. But this can only be a very general guide, because the exact point of no return depends on how much blinking occurs and how well your tear ducts are working. It's good to work it out as closely as possible because once the bubbling starts, it only takes ten minutes before your entire eyes will have boiled away.

Give or take a minute.

Similarly, your lungs will begin to melt from the inside after one hour fifty, in fact, just about as soon as the eyes have finished pooling on the floor. But again, this all depends on how healthy the subject is, how prone to hyperventilation, and whether their lungs have already been ravaged through smoking.

The best anybody could give me for these variables was a guide – a ballpark figure. And the other factor is size of the room. The smaller the room, the more concentrated the available moisture will be, and the faster the body parts will surrender to liquidity.

How big was Foster's ballpark?

The monkey-puzzle tree looked parched – it was one of only a few real plants they had in this place – the rest were just dusty, but they wouldn't stop being green. The monkey-puzzle tree was starting to go brown around the edges of its bristles, and I figured that as I'd hired the entire place for a whole week, I should really water the plants.

Although I expected I had already forfeited my deposit.

I went off in search of a watering can. I put my hand on the door of the steam room and told Foster. I'm just going to find a watering can for this tree, ok?

He didn't say anything.

The door felt hot.

I walked along the corridor smeared with blood from the chase, and took the service elevator again, this time to the basement. I figured the basement was the most likely place I'd find a watering can because that's where the caretaker's quarters were. I thought the caretaker might enjoy a bit of time without his gag anyway – might as well kill two birds with one stone.

No rush.

By the time I got back to the steam room door, Foster had been in there for over half an hour, and the entire corridor was beginning to feel a bit tropical. I refreshed the monkey-puzzle tree and I swear it gave out a little sigh of gratitude.

As I sprinkled, I asked Foster how he was bearing up.

He didn't say anything, but that was nothing new – I could tell he was listening to me.

I could always tell.

I told Foster everything I've been telling you, Gulliver, that his regime of perfection, his aspirations for me to become flawless, was destroying me. I told him that it wasn't possible for me to continue like that, that I just didn't enjoy the hits anymore, that even the momentary thrill of dispatching our prey together was dead because I knew his nit-picking would outweigh any encouragement.

Foster,

I said, and I was speaking quite loudly and clearly now in case he was beginning to feel delirious.

I can't continue aiming for the perfection you want me to reach; I don't believe it exists, I've planned this final hit for both of us as the closest thing either of us will ever get to that pinnacle. You're going to see what a perfect pupil I've become, Foster.

I've learned so much from you.

Here it is in action.

Nothing about this is by halves, Foster, this is all one hundred and eleven per cent. Every detail considered, every second calculated.

Except – and you see Foster, how perfection is always going to be unattainable – for knowing how long it might take for your various parts to expire in there. But I have a ballpark, Foster – we'll see soon enough if it's a big enough ballpark.

I said that. Or something very similar.

Foster maintained his silence.

I pressed my ear right up against the door – the door was sweating some kind of viscous fluid and my face ran with my own perspiration.

It's getting hot out here,
>   I said, listening,
>   It must be quite uncomfortable in there.

I listened some more, I stayed very still, and I filtered out all the other noise – the humming light bulbs, the distant traffic, my beating heart. And I heard Foster breathing. His breaths were coming out slowly, methodically, timed. Not like the unregulated rise and fall I had come to know over the past ten years listening from the kitchen.

Foster was smart. He knew the best way to prolong his life. I told you, Gulliver, he and I, neither of us had the guts to surrender to the edge of the cliff – to launch into the unknown where perfection might just be attainable.

I bet he even had his eyelids shut tight in there.

Crouched there in the corridor, with my ear against the weeping wooden door, and the world zoned out save Foster's steady breathing, it was easy to lose track of the time. The humid atmosphere gently caressed me until I slipped imperceptibly from relaxed consciousness into smooth slumber – my head, rather than my feet, holding me up against the door.

Asleep in the corridor my mind played host to an anthropomorphic monkey-puzzle tree, eternally in my debt from saving it from drought. It stuck there at my side and shielded me from dark shadows creeping in from my peripheral vision. And I twisted fronds from it from time to time, to eat them because I was hungry. And every time I tore off a bristly frond, the tree would wince and seem sad, but I would laugh and water it a little.

When I came to, my face hurt. I opened my eyes gradually and the motionless monkey-puzzle tree swam into view. I stood up quickly but clumsily, and shouted out in pain as some of my skin stayed behind on the sticky door.

In frustration I thumped the door, and quickly looked at my watch. Foster had been inside the steam room for almost exactly 100 minutes.

I composed myself and grinned, because do you know something, Gulliver?

Despite everything, it was sort of perfect.

I twisted the key in the lock and wrenched open the door using quite a bit of force because the wood had bloated. The door popped open and swung outward, and the blistered head of Mutt Jenkins flopped onto the corridor carpet, Foster's revolver still embedded deep in his skull; blood mixing with boiling water.

I wonder if they ever got the stains out of that carpet.

With no chance of seeing more than a few centimetres through the swirling whiteness, I had to step back for a few seconds just to allow the air to cool a little, then I stepped over Mutt Jenkins's body and advanced into the room trying to bat the steam from my face as I went.

Foster was near the front of the room, naked and stretched out his back, obviously attempting to gain some relative coolness from the tiles.

Self-preservationist.

As I peered through the swirls I found his skin a sore sight for the eyes. Mountain ranges of ruptured flesh, oozing and cooked like meat, red trickles, green gungy eruptions, and yellow translucent areas pattern-printed across his entire body.

I watched his still form for a few seconds, knowing he couldn't be dead – knowing he was stronger than the average. Then I saw it, his chest rose then fell and I knew – he wasn't just not dead, he was still conscious, preserving his lungs from melting – he was holding his breath for as long as was humanly possible.

Afraid of the edge.

The humid atmosphere was already making me giddy, and my eyes were drowned with the sweat running from my hair like water draining from spaghetti. My eyes were beginning to tell me they couldn't take much more – so I backed out and braced myself against the wall. I twisted my head around and the monkey-puzzle tree stared back at me.

Good plan. I told it. And I snatched up the watering can.

Back at Foster's motionless, chicken fillet of a body, I sprinkled my head with the can using one hand, and grabbed hold of Foster's foot with the other. He groaned, and as I tugged the flesh began to abandon his bone like tender meat from a drumstick.

I dropped Foster's leg, and it landed on the floor with a splat. Two of his toes had parted ways with his foot, which was perfect because I needed to examine them. With a real thrill I witnessed another part of my research prove itself true – Foster's toes nestling in my palm, were as smooth and featureless as grapes.

I pocketed the toes, and knelt down to take his hand in mine; gently I patted it, I genuinely hope it brought a little comfort, but my ulterior motive was a glance at his fingertips, and there they were, smooth and bloated just like his toes.

Anonymous.

I dragged my own gently weeping foot out of the room – the atmosphere wasn't doing it any good at all, I can tell you. I shuffled off down the corridor to the massage temple, past the stucco stonework and the 12-volt whirring water features, I headed for the back of the place where the temple features suddenly gave way to cold white tiles and brushed steel storage units. Customers didn't have to see this – they stayed in the magical bit. The magic temple of massage and exotic aroma, and having needles stuck in your head.

The first cupboard yielded only pots, but I paused nonetheless and I read the labels. Chocolate and Orange, Lavender and Coconut, Lemongrass and Jasmine, Paprika and Apricot, Caramel and Banana. It made my mouth water but none of it was edible – they were body butter rubs that people paid to be covered with.

Vanilla and Thyme.

Mint and Pine-nut.

Perfect.

I grabbed the Mint and Pine-nut body rub, and swung open the next cupboard. There they were, rolls and rolls of thick, transparent body wrap.

As I dragged my aching leg back along the corridor, the monkey-puzzle tree appeared to wave at me, beckoning me onwards with urgency. I quickened my pace, wincing as the tenderised flesh of my bloated foot rubbed painfully in my shoe. It was only when I got to within a metre of the tree I realised it really was waving at me – only because Foster had managed to drag himself out of the steam room and stationed himself behind it.

Foster. What a trooper.

I'm telling you, Gulliver, I don't expect there are many men in the world who would have been able to manage to get that far out of the room in his condition – and it wasn't by way of physical strength or wonderful health. It was strength of mind, strength of will.

The desire to live, although life now offered him little. I told Foster. Don't think of this as your demise. You'll never be identified. Do you see? This beautiful hit will be attributed to you. It's my gift.

You'll endure.

Hunted.

Pursued.

Legend.

And me. I'll emerge, liberated, from years of imprisonment, torture, God knows what.

They'll speculate.

Missing Jasper, found, rescued. And I'll tell them all how magnificent you were. But I'll be confused. Why did Foster leave me?

I told him.

I'll do therapy.

They'll pity me.

They'll watch me.

And I'll let them.

Bits of Foster highlighted his path – torn flesh from his legs and stomach lay like whale blubber on the carpet. Foster himself lay facing me trying to muster the strength to move his arm, to grab my ankle. I think he thought that if he could grab hold of my bad foot, he might be able to overcome me. He'd been boiled alive, and it didn't look like he was seeing too well – his eyes looked a bit bumpy on the surface, and he kept grunting and blinking.

But he was still trying to fight me.

The monkey-puzzle tree was in danger of falling over so I moved it out of the way – it gave me better access to Foster anyway. I picked at the brand-new roll of body wrap and took a while finding the end.

I told Foster to be patient.

I had to tell myself to relax too because I knew he would probably regain some strength being out of the steam room, I just hoped he was cooked up enough to keep him docile while I hung him up.

But I'm getting ahead of myself.

I looped the wrap around Foster and used it to pull him out into the corridor without losing any more of his tender body bits. The open bits of him looked really gruesome pressed up against the clear plastic, some of them opened up more. In a couple of places the plastic even squashed right down to the bone and already there was a pooling of blood, sweat, pus, and liquid fat where the plastic sagged. I let him lie there for a second while I opened my special jar.

Mint and Pine-Nut, Foster. I said.

He didn't react. I don't think he got the joke.

You know, like a stuffing because you're cooked? I said.

He was just stubborn. I know he was impressed with little details.

I soon realised Foster's ruptured skin wasn't going to stand up to having the body rub smeared over it – the skin was just peeling off several layers as a time, so I took to slapping it on in globules and pressing it down. I figured if I dotted enough of it around him, the wrap would squeeze it out over him. The smell was almost overpowering, especially combined with the humidity coming from the steam room.

And it was making me hungry.

It made me realise I wouldn't be relying on Foster to feed me any longer. Did you have that feeling too, Gulliver? When you left us behind? You find your own way don't you? But it's different, strange at first.

Liberating, though.

I almost forgot the most important thing.

The climbing harness.

I had it in my bag, but I was just about to wrap Foster up nice and tight within several layers of thick plastic sheeting when I remembered that if I didn't put the harness on first I'd never get the bloody thing on him would I?

The straps inevitably cut through Foster's ravaged flesh like a blunt knife through crème-brûlée. But there was something still holding him together, in fact he was showing remarkable resilience. He started to moan and make vague signs of wanting to struggle, and I don't know if it was because of the fact that his eyeballs had been partially cauterised, but a tear ran down his cheek and made him look very sad.

A real tear.

Wrapping him up was a lot of fun – I rolled him over and over and over like rolling up my sleeping bag, at Foster's insistence, on his kitchen floor, every morning, trying to get it back into the impossibly tiny bag it originally came in. And just like the sleeping bag I kept him nice and tight, and I squeezed out the air bubbles. It was a lovely, neat job Gulliver – a work of art, and a joy to smell too. The red ooze was turned dark green by the body rub, so it didn't look too gruesome at this point. This was when I knew there was no chance of Foster suddenly finding some superhuman strength and rising up to strike me down. Nobody could break out of such a tight body wrap, and even if Foster managed to, his body would fall apart into lots of bits anyway.

Imagine that, Gulliver. Yeah – I know what makes you tick.

I didn't even notice the pain in my foot as I dragged Foster down the corridor towards the gym.

This was my victory.

Nothing was going to thwart the culmination of my six-year plan.

So this was the full circle bit – it took a lot of effort to clip the harness into the frame of the weights machine – but once it was done, it was sweet. Foster dangled there wrapped up like a fly in a spider's larder. And you know what? My timings were really good because by now he was really beginning to struggle – he seemed to have regained quite a bit of strength, and his writhing made him swing gently backwards and forwards.

Best of all – I knew he could hear me.

I told him again how lucky he was to have someone to give that extra push off the edge of the cliff into the unknown, into the only place where any person could ever hope to find perfection. And I had conducted the entire plan in as perfect a manner as I possibly could.

Foster,

I said,

I could have achieved the same result with a slap dash concoction of uninspired treacheries. But no, I did all of this for you. I listened to you. I respect you.

I took a little scalpel from my backpack, and I waved it under his swollen eyes. I don't know if he could see anything by now – I think so because his eyeballs swivelled to the scalpel as I crouched down at his wrapped, dangling feet.

So, the perfection,

I told Foster,

and the actual push off into a place beyond this life – those things are for you.

I slit open the plastic wrap around his toes – the eight of them that weren't already in my pocket.

But this bit,

I said,

Is for me. This is the full circle bit because, Foster, at the end of the day, when all's said and done, it was you who allowed my foot to rot like an apple in a forgotten bread bin, and it was you who killed my family letting them drain onto the floor over the course of several hours like defrosting freezer cabinets.

And I rapidly began to slash through the layers of plastic at his foot, soon hitting soft flesh and bone, and slicing veins and forcing through tendons – and then, Foster's dying lungs found voice to wail. And the plastic wrapping began to fill up with dark red and it seeped through the layers making beautiful patterns before trickling from the bottom of the cocoon and pooling onto the floor of the gym.

That was where they found me.

Wading through the gruesome aftermath of a disturbingly elaborate hit on an unidentifiable man.

Dragging behind me an understandable trauma, convenient in restricting my openness, except to describe how Foster planned it all, and lament having been abandoned by him at last.

I moved back into the Round-Table Terrace flat as soon as it was no longer deemed a crime scene. And I enjoyed the only barely concealed revulsion my willing presence there elicited; why would I choose to live in my prison of over a decade?

I must be a puppet, and Foster still my master.

When I walked back into the flat I found myself with a bedroom and bed of my own to sleep in for the first time since I was 8 years old. But I wasn't prepared to come face to face with Foster quite so quickly again.

There he was, standing next to me atop Calton Hill on our Edinburgh trip just weeks before, wearing something like a smile. He'd put it in the burnt umber fabric frame - perfectly straight.

I wept.

Thirty-Four

Friday, 8 March

Betrayed

It's a funny old world.

That's what I told Martha as I cried and cradled your brother's body.

I can hardly bring myself to write it

Michael is dead.

Perhaps you already feel it in your bones.

The events of yesterday have made me suddenly old, and my emotions are escaping, flowing thick and un-channelled as oil from perished rubber. I know now exactly how much I love you, and Michael.

It has bruised my heart to see one pitched, at last, so venomously against the other.

I pulled back the caravan curtains and the morning flooded in, such a rare one, so lovely, so still.

I boiled the kettle, mostly just to look at the steam dancing through the early morning sun's rays. I did fancy a cup of tea too, and I sat out on the step and bathed in the light, not very warm, but rejuvenating.

And presently, something I wasn't expecting.

I was no longer alone.

From across the wild grass, right against the forest's edge, a person was moving slowly towards me. The movement startled me, but I quickly realised it was familiar.

The elegant poise.

Effortless gait.

Unmistakably, Little Hye.

I watched her approach, and took a moment to congratulate myself on my part in raising such a graceful young woman. I flashed back to the little girl crouching in the shadows of that London house, uncoiling in her first silent strike, saving me. That discipline of posture and physical awareness only became more finely tuned as she grew older.

Of course, she diverted her path long before reaching me; nobody having exited the Crypt, would risk their own safety or mine by punctuating or culminating their journey at the caravan.

After Hye had almost vanished, I grabbed my jacket, and fired up Martha's 4x4. Bouncing over grass and along the muddy track. I overtook Hye, rushing past her in a manner that to anybody watching, would have seemed unreasonable.

A mile down the road, I pulled into a Forestry Commission track, and waited.

She was soon with me, and climbed in.

Good morning.

Good morning, Jasper.

Where are we going?

Where we first met.

I raised my eyebrows, but slipped the car into gear.

Twenty minutes later, we rolled onto that un-surfaced lakeside café car park. Like very little else, the café has survived, albeit with much faded signage, and a menu entirely composed of things that can be stored for a long time and heated up quickly.

It would be hours before the place opened.

We stared out of the car, looking at the spot where Hye-Kyoung's powder blue Land Rover had become her sepulchre.

Hye asked me,

Did you feel bad for taking my mother?

I felt good protecting you from your grandfather,

I replied.

And your mother wasn't looking after you. You won't remember?

That day? Every second, I remember my mother before that too.

Happy memories?

She didn't say anything.

It doesn't matter anyway. She was my mark. You know that. Hye was silent, motionless, staring from the window for thirty seconds or more. It felt longer anyway, and I couldn't bear it.

Why are we here?

I asked.

Closure.

She replied.

Then she reached behind her and slid something from her little bag.

Instinctively I stiffened, and felt naked.

Un-armed.

It was teddy.

His head firmly re-sewn onto his shoulders.

I relaxed.

Hye smiled at me. I smiled back.

Then in one fluid movement she tore teddy's head off, again, and there nestled inside his body, a revolver.

Well. He's full of surprises,

I said.

She trained the gun at my temple.

You took my mother away,

Said Hye,

You've exposed me to death, trained me to do terrible things.

I could hear her teeth grinding, she did that in her sleep too. And she clenched her fist around the handle.

She took a deep breath.

Thank you,

She said. And she lowered the gun.

Nobody's ever said that to me before, Gulliver. Nobody.

But, I need to explore,

She said,

Don't look for me like the other night, even if I'm gone a long time. OK?

OK.

She got out of the car, and walked over to the spot where Hye-Kyoung had met her end. She set Teddy down on the ground, body first, then his head placed on top.

She tucked her revolver underneath her waistband, and walked back over to the car.

I'm going to stay here for a while,

She said.

And then?

I don't know.

Peace, like the longest exhale.

I couldn't tell you how good it felt to drive away from Hye without an accompanying dread in my heart.

That's how you do it, Gulliver.

And later, I walked.

I pottered around between the trees that only a few nights previously, I would have been terrified to face lest I become swallowed.

I felt as though there was nobody else in the world with me. Not just alone among the trees, but alone in the world. And the feeling is all the more mysterious when I consider that as I walked over the soppy mulch at the forest's edge, enjoying the sight of my breath hanging in front of me like little clouds, there was already a small army among the trees, a malicious battalion of those who would seek to bring harm to me and my children.

And I, blissfully unaware.

And yet, I survive.

And for this, must I be thankful?

I'm sorry, Gulliver, you must understand I am grief stricken. I don't know what he meant to you.

The Crypt was compromised.

I didn't walk that way deliberately; after Willows' warning the other day, I've been very cautious, staying mostly at the caravan. But I found myself at the Crypt eventually, after I tracked the sun as it fell behind the trees, amazing this time of year, how the sun can be so vibrant in the morning, and quickly so white and weak from only a few hours past midday.

Brief candle.

I was throwing caution to the still cold air if I'm honest; I was lost in a happy reverie, repeating Hye's words in my mind.

Thank you. Thank you. Thank you.

It couldn't last for long. People like us don't deserve peace.

Nothing is accidental, Gulliver, it's all for a reason, and therefore, all perfect.

Correct?

Perfection, despite mediocrity?

I don't know any longer, Gulliver. So many faces float in my head, in the day sometimes as well as the night. All those marks we hit together, all those I hit alone, all those I hit with the others.

Never with Michael, though.

I'm weary of the poisonous memories, they're beginning to infect the pure ones, to feed off them.

How can it be that my good memories are turning into bad?

I'm haunted, Gulliver.

And I'm sad.

And yet.

Yet.

There is still light in the living.

Sweet rest for the living.

And the dead have an eternal home here.

I did take comfort in that, Gulliver.

I will again.

Martha was there.

When I arrived at the Crypt, even though I tried not to be there. Still, I entered, and all was silent, so, silently I went down the stone steps, and I felt the warmth of the fire set against the coldness of the day.

Martha was there and she was pleased to see me.

She was sitting in the chair that Michael found for Hye, the one with Peter-Pan painted on the seat, and Tinkerbell on the back at the top. She put her finger to her lips.

Shh.

Seaburn was curled up a little too close to the fire for my liking – if she was a longhaired cat she would have become a fireball long ago. And all the children wrapped up on their plinths, one or two stretching and yawning. Sarah was reading as usual. She's in the middle of a Poe anthology. I don't think she sleeps.

Hye had not returned.

And that, was OK.

Martha knew something was wrong. She always knows. Those ghosts of the ones I committed to the wind, they encircle her within the Crypt, they're always present and they tell her what they know. But Martha was smiling, she beckoned me to her, and I sat next to her on the rug. We didn't talk for a few minutes, and I just enjoyed the Crypt – you know how I love to come back after a few days in that caravan.

Martha told me,

Don't worry, you're supposed to be here.

And she put her hand on my shoulder.

I suddenly had the strangest desire to show to Martha all the letters I've been writing for you – reveal myself to her in a new way. But an icy blast blew across the floor. Seaburn sprang to her feet and her tail stiffened like a snooker cue.

Then, soft footsteps.

I was ready for you, Gulliver, I believe I was as ready as I could be. Martha's words of comfort were strange to me, unsettling in a way because I didn't know what they meant, but they made me realise too, that if you were coming for me I would rather be here than anywhere else. And if it was your intent to harm those little ones, I would face that intent.

Stare the monster down, or die in the attempt.

Martha tightened her grip on my shoulder, and Sarah put down her book as the footsteps came closer. None of them knew my fears – none of them knew about the gun inside your poor Woodward, none of them knew about the blood-filled wine glasses.

I kept these things to myself to protect them from the truth.

But the truth I was protecting them from was no truth at all.

Our visitor from the cold was not you, Gulliver.

It was Michael.

He was always a tall boy.

He seemed ten feet high to me as he stepped into the Crypt, with me sitting on the floor and the flames flickering on his face. He looked, grown up. I mean, he was grown up, but, you know what I mean.

He'd gained a man's frame, the fully realised version of what I'd seen half-baked in the dying sunlight twisted by the gas burner heat haze on the day you couldn't cut off my fungus addled stump.

And Michael could.

Martha's hand still gripped my shoulder, and Seaburn continued feigning taxidermy, but I don't have their intuition and I leapt up with my arms wide. He hugged me back, Gulliver, it felt good to have him back and I told him so, I hugged him tight towards me. But over his shoulder a pale face materialised from the darkness, a face I thought it was impossible to see inside the Crypt.

Sgt. Willows.

I know you're not surprised Gulliver, because I know the truth, now.

You're languishing in a cell.

God knows where.

How did Michael contain you, Gulliver? I would never have thought it possible. I can only imagine that you maintain a sliver of a brother's love.

I wished you to love Michael as a brother.

Has love become your suppression?

If so, I hope he hasn't destroyed love within you, Gulliver.

Love is very hard to destroy.

When Willows entered the Crypt my first thought was that poor Michael had been trailed; that Willows had followed him through the darkness among the twisted trees.

But Willows placed his hand on Michael's shoulder, and the truth crushed the wind out of me.

And Willows said,

Go straight to jail, do not pass go, do not collect two hundred pounds.

How long do you think he'd been planning that?

He whistled,

So this is your kiddie-snatch dungeon, Flint.

Like I was something disgusting.

He said,

This is the lair where you bring your victims.

Do they look like victims?

My words caught in my throat.

Willows just shrugged his shoulders and grinned. Big day for Willows.

What's to stop me from making sure you're never seen again? I said.

Six good men outside, six semi-automatic rifles.

Classy,

I muttered.

He laughed because he didn't know if I was being sarcastic or not. Even now, I think he still wanted me to like him – still thought we were buddies playing some kind of brutal game of tag in the dark.

But my mind wasn't really on Willows and his team of armed flatfoots outside hoping for the chance to gun me down, it was firmly on Michael and the fact that he'd brought them into the Crypt.

Into this sacred place.

I choked. I told him,

Michael, I'm sorry.

He avoided my eyes, and looked at the ceiling.

I'm sorry about your birdhouse. I knew Gulliver didn't make it himself, but I didn't say anything.

He just kept looking at the ceiling. So I asked him,
    Why are you doing this, Michael?

You've had some revelations during your therapy, haven't you, Mr. Granton?
    Said Willows.

Michael looked me in the eye, and said,
    I hate you.

He said he hated me, Gulliver.
    Like he was telling me he'd forgotten to buy milk.

Willows said,
    Mr. Granton's therapist says he's cradling a deep-seated inadequacy. Also, you killed his Mum, so, you know...

Michael sighed, and fixed his gaze on the ceiling. Willows patted him on the shoulder.
    Like his Dad. Or something.
    Mr. Granton has been assisting us with our enquiries for a while now, Flint,
    Said Willows,
    At first he was reluctant weren't you, Mr. Granton?

But turns out he just needed a pen and paper, and a therapist. Started writing about his brother – the one with pointy teeth and a bald head. Almost, an animal.

I know you'll enjoy that, Gulliver.

Willows continued with his nose in the air, and he started to wander slowly around the room like a plasticine Columbo, and he kept peering down at the little faces staring up at him from the plinths.

The fellow,

He said,

Who I believe you know as...

And he paused, just for effect, and took a tiny little notebook out of his breast pocket, also extracting a pair of half-moon reading glasses from an impossibly small tube. He put them on, peered at the notebook, holding it at arm's length and squinting, and he said,

...Gulliver. Yes, your Gulliver fellow fell for the lure of meeting Mr. Granton, who, I must say, really has the guts for a mission. Anyway, in we swooped and caged the beast. He's a victim too of course... but he's also linked to some pretty unhinged crimes... Still, if he spills his guts about you, Flint, he might get some sympathy, so, you know, the future's bright really. Except yours.

I turned away from the ridiculous sight of Willows, the wrong sight of him here at all. I spoke to Michael and found I wasn't angry.

Michael,

I said,

What about the gun inside the dog? And the wine glasses from the Allegro, with the blood?

Slips, Jasper, in Mr. Granton's therapy,

Cut in Willows,

You have to understand, Mr. Granton has been through a terrible ordeal lasting more than a decade.

I was gritting my teeth.

Now, Gulliver, you're probably wondering why you haven't seen Sgt. Willows gloating over his victory. You're probably sitting in your jail cell right now, going out of your mind with the frustration of being locked up without access to firearms.

An impotent assassin.

Sorry about your dog... by the way.

I feel for you Gulliver. I promise, I'll try to spring you. The truth is, Sgt. Willows may well be dead. I don't know. The last anybody saw of him was running into the forest in the still darkness of night, as fast as his little legs would carry him, screaming for his life.

Thirty-Five

Friday, 8 March

The Stand Off

The first sign that Willows' rifle-wielding bobbies were no longer the scariest thing outside the Crypt, was Seaburn suddenly going stiff and spitting again.

She mewled really loudly then hot-footed it off down her favourite tunnel.

Then we heard the first crack.

It was music to my ears, because I recognised that crack, it was one of my favourites.

Do you know what I thought, Gulliver? I thought it was you. I thought you'd broken out of prison, and you were coming to rescue us from Willows and his goons. I'd gone from being deadly afraid that you were coming here to get me, to wishing you to be here with a smoking gun and a malicious grin.

It wasn't you.

Some confused shouting, five more cracks, and each one followed by a dull thud. Willows' face drained of colour – he knew.

Six local coppers.

Six hero funerals.

Six grieving families.

And then it was time for the rest of us to face whatever had come to visit.

There were eight of them.

They were organised to perfection.

Foster would have been awestruck.

They descended the stone staircase without a sound.

Shadows of death.

My past, come back to haunt me.

Mr. Yang's own brood had hunted me down at last, led here by Willows' good men.

They were seriously impressive, Gulliver, decked out in black body suits with red belts and these tight hats that came down over their faces if they so wanted, like a really flexible motorcycle helmet.

The first six to come down the steps held onto the hilts of long swords at their hips, lightly curved, sheathed, elegant.

Why did Little Hye's mum never have any of those beautiful swords for sale among her perfumes and cosmetics?

Of the final two, one sported a sword too, but also brandished an XK8 assault rifle.

Less elegant, but it certainly held the attention of everybody in the room.

Those last two were obviously special, though they didn't dress any differently – the one with the rifle was a guard for the other, who didn't carry anything at all.

The other six parted like the Red Sea before these two, and the leader stood at the head of the group; arms folded.

My poor children; some immediately coiled like springs, others focused on not turning to mush.

Poor Willows. Thunder, well and truly stolen.

I rolled my eyes as he straightened his back and, loudly, gracelessly, cleared his throat.

Excuse me,

A step forward and immediately, one of our visitors became a blur and spun around a neat 360-degree pirouette.

Willows immediately recoiled against the wall, his knees bent. We saw the blood before he felt the cut; a crimson thread connecting his brow to his nose. A superficial wound that dribbled blood into his eye as he brought his hand up to touch his face.

He stared, bewildered, opened his mouth, then wisely, shut it again and slumped sulkily against the wall.

Adept in theatrics, our eight visitors took silent command of the room. Every tiny movement appeared huge, our senses tuned to their frequency. We watched transfixed as the leader executed a slow, graceful turn of heel to reveal unmistakable, elegant, femininity.

She bent past the curtain in the corner of the crypt, and picked something up, rolling it between thumb and forefinger; Hye's lipstick.

To be truly accurate – her mother's lipstick.

Oft opened, never used.

Branded 'Yang'.

The graceful leader pretended not to see the brand, but I saw a little light dance in her eye.

She was running black-clad fingers through Little Hye's dresses.

I shivered.

She brought one of the dresses up to her nose, and inhaled deeply.

I couldn't bear it.

I started forward in anger, and Martha put her hand on my wrist to stop me.

Always surprisingly strong.

But their leader didn't flinch anyway. Instead, ignoring me, she held the lipstick aloft, turned again on her heel, and held it up in front of the whole room.

She spoke with a voice like double cream, free flowing, smooth, lacking colour.

Who does this belong to?

And Sarah Greenleaf said,

It's mine.

Bless her.

With imperceptible speed, Sarah was forced into Hye's chair.

Show me,

She said.

Crouching in front of her, holding up the lipstick.

Slowly twisting it.

The bright pink tip sliding smoothly upward

Sarah, rigid with fear.

She held the stick in front of her, and with her other hand, she stroked Sarah's hair.

Revulsion. We all felt it.

Show me.

Sarah took the lipstick, and with remarkable grace, she applied it to her lips, just as if it was her own. To my knowledge, Sarah has never before worn lipstick.

Beautiful. Said the leader. Do you have nail polish to match?

Sarah shook her head.

That's ok. I do.

And from the tiny pack clinging to her back, she withdrew a slim bottle.

Same hue.

Same logo.

Isn't that a coincidence?

Please. Allow me.

Gripping Sarah's hand, she painted Sarah's nails with terrifying dexterity. The same bright pink of her lips.

Very pretty.

But I'm afraid I don't believe you.

Sarah screamed, and with fluid grace, her black-clad tormentor was beside me, a hard, round, splash of pink pinched between her fingertips, held aloft.

No blood.

Sarah clutched her stripped finger, enclosing it in her other hand, and gritting her teeth against the pain.

Mr. Flint, do you recognise this colour?

Yes.

Where is the girl whose lips are this colour?

She never used it. I told them. Sometimes she looked at it, for a long time.

You watch her?

I protect her.

Where is my sister's child?

I don't know.

Silently, she stepped back to Sarah and gently, tenderly, took her hand, and uncurled her fist. She laid Sarah's palm upon the table. Her fingers bloodied, impossible to see which nail was missing.

A sudden movement.

Sarah stiffened.

Stole herself against the pain.

She barely moved an inch, defiantly stared ahead.

Can you imagine my pride, Gulliver?

You must take some credit too.

Would I then break down and weep? Would I beg for mercy on Sarah's behalf? Is that what I had taught her to do? Her strength became the solid platform that supported me in my own resolve.

Also, I didn't know.

Not everybody in that room had such a strong conviction towards calm in the face of torment. I confess, I'd forgotten Willows was even there – Willows, a distant spectator in his own hero story; poor man, he couldn't have dreamed such happenings.

But Willows, though trembling, was not the one to break.

That, Gulliver, to our shame, was Michael.

It isn't that his actions were dishonourable, they were brave, of course, but they were ignorant of the need for stealth and stillness. Only at that moment, did I truly admit to myself, that I had failed Michael.

And as I watched him take a stride towards Sarah's tormentor, I knew, I had killed him by holding him back.

Never believing it was worth the effort to give him his turn. We failed to see the man emerging from the inept little boy. And by the time his true potential had started to break through, it was already too late.

I see, now.

Did he know that he allowed Sarah's escape?

I hope the world slowed down in his final moments. I hope he gained some clarity.

I hope.

For us looking on, there was no such slowing down of the scene. Michael's lunge was met almost immediately by the unmistakable crack of that discharging XK8 rifle.

He folded neatly onto the stone floor.

Shot through the heart.

Sarah saw her opportunity immediately.

Before Michael's body had settled, she was up on a ledge with Lynette, and silently capitalising on that brief distraction among the Koreans, Sarah took control. The eyes of my brood looked for her command, even Vinnie.

The flash in her eyes said, pick a target.

And hold it.

Perhaps, perhaps... if I had managed to raise my own eyes only a fraction of a second earlier from their bemused fix on Michael... perhaps I could have given guidance to Sarah.

Warned her.

She was following her training impeccably, and so I find myself at fault again, Gulliver.

Engage in a stand-off when you're certain you have the upper hand. Yes, but in our field, where we inhabit the shadows and spring upon our prey like foxes on caged hens, when have we not had the upper hand?

She was counting guns.

Six ex-military revolvers versus one Korean assault rifle.

But you will know, Gulliver, what Sarah had missed; in a stand-off, you don't weigh up firepower, you weigh up reaction times.

And when your opponents are assassins highly trained in a brand of agility allowing them to dispatch targets at close range without using ballistics, and without being seen, then a stand-off relying on your own lightning-fast reactions being better than theirs, probably isn't the way to go.

In my defence, it's a very unlikely situation, but I'll make certain to cover it fully in future.

For a long while, stale mate.

I felt, initially, that as my plucky brood on their stone ledges numbered only six, with eight shadowy assassins below them, then Martha and I should make sure to lock eyes with one each too, to give the stand-off its best chance of success.

But soon enough, I realised, most of the Koreans were fixed upon Sarah or Vinnie, having perfectly deduced which of the armed fierce-eyed children staring them down constituted any real threat.

I decided instead, to fix my gaze on Sarah in case she needed guidance, and in case I could work out how to impart guidance with only a flicker of my eyelids.

She never looked in my direction anyway.

To the untrained eye, she was unflinchingly poised, focused, alert.

To my eye, she was all of these, and yet, I could sense her fear.

She knew.

It was too late, but she knew she'd made an error entering this stand-off. The Koreans stared down the barrels of the children's guns, calm, unwavering. And I knew, they were just waiting, certain they wouldn't need to make the first move. My brood is trained well, but they are still children. Perhaps we trained them too well; we gave them a self-belief justified in most cases.

Not all.

The Koreans were waiting for the bullet.

My mind raced through the options, and there it was.

If we all waited long enough, one of my brood would break and fire, thinking the others would follow suit and they could dispatch the intruders in one single round of glorious gunfire.

The naivety of youth.

When you're laying in the dark, or tucked away in the shadows waiting for your hit to shimmy into your line of sight, you can feel like you're the king of stillness, even your breath impressively controlled, a passing fly landing on your lip would not induce a modicum of movement. But really, you're still slowly flexing your toes, clenching and unclenching your hands, your teeth, your buttocks. You can, because you're hidden; your aim is to remain so.

A stand-off is different. This kind of stillness demands serious self-control; and the slightest twitch, like a raised eyebrow in an auction house, can mean endgame.

The Koreans had masks over their eyebrows.

Nothing remotely twitchy about them.

Children twitch.

Especially trained assassin children, hyped up from the death of one of their own in front of their eyes. I looked to Vinnie, I caught a flash of you in his eyes, Gulliver.

I scared myself.

He was gone, a lone sniper disconnected from everybody, excited fury flashing in his eyes. He would shoot long before the Koreans made their move, but weighing up the odds in my head, I couldn't put my chips on Vinnie.

Stephen was an interesting possibility, as keen as he'd been to learn the job, especially the firearms aspects, he wasn't always fully focused; a lot going on in his mind, I think. Right now his eyes were twitching feverishly between our visitors, and Michael's motionless form on the floor. More fear than outrage; no, it wouldn't be Stephen.

Lynette, poor thing, frozen with fear. Sarah was right to be with her – she would take Sarah's cue and nothing else. It wouldn't be Lynette. Ditto Jason, he was twitching alright, but only to look sideways at Vinnie; they may not see eye to eye on a lot of things, but in combat, Jason would mirror Vinnie, unless Vinnie went completely mental, which is always a distinct possibility.

And suddenly, I could see exactly how it would happen. My mind's eye flashed back to a perfect replay of our rescue mission deep in the clutches of the forest only a few nights past. The tired little boy with his energy sapped, padding along dejectedly with no will to go on. The genius stroke of Sarah, scooping him up to her shoulders, knowing his reaction would be anything except compliance. The little boy, once set down, determined to prove himself a little man among the rest, leading the way with renewed fire.

I suddenly realised, that finding Hye that night (or her finding us) had marked the end of our mission, but only the beginning of his. I saw in Arthur's eyes as he lay on his stone ledge, not the frightened cower of the little boy I was used to, but the fierce independence of the little man born that night in the forest.

He wouldn't deign to sit upon Sarah's shoulders today either.

He isn't driven by morbid excitement, as Vinnie or you might be.

He isn't driven by the rule book, like Sarah or Stephen.

Arthur is driven by righteous indignation.

Righteousness is slow to act, but indignation has an itchy trigger finger.

The Koreans were on to him.

That bead of sweat rolling down his temple; they saw it.

That quickening of his breath; they felt it.

And one by one, they fixed their eyes on Arthur, willing him to break, like mice dancing limbo beneath a trip wire; their eyes taunted him with subtle incredulity.

And then, the masterstroke. Achieved through the slightest relaxing of a thigh muscle, the long-curved sword of one of our black-clad visitors, shifted, the movement itself imperceptible to our eyes, but the effect was to bring the blade flat into the path of light from a naked bulb above.

The beam reflected directly across Arthur's face.

Recoiling from the flash, his hair trigger released, and his shot blasted through the crypt. Hopelessly off mark, his bullet hit the ceiling, splintered rock its only effect, but it was the starting pistol.

Even before Arthur's bullet hit the ceiling, the Korean assassins flexed their muscles ready to take flight across the Crypt. Arthur's shot was predictably followed by the same multiplied five times as the others gratefully took aim and fired.

To no avail.

Only their leader remained motionless, the other seven lithe intruders sprang into a deadly formation, artfully dodging the bullets that seemed to flop through the air compared to the grace of their intended targets.

Floor, walls, ceiling, all simply equal surfaces to use as springboards as those long-curved swords were held aloft with two hands each, slicing through the air towards young jugulars.

You know when somebody says they keep replaying a moment in their mind? I never understood it properly.

Until now.

It doesn't just mean replaying a tape in your head, experiencing the same thing again as witnessed – it means zooming in from different angles, it means hearing things that only your subconscious witnessed first time around. Amazing, the potential for us to replay every moment of our lives in this multi-layered, rich manner; it's nestled there somewhere in the subconscious mind. But once in a blue moon, the mind chooses to force open the gates of the dark memory palace and allow perfect recall.

For instance, I didn't realise at the time, that I could hear Martha singing. The only sounds I thought were present in my ears after the gunshots were my own heartbeat and the swish of soft footfall on rock. But Martha was singing, I think she'd been singing for a while, gradually raising her volume.

Sáitheán an soladach agus an scagach,
an dorchadas agus solas,
a thabhairt amach do ruin.

No, at the time, I didn't hear Martha singing.

At the time, the next thing I heard was the almighty crash from above.

You know those intense thunder claps you can almost physically feel? That's the closest I can get to describing the devastating crash that tore through the crypt.

With the swords of our intruders inches from the necks of my terrified brood, all seven of the striding Koreans jolted to a stop in their tracks and wheeled around.

Their statuesque leader appeared at last genuinely flustered; but still beat all of us to a realisation of what was happening. A sharp glance directly upwards, and she side-stepped out of the way of a huge section of the ceiling that plummeted from directly above her dragging soil and roots down with it, and breaking into three huge pieces on the floor of the crypt so the floor and walls visibly shook.

Arthur's premature bullet had found a worthy target after all; that splintered rock dislodging a ceiling slab that must surely have been ready to fall for a long time.

The black-clad leader peered upwards as we all did save Martha. I expected to see stars. Waving branches, scudding clouds in moonlight.

Instead, an un-lit void.

A hidden space.

Peering into the darkness, it was impossible to tell what hid there, above our heads. My eyes fancied they perceived a metallic glint.

Suddenly, a sound like a swift blade cutting the air, and I was filled with dread as I assumed one of those swords had found its mark midst the confusion.

But it wasn't a sword.

It was a strikingly colourful shard of stained glass, three-feet wide at the top, six-feet tall tapering to a point. It sliced through the air from high up above within the newly opened chamber, its deadly speed barely slowed as it found purchase between the vertebrae of the Korean leader's neck.

Head and shoulders virtually severed from behind.

With hardly a sound.

Nobody's mind had been quick enough to process the shard drop from the dark void above, but one and all watched transfixed as the graceful Korean leader crumpled onto the stone floor beneath its weight and momentum, first onto her knees, and quickly bowing forward until her head touched the floor. And when her body couldn't bend further, the stained-glass shard wavered above her for a moment before yielding to break into a shower of smaller colourful shards falling around her.

A beautiful shrine.

I call them 'my' brood.

I call it 'my' crypt.

All of that is ridiculous now.

The wound where my lower leg used to be, burned with unbearable pain as I stood dumbfounded staring at Michael, surrounded by these would-be assassins, laid bare before Willows, less sure of my place in any world than I have ever been.

To feel any kind of equality with Martha, right from the start, has been a delusion, Gulliver. My brood resides within the Crypt, and the Crypt is hers to guard.

I feel the children are under her protection, and Little Hye has become her protégé instead of mine. And so, what part can I possibly play in their lives?

Martha stopped singing.

As soon as the shard fell upon the Korean leader, Martha's song stopped. The old wound Michael had wrought at my shin burned excruciatingly, and suddenly I felt the pain rise up through me, my blood boiled, and I converted it willingly into blind rage.

I roared like a caged beast, I clawed at the air in front of me and I strode up to Willows, still wiping blood from his eye. Wrenching his gun from his grasp, with no plan, no rationale beyond filling some kind of void, I fired at the floor by Willows' feet. He did a little dance, but he needed no further encouragement, virtually throwing himself up the steps.

I followed.

Do you wonder why, Gulliver? Why was I so led to chase Willows when down below lay the immediate threat of those quiet assassins?

Against them, I could do nothing.

Anyway, they had come to collect Little Hye – to return her to her grandfather. I could understand that.

Willows filled our Michael's head with rubbish.

Gulliver, he turned Michael against us.

It's his fault Michael is dead.

I followed Willows to the top of the steps, and the forest seemed so close. In the darkness, the denseness of the trees just slammed into me; an insurmountable barrier, and I felt winded, and unable to continue.

My rage was gone.

Willows didn't understand, he fled directly into the deep foliage, and right away, I couldn't see him.

I don't know, Gulliver, whether he's alive, or dead.

Deflated, I slunk down the steps, and there I found myself face to face with our visitors. Their burden was the body of their fallen leader, with as much dignity as possible, they bore her among them, swords sheathed, and I knew — they couldn't leave like that.

I lay down Willows' gun and motioned for them to stop. To wait.

I walked to the back of the crypt, to that darkness charred by Martha's furnace, the endless source of Seaburn's treasures.

Everything macabre had been charred and committed to the wind. Now, there was only folded bedding.

I selected a large, coloured, quilt. It smelled of lavender. Silently, I laid it flat over the parts of the collapsed ceiling, among the circle of coloured glass shards and blood that marked where she had fallen.

And I stepped back.

The assassins lay their leader's cloven body on the quilt, which they folded gently, and hoisted her above their heads. The last to leave nodded to me, almost imperceptibly.

I nodded back.

And they were gone.

Michael remains.

Michael's remains.

Gulliver, we're coming.

I will put this letter into your hand.

I remain,

Jasper Flint.

DECADES

Donovan
in the 1960s

Jeff Fitzgerald

sonicbondpublishing.com

Sonicbond Publishing Limited
www.sonicbondpublishing.co.uk
Email: info@sonicbondpublishing.co.uk

First Published in the United Kingdom 2022
First Published in the United States 2022

British Library Cataloguing in Publication Data:
A Catalogue record for this book is available from the British Library

ISBN 978-1-78952-233-4

Typeset in ITC Garamond & ITC Avant Garde
Printed and bound in England

Graphic design and typesetting: Full Moon Media

DECADES

Donovan
in the 1960s

Jeff Fitzgerald

sonicbondpublishing.com

Preface

On a warm evening in the summer of 1985, I took my seat at the Ontario Place Forum, a large outdoor amphitheatre with a revolving stage in Toronto, Canada. Some 2,500 people filled the benches, with many more sitting on blankets and lawn chairs on the hillsides surrounding the Forum. There was a sense of anticipation in the air as we all waited for the show to start.

First up was a Beatles cover band called 1964 the Tribute, an act that focused on re-creating the early Beatles experience when they were still performing live. They set the nostalgic tone for the evening. But we were all there for the main act. We all clapped and cheered as Donovan walked out on stage.

I was 20 years old. To me, at that age, the 1960s were some long ago, almost mythical time. While many my age were enthusing over synth-pop, punk and new wave, I was diving headlong into the past. I viewed the age I found myself in as often vapid and meaningless. The music of those times just didn't speak to me, or at least not in a language I could understand at the time. Over the years, with retrospection and the benefit of age, I've come to appreciate the times and much of the music of the era I grew up in. But during that time, I was hungry for identity, something I could hold on to and proclaim, 'This is me!' I found that in the culture of the 1960s and especially in the music of Donovan. During that period, I went to see any artists from the 1960s that I could. I saw Richie Havens, Bob Dylan, the Grateful Dead, Joan Baez, the Moody Blues, Eric Clapton, John Prine, The Who and others. But seeing Donovan live that night was a bit like finding the holy grail for me.

During my latter years of high school, I did a radio show at the University of Waterloo's campus radio station CKMS-FM. They had a huge library of music there, some 15,000 albums, a wonderland for a young teen eager to discover new things to listen to. In the stacks, I found a copy of *Donovan's Greatest Hits*, a compilation originally released in 1969, the first collection of the kind that Donovan had released. Songs like 'There is a Mountain', 'Jennifer Juniper' and 'Hurdy Gurdy Man' inspired me with their poetic musings, bright melodies and almost dream-like quality. From there, I delved into the albums *Sunshine Superman* and *The Hurdy Gurdy Man*.

Despite having only a young child's memory of the 1960s and having never gone through any of the life experiences that Donovan had that had so informed his music, I still related to it. His music spoke to me. His words and sounds were the fragments of an identity I wanted to forge for myself. By the time I was in college, I started playing acoustic guitar and writing my own songs while often wearing tie-dyed shirts, finding myself as a self-styled hippy during a time when it was completely uncool to be such a thing. Yes, the Paisley Underground that existed in America and the nascent neo-psychedelic festivals seen in the UK would evolve into both the rave scene and a new era of psychedelia in the 1990s, but they were still just taking off.

The 1990s would see a re-appreciation of the 1960s and of Donovan and his music. After the heyday of the 1960s and the more low-key period for Donovan in the 1970s, he fell out of favour with the general public, his songs seen as quaint and naïve. And yet, many true fans still followed him, as was evidenced by the crowds at that show at Ontario Place in 1985. But he had ceased to be the phenomenon he'd been in the 1960s. I think it's fair to say that, looking back now, Donovan was one of the true cultural icons of the decade, a troubadour to the hippies and the King of Flower Power. Reflecting back on that magical evening in 1985, it's almost surprising to me now to think that Donovan had only just released his first single a scant 20 years earlier.

During the writing of this book, I had the pleasure of chatting with John Cameron about Donovan's music for several hours. John was instrumental in helping to create Donovan's sound in the 1960s, arranging many of his classic songs, including 'Sunshine Superman', 'Legend of a Girl Child Linda', 'Writer in the Sun', 'Jennifer Juniper' and many others. He also performed on a number of Donovan's songs and acted as musical director on tour with Donovan, conducting orchestra sections and playing keyboards. He has offered up some of his own insights and stories on Donovan's music which are included in the book as well.

I would like to thank Mr. Cameron, as well as others, past and present, who made this book possible. First, Dave 'Doc' Hight, my musical mentor at CKMS-FM. He opened my mind to so many new styles of music and instilled in me a desire to discover and appreciate them all. I have a memory of a night when I was not feeling well, and I was at home listening to Doc's Monday night jazz show on the radio and I decided to call in. I said I had a bit of a strange request. I asked him if he would play Donovan's song 'Get Thy Bearings'. Even as a teenager, I could hear the brilliance in Donovan's music and how it would fit nicely amidst the rest of the music being played and Doc, with the words 'Here's something a little different on the show tonight. This is … Donovan,' played the song. I think Donovan himself would have appreciated hearing his music playing on a jazz show!

I would also like to thank my college teacher in broadcasting, Larry McIntyre, who stoked my interest in history, especially that of the 1960s. He gave me insight into the myths and also how to look beyond the myths. Larry gave me context to the music I was falling in love with at the time. Deep discussions with him in his office were brilliant and I will always remember them.

Thanks as well to Roger Goodman for contributing photographs and scans for the book and to Eileen Jennifer and Anthony Lymp, administrators of the Facebook group 60s 70s Folk Music Group, for facilitating it.

I'd very much like to thank my friend and fellow musician and Sonicbond author Stephen Palmer for his advice and encouragement and my publisher at Sonicbond, Stephen Lambe, for giving me this opportunity and for his patience with someone who had always wanted to but had never taken on a project of this scope before.

And of course, I can't forget Jeff, James, Rebecca, Tim, Adrian, Rob and Patricia for their many, many years of friendship and for always believing that one day I would do this.

Most of all, I would like to thank my wife, Stephanie. Her encouragement, her assistance, her thoughts and love were what kept me going, and simply put, this book would have never come to be without her.

DECADES | Donovan in the 1960s

Contents

Introduction

Writing a book about Donovan's life and music in the 1960s is no easy task. There's a lot of information out there in various books, articles and on websites, and many of the facts seem to conflict with each other. Remember, we're talking about events that took place five to six decades ago.

Donovan himself was a very busy lad in the 1960s, especially between the years 1965 to 1969. A great deal happened in his life, and sometimes it's difficult to untangle it all. I've done the best I can here in this book by looking at different accounts and dates and trying to find either a middle ground or the most frequently cited versions of events. I didn't include everything that happened to Donovan in that period, but most of the events and people that influenced his music are here. After all, this book is about his music. But Donovan's lyrics draw deeply from his experiences and help to tell the story of his life.

The reflections in this book are my own interpretations of Donovan's songs from the 1960s, backed up by as many facts as I could find in my research and interspersed with details of Donovan's life during those times that give context to his music. I felt that every song of Donovan's told a little part of the story but also felt that there was many stories to be told beyond that. You will see that I've used elements of both the Decades series, which this is part of, and the On Track series, also by this publisher, to tell the full story.

Rather than organising the sections of the book into one chapter per year, I organised the chapters into the various phases of his career as I saw them. The first chapter covers four years, from 1960 to 1963, in somewhat compressed fashion. This is when Donovan was a very young teenager, before his career began. They are still interesting years, however, as some of the events in his life, even at that age, went on to inform and influence his music throughout the rest of the decade. Other chapters overlap years a little, because the different phases of his career don't always align exactly to the beginnings and ends of years.

As of the writing of this book, we are still blessed to have Donovan alive and still doing music today. But I've chosen the decade of the 1960s to cover because these were his most prolific and influential times. The book covers his story and his music, from when he first picked up a guitar in 1960 and began learning how to play, to when he was a young lad with big dreams to his ultimate rise to become an icon of his times. His story is one filled with tales of romance, legendary friendships, hit records and screaming fans. But it's also the story of a spiritual journey and of a personal mission to bring his message of peace, love and beauty to the world.

My hope is that, whether you are new to Donovan's music and looking for a guide to take you through it, or a seasoned fan who's been listening to him for decades, that you may gain some insight into his music that you didn't have before, and that you may learn some things about his life that you never knew.

I hope you enjoy the trip as much as I enjoyed writing it.

Jeff Fitzgerald
Edmonton, 2022

1: Just a Dream 1960–63

They sat on the sea wall together, Donovan and his friend Gypsy Dave, sharing a cigarette and gazing out at the St. Ives harbour and the bay beyond. The sound of the waves crashing on the rocks lulled them, with the gulls crying as they wheeled in the blue Cornish skies above, the smell of the salty sea in the air, the taste of recently consumed saffron cakes from the nearby bakery still on their tongues. Beside Donovan lay his acoustic guitar. He started playing it when he was 14 and he was getting quite good at it, learning everything from traditional folk songs to more recent popular tunes. He'd even started to write a few of his own original songs.

It was the summer of 1963. Donovan and Gypsy (David John Mills) had hitch-hiked down to St. Ives from Hatfield in Hertfordshire, where Donovan's parents lived. Donovan had recently celebrated his 17th birthday.

This bohemian lifestyle is what he had desperately desired. So much so that he had dropped out of art school to pursue it. It was a mostly carefree life of sleeping on the beach, smoking, getting high, swimming, chatting up the girls and even making love to some of them. He and Gypsy hung out with the other young people who were inspired by the ideas of the Beat Generation to hit the road and live free. On warm summer evenings, Donovan would take out his guitar and play songs by the artists that inspired him, such as Woody Guthrie and Jesse Fuller.

Few of the friends he met that summer would have any inkling of what was to come for this affable Scottish teen. Perhaps Donovan himself did. He had dreams and he had ambition. But likely, not even he would have foreseen his meteoric rise to fame that was less than two years away. The rise would see him transform from a teenage beatnik vagabond into an icon of the 1960s, creating music that would enchant the youth of his time, not only in England but across the pond as well in North America and around the world. He would rub shoulders with the likes of The Beatles, Bob Dylan and Joan Baez and turn a generation on to 'Flower Power'.

But in that idyllic summer of 1963, the future was still just a dream.

He was born Donovan Phillips Leitch on 10 May 1946 in Maryhill, Glasgow to working-class parents Donald and Winifred (née Phillips) Leitch. Growing up in post-war Glasgow, he played in the dirty streets and explored the ruined buildings left over from the war. His father was a larger-than-life man who loved stories and especially poetry. The young

Donovan sat enraptured as Donald recited poems, from memory, by the likes of Percy Bysshe Shelley, Lord Byron, Robert Service, William Butler Yeats, William Blake and Scotland's own Robert Burns.

As a child, Donovan bore a limp, the result of contracting polio at the age of three, and sometimes the other kids would make fun of him. But it only hardened him in preparation for some of the ridicule he would face later in his life and ultimately triumph over.

A pivotal moment came for him in 1954 when his father brought home a present for him, the new record by Bill Haley and His Comets. He was transfixed by this new kind of music, rockabilly. Rockabilly significantly influenced not only Donovan but also Bob Dylan and The Beatles whom he would be compared with. It was his first musical shock and planted the initial seeds that would grow into something far greater than anyone could have imagined at the time.

At the age of ten, his father, following the trend of workers heading south, moved his family to Hatfield, Hertfordshire, a small town just north of London. Here, Donovan discovered the music of Buddy Holly and eventually formed his first band. Donovan played drums, with his friends Mick, playing guitar, and Dippy, playing saxophone. They had three songs in their repertoire. Needless to say, the band was short-lived.

At 15, Donovan finished his secondary education (a normal age for this to happen in England during that time) and started at The Welwyn Garden City College of Further Education with the hope of getting into art school. His time at Welwyn was short-lived, though. Restless and filled with dreams, Donovan longed for something more. He'd been inspired by the Beat poets and writers such as Allen Ginsberg and Jack Kerouac. He'd also delved into the works of poets such as Dylan Thomas and W. B. Yeats. Yeats especially fired his imagination, a poet who had explored pagan myth, especially the lost Celtic faith. He was also fascinated by the spiritual writings of Alan Watts and Lao Tzu.

Donovan was passionate about art and wished to get into art school. But in order to do so, he was also required to pass exams in other areas of study that he was not interested in. Frustrated by it, and against his parents' wishes, he dropped out of Welwyn.

He pursued a series of jobs, never lasting very long in any of them. When he worked at a cake stall in St. Albans, he met David Mills, a boy his own age who would become his lifelong best friend. Mills became better known as Gypsy Dave. After only a brief meeting, confounded by a misunderstanding, Donovan ran into Gypsy again at the Cherry Tree pub, a jazz club in Welwyn Garden City. They found that they had a lot in common. They shared their ideas and their dreams of being on the road. A plan slowly began to hatch.

In the spring of 1963, Donovan and Gypsy hit the road, again, to his parents' protests. But the young Donovan wanted to follow in the footsteps of his Beat heroes. For many young people who did this at the time, it never worked out. But for Donovan, this journey would see him actually become one of those heroes to his own generation.

The pair spent the summer in St. Ives, Cornwall, a picturesque little fishing town and seaside resort with a bay of sparkling ocean waters nestled between two white sand beaches. Donovan wandered the narrow, cobbled streets, drinking in the images and hanging out on the beach, smoking and talking with the other young beatniks who had decided to hit the road too. He and Gypsy lived on the beach, eating free saffron cakes they got from a local bakery. It was an idyllic summer for both of them and gave them the taste of freedom they both desired. But Donovan had also been working hard on learning how to play his guitar, the only possession he'd brought with him. In his mind, his future began to slowly take shape. That summer would change the teenage Donovan forever.

2: The Folk Years 1964–65

After the summer, he returned to St. Albans, settling there. There was a thriving folk scene with a number of clubs in St. Albans at the time, and here, Donovan would watch the more experienced musicians performing, not only to enjoy their music but to carefully observe their guitar picking techniques. He listened to records over and over again, trying to replicate what he was hearing. He learned all the popular songs by artists such as Woody Guthrie, Derroll Adams, Davy Graham, Bert Jansch, Jesse Fuller and Ramblin' Jack Elliott. Donovan slowly built his own repertoire.

One weekend, a local popular R&B band called Cops 'n' Robbers got a gig just south of St. Albans in Southend-on-Sea. Much of the St. Albans crowd went down to support them and Donovan was given the opportunity to play a song between sets, so he got up on stage with his guitar and harmonica and played Jesse Fuller's classic song 'San Francisco Bay Blues'.

Unbeknown to Donovan, two record managers, Geoff Stevens and Peter Eden, were sitting in the back. After his performance, Donovan felt a bit ill from too much beer and stage fright, so he went out back behind the club to get some air. The two managers followed him, saying they wished to talk to him. But the ill-feeling overwhelmed Donovan and he promptly puked all over them! They took it in good stride, though and asked him if he'd like to come up to London to record some demos.

On the day they had agreed upon, Donovan hitched a ride up to London and met the two managers in a recording studio in the basement of an old building on Denmark Street, the Tin Pan Alley of London.

With his Zenith acoustic guitar in hand, Donovan recorded a series of demos, some covers and some of his own original compositions. The demos weren't intended for release, just to be given to record executives to show them what Donovan sounded like. A couple of the demos did eventually appear on the *Troubadour* anthology in 1992 – covers of 'London Town' and 'Cod'ine'.

'London Town' had originally been recorded by Mick Taylor, an itinerant American folk-blues musician residing in London at the time, and released as a single in 1965. He, along with his partner Sheena McCall, would go on to design album covers, flyers and concert programmes for Donovan. Peter Eden had produced the Mick Taylor single. Eden was, of course, one of the managers who had discovered Donovan, and he played the song to the young musician in the studio, suggesting it would be a good one to cover. Based on a blues/folk song, 'Green Rocky Road', 'London Town' was in the traditional repertoire at the time and lots of people played it, often changing the lyric so that the writer's credit was 'Trad[itional] arr[anged] by …' But Donovan liked Taylor's version of it and decided to record it as one of his demos.

Canadian-American folk singer-songwriter Buffy Sainte-Marie wrote and first recorded 'Cod'ine'. It detailed her experiences after she became addicted to codeine that had been given to her for a bronchial infection. It appeared on her debut album, *It's My Way*, released just a few months before Donovan recorded his version and became a popular song to cover by artists in the 1960s and 1970s. Although Donovan's version was just a demo, he was one of the first to record a cover of it. Donovan's version follows the same arrangement as Sainte-Marie's version, but Sainte-Marie's displays a very unique vocal vibrato. Although that kind of vibrato would become one of Donovan's distinct vocal stylings later on, he doesn't use it in this song. His vocals are more akin to Dylan's vocal style on this track. Whereas Sainte-Marie's original version has a searing, desperate feel to it, Donovan's version is cooler and more detached, perhaps because Donovan wasn't singing from personal experience. Yet his version still hints at that disconnection from reality that the addict feels. Donovan would eventually record and score a hit in 1965 with a cover of another Buffy Sainte-Marie song, 'Universal Soldier'.

The rest of the demos finally saw an official release in 2004 on the appropriately titled album *Sixty-Four*. Some of the covers included the Jesse Fuller song 'Crazy 'Bout a Woman', the Ewan MacColl song 'Dirty Old Town' and a version of 'Keep on Truckin'', a song that would later appear in a different version on Donovan's debut album.

Two of Donovan's original demos appeared later in slightly different versions. He reworked 'Isle of Sadness' into 'Belated Forgiveness Plea', which appeared on the *Fairytale* album. Also, 'Darkness of My Night' was later re-recorded and renamed 'Breezes of Patchouli' around the time of the *Sunshine Superman* sessions, although it wasn't released until 1992 on the *Troubadour* anthology. 'Talkin' Pop Star Blues' was another original demo which Donovan played live on the 5 March 1965 broadcast of *Ready Steady Go!*

In fact, on the strength of Donovan's demos, the show's producer, Elkan Allan, booked him on the programme. *Ready Steady Go!* was a TV show oriented towards the youth market that featured performers playing their songs 'live' while the studio audience (of mainly young people) danced. Donovan, quite unusually, was invited to perform on the show despite not having an actual commercial release to his name yet. He first appeared on the show on 29 January 1965. While most of the performers on *Ready Steady Go!* would lip-synch to the studio versions of their records, Donovan insisted on performing live. His first three appearances happened prior to releasing a record and included performances of covers such as Jesse Fuller's 'San Francisco Bay Blues' and originals, such as the aforementioned 'Talkin' Pop Star Blues'. On his fourth appearance, Donovan would perform 'Catch the Wind', the song that would propel him to fame.

Donovan's managers secured him a recording contract with Pye Records. Pye wanted him to record a cover song as his first single, a song they'd found about a wandering hobo, which they felt fit his image at the time. But Donovan had been working on more new material of his own and insisted that his first single should be one of his originals. As he'd done with *Ready Steady Go!*, he pushed back with clear intent. Donovan had his own vision, one that didn't include his first single being a cover. As he told *Goldmine* in 1992, 'At the stage of late 1964, I had everything intact. I'd already had a year and a half of songwriting. So, everything that was to happen in 1965 was already formed and shaped in my mind in 1964.' 'Catch the Wind' impressed the execs at Pye records, who realised that this young musician was more than just another cookie-cutter teen pop star, so they agreed to let him have his own original song as his debut single.

On his 12 March appearance on *Ready Steady Go!*, he performed 'Catch the Wind', the same day as it was released as a single. After the show, in the green room, Donovan was hobnobbing with the show's hosts and the other musicians when he met a young woman who would go on to have an enormous impact on his life and his music. While chatting with one of the show's hosts, Michael Aldred, Donovan noticed a girl standing alone on the other side of the room. He pointed her out to Aldred, who happened to be a friend of the girl, so he introduced the young musician to Linda Anne Lawrence. It was to be a pivotal moment in Donovan's life. After hanging out together backstage, the pair went to Donovan's place and talked and listened to music till the sun was rising. Donovan, enchanted, asked for Linda's number before she left to go home.

While he thought of her over the next few days, 'Catch the Wind' stormed into the Top 40, rising to number four on the UK charts. It even made a serious dent in the US charts when Hickory Records released it there a few months later, reaching number 23. Donovan was on his way to stardom. His new love life, however, took an unexpected twist. He invited Linda to one of his gigs and that's when he found out that she had a son, and the father was Brian Jones of The Rolling Stones. She said she wasn't together with Jones anymore, but over the next few weeks, as Donovan got to know her more, he detected a certain sadness in her and began to torture himself with thoughts that she may still be in love with Jones.

Even as his love life wavered, Donovan's career was steadily growing. He had taken a bit of flak from some journalists in the music press, who called him a Bob Dylan imitator and a fake. But when *New Musical Express* (*NME*) conducted its annual readers' poll on the best artists and performances of the year for 1964–65, fans said differently. Donovan won the category of 'Best New Disc or TV Singer'. He was invited to perform before 10,000 screaming fans at the 1965 *NME* Annual Poll Winners' All-Star Concert at London's Wembley Empire Pool on 11 April, where he shared the stage with such artists as The Beatles, The Rolling Stones, Herman's Hermits, The Seekers, Them, Dusty Springfield, The Animals and The Kinks among others. In his review in the 16 April 1965 edition of *NME*, Alan Smith wrote:

This was the act so many fans had been waiting for, if only for its curiosity value. Would Donovan match up to his publicity? The roughly dressed folk singer answered in a way that should silence his critics forever. He came on stage to a fantastic barrage of screams. First number was his hit 'Catch the Wind', sung firmly and confidently, and he followed it with a slow wailer 'You're Gonna Need Somebody When I'm Gone'. Plenty of harmonica work here.

His rising star had not gone unnoticed in the US. After the enormously successful appearance of The Beatles on *The Ed Sullivan Show* the previous year, the British Invasion of America was in full swing and Sullivan was eager to get up-and-coming UK artists on his show. Donovan's management was contacted to ask if the young folk musician would be interested in appearing on the show. Donovan whisked off to America to perform on *The Ed Sullivan Show* on 11 April 1965, a scant five days after the *NME* concert. One of the millions of viewers he impressed that night was the American music manager Allen Klein who made a note to contact the young musician.

Hickory Records had apparently planned to rush the release of Donovan's debut album to coincide with *The Ed Sullivan Show* appearance, but for whatever reasons there may have been, it didn't see its release until June. Hickory also changed the title of the debut album to match Donovan's single, 'Catch the Wind'.

The canny move not only cashed in on the name recognition, but also captured the romantic tone of Donovan's music, more so than the more politicised UK title. Nonetheless, over the years, *What's Bin Did and What's Bin Hid* is the title that has ultimately become the standard one for re-issues on both sides of the Atlantic.

What's Bin Did and What's Bin Hid
(released in the US as Catch the Wind)

Personnel:

Donovan Leitch: vocals, acoustic guitar, harmonica

Brian Locking: bass

Skip Alan (Alan Skipper): drums

Gypsy Dave (David Mills): kazoo

Produced at Peer Music, Denmark Street, London, February–March 1965 by Terry Kennedy, Peter Eden and Geoff Stephens

UK release date: 14 May 1965; US release date: June 1965

Highest chart places: UK: 3, US: 30

Running time: 31:50

TrackListing:

1. Josie (Leitch); 2. Catch the Wind (Leitch); 3. Remember the Alamo (Bowers); 4. Cuttin' Out (Leitch); 5. Car Car (Guthrie); 6. Keep on Truckin' (trad. arr. Leitch); 7. Goldwatch Blues (Softley); 8. To Sing for You (Leitch); 9. You're Gonna Need Somebody on Your Bond (trad. arr. Leitch); 10. Tangerine Puppet (Leitch); 11. Donn Donna (Zeitlin/Secunda/Kevess/Schwartz); 12. Ramblin' Boy (Leitch)

The 'Catch the Wind' single was just a teaser. Donovan's first album, *What's Bin Did and What's Bin Hid* hit the UK record shops on 10 May 1965, just four days after Donovan turned 19. Hickory Records released it in the US a few weeks later.

Recorded through February and March of 1965 at Peer Music on Denmark Street in London, *What's Bin Did and What's Bin Hid* definitely displayed the influence of his idols such as Woody Guthrie and Ramblin' Jack Elliott, as well as his contemporaries such as Bob Dylan. Much has been made over the decades of Donovan's supposed rivalry with Bob Dylan. In reality, no rivalry existed at all. Dylan had already well-established himself a few years before Donovan put out his first album. Both were influenced by the same stars of American folk music, so it's not surprising that Donovan sounded a bit 'Dylanesque'. *What's Bin Did and What's Bin Hid* had Donovan clearly imitating his influences, but it also displayed a certain individuality, Donovan saying he was not your average pop star, and here and there, his own voice can be heard as it begins to emerge.

'Josie'

This Donovan composition opens the album. Despite Donovan's Dylanesque delivery on this track, with its pastoral and poetic moments, it lyrically shows Donovan's own style emerging, as the narrator of the song begs for another chance with his lover who has apparently left him.

'Josie' is a sweet, little folk song with a catchy melody and pop sensibility to it. Donovan strums a simple acoustic guitar rhythm with a melodic picking for both the main melody and a countermelody. Brian Locking provides a subtle acoustic bass accompaniment and Donovan plays two harmonica solos during the course of the song. 'Josie' was released in the US as the B-side to Donovan's second major hit, 'Colours', from his *Fairytale* album. In response to Donovan's move to Epic Records, Pye Records released it as a UK single, in its own right (without Donovan's consent), in February 1966, with 'Little Tin Soldier' from *Fairytale* as the B-side, but it failed to chart. It also appeared prominently in the film *A Boy Called Donovan*, where Donovan is seen playing it to a group of friends.

'Catch the Wind'

While Donovan had already accrued a following with his live shows and appearances on *Ready Steady Go!*, 'Catch the Wind' broke him onto the scene and made him an international hit. As his first single, it reached number four in the UK and number 23 on the *Billboard* Hot 100 in the US. Both singles were backed by the non-album track 'Why Do You Treat Me Like You Do?'

It's a poignant love song about longing for someone who is out of reach. The narrator likens gaining her love to trying to catch the wind. Donovan has said that this song is about Linda Lawrence, though he had not met her when he wrote it. He still feels it perfectly captures the nature of their relationship in the early days.

Like 'Josie', 'Catch the Wind' features Donovan strumming a rhythm on his acoustic with a gently picked melody. It's a little more languid and dreamier than the previous song, particularly in Donovan's singing. Brian Locking again accompanies on bass. The song features a harmonica solo during its latter half.

'Catch the Wind' had two other studio recordings made: the original single, which features reverb on Donovan's voice and a string section accompanying him (along with Locking on double bass) and has no harmonica solo. The London folk purists were apparently upset with him for using a string section, but Donovan wanted to experiment and try new ideas, a foreshadowing of the things to come in his music.

The third studio version of the song was recorded for the *Donovan's Greatest Hits* compilation record, released in early 1969. His label, Epic Records, was unable to obtain the rights to the original Pye Records versions of both 'Catch the Wind' and 'Colours', so new versions were recorded in 1968, specifically for the compilation.

This version of 'Catch the Wind' has a lavish production by Mickie Most and features a whole band (Big Jim Sullivan on guitar, John Paul Jones on bass and keyboards and Clem Cattini on drums). It's a much slower, dreamier version, which stretches from its original three minutes to five minutes in length. John Paul Jones's piano is particularly effective on this version.

Yet when all is said and done, I think the stripped-down album version, in its simple purity, best represents the themes in the lyrics.

'Remember the Alamo'

At the time he recorded 'Remember the Alamo', Donovan had never visited the United States, but he had already immersed himself in the American folk tradition. It's therefore not surprising that he picked a song like 'Remember the Alamo' to cover. Written by American songwriter Jane Bowers, 'Remember the Alamo' was first recorded by the legendary country star Tex Ritter in 1955 and was also covered by Johnny Bond and Johnny Cash. However, the Kingston Trio's version in 1959 propelled the song into popularity and made it a favourite to play by professional and aspiring folk musicians alike.

Donovan's version strips the song down to its basics. Gone are the whoops and hollers, the horns and strings, the martial beats and multi-voiced choruses of previous versions. It's just Donovan and his guitar. Surprisingly, he delivers an emotional performance that rivals his American counterparts. In particular, he sings the chorus with a fiery passion and a little snarl as he sings the name of Santy Anno.

'Cuttin' Out'

During his time in the beatnik subculture, Donovan developed a real passion for jazz. He had it in his mind to somehow combine the aspects he loved about jazz with his folk and pop music. He would take this idea to fuller fruition on later albums such as *Mellow Yellow* and *The Hurdy Gurdy Man*, but he first tried it here on his debut. 'Cuttin' Out' is a simple song with a walking bassline and Donovan playing his guitar. He sings in a smoky, bluesy vocal style, which is closer to the vocal style he would eventually develop, compared to his more Guthrie/Dylan style vocal heard on most of the rest of the album. The lyrics speak to teenage coolness. In several situations, the narrator simply shrugs with an 'I don't care' attitude and cuts out. Josie makes an appearance again, or rather is mentioned, but she is absent, suggesting, possibly, that the narrator's hopeful plea from the opening song was not getting him anywhere.

'Car Car'

Alternatively titled 'Riding in My Car (The Car Song)', this is a cover of a children's folk song written by Woody Guthrie. Donovan can even be heard saying, 'This is for Woody,' in the opening of the song. It's a silly, fun little tune with Donovan making car sounds with his voice. At one and a half minutes long, it is the shortest track on the album. Donovan would go on to explore more children's music in later works, releasing several entire albums of songs for children, including one I'll cover later in the book.

'Keep On Truckin''

Donovan credits this song to one-man band Jesse Fuller; however, I can find no evidence of it being written by Fuller. It does not appear that Fuller ever even recorded the song. The music is originally from a song by American pianist Bob Carleton called 'Ja-Da', which had completely different lyrics. The earliest version of the song with the Truckin' lyrics appears to be by Piedmont blues musician Blind Boy Fuller in 1936 under the name 'Truckin' My Blues Away', so perhaps Donovan simply got the similar names of Jesse Fuller and Blind Boy Fuller confused. A popular version of it was recorded and released by bluesman Mance Lipscomb in 1964, but this was months after Donovan first recorded it for his demos. The version he recorded for *What's Bin Did and What's Bin Hid* is just as fast-paced as the demo version, in fact, it's half a minute shorter, showing off his growing guitar skills. It also features less reverb on his voice. He has Brian Locking on bass and Skip Alan on drums backing him up. Donovan's friend Gypsy Dave also contributes some manic kazoo to the proceedings.

'Goldwatch Blues'

English folk singer-songwriter Mick Softley wrote 'Goldwatch Blues', but would not record the song himself until 1971 for his *Street Singer* album. Donovan's picking style on this song shows him as an accomplished player. His voice echoes with reverb, giving the song a lamenting feel. The song tells the story of a man essentially signed up for life to a job he doesn't like, who is even told that his son could follow in his footsteps. Donovan may have seen himself in the lyrics. His father was a blue-collar worker and Donovan had been encouraged by his parents to work in labour jobs during his earlier teens. The chorus echoes this, and perhaps expresses Donovan's feelings about this kind of job, afraid that it would crush his dreams:

Here's your gold watch and the shackles for your chain
And your piece of paper to say you left here sane
And if you've a son who wants a good career
Just get him to sign on the dotted line and work for fifty years

'To Sing for You'

This song became infamous as the song Donovan played for Bob Dylan during the hotel room party in D. A. Pennebaker's 1967 documentary *Don't Look Back*, which chronicled Bob Dylan's 1965 UK tour. Some commenting on it later tried to promote the idea of a bitter rivalry between Dylan and Donovan. Others commented on how simple Donovan's song was when compared to Dylan's. After Donovan plays his song, he asks Dylan to play 'It's All Over Now, Baby Blue', and Dylan promptly blows away the room with a performance of the song. Much has been said about this scene over the years, mostly to the effect of how bad it made Donovan look alongside his 'rival'. But Donovan was early in his career, whereas Dylan was five years Donovan's senior and had five years of career experience over Donovan. Dylan himself says of the song as Donovan plays it, 'Hey man, that's a good song.' Derroll Adams is there with a look of pride on his face as he smiles at his young protégé. In fact, the whole room seems to enjoy Donovan's performance. Earlier in the film, ex-Animals keyboardist Alan Price talks to Dylan and says of Donovan, 'He's a young, Scottish bloke ... he was singing pretty folk music and he's been around and he plays very good guitar. He's a very good guitar player. He's better than you!' As if to counter what was being said in the press at the time, Price adds, 'He's all right ... he's not a fake.'

Donovan was just a teenager, clearly thrilled to be hanging out with one of his idols and excited to play one of his songs for Dylan and the other people in the room. It is such a shame that, over the years some people have twisted this wonderful moment into something ugly, when it really isn't.

'To Sing For You' is actually one of Donovan's first declarations of what would become his mission in life, to be the wandering musician bringing peace, love and good vibes to the world with his message and his music, reflected in the lyrics:

When you're feeling kind of lonesome in your mind
With a heartache followin' you so close behind
Call out to me as I ramble by
I'll sing a song for you
That's what I'm here to do
To sing for you

'You're Gonna Need Somebody on Your Bond'

This old blues/gospel standard was first recorded by Blind Willie Johnson in late 1930. The year before Donovan recorded it for his debut, he had recorded the Buffy Sainte-Marie song 'Cod'ine' as a demo after hearing it on her debut album, *It's My Way!* (1964). It's probable that he was inspired to include 'You're Gonna Need Somebody on Your Bond' after hearing Sainte-Marie's version of it, as it was also on her debut.

Donovan gives his own version a loping rhythm built around an elastic bassline from Brian Locking and a swing beat from Skip Alan on the drums. Here again, Donovan experiments with a jazzy kind of feel to great effect. While Sainte-Marie's version was done more seriously, Donovan seems to have fun with it, giving it a cheeky vocal delivery. During the intro to the song, he can be heard saying offhandedly, with a little laugh, 'The wine's just fine.'

Hickory Records released it as a single in November 1965, with the Shawn Phillips composed 'Little Tin Soldier' as the B-side, but it failed to chart.

'Tangerine Puppet'

As one of the highlights of *What's Bin Did and What's Bin Hid*, 'Tangerine Puppet' is an instrumental (save for a spoken word introduction where Donovan says, 'This is the fairy story of a tangerine puppet.'). It shows off just how accomplished the young Donovan was becoming at the fingerpicking style of guitar playing. More importantly, in its mystical mood, Donovan hinted at the direction that he would take his music in the near future. Introduced as a fairy story, 'Tangerine Puppet' foreshadowed the title of his next album and offered up the most complex composition and playing on *What's Bin Did and What's Bin Hid*.

'Donna Donna'

Sholom Secunda and Aaron Zeitlin originally wrote this song (as 'Dona Dona') in 1940 for Zeitlin's stage production, *Esterke*. Many versions of the song have been recorded, including one by American folk group The Chad Mitchell Trio on their album *Mighty Day on Campus* (1961) and a version by the English duo Chad & Jeremy that was on their album *Sing For You*, released in January 1965, just a few months before Donovan recorded his version. Likely it was Joan Baez's version, which had appeared on her self-titled debut album in 1960, that caught Donovan's ear. The song tells the story of a calf bound for slaughter. Possibly, Donovan was attracted to the song because of its use of birds (in this case, swallows) as a symbol of freedom. Donovan would go on to use birds, especially seagulls, as symbols of freedom in his own compositions. Although the three other versions mentioned were all played with a fingerpicked acoustic guitar, Donovan chooses to play his guitar sharply, with edgy strumming that adds dramatically to the creeping tension of the piece as the calf gets closer to the market to be slaughtered.

'Ramblin' Boy'

Here Donovan once again takes on the persona of the wandering musician, though this time, instead of offering comfort to those in pain, he recognises the pain of someone he hurt personally by leaving. His words have a weary resignation as he accepts the way he is and that he couldn't help hurting the woman he loves because of it. Donovan was possibly influenced by the Bob Dylan song 'Don't Think Twice, It's All Right', from his 1963 album *The Freewheelin' Bob Dylan*, which tells a very similar story.

The track features Donovan on guitar and vocals, along with Brian Locking on bass. The pace is quick, but the melody is wistful and sad. Donovan picks an accompaniment along with his singing, getting an almost percussive feel from his guitar.

What's Bin Did and What's Bin Hid was released in the UK on 10 May 1965, a few weeks later in the US, reaching number three on the UK charts and number 30 on the *Billboard* Top 200 album charts. Donovan gains a firm footing with his debut album. While he may still be struggling to find his own voice, he nonetheless displays his talent not only as a guitar player, but as a thoughtfully romantic songwriter.

There were two tracks recorded around the same time that weren't on the album and weren't released as singles but did get released in various other forms such as EP tracks and B-sides of singles. 'Every Man Has His Chain' is a Donovan composition that first appeared on a four-track EP called *Catch the Wind*, released only in France on 1 April 1965, which also included 'Why Do You Treat Me Like You Do?', 'Josie' and the title track. The guitar-playing on 'Every Man Has His Chain' sounds very similar to 'Catch the Wind', though the overall melody is quite different. The lyrics have a few nice, poetic turns, but overall, it's a lesser track in Donovan's discography. Donovan can be heard in the intro to the song talking to bassist Brian Locking where he says, 'I think a lot of this song, Brian. It's called "Every Man Has His Chain". I come to conclusion one day, ya know.'

'Why Do You Treat Me Like You Do?' is a Donovan-penned song that first appeared as the B-side of the UK single of 'Catch the Wind', released on 12 March 1965. The song details the narrator's experiences in a broken relationship with an abusive girlfriend, a woman he still loves despite the pain she has caused him.

The melody is very similar to Bob Dylan's 'Don't Think Twice, It's All Right', from his 1963 album *The Freewheelin' Bob Dylan*. Dylan himself adapted the melody from the tragic American folk singer Paul Clayton's song 'Who's Gonna Buy You Ribbons (When I'm Gone)', which had appeared on his 1960 album *Paul Clayton Sings Home Made Songs and Ballads*. Clayton himself borrowed the melody from a traditional folk song called 'Who's Gonna Buy You Chickens When I'm Gone?' This kind of sharing, adapting and reusing songs or elements of songs was common amongst folk players of the time, a tradition going back several centuries or more.

Donovan's swift rise to the charts and to success was clouded during this time by the many comparisons being made of him to Bob Dylan, including a manufactured rivalry between the two. The apparent rivalry was largely created by the music press, who dubbed Donovan 'the UK's answer to Bob Dylan'. His detractors ridiculed the teenager, claiming he was a fake and all just hype. But Donovan didn't see it that way at all. As he told Dawn James in *Rave*, June 1965, 'I don't preach such positive things as Dylan. I look at it like this. There are people in the middle of a circle who are unsure and whose minds are still open. Then there are people around them whose minds are closed. And then there is me and there is Dylan and a few others outside the circle trying to get at those in the centre through those around them. Dylan writes about positive things that shock and are easy to grasp. I write about beauty.'

Donovan clearly had his own vision.

For example, let's compare two similarly themed songs, 'North Country Girl' by Bob Dylan, from his 1962 album *The Freewheelin' Bob Dylan* and 'Josie' by Donovan from *What's Bin Did and What's Bin Hid*. Both songs deal with the end of a relationship. In the case of Dylan's song, it's possible that it was about his then-girlfriend Suze Rotolo. He had gone to Italy to meet up with her, but she had just left for the United States. With the relationship apparently over, Dylan wrote the song as a lament, although he did ultimately catch up with her in the US and persuaded her to restart the relationship.

In Donovan's song, the narrator seems to have made some mistake that ended the relationship with 'Josie'. Lamenting, he tries to win her back by telling her he won't fail her.

Both songs use the symbolism of night and day. In Dylan's song:

I'm a-wonderin' if she remembers me at all
Many times I've often prayed
In the darkness of my night
In the brightness of my day

In Donovan's:

The meadows they are bursting,
The yellow corn lies in your hand,
And with the night comes sorrow
As the tide of dawn sleeps on the land

Both have exquisite turns of phrase, poetry expressing deep and profound emotions, but Dylan's is more inward-looking and soul-searching, whereas Donovan's evokes pastoral imagery to express his feelings. Dylan was often earthier, a relatable everyman whose words were unflinching in their honesty, whereas Donovan's are more romantic as he expresses his thoughts through an ever-expanding palette of imagery. I'm not claiming that one is better than the other, but that they are different. Calling Donovan 'the UK's answer to Bob Dylan' is a misnomer. It's just not a good fit, despite how it may have looked.

And even if there was any truth to those accusations in 1965, Donovan very quickly found his own voice. Less than a year later, he was recording *Sunshine Superman*, an album so innovative and original that it started a whole subgenre of music still going strong today. And he only continued to grow from there. Musician and producer Steven Wilson, on his podcast *The Album Years*, when talking about *For Little Ones*, which came out just two years later in 1967, said:

> I think he's not someone that springs to mind when you talk about … the great singer-songwriters of the late sixties and early seventies. Donovan is not a name that comes up a lot. Maybe part of the problem was he started off fashioning himself very much after Bob Dylan … perhaps too much … but even as early as 1967, which is only what, two to three years into his recording career, he's completely out on his own. I mean, this is so far away from Dylan now, isn't it? When you consider just two years earlier, he's been writing these Dylan pastiches … this album is absolutely divine. I mean, you listen to a song like 'Blackbird' on *The White Album*, which obviously came out the year after, and I just think to myself … it's like a whole album … of songs of that kind of magical childlike quality with similar kind of arrangement. Even the use of … the sound design on 'Blackbird' with the sound of the bird singing … it's all over this album.

Fortunately, in 1965, Donovan was able to personally shrug off the controversy and plough ahead with headstrong determination, as he said in an interview with Dawn James for the June 1965 edition of *Rave*, 'I am trying to handle myself so that I am not hurt by people or upset or angered. Feelings of that sort are a form of self-adoration. It doesn't hurt me now when I am called a fake and a copy. I feel only pity for those who are shallow enough to call me these things because they cannot see me properly.'

Talking to Keith Altham in the *New Musical Express Summer Special* in 1968, Donovan reflected back on the controversy: 'I admired Dylan tremendously. I respected him even more after we had met but I never consciously set out to imitate him in any way. Naturally, I was influenced by some of his early work, and you cannot shut an immense talent like that out of your mind. It takes time to realise what your own "thing" is.'

Pye Records issued Donovan's second single, 'Colours' on 22 May. Just as 'Catch the Wind' had, 'Colours' zoomed up the UK charts peaking at number four. Hickory issued it in the US in June, where it was less successful, only reaching number 61 on the *Billboard* charts. It peaked at a moderately better number 40 on the *Cash Box* charts. But that wasn't going to stop Donovan. In the summer of 1965, he appeared a number of times on TV in both the UK and the US. All of a sudden, Donovan's name was everywhere and fans were eager for more. He made a surprise appearance at the Newport Folk Festival that summer to sing a duet of 'Colours' with Joan Baez. Baez would go on to record a cover of 'Colours' for her album *Farewell, Angelina*, released later that year. While at the festival, A&R man John Hammond, at the behest of Clive Davis, administrative vice president and general manager of Columbia Records, a division of CBS, approached Donovan about possibly signing on with CBS Records. Davis, a huge Bob Dylan fan, had been intrigued by Donovan's music, especially his lyrics.

Amidst the appearances on TV and live performances, Donovan returned to the studio to record an EP. Vogue Records, a sister label of Pye, had some success with the EP *Catch the Wind* that had been released in France, so Pye decided to take another shot at it for the UK market, this time with all-new, non-album songs based around the theme of war. The *Universal Soldier* EP was released on 15 August 1965. Three cover songs, Buffy Sainte-Marie's 'Universal Soldier', Bert Jansch's 'Do You Hear Me Now' and Mick Softley's 'The War Drags On' were featured. It also included one Donovan original, 'Ballad of a Crystal Man', which Donovan would re-record for his next album, *Fairytale*. The EP's explicit anti-war sentiments were unusual for Donovan, but they obviously resonated with the British public and the EP reached number five on the UK charts. Because the EP was not a popular format in the US at the time, Hickory Records decided to release 'Universal Soldier' as a single with 'Do You Hear Me Now' as the B-side. This did somewhat better than Donovan's previous single, 'Colours', rising to number 53 on the *Billboard* charts.

Keeping the momentum going, Pye Records got Donovan back into the Peer Music studios in September to record his second album, *Fairytale*.

Fairytale

Personnel:

Donovan Leitch: banjo, guitar, harmonica, vocals

Skip Alan (Alan Skipper): drums

Brian Locking: bass

Harold McNair: flute

Shawn Phillips: guitar, 12-string guitar

Produced at Peer Music, Denmark Street, London, September 1965 by Terry Kennedy, Peter Eden and Geoff Stephens

UK release date: 22 October 1965; US release date: November 1965

Highest chart places: UK: 20, US: 85

Running time: 35:17

Tracklisting:

Original UK album: 1. Colours (Leitch); 2. To Try for the Sun (Leitch); 3. Sunny Goodge Street (Leitch); 4. Oh Deed I Do (Jansch); 5. Circus of Sour (Bernath); 6. Summer Day Reflection Song (Leitch); 7. Candy Man (trad. arr. Leitch); 8. Jersey Thursday (Leitch); 9. Belated Forgiveness Plea (Leitch); 10. The Ballad of a Crystal Man (Leitch); 11. Little Tin Soldier (Phillips); 12. The Ballad of Geraldine (Leitch)

1965 Hickory Records US version: 1. Universal Soldier (Sainte-Marie); 2. To Try for the Sun (Leitch); 3. Sunny Goodge Street (Leitch); 4. Colours (Leitch); 5. Circus of Sour (Bernath); 6. Summer Day Reflection Song (Leitch); 7. Candy Man (trad. arr. Leitch); 8. Jersey Thursday (Leitch); 9. Belated Forgiveness Plea (Leitch); 10. The Ballad of a Crystal Man (Leitch); 11. Little Tin Soldier (Phillips); 12. The Ballad of Geraldine (Leitch)

With hints of his own voice on his first album, *Fairytale* really begins to show Donovan's personality. It shines through in his lyrics, his composition and his performance. Comparisons to Dylan would be left behind in the past. Donovan here establishes such symbols as colours, sunshine and seagulls; all would feature prominently in many of his songs over the rest of the decade.

Skip Alan and Brian Locking return on drums and bass, but now Donovan expands his musical palette by bringing in Shawn Phillips on 12-string guitar and Harold McNair on flute. Shawn Phillips would go on to a successful career in the 1970s with albums such as *Second*

Contribution (1970) and *Faces* (1972), but he had already made a name for himself on the live circuit alongside Tim Hardin. Phillips spent some time in Canada as well, where he met a young aspiring musician named Joni Anderson and taught her some guitar techniques. She would later change her name to Joni Mitchell and go on to stardom as well. Donovan includes a cover of Phillips's 'Little Tin Soldier' on this album. Phillips would also make significant contributions to the next album Donovan would release.

On *Fairytale*, Donovan first worked with Harold McNair, a musician who would become one of the most important contributors to Donovan's sound through the rest of the decade. McNair was both a saxophonist and a flautist and was an in-demand session and live player in the 1960s. Born in Jamaica, McNair spent his early years playing calypso music in The Bahamas. After recording his first album *Bahama Bash,* in 1960, he moved to Britain. McNair would record several albums with his own band, as well as performing with a number of other artists, including the great Charles Mingus. He also did film soundtrack work, notably contributing saxophone to the soundtrack of the original James Bond movie *Dr. No* in 1962. He was brought in on the *Fairytale* sessions to play flute on the song 'Sunny Goodge Street'. After McNair returned to record flute for an early version of 'Museum' done during the *Sunshine Superman* sessions, Donovan realised the importance of the flute to his music and McNair would end up playing on all of Donovan's albums for the remainder of the 1960s.

While six of the 12 songs on *What's Bin Did and What's Bin Hid* were either cover songs or traditional folk songs, only four of the 12 on *Fairytale* are. Donovan's songwriting began to come to the forefront and lyrically found him edging away from more traditional folk themes to explore the kind of psychedelic imagery that would blossom on his next album. In fact, the album cover even highlights this; printing a small portion of the lyrics of 'Sunny Goodge Street' on the front beside a photo of Donovan:

> The magician, he sparkles in satin and velvet
> You gaze at his splendour with eyes you've not used yet
> I tell you his name is Love, Love, Love,

as if suggesting that the young musician himself was becoming the 'magician' whose name is Love. And indeed, he was.

'Colours'

The opening line of 'Colours', 'Yellow is the colour of my true love's hair', was possibly inspired by the title of 'Black Is the Colour of My True Love's Hair', an American traditional Appalachian folk song believed to have Scottish origins. It's a cute bit of symmetry as Donovan was a singer of Scottish origin with a deep interest in American folk music. But whereas the traditional song captures the quiet and mysterious beauty of black, Donovan's song in turn, captures the mellower, sunnier vibe of yellow, a vibe that would figure prominently in his music later on.

Pye Records released 'Colours' as a single in the UK on 28 May 1965 (with a B-side of 'To Sing For You') just two weeks after the release of Donovan's debut album *What's Bin Did and What's Bin Hid*. It shot to the upper reaches of the British music charts, peaking at number four. The Hickory Records version released in the US a few months later (with a B-side of 'Josie') was somewhat less successful, only reaching number 61 in the *Billboard* Hot 100. It did, however, see much more success in Canada, peaking at number eight on the RPM charts.

Like 'Catch the Wind', 'Colours' is a love song. But where the former captured the youthful ache and yearning for a love unfulfilled, the latter is a much more comfortable song of a love in full bloom. 'Catch the Wind' is a song of potential; 'Colours', a song of potential achieved. In the final verse of the song Donovan sings:

Freedom is a word I rarely use
Without thinking, oh yeah
Without thinking, m-hmm
Of the time, of the time
When I've been loved.

On the surface, it speaks to the freedom one may feel after the potential has been achieved, when one is free from the search for love because one has found it. In its broader sense, the first line, 'Freedom is a word I rarely use without thinking' is a stunning statement. In fewer than ten words, Donovan captures the mindset of the 1960s hippy movement; that yearning for freedom, but also the many questions of what that freedom will cost to achieve. He makes it stand out by separating it with the repetition of 'without thinking' before bringing it back to the love theme of the song.

Musically, Donovan plays some lovely picking on the acoustic guitar. He also accompanies himself in an overdub, playing his White Lady banjo in the style of Derroll Adams.

Like 'Catch the Wind', several versions of 'Colours' were recorded. The version released as a single included a harmonica solo in a sucked blues style instead of the Guthrie 'blow method', which was taken out of the album version. Unable to obtain the rights to an original version of 'Colours' from Pye Records, Epic had Donovan re-record 'Colours' for the 1969 compilation *Donovan's Greatest Hits*. The Epic version was produced by Mickie Most and featured a whole band, including Big Jim Sullivan on guitar, John Paul Jones on bass and keyboards and Clem Cattini on drums. The much longer version (by about one and a half minutes) features a lumbering rhythm section, backing vocals echoing Donovan's voice in the chorus and an organ solo in place of the harmonica solo. As with 'Catch the Wind', I find the original album version to be the best. With just the guitar, bass and banjo, it's much cleaner, with Donovan's voice in the forefront, where it should be.

'To Try for the Sun'

Donovan's writing in this song provides one of the purest evocations of his days in St. Ives with Gypsy Dave in 1963. Once again, the song exemplifies that youthful yearning, but this time instead of love, Donovan talks about dreams in general. On one level, he could be talking about his teenage dreams of being on the road, like one of his heroes Jack Kerouac, being the rambling man, the wandering musician. While those adventures would become insignificant to the general public in light of what he would become, to Donovan, especially in 1963, they were the culmination of everything he wanted to do. He was living the dream.

In the larger sense, of course, he may be talking about more distant dreams, those horizons that lay beyond the hills of St. Ives, the big dreams he was going to try for in the near future, those not just of stardom, but those of incorporating his current dreams into a larger picture.

In the chorus, he both looks back on those dreams of early youth and those days in St. Ives, but also looks forward to the larger dreams of the future. The sun symbolises those dreams he's reaching for, something clear and visible to him, something bright and beautiful but ever so far away. Though he acknowledges that even in 1963 in St. Ives, he was at least close enough to feel the sun's warming rays of light and writes:

And who's going to be the one
To say it was no good what we done?
I dare a man to say I'm too young,
For I'm going to try for the sun.

The song also expresses the love he feels for his friend, Gypsy Dave, who would continue to be his stalwart companion throughout the 1960s and onwards throughout Donovan's life.

While drawing from the American folk traditions that had been the hallmark of his early sound, 'To Try For The Sun' finds Donovan emerging from that paradigm, asserting his own personality and style. As a high-pitched harmonica drone in the beginning of the song shifts into a simple melody, Donovan sings a plaintive vocal over some deftly fingerpicked acoustic guitar. It's simple and yet complex at the same time, just as the lyrics are both filled with youthful innocence and the more mature outlook of a boy who was becoming a man, as Donovan was leaving behind his days of trying to sound like his heroes into times where he was sounding more himself.

'Sunny Goodge Street'

The song 'Sunny Goodge Street' solidifies what Donovan saw as his mission in life. As he said in his autobiography, 'The pure line that opens the first track of Miles [Davis's] album *Seven Steps to Heaven* had been a call to me in 1963 in St. Ives, a herald announcing a new consciousness in music. We all heard it. Now, a year or so later, at 18 years of age, I wanted to project a new meaning into music: "love and compassion". I began a song in the jazz feel that spring of 1965, called Sunny Goodge Street.'

Lyrically, the song took a huge step forward for Donovan. The influence of Allen Ginsberg, a poet that Donovan had discovered while he was in art school when he was 15, is quite apparent. Goodge Street is a Tube station in the West End of London and serves as the setting for the song. In beat-style poetry he conjures up scenes from the chaotic, loud, beautiful city while invoking mystical figures such as 'the goddess' and 'the magician', as well as a mention of jazz legend Charles Mingus. It was also one of the earliest songs to explicitly mention marijuana: 'Violent hash-smoker shook a chocolate machine'. The word 'mellow' crops up again, as it does in 'Colours', and would again most memorably in the title of a much more well-known hit single by him that was yet to come. Donovan reflects on the emerging underground that he sees happening and is himself a part of.

Musically, Donovan takes another massive step forward and shows his new direction. Co-producer Terry Kennedy made a jazz arrangement for the song around Donovan's descending waltz-time finger style. Echoes of it can be heard on the *Sunshine Superman* album, and it would not have been out of place at all on the *Mellow Yellow* album. Harold McNair makes his first appearance on a Donovan album, providing a short but effective flute solo in the middle of the song.

'Oh Deed I Do'

Bert Jansch, famous not only as a solo artist but also as a founding member of Pentangle, wrote, but never recorded, this song. Donovan most likely first saw Jansch playing at Pete Frame's club in Luton on 28 April 1965, after Donovan had recorded his first album but before it had been released. Donovan's management were hoping to sign Jansch to their label.

Donovan was fascinated by Jansch's playing, which was far more advanced than his own and far more advanced in fact, than most of his contemporaries. Despite the folk crowd not liking the fact that Donovan had the audacity to have a hit record and to appear on a television show, Jansch liked the young musician and was happy to teach him guitar techniques. For his part, Donovan always championed Jansch in the press and included a number of Jansch's tunes in his live repertoire. 'His use of traditional language to convey a traditional mood with a modern experience absolutely blew my mind,' Donovan said of Jansch in his autobiography. Donovan wanted to record something by Jansch, so when his management came to see the musician, Jansch gave them 'Oh Deed I Do'.

'Oh Deed I Do' is actually a relatively simple love song based around a repeating chord progression and features only verses, no chorus, with the opening lines repeated at the end. It is nonetheless a beautiful little folk song, perfectly in tune with the direction Donovan was heading with his own music. The US edition of *Fairytale* replaced it, however, with Donovan's cover of Buffy Sainte-Marie's 'Universal Soldier', most likely because Sainte-Marie was a more well-known name in the US and Donovan's cover of her song had scored him a minor hit in the US two months before the American release of *Fairytale*.

'Circus of Sour'

Seemingly the only recorded composition by Paul Bernath, 'Circus of Sour' is a quirky take on life as a circus where the listener is expected to appear in ring three. At just under two minutes, it's the shortest song on the album. Donovan plays it with a sense of humour and even gives a small laugh midway through. At the end of the song, it is revealed to the listener that they are part of the show as Donovan vocalises the 'sad trombone' womp womp sound, as if someone has just taken a pratfall.

The song was also recorded by American folk duo Chuck & Mary Perrin for their debut album, *Brother and Sister,* in 1968.

'Summer Day Reflection Song'

Like 'Sunny Goodge Street', the 'Summer Day Reflection Song' is another example of Donovan's earlier lyrical explorations of a more psychedelic bent. The elements and symbols that would become a familiar aspect of his writing: the sun, colours and fairy-tale imagery, are intertwined with modern words and images.

It makes for an ideal environment to reflect; to look into oneself, and some of the lines sound as if they are coming straight from the subconscious. Brilliantly, though, the word 'reflection' has a double meaning, as the cat, a constant character throughout the song, in its behaviour 'reflects' the narrator's thoughts. In the song, Donovan shows off some of his most advanced fingerpicking style to date and it also features some lovely guitar fills courtesy of Shawn Phillips playing a 12-string, vibing along perfectly to the song. It's a wonderful, evocative piece of music, an early classic of Donovan's, to be sure, showing both his performing skills and the growth of his songwriting.

In 2000, Castle Records released a compilation of all of Donovan's Pye Records recordings called *Summer Day Reflection Songs.*

'Candy Man'

This traditional song is sometimes attributed to the legendary bluesman Reverend Gary Davis. Davis told a number of different stories about where he learned it, including from local players in his hometown of Spartanburg, SC, from a travelling medicine show and from a rambling musician everyone called 'gittar man'. Often though, Davis played it as an instrumental, claiming the lyrics were sacrilegious.

It was first recorded, however, by blues player Sleepy John Estes in 1928. 'Candy Man' was later popularised by artists such as Jack Elliott and Dave Van Ronk, both of whom were influences on the young Donovan. Donovan, however, reportedly learned the song from John Renbourn. Often, the lyrics are changed from version to version depending on who is singing it. Some versions seem to be sung from a woman's point of view, as she waits for her 'candy man' to come home and give her some candy (i.e. sex). Often though, the 'candy man' of the song is a drug dealer. While John Renbourn's version of the song seems to express the sexual variation, Donovan's version definitely uses the drug-dealer interpretation with his additional lyrics referencing 'scoring', 'Morocco' (a place where drugs came from) and, in particular, the line 'Yeah, my Candy man, he gets me high'.

Donovan infuses an enthusiastic energy into his playing and singing, overdubbing his voice into the chorus, crying out 'Candy Man!' while singing 'Run, fetch a pitcher, get the baby some beer' and harmonising with himself during the chorus, giving an old blues tune some catchy, pop sensibility.

'Jersey Thursday'

As one of Donovan's early masterpieces, this minor-key folk song captures a beautiful moment in time. With its symbolic use of seagulls and some vaguely psychedelic imagery, it also points the way forward for Donovan as he creates his own unique voice. In his autobiography, Donovan referred to this one as 'a gaze into a crystal and a weekend on the Isle of Jersey'.

Jersey is an island and self-governing British Crown dependency near the coast of northwest France. At 22 kilometres (13.5 miles) across, it's the largest of the Channel Islands. The crystal that Donovan mentions, in the song 'a tiny piece of coloured glass', is likely referring to sea glass. Sea glass (or beach glass as it is sometimes called) is pieces of glass that have ended up in the ocean and, over time, are shaped and polished by the currents, ultimately washing up on the shore where they look like little sparkling gemstones. Many people enjoy collecting them and the beaches of Jersey are known to be a particularly good place to find them.

As with the song 'Colours', 'Jersey Thursday' mentions a number of different colours as if Donovan is using them to paint a picture of his moment in time. He would also continue to do this in later songs.

'Belated Forgiveness Plea'

This is a new version of an original song that Donovan first recorded as one of his demos in 1964. The demo was titled 'Isle of Sadness'. 'Belated Forgiveness Plea' tells the story of a pilgrim who arrives on the shores of Trist la Cal. Trist la Cal would seem to be an imaginary place, but 'trist' means 'sad' in Spanish, echoing the original title of the song.

The narrator of the song, the pilgrim, is both old and weary but young and perhaps even crazy as well. Although Donovan was a teenager when he wrote it, he seems to capture something ancient and sad in his words. Dawn James wrote in an article for *Rave* in June 1965, 'The cap and the faded jeans and the sad little voice are just a front covering for a boy who is strangely old. You can't put a date on Donovan. He could have stepped out of the Old Testament, or the ancient Chinese civilisation, or the year two thousand.'

Maybe it's this persona, the young lad with the strangely old mind, that Donovan evokes here. A kind of archetypal traveller, weighed down by the past, seeking redemption. But Trist la Cal is not where he will find it. Donovan here uses the symbols he will continue to use throughout much of his songwriting, symbols such as seagulls and the sun. While he may create a fairy-tale setting in Trist la Cal, in 'Belated Forgiveness Plea', he pushes it off-kilter. Here, the seagulls have all gone and the sun blazes madly insane, conjuring up impressions of loneliness, sadness and a loss of freedom, though perhaps not a physical loss, but a mental prison of sorts, a man trapped by guilt for someone he has hurt, feeling it to be too late for him to actually receive forgiveness.

Musically, the song is a typical but definitely catchy little folk song with a very Dylanesque melody to it, but Donovan's lyrics and his delivery on this one are all his own.

'Little Tin Soldier'

'Little Tin Soldier' (not to be confused with The Small Faces song 'Tin Soldier') is a Shawn Phillips composition. Phillips himself recorded his own version of it on his debut album *I'm A Loner,* released the same year as *Fairytale*. The song may have appealed to Donovan because of its magical, fairy-tale-style story. It's the tale of a tin soldier in a small shop, sadly missing a leg, but in love with a toy ballerina on the shelf across from him. When she is sold, because he is broken, the soldier is discarded but ends up travelling the lands, bringing happiness to many children and finally reuniting with his love. There is even the image of the dove of peace in the final lines of the song, making it a more universal kind of tale. Donovan may have seen himself as the little tin soldier, a wanderer missing a leg (from his bout with polio as a child, Donovan had a limp), missing his true love (Linda), and travelling the lands bringing happiness to others. It may be that he saw the happy ending of the song as the happy ending he wished for himself.

'The Ballad of Geraldine'

Intriguingly, Donovan leaves behind his fairy-tale notions for the final cut on this album, a stark and gritty tale that is the flip side to his previous album closer 'Ramblin' Boy'. Whereas that one was told from the point of view of the wandering musician who feels he must leave his love behind to answer his call to the road, 'The Ballad of Geraldine' is from the point of view of the woman he leaves behind and it paints just as sad a scene as 'Ramblin' Boy' did, but one totally devoid of any romance. Geraldine is left pregnant, hurt and wandering alone. She still can't help loving the ramblin' boy, but in the end, she concludes that life has no fairy-tale ending; that even if he returns to her, she would be hurt again.

It's a stunning reversal to the conclusion of his first album and possibly again may be a reference to Linda and her relationship with Brian Jones.

Fairytale was released on 22 October 1965 in the UK. Hickory Records issued it the following month in the US while Donovan was on tour there. It's arguably a better album than *What's Bin Did and What's Bin Hid*. Donovan edged away from his American influences and started to draw more on British folk influences, but the album also sees him emerge as a gifted songwriter. Key symbols cement themes that would reappear in Donovan's music during the rest of the decade, including seagulls and references to colours. It's more complex lyrically, with suggestions of psychedelia in songs such as 'Sunny Goodge Street', 'Jersey Thursday' and 'Summer Day Reflection Song'.

Unfortunately, *Fairytale* didn't do as well in the charts as the previous album had but was still a success. It reached number 20 on the UK charts. Based on the strength of Donovan's previous single, 'Universal Soldier', Hickory Records decided to replace Bert Jansch's 'Oh Deed I Do' with the Buffy Sainte-Marie cover song. Despite the addition of the successful single, the album only peaked at number 85 on the *Billboard* charts. To some, it may have looked like Donovan himself had already peaked and his career was in decline. However, he was still a popular live attraction, and he was working on a new batch of songs and ideas for his next album, the album that would change everything and turn Donovan into a superstar.

Pye continued to release singles in the UK, this time the non-album track 'Turquoise' with 'Hey Gyp (Dig the Slowness)' as its B-side, but it failed to achieve the success that 'Catch the Wind', 'Colours' and 'Universal

Soldier' had, still doing reasonably well, peaking in the charts at number 30. 'Turquoise' is actually a beautiful little song that Donovan wrote for Joan Baez. Baez, in turn, recorded a version of it for her 1967 album *Joan*. 'Hey Gyp (Dig the Slowness)' is a groovy little rock tune, signalling Donovan's growing interest in expanding his horizons beyond folk music. He learned the song from someone, but he couldn't remember who it was, so he was unable to credit it. He changed the title to 'Hey Gyp' in tribute to his friend Gypsy Dave.

Things seemed to be going fairly smoothly for Donovan, but starting in the autumn of 1965, a series of events occurred, and a number of decisions were made that would not only propel Donovan's career forward but also plunge him into a legal entanglement that would affect his career for the rest of the decade. Without access to the actual contracts and their details, it can be difficult to untangle everything that went down during this period, but I'll give it a shot here, at the end of this chapter and the beginning of the next, to hopefully help make sense out of it.

Donovan headed out on tour in the US in November to generate interest in the coming US release of *Fairytale*. Hickory released their version of *Fairytale*, with 'Universal Soldier' replacing 'Oh Deed I Do', in late November. Despite the album not doing as well as the first one, Clive Davis was still interested in signing Donovan to Epic Records. Columbia Records (part of CBS) set up Epic Records to originally specialise in jazz and classical music, but they began signing new, young artists in pop during the 1960s.

Sometime during this period, Shawn Phillips introduced Donovan to Ashley Kozak, who was a jazz bassist turned record producer and artist manager. Kozak worked at Brian Epstein's NEMS Enterprises, which was Donovan's concert booking agency. Kozak also knew manager and accountant Allen Klein, who had been impressed with Donovan's performance on *The Ed Sullivan Show* and had an interest in working with the artist. They convinced Donovan to split with Geoff Stephens and Peter Eden, the two managers who had discovered Donovan originally and Kozak became the young musician's new manager, with Allen Klein in charge of the legal and financial negotiations. Kozak was aware of Clive Davis's interest and was eager to get Donovan to sign with Epic Records, so he and Klein began negotiations with CBS to get the artist on one of their labels.

Around the same time, a young hotshot record producer named Mickie Most signed an exclusive production contract with EMI, which, like Epic, was a subsidiary label of Columbia Records. Most had had considerable success with groups such as The Animals and Herman's Hermits, producing some of their biggest singles. In fact, he had a reputation for being able to recognise the songs that would be hits for the artists he was producing. Mickie Most was behind some of the top singles for acts such as The Animals, Herman's Hermits, Suzi Quatro, Lulu, Hot Chocolate, the Jeff Beck Group and, of course, Donovan.

Most was born Michael Peter Hayes on 20 June 1938 in Aldershot, Hampshire, England. At the age of 15, Hayes formed a vocal duo with Alex Wharton called The Most Brothers. They recorded one single with Decca Records but soon disbanded. In 1959, Hayes went to South Africa. Changing his name from Michael Hayes to Mickie Most, he formed the band Mickie Most and the Playboys, scoring 11 consecutive number one hits in South Africa. Returning to the UK in 1962, he continued to tour as a solo artist, but major success eluded him. Tired of the endless club dates he found himself playing, Most turned his interest to producing. He offered to produce The Animals' first single, 'Baby Let Me Take You Home', which did quite well in the charts. But the next single that he produced for them, 'House of the Rising Sun', would really make the music industry sit up and take notice. The song reached number one in the UK, the US and Canada, and cracked the Top 10 in many other countries worldwide. Most's name became so well known, not just to musicians and music executives, but also to music fans, that it was considered a selling point to put 'A Mickie Most Production' on the covers of albums he produced.

Donovan's and Most's paths were to cross shortly, and music history was about to be made. Meanwhile, Pye Records in the UK released the next single to be culled from *Fairytale*, the Shawn Phillips-composed 'Little Tin Soldier' with 'Hey Gyp (Dig the Slowness)' once again as the B-side, but it had little success, even failing to chart. It was a bit of a blow for Pye, but they had confidence in the Scottish musician and announced near the end of 1965 that Donovan's next single would be called 'Sunshine Superman'.

3: Psychedelic Superstar 1966–67

Sunshine Superman
Mellow Yellow

This would turn out to be a pivotal year for Donovan that would see his star rise high, putting him in the upper echelons of British pop stars, but also see him run into legal troubles and record label disputes.

Allen Klein thought producer Mickie Most and Donovan would work well together, so he introduced them to each other and the two hit it off. Donovan felt that Most would be able to help him realise the grand vision he had for his next album. Most had been impressed with 'Sunny Goodge Street' on Donovan's *Fairytale* album with its elaborate jazz arrangements and was eager to explore more of that kind of thing with Donovan. It was agreed that he would produce Donovan's next album, starting with the single 'Sunshine Superman'.

However, this ruffled feathers at Pye Records and they withdrew 'Sunshine Superman' from their release roster, claiming that they did not have the rights to release a Mickie Most production in the UK because he was signed exclusively to EMI. Due to Donovan being too young to legally enter a contract at the time, Donovan's father had signed the contract with Pye that had given them the rights to release Donovan's albums (how many he was contracted to is uncertain) in the UK. Pye had a long-running partnership with Hickory Records in the US and would often use them to distribute records across the pond, as they had done with Donovan's singles and albums. Clearly, Pye didn't want to lose Donovan, as his hit records in 1965 had made them a lot of money.

But Ashley Kozak and Allen Klein finally negotiated a deal to sign Donovan with CBS and release his upcoming single and album on their Epic label in both the US and the UK. Pye Records said that they had the exclusive rights to release Donovan's music in the UK, thus putting them in conflict with CBS. The agreement also put them in conflict with Donovan's US distributor, Hickory Records, and Donovan was forced to acrimoniously part ways with the American label. They still retained the rights to his 1965 recordings, however, and would continue to release various compilations in order to compete with the Epic releases that were to come.

In January 1966, BBC Television aired a documentary titled *A Boy Called Donovan*, which depicted Donovan's life just before his fame, recreating the times he spent in St. Ives in the summer of 1963 and going on to his *Ready Steady Go!* appearances which helped propel him to his initial fame. One scene depicted Donovan smoking marijuana with friends, something that was quite shocking for the time. This particular scene would become dramatically more significant later in the year.

Donovan and Most then headed into the studio to record the initial tracks for *Sunshine Superman*. Ashley Kozak felt that a talented arranger could help with the elaborate productions the musician and producer had in mind. He knew a jazz bassist named Spike Heatley who he thought could help. Heatley was playing in a supper club house band at the time with a young musician just down from Cambridge named John Cameron. Cameron recalls:

I came down, and originally, I did some cabaret … I wanted to be a musician. I wanted to write, to arrange. So I ended up doing a turn at a place called The Take One in St. Martin's Lane. This was like an American supper club. It's good food, wine, whatever. The Ronnie Ross Band was the resident band there. And the bass player was a guy called Spike Heatley who was a pretty famous jazz bass player at the time … I was right ready to get moving on to something different. And Spike came in … Do you fancy having a shot with Donovan? And I said, what's happening? He said, well, he's just split with his current producer and management set-up … and he's going to record with Mickie Most … do you fancy having a shot at a couple of numbers with him? Yeah. Why not? So we pitched up at Don's manager's apartment … Ashley Kozak, his new manager who was an old bass player and an old friend of Spike. That was where the connection was. So Spike and I picked the pitch up at Ashley's place … he was totally psychedelic. It was stars on the walls … purple and lots of velvet, lots of … very plush kind of Oriental decor … anyway … we set to and we talked to Don … and we came up with the idea of using two basses, the bass guitar and the (double) bass and the harpsichord and the kind of bluesy slide guitar … and we put it together between us.

Donovan impressed Cameron with some of his ideas for a few of his other songs, including 'Bert's Blues', a tribute to his friend Bert Jansch. 'He (Donovan) would feed me ideas and I would interpret them', Cameron said. 'And he was very open. If I said let's make this a jazzy thing and in the middle of it I'll suddenly do a Baroque harpsichord solo, which happens in 'Bert's Blues', he was yeah … great!'

But what they found was that the three of them, Most, Cameron and Donovan, working together made the magic happen. 'Mickie was then the editor,' Cameron says, 'because we go in with all these crazy ideas, and sometimes they worked … Mickie was a great editor … he had a vision of how it could be commercially successful. Don had a vision of how he wanted it to be, and I was kind of the midwife in between. It wasn't creatively stultifying in any way. I think this is why I've always enjoyed working in movies and in theatre because all those processes are just very organic. Nobody can say, "That's my absolute image of what it should be, and you can't change it," because you'd never get anywhere. I love working with people. They feed me ideas. I feed them back. We stir it up in a big pot … I love the process.'

They recorded four tracks in the EMI Studios (renamed Abbey Road Studios a few years later) in London: 'Sunshine Superman', 'Legend of a Girl Child Linda', 'Bert's Blues' and 'Museum'. 'Museum' didn't end up on the final album but did make it on to the next album with a different arrangement.

Then Donovan headed off to Columbia's studios in California to finish the rest of the album with a set of different musicians, including Shawn Phillips. Cameron wasn't involved in those sessions (though he would return on the next album), but Mickie Most was at the helm, like a conductor of an orchestra, guiding the elaborate production.

Most predicted 'Sunshine Superman' as the song that was going to be a hit. But Pye and CBS were still at odds with each other, and it looked like the album was not even going to be released. Exhausted after the recording sessions and frustrated by the ongoing legal hassles, Donovan sought a break and joined some friends in Mexico, a trip that would inspire the song 'Sand and Foam'. But upon return, Pye and CBS had not resolved anything. The legal battle continued.

Without much else to do, Donovan spent his time lazing around his flat writing songs or going over to hang out with Paul McCartney and George Harrison, whom he had become friends with, even contributing some lyrics to a song McCartney was working on, 'Yellow Submarine'. Unbeknown to Donovan, unless you consider his song 'Season of the Witch', already recorded, as some kind of prophetic vision, things were about to get darker. The police had their eyes on busting some of the bigger pop stars for drugs in order to make it clear that no one was above the law. The previously mentioned scene in *A Boy Called Donovan*, where the musician was seen smoking marijuana, had caught their interest.

After a trip to America, Donovan returned, unaware that the police had been watching his place closely, where two girls he had temporarily rented his flat to had been hosting a number of parties. The quiet, often shy young folk musician from Glasgow became their first target. George Harrison warned Donovan in a phone call that something was going down, but it was too late to do anything. In a dramatic raid, Donovan and Gypsy were arrested for drug possession. Donovan had only smoked marijuana and occasionally tried LSD and mescaline and did not use any of the hard drugs. But marijuana, at the time, was just as illegal. The news story made front-page news, not just in the music press, but in the general press too. Donovan was the first of a number of pop and rock star arrests for drugs that would take place.

With all the legal hassles preventing the release of his album and now the bust, Donovan believed his career was basically over. Despondent, he and Gypsy Dave packed up and headed for Greece, a retreat of sorts where Donovan would compose 'Writer in the Sun', a song lamenting that at the age of 20, it looked as if he was now retired. Based on Most's recommendation, though, CBS released the single 'Sunshine Superman' with 'The Trip' as its B-side, in the US and other countries where they had the rights to, but not in the UK due to the ongoing label issues. To everyone's surprise (except maybe Most's), the record shot up the charts, reaching the number one position on both The US *Billboard* Hot 100 and The US Cashbox Top 100. It flew up the charts in many other countries as well, coming into the Top 10 on numerous charts worldwide.

Donovan was completely unaware. He and Gypsy were relaxing on an island in the Mediterranean that had only one phone on it in a small taverna. One day a call came through for them. Donovan's manager, Ashley Kozak, told the young musician that he had to come back because his record was number one! Stunned, Donovan and Gyp made immediate plans to go to London.

The single, 'Sunshine Superman', had been released on 1 July, everywhere except in the UK due to the ongoing legal dispute. The album followed hot on its heels, released on 26 August 1966.

Sunshine Superman

Personnel:
Donovan Leitch: vocals, acoustic guitar, electric guitar (track 6)
Bobby Ray: bass (tracks 4, 6, 7, 9, 10)
Fast Eddie Hoh: drums (tracks 6, 7, 10)

Shawn Phillips: sitar (tracks 3, 4, 8, 9, 10)
Cyrus Faryar: bouzouki (track 10)
Peter Pilafian: electric violin (tracks 3, 7, 8, 10)
Jimmy Page: electric guitar (track 1)
Eric Ford: electric guitar (track 1)
Don Brown: electric guitar (tracks 6, 7)
John Cameron: keyboards, arrangement (tracks 1, 2, 5)
Lenny Matlin: organ (tracks 6, 10)
Spike Heatley: acoustic bass (track 1)
John Paul Jones: electric bass (track 1)
Bobby Orr: drums (track 1)
Candy John Carr: bongos (tracks 3, 4, 8, 9)
Tony Carr: percussion (track 1)
Produced at Columbia Studios, Hollywood and EMI Studios, London, January–May 1966 by Mickie Most
UK release date: June 1967. US release date: 26 August 1966.
Highest chart places: UK: 25, US: 11.
Running time: 42:59
Tracklisting:
Original US album: 1. Sunshine Superman (Leitch); 2. Legend of a Girl Child Linda (Leitch); 3. Three Kingfishers (Leitch); 4. Ferris Wheel (Leitch); 5. Bert's Blues (Leitch): Side 2: 6. Season of the Witch (Leitch); 7. The Trip (Leitch); 8. Guinevere (Leitch); 9. The Fat Angel (Leitch); 10. Celeste (Leitch)
1967 UK album: 1. Sunshine Superman (Leitch); 2. Legend of a Girl Child Linda; 3. The Observation (Leitch); 4. Guinevere (Leitch); 5. Celeste (Leitch); 6. Writer in the Sun (Leitch); 7. Season of the Witch (Leitch); 8. Hampstead Incident (Leitch); 9. Sand and Foam (Leitch); 10. Young Girl Blues (Leitch); 11. Three Kingfishers (Leitch); 12. Bert's Blues (Leitch)

This much I knew then: I was making the music and writing the songs that reflected the emerging consciousness of my generation. I was here to do this. Knew instinctively I should present the Bohemian Manifesto to the world.
Donovan from his autobiography, *The Hurdy Gurdy Man*

If *Fairytale* showed Donovan slowly starting to craft his own style, moving away from the American folk influence, *Sunshine Superman* was a quantum leap forward for the young musician. The *Sunshine Superman* album exists in a very unique time and space, a dreamland somewhere between the sunny coast of modern California and the misty landscapes of ancient Britain, both of which are steeped in their own very different mythologies.

'Sunshine Superman'

'Sunshine Superman' was one of the first four tracks cut for the album. Mickie Most brought in Eric Ford and Jimmy Page again on electric guitars (as they had been on 'Museum'), with the addition of drummer Bobby Orr and percussionist Tony 'the Maltese Falcon' Carr. Unusually, the song was scored for two basses, one acoustic and one electric. Spike Heatley played the acoustic and while there is some uncertainty as to who played the electric bass, John Paul Jones says it was he who did.

John Cameron came up with the idea of playing 'rock harpsichord' on the track. Harpsichords, a piano type of instrument that plucks the strings rather than hits them, were widely available in recording studios of the era but were rarely used in pop music. One of the first pop rock songs to use it was The Jamies' 1958 hit 'Summertime, Summertime'. 'Nobody had really used funky harpsichord before,' John Cameron says, recalling how they came up with the unique arrangement, 'There were no synthesisers … there was no way of manufacturing different sounds. You had to kind of think: now, how can we make something that's a different noise? Spike and I felt that we could make a different sound with two basses because one of them had the pluckiness to it, and the other one had the click to it. And that's how it kind of came about … the combination of that and the harpsichord to me gives it a totally off-the-wall vibe.'

Mickie Most recognised almost immediately that 'Sunshine Superman' would be a hit. Cameron recalls, 'I just remember being in EMI 3. We probably didn't record them in any particular order, but when he got to 'Sunshine Superman', Mickie kind of went, "Hey, we've got something here!" And he was right.'

Most, for his part, recalled in an interview in the 1983 book *The Record Producers*, 'I was happy with it because it sounded different, and it sounded as though Donovan had got his own sound, which I was pleased about, because it was away from his acoustic folk guitar sound – a mysterious electronic sound, which wasn't just electronic rock 'n' roll, and 'Sunshine Superman' was the start of that mysterious sound.'

'Sunshine Superman' is a three-chord rock song with a Latin vibe. While 'Sunshine' was a slang term for LSD at the time and the lyrics often sound very trippy, the reality is like 'Catch the Wind', it's a song about yearning for love just dressed up in psychedelic imagery. Donovan's relationship with Linda, or lack thereof, inspired the song's lyrics. Feeling like she was unable to commit to a deeper relationship with Donovan, she had left for the States to try a career in modelling. At the time, Donovan was not ready to give up on their potential relationship and he fully intended to do anything he could to be with her:

I'll pick up your hand and slowly blow your little mind
'Cause I made my mind up you're going to be mine
I'll tell you right now
Any trick in the book now, baby, all that I can find

The song is filled with references to Donovan's own life. Superman and Green Lantern come up, as Donovan loved the comic books when he was younger. References to standing on the beach at sunset and diving for pearls in the sea may have been recalling his time in St. Ives in the summer of 1963 when he lived on the beach. For a short time while there, he worked as a dishwasher at a local restaurant. 'Pearl-diving' was the slang they used to describe the job of a dishwasher.

The enduring popularity of 'Sunshine Superman' has seen it covered by over 70 artists ranging from punk band Hüsker Dü to jazz crooner Mel Tormé! Recently, The Mona Lisa Twins covered it in 2020 on their *Live At The Cavern Club* album.

'Legend of a Girl Child Linda'

Fairytale may have hinted at things to come for Donovan, but 'Legend of a Girl Child Linda' brought that fairy-tale vision into full bloom. Sung in nine verses with no chorus, Donovan tells the tale of children living in a magical land who need to save their world from sadness. In his autobiography, Donovan said, 'Strange to say, I had dreamt the writing of this song, waking Gypsy up and playing it to him one night in a hotel in Sweden. I had seen and heard myself composing in the dream.' Indeed, the song reflects its dream origins by evoking an enchanted land of seashell trees, velvet hillsides, dancing crystals and parrots who are 'talking their words with such ease'.

Three wizards call upon a group of children to undertake a quest to the White Queen's palace. They must try to wake the princess, who has fallen into a deep and sad sleep, in order to make all the sadness in the kingdom go away. Along the way, they are aided by a prince who has dreamt that his princess would awaken.

The influence of his relationship with Linda Lawrence comes out in the open here, with Linda as the princess and Donovan himself as the prince. The princess asleep becomes a metaphor for their relationship, which at the time was 'asleep' (they had just broken up, which Donovan was very sad about). In the song, the prince goes into battle 'with his confused mind'. There is a possible double meaning here, as Donovan takes a personal look at his own mind, confused as to how Linda really feels with him trying to figure out why she broke up with him. But in a more worldly sense, Donovan may be talking about soldiers ordered to go into battle, not sure exactly what they are fighting for, echoing the sentiments of Buffy Sainte-Marie's 'Universal Soldier', which Donovan had had a hit with the previous year.

The song draws on and solidifies the motifs and symbols that Donovan had already used in previous songs and would continue to use quite often in his music, especially on his 1967 album, *A Gift from a Flower to a Garden*, those of children, crystals, seagulls and medieval imagery.

At almost seven minutes in length, 'Legend of a Girl Child Linda' is replete with John Cameron's lush and evocative orchestral arrangements, which add to the dreamy and magical feel of the song. Donovan played acoustic guitar live in the studio as part of the orchestra rather than doing overdubs, with John Cameron conducting. Cameron also played harpsichord again, but in a more traditional way this time, to bring an extra romantic medieval vibe to the piece. 'The whole thing about working with Don,' Cameron remembers, 'his charm was in quite a fragile, beautiful centre. And you didn't want to intrude on that. So everything that I wrote tended to … was trying to enhance it, trying delicately to bring out a lyric … I always wanted to write things that would generally amplify, assist, colour. I used to marvel at how Don wrote these little jewels because it was not with a huge, expansive musical palette. It was quite small. It was quite intimate. I was off listening to Thelonious Monk, Charlie Mingus and Shostakovich. And then there was this beautiful little sound Don was making and my world had to come right down into it to kind of encapsulate that world.'

Joan Baez, Judy Collins and Joan's sister Mimi Fariña recorded a cover of the song for a 1967 benefit album called *Save the Children*.

'Three Kingfishers'

Some suggest that the title of the song is the result of a typo. In the song, Donovan sings 'Twelve kingfishers' in the opening line with no mention of three. Be that as it may, this seminal song is a masterpiece of psychedelia, bringing together Donovan's acoustic guitar with Shawn Phillips's gorgeous sitar, John Carr's hand drumming and Peter Pilafian's electric violin. Donovan claims that this was the first time anyone had ever plugged a violin into a pickup, but in fact, it had been done a number of times before this, going back to jazzman Stuff Smith on the song 'You'se a Viper', recorded in 1920. Nonetheless, it adds nicely to the exotic feel of the song. The lyrics repeat twice in the slower first half of the song. Midway through, the musicians break out into an Eastern jam, with Phillips's exquisite sitar leading the way, which takes us all the way to the end of the song. The elements of 'Three Kingfishers' may have come to be a cliché of 1960s psychedelic music, but when Donovan did it in 1966, it was a new thing and quite groundbreaking for its time and remains to this day arguably Donovan's most psychedelic song ever.

Lyrically, it is drenched with acid imagery involving not only the titular kingfishers but also the ocean. The kingfisher, despite being a somewhat shy bird, figures in many mythologies and Donovan certainly had a keen interest in mythology. In Polynesian mythology, the sacred kingfisher was believed to have power over the seas and waves. In the song, Donovan holds the oceans in the palm of his hand:

> Look at the tiny
> Oceans in my hand.
> Waves of liquid
> Colours touch the sand.

In ancient Greek myth, a pair of minor gods named Alcyone and Ceyx were in love with each other but had the audacity to refer to themselves as Zeus and Hera, a sacrilegious act, as these were the two primary gods of Olympus. For this, they had to die, but out of compassion, some of the other gods turned the two minor deities into Halcyons or kingfishers. They were also given the halcyon days, a few days on either side of the winter solstice without storms. Eventually, the term 'halcyon days' came to mean an idyllic and peaceful time in the past. Therefore, the kingfisher may represent days like those for Donovan, possibly his days in St. Ives.

Kingfishers usually have a colourful crest of feathers upon their head that, from the right angle, looks like a jewelled crown (hence the 'king' part of their name). In the song, Donovan sings,

Oh, I dreamed you were a great jewel
Sitting on golden crown on
My head

The song was notably covered by jazz guitarist Gábor Szabó as an instrumental on his 1968 album *Bacchanal* (he also covered 'Sunshine Superman' on the same album) and weirdly, but quite successfully, by stoner rock band Monster Magnet on their 2013 *Last Patrol* album.

'Ferris Wheel'

'Ferris Wheel' was recorded in Los Angeles and, while its lyrics may seem strange and trippy, they actually have a very prosaic origin. As Donovan explained in a 2011 *Mojo* magazine interview: "Ferris Wheel' was about a girl we met that got her hair caught in a Ferris wheel and had to cut it off.' Nonetheless, Donovan turns that simple story into a metaphor for not giving up on your dreams. The hair getting stuck in the Ferris wheel symbolises any number of snags one might encounter in the pursuit of one's dreams. He suggests not to dwell upon it, that the hair will regrow, and that everything happens for a reason. In the song, a seagull comes to build its nest with the hair that was torn off and remains on top of the Ferris wheel. The seagull often symbolises freedom in Donovan's songs, and here represents the letting go of past mishaps, the freedom to move on and continue your pursuit.

The song features Donovan on a strummed acoustic guitar, John Carr on hand drums, Shawn Phillips on sitar and Bobby Ray on bass. Ray provides a repeating bassline that is very prominent in the mix. The bassline provides a captivating countermelody to Donovan's vocal melody and is just as memorable as the latter.

'Bert's Blues'

'Bert's Blues' was one of the first songs Donovan played for producer Mickie Most and arranger/keyboardist John Cameron, and it was the first to be cut for the album. Donovan claims that this song excited some of the jazz musicians around the scene with its possibilities of blending jazz with other forms of music such as classical and pop. It caught the attention of bassist Danny Thompson, whom Donovan would develop a lifelong friendship with and collaborate with many times.

It's an interesting song in and of itself, but what really sets it apart is the loopy arrangement by John Cameron. 'In the middle of it, I go into this bizarre, improvised baroque eight bars,' he says, '... where that came from, I don't know, but it was just something that maybe Don wanted. And in a way, if you like, it was a bit of a benchmark for what happened on *Mellow Yellow*, because it was that sudden change of direction. Once again, it's cinematic.'

'Bert's Blues' adds a jazzy twist to the *Sunshine Superman* album, but it could have just as easily fit on *Mellow Yellow*. As Cameron says, '... almost more so, because ... looking at the rest of what was on the first one (*Sunshine Superman*), they were much simpler. Even one that had a kind of fairly full arrangement, like 'Celeste', was just big block keyboard sounds. It didn't have the intricacy that we got into later.'

The narrator of the song is looking for 'a good girl' but laments that it's taking time. It is possibly Linda he is referring to, especially in the lines:

> You know time could bring a change, girl,
> It ain't for me to say,
> You'll soon be out of range, girl,
> A-this could only be the way it's meant to be.

But the search for the 'good girl' seems to lead the narrator on a journey through a phantasmagoric world with fairy castles, seagulls and even Lucifer, suggesting that the search will not be an easy one and that while the narrator is searching, both he and the girl could change.

'Season of the Witch'

Recorded in Los Angeles, 'Season of the Witch' remains to this day one of Donovan's most popular and most covered songs, despite having never been released as a single. It's very different from the other songs on the album. While other songs present a groovy world of sunshine, myth, beauty, melancholy and magic, 'Season of the Witch' has a much darker streak running through it. Like other songs he wrote, such as 'Catch the Wind', Donovan sees it as prophetic in nature. In the liner notes from his *Greatest Hits* album, he writes, 'Spooky but true. I was the first pot bust in London, followed by The Stones and The Beatles. I wrote this song before the bust. Prophecy again. How dare I be so cool? It's a magic track.' 'Season of the Witch' taps into the paranoia of the times, especially when it came to illegal drug use. Someone famous was going to be busted. It was inevitable. The question was, who would it be? The lyrics perfectly encapsulate this paranoia in the lines:

When I look over my shoulder
What do you think I see?
Some other cat looking over
His shoulder at me.

Here Donovan captures the darker side of 1966. In a larger sense, Donovan could also be commenting on the social changes that were on the horizon. They were strange times for many, especially those who had difficulty accepting those changes. In a sly little comment he mentions, 'Beatniks are out to make it rich', referring to the Beat Generation he had emerged from looking down at the commercialisation of art that Donovan was now embracing. Later in some live performances, he would sing the line as 'Hippies are out to make it rich'.

Donovan sets aside his acoustic guitar on this song in favour of his white Telecaster electric guitar. While Donovan has the credit for writing it, Shawn Phillips has said over the years that he actually wrote most of it. Donovan recalls stumbling upon the main riff of the song and playing it for seven hours straight in Bert Jansch's kitchen. Shawn Phillips was there at the time as well. In a 2018 interview with the *Stone Cold Crazy* blog, Phillips said, 'Basically, the way we wrote together is that I would sit in the room and I would play the guitar. Don would make up lyrics. And that's the way – especially, 'Season of the Witch'. I mean, I completely wrote the music on that. And then for things like 'Guinevere', stuff like that. 'Season of the Witch' is the one I wrote the music to completely. Don had a set of chords. And basically, what I would do is I would play sitar and do an arrangement with the sitar while he played those chords.'

On the recording, Don Brown played electric guitar as well, Bobby Ray played bass, Fast Eddie Hoh was on drums and Lenny Matlin played the organ, including the outstanding organ solo in the middle of the song.

'The Trip'

'The Trip' is a bluesy little folk-rock romp with a rollicking beat. It tells the story of one night in Los Angeles when Donovan was hanging out with a guy named Bernie. They tripped together and watched themselves drive down into LA onto Sunset Boulevard, where a sign that read 'Strip, Strip, Strip' was misread by Donovan as 'Trip, Trip, Trip'. Part of the inspiration may also have come from a club in LA that Donovan liked, called The Trip. The Trip was a club on Sunset Boulevard which saw many artists of the times perform there, especially those who played in the folk-rock vein.

In some ways, this song is the perfect example of the blending of the mythology of California with ancient Celtic mythology, as the lyrics shift from images of Sunset Boulevard to images of Arthurian myth, strangely connected through the films of Fellini, as a woman Donovan dreams (or hallucinates) about, who seems to have stepped out of one of the Italian director's films, transforms into the queen in Arthurian myth, via Lewis Carroll's *Wonderland*! The silver goblet of wine held in a bejewelled hand is similar to the image in the song 'Guinevere' as the queen sips her wine.

Musically, it begins with a folky, acoustic intro before Bobby Ray's heavy, throbbing bass; Fast Eddie Hoh's jaunty drums and Don Brown's twangy, searing electric guitar kicks in. Peter Pilafian is also present, adding in some wailing electric violin touches. Donovan sings during the first verse with a stuttering affectation, often used in rock 'n' roll to help the lyrics fit in with the music. In this case, along with heavy reverb on the vocals, it heightens the weird, disconnected vibe of a 'trip'.

'Guinevere'

Steeped in rich, ancient and mythological imagery, 'Guinevere' is a slow, atmospheric and beautifully melodic piece that finds Donovan tapping into his Celtic heritage, as well as his interest in New Age mysticism. It centres on the titular character, known as the wife of the legendary King Arthur. In his biography, Donovan says she is intended as an aspect of the 'Triple Goddess', a figure in both ancient belief and neo-paganism who exists in three aspects, 'The Maiden', 'The Mother' and 'The Crone', representing the three stages of a woman's life.

It's an interesting take as historically, Guinevere has usually been seen as everything from a villainous traitor to a flawed but virtuous noblewoman, not as a goddess or one of the fay. And yet, her name translates as 'The White Enchantress' or 'The White Fay/Ghost', suggesting a supernatural or magical nature and a connection to the realm of the Faerie from English and Scottish folklore.

Some pagan and literary traditions do include Guinevere as a figure of divinity or at least supernatural origins, sometimes as the 'Flower Maid', a 'Faery Goddess' of love, growth and fertility; sometimes as a 'Goddess of Sovereignty'; and other times as a kind of 'Earth Mother', the aspects representing the 'Triple Goddess'. In some traditions, Guinevere is known as 'The White One', another name for a 'Faery Goddess'. At one point in the song, Donovan sings:

Maroon-coloured wine from the vineyards of Charlemagne
Is sipped by the queen's lip and so gently

Unlike Arthur, Charlemagne is a real historical figure who ruled over
Europe in the 8th and 9th centuries AD. Yet if Arthur, and hence
Guinevere, did exist historically, they would have existed in the 5th to 6th
centuries AD. Perhaps Donovan is suggesting that Guinevere is a magical
being, after all, immortal, existing in two places 300 years apart. In the
lines that follow the ones above, he mentions that there is a silence over
Camelot, Arthur's traditional court and castle, suggesting that its time has
passed. The chorus talks of the 'Jester' sleeping, again, suggesting the
time of life and laughter in Camelot is gone, but the 'Raven' is peeping
through dark, foreboding skies. Ravens have traditionally been a symbol
of death, especially after a great battle, once again suggesting the passing
of Camelot.

On the song, Donovan picks a slow finger-style pattern on his acoustic
guitar, while Shawn Phillips joins on sitar, giving the song a bit more of a
mystical vibe. Candy John Carr plays bongos and Peter Pilafian effectively
adds a brooding atmosphere with his electric violin.

'The Fat Angel'

This is certainly one of the dreamier, trance-inducing pieces on the album,
built around a similar riff to the one in 'Season of the Witch'. The song
was written for Mama Cass Elliot, whom Donovan met and befriended
in LA. Mama Cass was a member of the group The Mamas and the Papas,
but also a very popular social figure amongst musicians of the 1960s.
Many rock stars, from both the US and the UK, were said to often gather
at her house in Laurel Canyon, where they would hang out, getting high
together. The song is filled with drug references, from the dealer who
brings 'happiness in a pipe' to Donovan referring to himself as 'Captain
High' near the end of the song, making it one of Donovan's most upfront
songs about drug use.

The song also specifically mentions the US band Jefferson Airplane,
seemingly as an analogue of Donovan's Trans-Love Airways. Consequently,
Jefferson Airplane did a notable cover version on their 1969 live album
Bless Its Pointed Little Head.

There's a possible intriguing connection to the song "Ferris Wheel'.
In 'Ferris Wheel', Donovan sings, 'A silver bicycle you shall ride, to
bathe your mind in the quiet tide.' In this song, he sings, 'He will bring

happiness in a pipe, he'll a-ride away on his silver bike.' Donovan seems to have enjoyed throwing in these little phrases and images that connected his songs, and this continued to an even greater extent as his music developed through the late 1960s.

Recorded during the LA sessions, the song features Bobby Ray on bass, Candy John Carr on bongos, along with Shawn Phillips, once again providing psychedelic sitar.

'Celeste'

There could not have been a more perfect final track to end *Sunshine Superman* than 'Celeste'. With its languid pace and lush, complex production from Most, saturated in a mood of dreamy melancholy, 'Celeste' sums up everything that has come before. It's been suggested that the song was about a girl named Celeste that Donovan met and stayed up all night talking to. But considering how much his feelings for Linda pervade his music on this album, it's more likely that it's about her, as Donovan reflects, in the first verse, on the changes in his own life, likely both referring to his rising career as a pop star, but perhaps also to the deep longing he felt for a girl just beyond his reach; still one that he was not going to give up on. The second verse may reference the origin of the song 'Legend of a Girl Child Linda' coming to him in a dream and it paints a fairy-tale version of the images he conjured up in the first verse, as he muses over memories of their relationship. Unable to sleep, he watches the dawn, coming down to reality in the final verse, explicitly talking about Linda and how she left for America but reaffirming the pledge he made in the opening song, 'Sunshine Superman', to make her his:

Dawn crept in unseen to find me still awake
A strange young girl sang her songs for me
And left 'fore the day was born.
That dark princess with the saddening jest
She lowered her eyes of woe,
And I felt her sigh, I wouldn't like to try
The changes she's going through
But I hope love comes right through them all with you

With the legal situation worked out, at least on the American side, the single, 'Sunshine Superman', was released on 1 July 1966. As a fresh, new sound for radio, it was groovy and hip. The youth of the time embraced it, as did the disc jockeys, and they propelled it to number one in the charts. Epic followed the single with the release of the *Sunshine Superman* album the following month, on 26 August 1966. Record stores in America reported advanced orders for the album at a quarter of a million copies. The album reached number 11 on the US charts.

Sunshine Superman has often been cited as one of the first psychedelic albums. The Beach Boys' *Pet Sounds* album had come out shortly before, in May 1966, but although a huge step forward sonically, it didn't quite embrace psychedelic imagery in its lyrics like *Sunshine Superman* did. The Beatles album, *Revolver*, which featured the very psychedelic 'Tomorrow Never Knows', came out on 5 August, a few weeks before Donovan's album. But it was actually largely recorded after Donovan had recorded the songs for *Sunshine Superman*.

But still, *Sunshine Superman* sounds like nothing else of its time and can rightfully be called the album that started the psychedelic folk genre, which is still going strong today. But make no mistake, it was far more than just a folk album, drawing in elements of rock, blues, jazz, classical and world music, overflowing with lush, psychedelic imagery embedded in thoughtful, poetic lyrics. It was and remains a masterpiece, and Donovan still cites it as his favourite. As French critic Jacques Vassal said in 1976 in his book *Electric Children: Roots and Branches of Modern Folk Rock*, 'The influence of *Sunshine Superman* since its release cannot be overstated. Although in Great Britain, it did not immediately make a huge impact, it has become one of those albums that practically everyone interested in pop music owns. Certainly, it has now become recognised as the absolute acme of Donovan's writing career.'

Hickory Records were still sore after the acrimonious split with Donovan, but they still retained the rights to Donovan's 1965 recordings, so they decided to release the first Donovan compilation album, *The Real Donovan*, in September, to compete with *Sunshine Superman*. It included some of the usual hits like 'Catch the Wind' and 'Colours', but also some songs that the US market hadn't heard yet, like 'Oh Deed I Do', which had been originally replaced on *Fairytale* by 'Universal Soldier'. The three other songs from the UK EP of *Universal Soldier* were also included, as previously Hickory had only released the song as a single. It barely crept into the *Billboard* chart, only peaking at number 96.

On Donovan's end, everything seemed to be back on track, but it was not all sunshine in Donovanland. He worried, rightly so, that the drug bust would have a negative impact on his records getting played on the radio. He was also distressed over the continuing record label hassles which prevented the *Sunshine Superman* album from being released in the UK. And he was also unhappy about how things had gone with Linda. As she had appeared in some form in many of the songs on *Sunshine Superman*, she would continue to influence Donovan's songwriting, although to a lesser extent, perhaps. With her in the US and their relationship apparently over, Donovan turned his interest to other women, especially a young American model named Enid Stulberger. Still, his feelings for Linda lingered and both women would make appearances on his next album as Donovan wrestled with his conflicted feelings through songwriting.

Rather than releasing another single off *Sunshine Superman*, Epic wanted something new, something no one had heard before, and Donovan gave them 'Mellow Yellow'. Epic released the single on 24 October 1966 and like 'Sunshine Superman', it rocketed up the US charts reaching number two on the *Billboard* Hot 100 and number three on the *Cash Box* charts.

Donovan, of course, had much more than a single to give them. He'd been back in the studio through September and October with Mickie Most and John Cameron, recording the tracks for his next album, which would, as with *Sunshine Superman*, use the name of its first single as the title of the album as well.

Pye finally reached an agreement with Epic Records and released the single, 'Sunshine Superman', in the UK, where it peaked at number two on the UK charts on 29 December 1966, prevented from reaching number one by the Tom Jones classic 'Green, Green Grass of Home'. Pye followed 'Sunshine Superman' less than two months later with the release of the 'Mellow Yellow' single in February 1967, around the time the full album was released in the US. An agreement had not been reached as far as albums went, so once again, Donovan's album did not see a UK release … at least not yet.

In December 1966, Donovan recorded a one-off song not intended for the album and Epic released it as a single in the US in January 1967. 'Epistle to Dippy' was an upbeat number with a tight, punchy arrangement from John Cameron and saw Donovan stepping even further away from his pure folk roots. The song was an open letter to his school chum 'Dippy' whom Donovan had heard was in the army stationed in Malaysia. It's replete with psychedelic imagery, but as with most of Donovan's songs, the imagery all has meaning. The 'young monk meditating' may be a reference to the fact that Dippy's nickname had been a derivation of the name of a monk whose works he'd been interested in back in school. The rhododendron forests he mentions can be found in Asian countries such as India and Nepal, but also in Malaysia. One of the more curious images comes with the line:

Through all levels you've been changing
Elevator in the brain hotel
Broken down a-just as well-a

Donovan may be acknowledging the changes that had happened in their lives since their schooldays, recalling Dippy's interest in the monk's teachings. 'Elevator in the brain hotel' suggests an upward path to enlightenment, changes coming with each new level passed, but he says that the elevator is broken down, possibly seeing Dippy's journey towards enlightenment having stalled after he joined the army. Donovan, of course, was a pacifist, and could have easily seen his friend's involvement with the military as a barrier to achieving that enlightenment. Dippy actually heard the song and contacted his old friend asking him for help and Donovan happily bought his friend's way out of the army.

Donovan tunes his guitar down to a modal D chord in 'Epistle to Dippy', giving the riff around which the song is built a vaguely Eastern feel, reflecting the lyrics and Donovan's own growing interest in Eastern spiritualism. John Cameron's string arrangement adds to the effect. 'Oh yeah, that was fun,' Cameron recalls. 'It was with a string quartet and … electric guitar. We were trying to do a trance kind of vibe to it … that's why the strings were doing the kind of dang, dang, dang, dang … dang, dang … dang … dang, dang. It was … to give it a kind of mantra feel to it.' The song features Jimmy Page on electric guitar, Tony Carr on drums, John Cameron playing harpsichord and Danny Thompson on bass. Thompson would contribute to many other Donovan songs and albums going forward.

Catchy, bristling with energy, and overflowing with intriguing lyrics, 'Epistle to Dippy' was just another example of Donovan tapping deep into the pulse of the times and coming up with something that not only echoed those times but fed into them as well. While it didn't reach the chart heights his two previous singles had, it did respectably, peaking at number 19 on the *Billboard* Hot 100.

In February, Pye released the 'Mellow Yellow' single in the UK and it shot up into the Top 10 there, peaking at number eight. On 9 February 1967, Donovan attended the EMI session during which the orchestral parts of The Beatles' song 'A Day in the Life' were to be recorded. The film of these sessions certainly makes it look like a huge party and Donovan can be seen several times during the course of it. A blink and you'll miss it moment in the film features a close-up of the Epic release of the *Sunshine Superman* album spinning on a turntable!

The next day, on 10 February, Epic released the album *Mellow Yellow* in the US and it rose to number 14 on the *Billboard* charts and number 12 on the *Cash Box* charts.

Mellow Yellow

The lyrics of these songs provide a diary of my changes then. Linda Lawrence had been present in most of my songs on the *Sunshine Superman* album. I thought she was less apparent on Mellow Yellow, but she was there, even though I had tried to forget her.
Donovan, from his autobiography

Personnel:
Donovan: acoustic guitar, vocals
John Cameron: piano (tracks 4, 5, 10), harpsichord (track 10), organ (track 10)
celesta (tracks 2, 6), arrangements (tracks 2, 4, 5, 6, 9)
John Paul Jones: bass, arrangement (track 1)
Danny Thompson: bass
Spike Heatley: bass
Phil Seamen: drums
Bobby Orr: drums (tracks 1, 10)
John McLaughlin: rhythm guitar (track 1)
Joe Moretti: rhythm guitar (track 1)
Danny Moss: saxophone (track 1)
Ronnie Ross: saxophone (track 1)
Big Jim Sullivan: electric guitar (track 5)
Eric Ford: electric guitar (track 10)
Shawn Phillips: sitar (track 10)
Pat Halling: violin (track 8)
Harold McNair: flute (tracks 2, 4)
Paul McCartney: uncredited backing vocals (track 1)

Produced at Abbey Road Studio, London and Lansdowne Studios, London,
September–October 1966 by Mickie Most
US release date: February 1967
Highest chart place: US: 14
Running time: 34:13
Tracklisting:
1. Mellow Yellow (Leitch); 2. Writer in the Sun (Leitch); 3. Sand and Foam (Leitch);
4. The Observation (Leitch); 5. Bleak City Woman (Leitch); 6. House of Jansch
(Leitch); 7. Young Girl Blues (Leitch); 8. Museum (Leitch); 9. Hampstead Incident
(Leitch); 10. Sunny South Kensington (Leitch)

While *Sunshine Superman* existed in a dream world somewhere
between the sunny coast of California and the misty lands of ancient
Britain, *Mellow Yellow* is a very different album, one that embraced the
swinging 1960s scene of contemporary London. While 'Bert's Blues' on
the previous album followed in the footsteps of 'Sunny Goodge Street'
from the *Fairytale* album, the song's true successor was the album
Mellow Yellow. With its colourful portraits of contemporary life mixed
with the loopy Carnaby Street pop psychedelia that was currently the
rage, Donovan had his finger on the pulse of swinging London and truly
captured the zeitgeist of the era. Some of the songs on the album did,
however, take time out for a few vacations in the sun. *Mellow Yellow* also
saw the musician delving deeper into the jazz stylings that fascinated him.

'Mellow Yellow'
This is certainly one of Donovan's most infectious and catchy tunes and
is quite possibly the song he is most remembered for in current times,
partially due to its frequent use in advertising campaigns. Very few songs
capture the vibe of Carnaby Street and Swinging London as well as
'Mellow Yellow' does, and yet it was not Donovan's intention at all.

In nearly every single one of Donovan's songs, the lyrics are
carefully thought out such that every line has meaning, even in his
most psychedelic moments. But on 'Mellow Yellow', he used a collage
technique, drawing various words and images from magazines,
newspapers and even billboards. Donovan has said on a number of
occasions that 'the electrical banana' referred to a type of vibrator that
had become available for mail order in the back pages of 'certain types of
periodical'. There's a reference in the song to the saffron cakes he used to
enjoy in St. Ives during the summer of 1963 and a nod to his female fans

who, on average, were around 14 years old at the time.

The song became part of an urban legend that said if you smoked dried banana skins you could get high. So the story went, this is what Donovan was referring to when he said that electrical banana would be the very next craze. How the rumour got started is unclear. Possibly it began with a letter from one Jesus Cacahuete that was printed in the 15 February–1 March 1967 issue of *The East Village Other*. Cacahuete may have been referring to an earlier article in *The Barb*. Others claim it began with a hoax perpetrated by Joe McDonald of Country Joe and the Fish as a publicity stunt. Wherever it came from, the rumour spread quickly and Donovan's new song had been released at perhaps exactly the right time to get unwittingly caught up in the controversy.

'Mellow Yellow' was arranged by John Paul Jones, who also plays bass on it, and features a number of other players, including Joe Moretti on guitar, Bobby Orr on drums, and Danny Moss and Ronnie Ross both on saxophone. A most unlikely participant was fusion and jazz guitarist John McLaughlin (Shakti, Mahavishnu Orchestra), playing rhythm guitar! He went on to play guitar on Georgie Fame's jazz cover of 'Mellow Yellow' on the 1968 album *The Third Face of Fame*. Paul McCartney is somewhere in the mix, likely as part of the revelry near the end, but the persistent rumour that it was he who whispers 'quite rightly' in response to Donovan singing 'They call me Mellow Yellow' is untrue. Donovan sang that part himself.

Epic released the single 'Mellow Yellow' in the US in October 1966 and Pye released it in the UK in February 1967.

'Writer in the Sun'

As the contractual dispute between Epic Records and Pye Records dragged on, preventing the release of the *Sunshine Superman* album in the UK, a somewhat despondent Donovan retreated to Greece, resigned to the possibility that, at the age of 20, his career might be over. Here, he wrote 'Writer in the Sun', a sad but beautiful lament about being a retired writer, lounging in the sun, his 'days of wine and roses' behind him.

John Cameron did the arrangement and played celesta on the track, but the real star on this piece is Harold McNair. Although Cameron penned the flute parts, McNair's performance is something undeniably unique. Cameron explains, 'In the sixties, there was a feeling that British session musicians were incredibly accomplished. They would essentially, you know, you'd give them the part … and they'd play the whole thing perfectly. First time. Second, third time. It didn't change. Whereas American musicians tended to not be quite so quick on getting it right … they'd take a couple of times and then they'd start to interpret. Now, I found with people like Harold and with people like Ronnie Ross and Danny Moss who were jazz players, the same thing. I would write it for them, but then I'd get input from them back. 'How about if I play it like this?' … and we would discuss it … so there was always a personal thing in the playing, especially from the woodwind players and especially the jazz players and Harold, probably more than anybody else, would add his feel. The notes on the page might be the same, but the way he played them was his.'

'Sand and Foam'

'Sand and Foam' is a brief return, at least musically, to the essence of his first two albums. It's one of only two songs on *Mellow Yellow* that are stripped down to just Donovan singing and playing his acoustic guitar. It's a stunningly evocative piece, recalling a trip that he and Gypsy Dave and others took to Mexico shortly after finishing recording the *Sunshine Superman* album.

While the song is quite simple, Donovan's finger style is in fine form, especially between each verse when he throws in a gritty little descending bass-string fill that adds heft to the song. The minor key makes this song reminiscent of 'Jersey Thursday' from *Fairytale*. The lyrics conjure up imagery from Mexico but also allude to the experiences they had there smoking weed and using mescaline. Donovan references a mescaline-fuelled hike that he took into the surrounding jungle with Shawn Phillips. For a time, they sat staring at some crystal-encrusted rocks they found – 'That crystal thought time in Mexico' – and Donovan watched a bunch of stinging ants as they walked over him – 'Kingdom of ants walk across my feet'. Donovan again combines mystical or fantastic imagery with more realistic, down-to-earth imagery. Donovan also makes reference to a boat trip they took one night. He explained it to Keith Altham for *New Musical Express* on 14 January 1967: 'It was beautiful out there. We took a little boat out at night and when you dipped an oar into the water, it sparkled like a million diamonds in the night – that was the plankton, little tiny living creatures.'

'The Observation'

Despite the upbeat and cheerful title track, a certain darkness pervades the *Mellow Yellow* album, more so than on *Sunshine Superman*, from

Above: Donovan pictured early in his career.

Below: Donovan appearing on *The Smothers Brothers Comedy Hour* in 1969. *(CBS)*

Left: The 1969 reissue of Donovan's debut album *What's Bin Did and What's Bin Hid*. (*Marble Arch Records*)

Right: The first US edition of Donovan's debut album from 1965, retitled for the US market. (*Hickory Records*)

Left: The first UK edition of Donovan's debut album in 1965. (*Pye Records*)

Right: First UK edition of *Fairytale* in 1965. (*Pye Records*)

Donovan
Fairytale
Jersey Thursday · Sunny Goodge Street · Candy Man
The Ballad Of A Crystal Man · And Others

Left: The 1969 reissue of *Fairytale*. (*Marble Arch Records*)

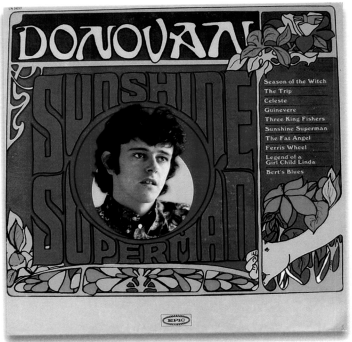

Left: The US Edition of the *Sunshine Superman* album from 1966. (*Epic Records*)

Right: The US Edition of the *Mellow Yellow* album in 1967. (*Epic Records*)

Right: Donovan performs at the 1965 *NME* Annual Poll Winners' All-Star Concert at London's Wembley Empire Pool. (*NME*)

Left: Donovan plays his hit single 'Catch the Wind' at the 1965 *NME* Annual Poll Winners' All-Star Concert. (*NME*)

Right: Donovan on US TV in 1966.

Above: The cover of Donovan's programme from Windsor Festival in 1967. (*Courtesy of Roger Goodman*)

Right: Praise to the 'Queen of All Living Things': Donovan's programme from the Windsor Festival, 1967. (*Courtesy of Roger Goodman*)

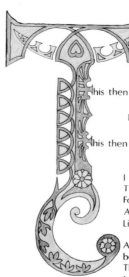

This then is the last minstrel,

Donovan

This then is his praise :

I thank the Queen of Living Things
For showing me each day
All the pretty beauty things
Living in her day

And I thank her kindly for bestowing upon me
The simple gift to daily lift
My tiny eyes to see

Left: A classic photograph of Donovan from the programme from the Windsor Festival in 1967. (*Courtesy of Roger Goodman*)

ERHAPS
Today is your day
Today you have love
(You only hired your seat)
My name is voice
Your name is ear

Where are you going
Oh wind of the morning
Your slippers are showing
and you're still yawning

To waken the wee ones
To tickle their lashes
For breakfast of milk buns
Toy spoons and splashes

Where are you going
So tinyly singing
Where are you blowing
the kiss you are making

To ponds to make ripplings
To blow out the matches
To lift up the gull wings
When the plough scratches

Left: Early lyrics for the song 'Mr. Wind' from Donovan's programme from the Windsor Festival, 1967. (*Courtesy of Roger Goodman*)

Right: Words from Julian McAllister of the band Amber in the same programme. (*Courtesy of Roger Goodman*)

BOUT
nineteen years ago Donovan was born into the streets of Glasgow impressions from the strap and glass eyed Saturday night man, left perception of a quality rare. Don is an occult of the religion music, someone who is part of a deeper thing than a revival of something that was dying. more like the opening into a new world of expressing things that many people understand and are now feeling. Some people know what happenings the open road holds and the expectancy of each town as you brush the rain out of your eye and maybe sleep in its park. Don has known and felt all these things and the expanse of freedom it gives anyone who has travelled and dug mind changes. Freedom of mind is the greatest liberation.

Julian McAllister
1965

Right: Art for the programme was done by Mick Taylor and Sheena McCall. (*Courtesy of Roger Goodman*)

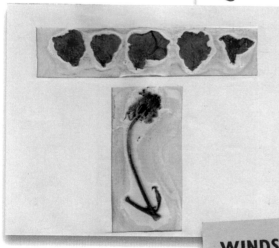

Left: A dried and pressed rose, distributed at the 1967 Windsor Jazz and Blues Festival headlined by Donovan. (*Courtesy of Roger Goodman*)

Right: A ticket stub from the Windsor Festival 1967. (*Courtesy of Roger Goodman*)

Left: *A Gift From a Flower to a Garden*, released in 1967. (*Epic Records*)

Right: The Boxset features a photo of Donovan's meeting with the Maharishi in LA. (*Epic Records*)

Left: Inside the boxset from the re-issue, released around 1979. (*Epic Records*)

Right: *The Hurdy Gurdy Man,* first released in 1968 and on CD in 2005. (*EMI*)

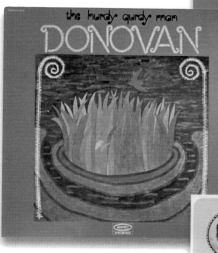

Left: The 2013 re-issue of *The Hurdy Gurdy Man* mono version on green vinyl. (*Epic Records*)

Right: The *Barabajagal* album, released in 1969. (*Epic Records*)

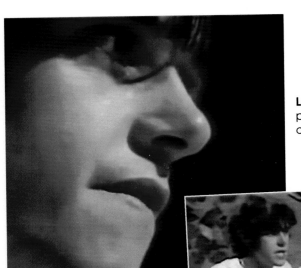

Left: A close-up of Donovan performing 'Hurdy Gurdy Man' on British TV.

Right: Another shot from the same performance.

Left: The Hurdy Gurdy Man himself.

Right & below: Donovan performs 'Lord of the Reedy River' in the movie *If It's Tuesday This Must Be Belgium* in 1969. (*United Artists*)

Right: Donovan also wrote the title song of the movie, performed by J. P. Rags. (*United Artists*)

Left: The *Donovan in Concert* live album, released 1968. (*Epic Records*)

Right: A four-song EP for 'Catch the Wind' released in France in 1965. (*Pye Records, Disques Vogue*)

Left: The single 'Sunshine Superman' released in 1966. (*Epic Records*)

Right: The colourful picture sleeve for 'Mellow Yellow' released 1966. (*Epic Records*)

Left: The 'Hurdy Gurdy Man' single released 1968. (*Epic Records*)

Right: A four-song EP for 'Universal Soldier' released in the UK. (*Pye Records*)

230 Bishops Rise
Hatfield
Herts

★ ★ ★

'Hi' Roger,

Just in the final stages of an India visit.

Glad you dug the Lella Show it was great fun as she is a fabulous person. So plain Jane and beautiful. I did write the other song doing so for that show. Pye tell me they hope to issue my double L.P. package in a few weeks. I had arguments with C.B.S. over this as they claimed it would be too expensive now they are agreeably surprised with around 200,000 sold to date. My record scene is a bit complicated on account of legal hustles but it will iron itself out. Have just edited an L.P. of a live show in America on which 'Rules' is featured. "Be Not Too Hard" is another ticklish legal issue and I don't think I'll do a collaboration job again with either a lyricist or writer. Hope your scene's groovy

Donovan

Above: A Handwritten letter to a fan from Donovan. (*Courtesy of Roger Goodman*)

melancholy songs such as 'Writer in the Sun' and 'Young Girl Blues' to the shadowy, gothic feel of 'Hampstead Incident'. 'The Observation' takes a gritty look at the emptiness of the hustle and bustle of life in the city, a prelude perhaps to Donovan's decision to move out to the country the following spring.

In the song, Donovan sings of 'the great community lie'. What he's possibly saying is that the constant rush and mindless going on of this mad city life (and the crazy world it is creating) is not really living, it's just 'filling in the space between life and death'. People may see it as living, even believe that it is what life is all about, but that's the great community lie.

Donovan flirted with jazz as early as his first album with the song 'Cuttin' Out', and with the help of John Cameron, he skilfully blended jazz with pop and folk on songs such as 'Bert's Blues' on *Sunshine Superman* and a number of the songs on *Mellow Yellow*. 'The Observation' takes it one step further, dispensing with pop and folk for a true jazz number with some blues overtones. John Cameron, whose background was in jazz, had a fun time recording this one: 'That's Tony Carr playing drums with his hands (on) the tom toms … at the start, when Spike Heatley opens it and then TC starts to play all around it. That was fun. That was one of the more straight-up and forward jazz-feeling pieces. I suppose that one and 'Preaching Love' were the two that were just, let's do it as a jazz number.' Cameron plays piano on it while Donovan sets his acoustic guitar aside to simply sing.

'Bleak City Woman'

'Bleak City Woman' was the last song done for the *Mellow Yellow* sessions because Mickie Most wanted the song count up from nine to ten. So Donovan wrote a song about his girlfriend, model Enid Stulberger but also referred to his relationship with Linda. The 'bleak city' of the title was New York City, where Enid was from.

Donovan slowly accepted that his relationship with Linda was over. In the song, he mentions it briefly when he says, 'I tidied up my last affair,' and puts his focus now on this new woman in his life.

Donovan includes some veiled references to sex, but in the end, he sees love. Although the album was recorded in the autumn of 1966 and Donovan didn't retire with a pregnant Enid to the English woods until the spring of 1967, the cracks were already appearing in Donovan's life, referenced in various songs on the album: the drug bust, the record label disputes, the failure of his relationship with Linda and her rejection of him, and his growing disillusionment with the pop star music scene. He was looking for something more. Not just peace but a reconnection to nature and love, the themes that would prevail on his next album. In the last verse of the song, he sings:

I took her to the fair green country
I'm so weary of the life I've led
I'll tell you what we're gonna do
We're gonna live and love so true.

Arranged by John Cameron, the song plays in a barrelhouse jazz style, a particular type of swaggering, bluesy jazz that took its name from the rural clubs where people used to come to dance and drink. As John Cameron recalls, 'It's real barrelhouse. I said, I'm fine with that … suddenly I'm playing barrelhouse piano … it's weird … I went through Cambridge listening to John Coltrane and Quincy Jones and Ray Charles … a very kind of in-your-face funk thing. So even when I was doing delicate folky things … I couldn't resist putting a bit of barrelhouse in, you know, Leon Russell, if you like. Jim Sullivan was the blues guitarist on it. Mickie (Most) was very good at just bringing somebody in for a session or for a number, just giving it that extra kind of vibe to it.'

'House of Jansch'
Donovan recorded two songs penned by Bert Jansch, 'Oh Deed I Do' from the UK version of *Fairytale* and 'Do You Hear Me Now' from the *Universal Soldier* EP, both fingerpicked folk pieces, and he also recorded a tribute to Jansch on *Sunshine Superman* called 'Bert's Blues', a wild mixture of jazz, baroque and blues styles. 'House of Jansch' combines bits of all of this with its complex fingerpicking on acoustic guitar and jazzier ruminations in the elaborate arrangement.

During this period, Jansch's house had become a sort of gathering place for many people in 'the scene' and Donovan spent many days and nights hanging out there. It was at a time when his relationship with Linda had come to an end. She had moved to the US to pursue a career in modelling and Donovan had yet to form a serious relationship with Enid Stulberger.

In his autobiography, Donovan mentions that he and Jansch both shared the affections of singer Beverley Kutner (Donovan refers to her as Beverley Chamberlain). Jansch taught Beverley how to play guitar.

Beverley would go on to record and release Donovan's song 'Museum' as a single in 1967.

In 'House of Jansch', he associates this love triangle with those times, but also says there were a lot of party girls floating around too, and that if he was unable to find love, he would at least have some fun. Donovan didn't likely see any of these relationships at the time as very serious, but nonetheless necessary. In the song, he says, 'the girl ain't nothing but a willow tree'. In Celtic mythology and the Bible, the willow tree is seen as a symbol of loss with the hope for a better future or rebirth. The willow tree has been seen as a symbol of hope and belonging. Its imagery is associated with the ability in people to let go of their pain and to grow anew. In the context of the song, Donovan possibly sees these fleeting relationships with party girls as a way to overcome his feelings of loss when it comes to Linda, a necessary step in order to let her go and begin searching for love once again.

'Young Girl Blues'

With 'Young Girl Blues', Donovan possibly provides his most scathing indictment of 'the scene' and how it uses up young people, shaping them into stars before tossing them aside to move on to the next one. Framed as an observation of how he saw Linda Lawrence's life in the US as she worked towards being a model, 'Young Girl Blues' provides an unflinching look at sad desperation and the willingness to degrade oneself just to become famous. Donovan wasn't denouncing Linda or her choices, but he sees her as just as much a victim as any of those caught up in the machinations of the fame industry, himself included. These feelings propelled Donovan towards his great escape into nature but never on any other song had they been spelt out in such a raw and affecting way. Donovan plays it alone on his acoustic guitar with the sound muffled and distorted as he sings of loneliness, flowers wilting and assorted 'phoneys' and 'losers' moving about in a narcotic, dreamlike world.

Donovan again pushes the boundaries of what can be sung in a song. In 'Sunny Goodge Street', he made the first reference to hash smoking in a popular song. In 'Young Girl Blues', some consider the lines of the chorus:

Yourself you touch
But not too much
You hear it's degrading

... to be a reference to masturbation. In this context, it would certainly emphasise that feeling of being alone on a Saturday night. But just before that line in the chorus is the line 'Cafe on, milk gone/Such a sad light unfading', a reference to the milk having gone bad, or in a sense, degraded. It hints at the nature of fame and how many feel that they must degrade themselves to attain it.

Marianne Faithfull notably covered 'Young Girl Blues' on her 1967 album *Love in a Mist*, but she changed the point of view to first person. In a way, it was, sadly, the perfect song for Faithfull. She was also caught up in the whirlwind of the same scene that Linda had found herself in, having also had a notable relationship with a Rolling Stone, and in her case, it all led to a breakdown in her life where, in the 1970s, she found herself a homeless heroin addict. Knowledge of what happened after she recorded the song certainly adds a poignancy to it.

Julie Felix released her version of it as a single from her 1967 album *Flowers,* but used Donovan's original title for the song, 'Saturday Night'. It featured a gloriously sombre orchestral arrangement by none other than John Cameron. Montrose frontman Sammy Hagar also covered it as a moody, bluesy power ballad on his 1976 debut solo album *Nine on a Ten Scale*.

'Museum'

'Museum' was one of the first few songs that Donovan had played for Mickie Most and John Cameron back during the *Sunshine Superman* sessions and was even recorded then, but it didn't make the final cut for that album. John Cameron created a completely new arrangement for the song during the *Mellow Yellow* sessions. With its swing beat and a deliciously strange blend of jazz and country elements, spacey violin and trippy, tribal hand drumming, the song becomes a glorious, sunny, psychedelic confection.

The museum in question is the Natural History Museum in London. The line 'meet me under the whale' refers to one of the most famous specimens in the museum, a blue whale skeleton that first went on display in 1938.

The song would have fit well within the context of the *Sunshine Superman* album, with its trippy lyrics. At one point, Donovan sings, 'A-maybe you should go get a power ring/You'd make all your troubles go'. The superhero Green Lantern is known for his power ring, which gives him the ability to create anything. Green Lantern, of course, also makes an appearance in the song 'Sunshine Superman': 'Superman and Green Lantern ain't got a-nothin' on me'.

Yet its London setting also makes 'Museum' a perfect fit for the *Mellow Yellow* album. When composing the arrangements for the *Mellow Yellow* album, John Cameron wanted to create a more cohesive kind of album. 'With albums in those days,' he says, 'you would very much concentrate on about four or five numbers. And then, Mickie (Most) would just pitch in the rest to make up the numbers a little bit, you know? Whereas I think with 'Mellow Yellow' it was much more of a planned thing. We were looking to make it a concept.'

Some lyrics excised from the original version seemed to explicitly reference an LSD trip, with mentions of liquid sunshine and references to *Alice In Wonderland*:

A-blue is a pretty colour
The sky's so very large
Our love it is a liquid sunshine
So drink up all you can
Our last dreams of the time
The queen soldiers know where it's at
The flowers even sing
Where our friend the caterpillar sat.

Because taking LSD had changed Donovan's life and perspective in many ways, the original lyrics seem to suggest that the girl he is meeting at the museum could have it change her life too. The trippy middle verse, however, was taken out of the 'Mellow Yellow' version to focus more on style and fashion making a difference in the girl's life. The power ring is a metaphor for change. Of course, he says she doesn't have to do it, but if she does she could be like him, a Peter Pan figure, a child in the sun.

A small portion of the lyrics to the song are only on the demo version: 'Don't you think it's time, good people/Try and use your mind?' Whether it be hallucinogens or style, it was all down to making that decision in your mind to change, to transform and become free.

As mentioned, a version of 'Museum' was originally recorded during the UK *Sunshine Superman* sessions with a completely different arrangement that featured wild percussion from Tony Carr and Candy John Carr, electric guitar from Eric Ford and very prominent flute from Harold McNair. Unlike his previous work on 'Sunny Goodge Street', which was only a 15-second solo, on this the original version of 'Museum', McNair's flute is an integral part of the entire song. In fact, Donovan has said that it was on this recording that he realised how important the flute could be to his music. Indeed, Harold McNair's flute would become a significant part of Donovan's music through the rest of the decade, including here on the *Mellow Yellow* album.

Harold McNair's unique phrasing made him an in-demand session player on non-jazz albums. John Cameron first worked with him on Donovan's albums but went on to collaborate with him on a number of other projects as well, including his much-lauded soundtrack for the Ken Loach film *Kes* (1969). McNair's flute on the first version of 'Museum' is quite astonishing. John Cameron recalls, 'Harold was an amazing player because not only could he play really pretty lyrical flute and all that kind of thing … Harold was the only flute player who could halfway through a number, stop the bank completely and play three, four choruses, totally unaccompanied on flute. And it swung as hard as any other part of the song. His rhythmic playing was quite amazing. Harold actually added a whole new dimension to it.'

As to which version is better, I can't really form a judgement on that. They are both great and both quite different from each other. The original version would have fit nicely on *Sunshine Superman*, but this newer version of it is just perfect on *Mellow Yellow*.

The song was recorded and released as a single by Beverley Kutner in 1967 (going just by the name Beverley on the record). Kutner's relationship with both Bert Jansch and Donovan was partially the topic of the song 'House of Jansch'. Kutner later married singer-songwriter John Martyn.

'Hampstead Incident'

One of Donovan's masterpieces, 'Hampstead Incident' drips with Gothic atmosphere and intensity. Hampstead, an area in London that borders Hampstead Heath, has intellectual, liberal, artistic, musical and literary associations. On the origins of the song, Donovan says in the liner notes of the EMI 2005 remaster of *Mellow Yellow*, 'I was standing by the Everyman cinema in Hampstead, in the soft misty rain, on mescaline; melancholic over the continued estrangement from Linda; philosophic comments on Zen and the everlasting "now" of the teachings.'

Some comment that 'Hampstead Incident' sounds similar to Led Zeppelin's 'Babe, I'm Gonna Leave You', although that song was actually written by Anne Bredon in the late 1950s. Regardless, Donovan himself said the song arose from two completely different inspirations. He borrowed the chord progression from Davy Graham's seminal folk classic 'Anji' and he sang it in a style inspired by Nina Simone.

With the vivid imagery provided by Donovan and the haunting arrangement from John Cameron, the song has a great cinematic sweep to it. As Cameron says, 'I love the way that it's kind of all quite delicate, and then there's this string section that comes in and it builds up and builds up and halfway through it explodes. It goes into that "pow pow pow" feel … Tony Carr giving it his all on the drums and then it goes back to where it was before. It's very filmic. It's like a movie where … you're describing something quite intimate and personal between people, and then suddenly, you're in the streets and there's traffic everywhere, the people shouting … and then you're back to where you were before. That's another of our "movie scores", if you like.'

The result is a complex epic that is a swirling blend of folk, rock, classical, jazz and chamber pop. It's rich with a dark and melancholy atmosphere, due in part to the lyrics but also to John Cameron's brilliant arrangement. Explaining how he created the arrangement to match Donovan's dark lyrics, Cameron says, 'There was … always a little bit of darkness because these were early psychedelic type songs; there's drug references in them and whatever else … there is a darkness in there which I think probably makes it quite attractive now … I think quite a lot of this does come from the arrangement. I'm a great one for trying to follow lyrics. And if Don had a kind of quirky fey lyric, I'd like the arrangement to reflect that … Hampstead is obviously something fairly autobiographical and there is darkness in there … I think the solo violin that's then joined by the trem(olo) violins; the string section … that's all part of it.'

'Sunny South Kensington'

As if in contrast to 'Hampstead Incident', 'Sunny South Kensington' ends the album on the bright, playful kind of note it started on. With its hip lyrics and upbeat, psychedelic vibe, it's not that dissimilar to the song 'Sunshine Superman' and could have fit quite nicely on that album. It's not surprising then to learn that it was recorded during the *Sunshine Superman* sessions, featuring players from those sessions such as Eric Ford on electric guitar, Bobby Orr on drums, Spike Heatley on bass, John Cameron on rock harpsichord and Shawn Phillips on sitar.

The song abounds in pop culture references, even in the title. South Kensington is a cosmopolitan district of London that is popular as a tourist destination because of its many cultural sites and museums. As well, a few famous people are name-dropped in the song. Jean-Paul Belmondo was a well-known French actor who had starred in such films as Breathless (1960) and That Man from Rio (1964). Mary Quant was a British fashion icon in the 1960s. She is often credited with inventing the mini-skirt and hot pants, clothing that would come to be defining fashions of the decade. And the American poet Allen Ginsberg was, of course, an early influence on Donovan's lyrical style.

Mellow Yellow was released in the US on 10 February 1967 and rose in the *Billboard* charts to peak at number 14.

Mellow Yellow is a kaleidoscopic panorama of sounds and ideas where shadowy wizards walk down the colourful and gritty streets of London, beautiful women flit through the shadows, occasionally giving you a meaningful glance from the darkness, dreams of distant tropical paradises come to mind and where mellow is another word for cool. Donovan realises his ambitions of combining jazz, classical, folk and pop together to create his own unique sound.

4: The Wanderer 1967–68

A Gift from a Flower to a Garden
The Hurdy Gurdy Man

Perhaps, like 'Catch the Wind' and 'Season of the Witch', 'Bleak City Woman' has a prophetic element when Donovan sings:

> I took her to the fair green country
> I'm so weary of the life I've led
> I'll tell you what we're gonna do
> We're gonna live and love so true.

His place in southwest London was still a kind of party place with many people coming and going, and Donovan was getting tired of it. Enid had also told Donovan in February that she was pregnant. Donovan was thrilled and excited about becoming a father but felt that this hip, London pad was the wrong place to have a child. And so, Donovan, along with Enid, moved out of London to a cottage in the country, in Hertfordshire, near the place where he grew up.

Both impending fatherhood and the bucolic lifestyle seemed to have ignited Donovan's creativity. He spent the summer writing enough songs for two albums, with the idea in mind to release them both in one package as a box set, something not very common in those days and even less so in the realm of pop music. He still toured, though, doing a number of European, Australian and Far East dates in the summer and was planning a US tour for that autumn.

In June, Pye finally came to an agreement with Epic Records and released an album called *Sunshine Superman* to the British public. I say 'an album' because it was not the US version of the album. Since Epic had already released the *Mellow Yellow* album, Pye decided to play catch-up and issued an album comprising some of the tracks from *Sunshine Superman* and some from *Mellow Yellow*. The album featured the original artwork that Donovan had wanted for the *Sunshine Superman* album, done by Mick Taylor and Sheena McCall.

To the Pye record execs, this might have made sense. But artistically speaking, it is quite confusing. The two albums are very different from each other. Gritty, city-bound tales on tracks such as 'Bleak City Woman', 'Young Girl Blues' and 'Hampstead Incident' clashed with the more fairy-tale splendour of songs like 'Legend of a Girl Child Linda' and 'Guinevere'.

Donovan wrote much of *Sunshine Superman* from a very optimistic point of view. *Mellow Yellow* has much more of a streak of pessimism and disillusionment running through it. Still, the compilation album did manage to reach number 25 in the UK charts, but it was a far cry from the US charts, where the album *Sunshine Superman* peaked at number 11 and *Mellow Yellow* at number 15. Nonetheless, fans in the UK were finally able to hear more than just the singles. The British public would have to wait until 1994 to see the official releases of the full US versions of *Sunshine Superman* and *Mellow Yellow* (along with *The Hurdy Gurdy Man* and *Barabajagal*) in a 4 CD box set issued by EMI called *Four Donovan Originals*.

During the summer of 1967, Ashley Kozak brought in an up-and-coming photographer and designer named Karl Ferris to do the artwork for the next Donovan album. Ferris had been experimenting with photography techniques that created psychedelic effects. He'd also come into some fame as a fashion photographer, notably in the summer of 1966 when on a trip to the Spanish island of Ibiza, he began shooting the innovative and psychedelic fashions of designers Simon Posthuma and Marijke Koger, known collectively as The Fool. These photos ended up in the fashion section of the British newspaper, *The Sunday Times*. For the first time, psychedelic fashions and photography emerged onto the scene. Kozak thought Donovan could use a new image to coincide with the new album and Ferris would be the man to bring that into being.

Ferris went out to Donovan's cottage to meet him. The pair discovered that they'd both grown up in the same area and had both been part of the beatnik scene of the time, so they hit it off naturally. Donovan played the album *Sunshine Superman* for him, then, on his acoustic guitar, played some of the new songs he'd been working on. 'I asked for some samples of the kind of music that would be on the record,' Ferris recollects in his 2021 photography book *The Karl Ferris Psychedelic Experience*, 'and I envisioned a Psychedelic Pre-Raphaelite type of image of a Medieval Minstrel to illustrate the poetic imagery of his lyrics and music.'

They did the initial shoots in Cornwall. Donovan didn't have anything that looked medieval in his wardrobe, but Enid suggested a Jordanian robe that she'd bought in Israel. It was perfect. Further photography was done at Bodiam Castle in East Sussex. Donovan also asked Karl if he could shoot a promotional film for the album. Although, till this point, Ferris had only done still photography, he agreed.

The short film told the story of a wandering minstrel (played by Donovan) upon a horse, travelling through the countryside searching for inspiration, all shot in moody black and white. But then he discovers a secret cave and, going through it, emerges *Wizard of Oz* style into a colourful elvin world. He meets various elves, one of them played by Jenny Boyd, who would go on to be the inspiration for the song 'Jennifer Juniper'. The film ends at a garden party with Donovan playing songs with the elves and other friends, including Gypsy Dave, Graham Nash, Candy John Carr and others. The film features the songs 'Three Kingfishers', 'Oh Gosh', 'Wear Your Love Like Heaven' and 'Ferris Wheel'. It ends up truly capturing not only the essence of Donovan but the essence of the times in all their mystical innocence. Donovan loved it and it ended up being played on various music TV shows around the world.

In July of that summer, Donovan went into the studio to record a new non-album single entitled 'There is a Mountain'. The lyrics of the song came out of Donovan's growing interest in Eastern religion. He adapted the lyrics from a Japanese haiku that had been taught to him by Derroll Adams. The haiku had in turn, been inspired by the words of a Zen master from ancient China named Ch'ing-yüan Wei-hsin. Alan Watts, a writer and mystic that Donovan had been interested in since he was a young teenager, wrote in his seminal 1951 book *The Way of Zen* that the Zen master once said, 'Before I had studied Zen for thirty years, I saw mountains as mountains, and waters as waters. When I arrived at a more intimate knowledge, I came to the point where I saw that mountains are not mountains, and waters are not waters. But now that I have got its very substance, I am at rest. For it's just that I see mountains once again as mountains, and waters once again as waters.'

But rather than setting the words to some serene, peaceful Eastern-tinged music as you might expect, Donovan put it all together in a cheerful, upbeat Calypso number! To achieve this, he brought Harold McNair back to not only play the effervescent flute on the song but to also arrange the piece. Danny Thompson and Tony Carr join in as rhythm section. On paper, it sounds like it couldn't possibly work, but 'There is a Mountain' is one of Donovan's best singles.

Although a haiku may have been the inspiration for the song, 'There is a Mountain' doesn't have quite the same structure as a traditional haiku. Nonetheless, as author and poet Simon H. Lilly wrote on his blog, 'One of the best British lyricists and songwriters is Donovan. His lyrics are deceptively simple, even naive and childish sometimes, but they often embody the spirit of haiku.' 'There is a Mountain' captures that spirit in a refreshingly unique way, with exuberance and joy. It reached number 11 on the *Billboard* Hot 100 and was Donovan's fourth consecutive Top 10 hit on the *Cash Box* charts. Pye Records released it in the UK and it soared to number eight on the British charts. The Allman Brothers used 'There is a Mountain' as the basis for their epic half-hour-long 'Mountain Jam', which appeared on their classic *Eat a Peach* album in 1972. In 2009, Kenny Loggins, along with his daughter Hana, recorded a cover of the song for his children's album *All Join In*.

August brought Maharishi Mahesh Yogi to Britain; an Indian Guru who developed a spiritual growth technique called Transcendental Meditation. The Maharishi wanted to bring his teachings to the West, especially to the younger generation starving for new spiritual pathways. And the best way to do that was to get famous musicians on board. In Britain, he converted The Beatles, who claimed him as their personal Guru. He would also influence Donovan later in the year.

In August, Enid gave birth to a son whom the couple named Donovan Jerome Leitch. Donovan barely had any time to spend with his newborn son before he headed off in the autumn to tour the US. Donovan's popularity was at an all-time high. Rock journalist Lillian Roxon, who had seen him in February 1966 at a show where he played to a two-thirds empty Carnegie Hall, memorably commented in her *Rock Encyclopedia* when she saw him this time at the Philharmonic Hall in Lincoln Center in New York, '... in a piece of showmanship worthy of the Maharishi, Donovan stepped out on stage into a sea of massed flowers, feathered boas and burning incense, looking, in his floor-length white robe, like an escapee from the Last Supper (and for one chilly moment, not entirely unlike its Guest of Honor). Perhaps one group too many had come out in love beads and Carnaby frills. Perhaps it was just the luxury of not having the eardrums damaged for once. But whatever it was, and though it must have all been very contrived (he did the same things at every concert), it was a heady night. Donovan sang, the incense burned and no one could stop hallucinating.'

A similar scene was set at the Hollywood Bowl concert on 23 September. At this show, it started to rain, and Donovan famously encouraged the crowd to clap, saying it would make the rain go away and the rain did indeed stop for the entire show, only starting again as Donovan left the stage. It prompted radio personality Rhett Walker to refer to Donovan as 'the phenomenon of Donovan' in his introduction at the Anaheim Convention Center in November.

One of the fans at the Hollywood Bowl concert was a young music journalist named John Carpenter. While Donovan was in Los Angeles, Carpenter managed to get an interview with the musician. Carpenter was writing for a small, brand new, independent music journal called *Rolling Stone*. Donovan's interview with Carpenter spread across the first two issues of the magazine, which then was more of a newspaper format, on 9 December and 23 December. Donovan was the very first musician to have an interview printed in *Rolling Stone*.

Also, while in Los Angeles, Donovan was invited by a friend to attend a lecture by the Maharishi, who had now made his way to the States. The young musician had a chance to meet the Guru backstage and was invited to come to where the Maharishi was staying in Beverly Hills. Donovan, already interested in Eastern spiritual teachings, was curious and accepted the invitation. While there, the Maharishi initiated Donovan personally, guiding him through some meditation and it had a profound impact on the young pop star. He had an epiphany, coming to the personal realisation that he could achieve the same kind of spiritual experience he had with drugs like marijuana and LSD, but without the drugs. While he was there, a picture of him was taken with the Guru that would appear on the back cover of his next album.

In the John Carpenter interview with *Rolling Stone*, Donovan talked about playing his music for the Maharishi. 'It's beautiful,' he says. 'He said I bring him joy, and he brings me joy by saying that. He says the music is of a transcendental nature which his meditation's about, which I knew anyway and we were initiated. What I needed and actually need is a discipline of tradition which is lacking in our civilisation. Discipline of tradition and the ceremony of humbleness. He wrote it for me, you know, the meditation, which is diving into the well of me that I know is there anyway. And I knew I had to go in there sometime.'

Donovan had been busy recording the songs for his next album. When he told Mickie Most he wanted to do something different, an album of stripped-down acoustic songs, Most didn't like the idea and the two had a bit of a falling out. Donovan's idea would be realised in *For Little Ones*, the second disc of his upcoming album, produced entirely by Donovan himself. Donovan also produced most of the first disc as well, save for 'Wear Your Love Like Heaven' and 'Oh Gosh', which were produced by Most. These two songs would become the A- and B-sides, respectively, of the first and only single to be released from the album. Despite Donovan

producing the majority of the album, the producer credit still went to
Mickie Most, possibly as a selling point.

The box set had been a hard sell to Clive Davis. In classical music, the
format was not uncommon, but in pop, it was pretty much unheard
of. Donovan stuck to his guns though, and along with Karl Ferris and
art designer Sid Maurer, convinced Davis to give it a go, with a small
compromise. Davis wanted to also release the two discs as separate
albums as well. Donovan agreed, and in December 1967, Epic released
the albums separately as *Wear Your Love Like Heaven* and *For Little Ones*.
Their individual chart showings were dismal. But the box set *A Gift from
a Flower to a Garden* was released shortly after, by Epic in the US and by
Pye in the UK, and became an instant hit. Donovan had been vindicated.
While it didn't do quite as well in the charts as his two previous albums, it
was still a hit with fans.

A Gift from a Flower to a Garden

Personnel
Donovan: vocals, guitar, harmonica, whistling
Eric Leese: electric guitar
Cliff Barton: bass
Jack Bruce: bass on 'Someone Singing'
Ken Baldock: double bass
Mike O'Neill: keyboards
Keith Webb: drums
Tony Carr: drums, bells, congas, finger cymbals
Mike Carr: vibraphone
Candy John Carr: congas
Harold McNair: flute
Produced at CBS Studios, London, September–October 1967 by Mickie Most
Uncredited production by Donovan
Release date: December 1967
Highest chart places: UK: 13, US: 19
Tracklisting:
Wear Your Love Like Heaven (first disc): 1. Wear Your Love Like Heaven (Leitch);
2. Mad John's Escape (Leitch); 3. Skip-a-Long Sam (Leitch); 4. Sun (Leitch);
5. There Was a Time (Leitch); 6. Oh Gosh (Leitch); 7. Little Boy in Corduroy
(Leitch); 8. Under the Greenwood Tree (Words by William Shakespeare, music
by Leitch); 9. The Land of Doesn't Have to Be (Leitch); 10. Someone Singing
(Leitch)

For Little Ones (second disc): 1. Song of the Naturalist's Wife (Leitch); 2. The Enchanted Gypsy (Leitch); 3. Voyage into the Golden Screen (Leitch) 4. Isle of Islay (Leitch); 5. The Mandolin Man and His Secret (Leitch); 6. Lay of the Last Tinker (Leitch); 7. The Tinker and the Crab (Leitch); 8. Widow with a Shawl (A Portrait) (Leitch); 9. The Lullaby of Spring (Leitch); 10. The Magpie (Leitch); 11. Starfish-on-the-Toast (Leitch); 12. Epistle to Derroll (Leitch)

'Oh, what a Dawn Youth is Rising to. With all the Love in my Heart, I bequeath this gift from one flower to many.' Thus declares Donovan in the liner notes of *A Gift from a Flower to a Garden* to provide hope for both the parents and to the little ones of the future. He describes the first album as 'music for my age group, an age group which is gently entering marriage'. He continues to dedicate the second to the youth of the future, 'the children of the dawning generation are already being born'. All fine and good, but Donovan drops a bombshell. 'I call upon every youth to stop the use of all drugs and banish them into the dark and dismal places. For they are crippling our blessed growth.'

Donovan's recent transcendental experience with the Maharishi in which he had a similar experience to taking drugs, but with meditation instead, had profoundly affected him. Coupled with the drug bust and becoming a new father, it had changed Donovan's outlook on drug use. But to a young fan base who were in the midst of 'tuning in, turning on and dropping out' as Timothy Leary had famously encouraged, this must-have seemed a bit of a left turn for their psychedelic music hero.

But Donovan's vision went far beyond getting stoned and listening to trippy music. His was not just a revolution of the mind, but of the body and of society and the world. He saw a better future for both his generation and the generation that was just coming into existence, and the message woven into every song on the album was his gift to the world. He was the flower, everyone else was the garden.

A Gift from a Flower to a Garden was the first Donovan album to see a proper release in the UK since *Fairytale*. It was a Top 20 album in both the UK and the US, peaking at number 13 on the UK charts and number 19 on the US Charts.

'Wear Your Love Like Heaven'
As one of the two songs on the album that were produced by Mickie Most, 'Wear Your Love Like Heaven' was the leading and only single off the album. It peaked at number 23 in the *Billboard* Hot 100.

'Wear Your Love Like Heaven' is a celebration of spiritual love and the unity of the human race. It is a joyous paean to the hippy dream of peace and love for all mankind. Numerous exotic colour names pepper the lyrics of the song and are the names of different dyes and paints. Donovan explained in a 2016 interview with *Songfacts,* 'You can see in many of the British singer-songwriters that we were able to make images. John Lennon and George Harrison were artists, Paul also makes sketches, Pete Townshend went to art school, I kind of went to art school – for a little bit, in a college. Joni Mitchell is an artist, of course. Bob Dylan can paint. So we were in art school or close to painting in a big way. So 'Wear Your Love Like Heaven' is very, very paint-ily. When we put the painter's brush down and we picked up the guitar, a lot of the songwriters started 'painting' songs. You'd just have to think of John's 'Picture yourself on a boat on a river' – you're actually in a movie, or you're in a painting. 'Tangerine trees and marmalade skies' – he's painting. So, 'Wear Your Love Like Heaven' was really a paint-ily song – watching a sunset go down. 'Colour in sky, Prussian blue/Crimson ball sinks from view.' It's a painting, really. We were very fascinated with painting, and when we stopped, we put them in the songs.'

As exotic as the colour names are, they are all colours that can be seen in the sky at various times during the day. They mirror the many colours, cultures and spiritual beliefs of people all over the world, acknowledging our differences but also saying that every one of us lives under the same sky. Invoking the names of the great prophets of both Christianity and Islam, Donovan then has a vision, his own 'prophecy' for the future:

Cannot believe what I see
All I have wished for will be
All our race proud and free

Donovan sees the human race all coming together as one but also with the freedom to be proud of and to each express our individuality. It's one of Donovan's most joyous and celebratory songs and remains one of his most popular tracks to this day.

Amusingly, in *The Simpsons* season 13 episode 'Weekend at Burnsie's', the song is used in a scene where Homer uses medicinal marijuana and floats into a colourful, psychedelic sequence. While this scene has led some to believe that the song itself is about marijuana, the kind of psychedelic trip pictured is more associated with hallucinogens like LSD and magic mushrooms.

Never one to pass on an opportunity, Donovan licensed the song for use in Menley & James' Love Cosmetics advertising campaign. 'Wear Your Love Like Heaven' was the background music in TV commercials for such products as Love Colour and Cover, Love's Fresh Lemon Cleanser and Eau de Love Fragrance.

'Wear Your Love Like Heaven' has been covered by the likes of Richie Havens, Eartha Kitt and Sarah McLachlan, the latter of which was for the 1992 Donovan tribute album *Island of Circles,* which contributed to the revival of interest in Donovan and his music in the late 1980s and early 1990s.

'Mad John's Escape'

This song is about a friend of Donovan's who escaped from a mental health centre. The lyrics spin the tale of Mad John's wild adventures as he makes his way across England. The song isn't at all disparaging to the titular character, in fact, it cheers him on.

The song is upbeat, with a rock vibe (especially near the end as it is propelled along with John Carr's hand drums and a slick guitar solo from Eric Leese). There's a huffing and puffing sound at several points in the song, giving it an urgency and even a hint of desperation as its protagonist makes his way through the countryside.

'Skip-a-Long Sam'

A light and easy-going song, 'Skip-a-Long Sam' is about 'Sammy', an old-school chum of Donovan's. Sam and his 'lady fair' Lynn were two of the people that joined Donovan at his island commune on Mingay in late 1968.

It was recorded by the Canadian sunshine pop vocal group The Sugar Shoppe and released as a single from their 1968 self-titled debut album. It reached number 73 on the Canadian charts. Bobbie Gentry recorded a groovy, upbeat cover of the song during the sessions for *Local Gentry* (1968), but it didn't see the light of day until 2000 when it was released on *Ode to Bobbie Gentry: The Capitol Years.*

'Sun'

Throughout his career of more than five decades, Donovan has written and recorded a number of songs drawing attention to the preservation of our environment and ecosystems. While the majority of these songs were released on post-1960s albums, he had begun to dabble with the environmental song in the 1960s. Having moved to the country, Donovan had found a new appreciation for nature which weaves its way through many of the songs on *A Gift from a Flower to a Garden*.

'Sun' was one of the earliest songs he recorded that had a clear environmental message, as Donovan sees the trees standing tall and green, loved by the sun, only to be chopped down, leaving a kind of post-apocalyptic sun-baked world where the rivers and even the oceans are dry. Meanwhile, two people sit reading the paper and drinking tea, either uncaring or just not aware of what is going on around them.

Musically, the song is deceptively relaxing with its gently strummed acoustic guitar, dreamy call and response style vocals and jazzy organ all set to an easy-going rock beat. It is easy to get lulled into complacency, but as one line of the song states, 'Life's very unstable/It's built upon sand,' echoing the fable of the man who built his house on sand, only to see it washed away.

'There Was a Time'

As one of the more upbeat numbers on the album and perhaps the one most similar to the sounds of the previous two albums, 'There Was a Time' prominently features the harpsichord, presumably played by keyboardist Mike O'Neill giving it a bit of a gothic feel. The song tells the story of a selfish medieval nobleman who, one day in St. Albans' marketplace, has an epiphany and comes to realise he has a higher mission in life, to bring beauty and joy to 'a dreadful age'.

In a larger sense, this song could possibly be a metaphor for Donovan's own life. Although Donovan was not 'of high lineage', he did transition from a young musician wanting to make a name for himself to a modern-day troubadour who had a message to bring to the world. St. Albans is a cathedral city in Hertfordshire, England, that has a history stretching back to the Iron Age. Its marketplace was established in the 9th or 10th century and is still active to this day. Here, a young Donovan played in local pubs, learning his craft and coming to realise the nature of his own personal mission. Donovan draws a parallel between himself and the character in the song, both having had a spiritual awakening but hardly knowing where it would lead them:

On a windy Saturday
St. Albans' market day
Little did I know

The work I was to do
Or the love I had to show.

While the band plays fairly lightly in the song, the harpsichord, an instrument invented in the late medieval period, is very upfront in the mix, Mike O'Neill playing a countermelody during the verses and providing an exciting run at the end of each chorus.

'Oh Gosh'

'Oh Gosh' was one of two songs produced by Mickie Most on the album. It was the B-side of the 'Wear Your Love Like Heaven' single. Clocking in at just under two minutes, it's the shortest song on the album. It opens with Ken Baldock's jazzy double bass, Harold McNair's swirling flute joining in quickly, the song set to a leisurely pace with a spritely swing beat from Tony Carr on drums. 'Oh Gosh' has a similar feel to the other Mickie Most produced song on the album, 'Wear Your Love Like Heaven', but it's much lighter in tone, forsaking the grandiose visions of that song for a gentler, more personal happiness on Donovan's part.

Donovan wrote it while his girlfriend Enid was pregnant with their first child. Donovan was looking forward to becoming a father and the song expresses the joy and excitement he felt. The initial focus of the song is on Enid. 'With the baby in your belly' from the second verse, Donovan speaks to the overall theme of the album as songs for young parents or those who were about to become parents. In the latter half of the song, Donovan changes focus to the baby growing within her and he speculates that later while on tour, Enid and the baby may see him on television, and he assures them that he will be sending love from afar.

The second chorus speaks of miracles. 'Think about it, you'll agree/ Many miracles you'll see …' In the context of the first part of the song, he may be referring to Enid (and himself) experiencing the coming birth of their child, as birth is often called 'a miracle'. But in the context of the second part of the song, addressed to his child, he may be referring to the vision he describes in 'Wear Your Love Like Heaven', the beautiful world he sees the future as being, a world in which his child will grow and thrive witnessing the miracles to come.

'Little Boy in Corduroy'

This is another very light song. A swing beat played softly by Tony Carr using brushes provides a very old-timey feel to it, which becomes even more prevalent with its call and response chorus and its first break featuring whistling, which was popular in the music of the 1920s and '30s. It evokes a simpler time, a time of innocence, to describe the play of children.

Corduroy is a kind of ribbed fabric used in clothes. While still worn today, it had particular popularity in the late sixties and early seventies in pants for young boys.

Donovan re-recorded the song for his *Pied Piper* album (2002), which was a little longer and had some more lyrics. On that version, the response voices also included women and children and children's voices were also heard in some of the singing. The *Pied Piper* version also has various people, adults (including Donovan himself) and children making wishes at the end of the song.

'Under the Greenwood Tree'

'Under the Greenwood Tree' is the only song on the album not entirely written by Donovan. In fact, William Shakespeare provides the lyrics of the song. The Royal National Theatre commissioned Donovan to write music to a song from Shakespeare's play *As You Like It*, which they intended to use in a stage performance. When this fell through, Donovan recorded the song for his album.

In Shakespeare's play, Amiens, an attending lord and musician, sings the song as he extols the benefits of country life in the Forest of Arden, where the play is set. Despite having been written in 1599, the song fits in perfectly with the pastoral themes of *A Gift from a Flower to a Garden*. It's also a pretty fair description of Donovan's view on life since moving away from the city into a cottage in the country.

In the end of the song, he sings, 'Will you, won't you … join the dance?', a reference to *Alice's Adventures in Wonderland*, where, in the tenth chapter, the Mock Turtle and the Gryphon tell Alice about a dance called The Lobster Quadrille they used to do under the sea.

The mid-tempo song is just under two minutes long, played with the full band in a classic 1960s pop style.

'The Land of Doesn't Have to Be'

One of two songs that Donovan wrote and recorded with this title; this was the second one. The song details the existence of a magical land hidden behind 'a wall of doubt'. The implication being that you must believe in it to be able to get there. It echoes the film Karl Ferris shot for the album, which has Donovan discovering a magical land hidden from view and accessed through a secret cave. In the film, Donovan, the medieval-styled wandering troubadour, rides a horse. In the song, we are told that children can reach the magical land riding on a 'dreamy mare'.

Beginning with a simple seesawing piano melody, the band joins in with a lilting backdrop accentuated by a high-pitched, almost whistling organ that gives the piece a mystical atmosphere appropriate to a song about a hidden, magical land.

The title suggests that things don't have to be the way we see them, that we can open our minds and travel by 'natural velocity' to an existence better than this one, we just have to believe. It once again expresses Donovan's message wrapped in beautiful poetry.

'Someone's Singing'

The final song of the first album in the box set, 'Someone's Singing', is almost a kind of summation of all the themes Donovan has touched upon in the songs that came before. The opening lyrics re-express the exuberant joy heard on other songs like 'Wear Your Love Like Heaven' and 'Oh Gosh'. He even references the title of the latter in lyrics such as 'Someone's living and, oh, gosh, it's me'. Childbirth and new families crop up in the lines:

Into your life
There will come friends
Maybe a wife
Who to you sends
Love with no gain
Part of a chain
At the giving birth of a new child.

He touches upon the natural world with the lines:

People and flowers
Are one in the same
All in a chain
At the beginning of a new world

… which echoes the title of the album as well as the interconnectedness of the human race. 'Someone's painting and I think it's me' recalls the paint pigments in 'Wear Your Love Like Heaven'. And, of course, there's love too, throughout the song.

'For Little Ones'

I evoked the spirit of nature and sang of the sea and the mystery of Mother Earth. My inspiration had, of course, come from living in the country; but I also called up a simpler and happier time when I had lived on the beaches of Cornwall with my only possession, an old beat-up guitar.
Donovan from his autobiography, *The Hurdy Gurdy Man*

'Song of the Naturalist's Wife'

The recording opens with the sound of a baby crying which is actually Donovan and Enid's newly born son, Donovan Jerome. Over it, Donovan begins to sing a gentle but wordless lullaby-style melody, and the baby stops crying. In his autobiography, Donovan said, 'Critics of my gentle approach to music were still missing the point. In contrast to the wild exuberance of rock and roll, I was soothing with my songs. Peaceful music was needed then.' The opening bit of this song is a mission statement, if there ever was one.

The song is a simple tale of a naturalist greeting his wife as she returns home from a day by the sea collecting shells. 'Naturalist' is an older term for someone who studies natural history, plants, animals, organisms and their relationship to the environment. It has been replaced by more modern disciplines such as botany, zoology and geobiology. Evoking the term gives the song an old-timey, nostalgic vibe but also reflects Donovan's newly found appreciation of nature.

After I wrote this, my wife pointed out to me that it could very well be from the point of view of the naturalist's wife as she sees her husband returning home from a day of collecting seashells, but I rather like the notion of the naturalist at home doing his research, then seeing his wife returning with seashells she has collected for him, as she is then an interested and active participant in her husband's naturalist studies.

The song is simply Donovan singing and accompanying himself on a banjo. Using the banjo instead of an acoustic guitar cleverly enriches the wistfully nostalgic nature of the song. The lullaby intro has a strange resonance to it, filled with microtones that give it an otherworldly feel. Donovan achieved this by singing into the body of his acoustic guitar!

'The Enchanted Gypsy'

This is a beautiful, mystically inclined tale featuring one of Donovan's most recurring themes, that of the wanderer. In this song, though, the narrator is telling the story of the enchanted gypsy, but the story is really about the siren call the narrator feels to follow him, and to become a wanderer himself.

Unlike his earlier songs of wanderers such as 'Ramblin' Boy', which were infused with the grittiness of the realities of taking to a travelling lifestyle, 'The Enchanted Gypsy' is steeped in imagery drawn from fairy tales and other stories of old. The temptation to leave and the narrator questioning his choices remains, though.

Familiar images arise, such as the rubies on the fingers of the narrator's lady, suggesting that the narrator himself is well off, one of the privileged who is considering leaving it all behind to follow his calling, much like the hero of 'There Was a Time'. Gemstones and crystals had been a recurring symbol in Donovan's songs since the *Sunshine Superman* album, always hinting at a mystical kind of richness, wealth that went beyond material gains. Paints also figure in the song, this time used to create pictures on the side of the gypsy's caravan, which tell the tales of his journeys.

The choice of instruments on the song – acoustic guitar, hand drum, tambourine and flute – suggest a group of wandering musicians playing around a campfire, with an acoustic bass filling out the bottom end of the sonic palette. The overall rhythmic quality of the song suggests the movement of a wagon. Near the end of the song, the band breaks out into an upbeat tempo for a wonderful little instrumental jam that takes us to the close of the piece.

'Voyage Into the Golden Screen'

Recalling the enchanted fairy-tale setting of 'Legend of a Girl Child Linda', Donovan takes the listener into a magical realm hidden from the rest of the world. In this context, the 'screen' of the title means a covering or concealment, a sort of veil between the worlds. The theme is similar to 'The Land That Doesn't Have to Be' and also suggests the Karl Ferris promotional video that features Donovan as a wandering minstrel who discovers a secret passage to a hidden magical world. Before Ferris came up with the ideas for the album design and the video, Donovan played him some of the songs he was working on for the album to give him some inspiration. Possibly this was one of them.

Once again, it's filled with the images and symbols Donovan is fond of, like jewels, birds, the seashore, the moon, children and art. It's drenched in mythical and fantastic imagery, drawing on different cultures, such as the elves of Celtic mythology wearing cloaks of fine damask, a type of woven material from the Middle East and China, and finding mysterious, bejewelled casks in Mexico. This brings to mind the sentiments of 'Wear Your Love Like Heaven', that we are all different and yet all the same, as these images from different cultures can resonate within us all. There are some beautiful, mystical turns of phrase, such as 'Tread so light so not to touch the grass,' suggesting graceful, supernatural beings who float over the grass rather than walk through it.

The music displays Donovan's advanced fingerstyle and his use of unusual chords to create a mystical atmosphere that at first seems unsettling but, by the end of the song, is comforting. It perfectly captures the vibe of the lyrics as one experiences fear at first entering this strange realm, but soon finds it feels more like home than the land from which they came.

While there have been no cover versions of the song recorded, in 1968, Danish composer Per Nørgård wrote a symphony entitled 'Voyage into the Golden Screen' inspired by the title and lyrics of Donovan's song.

'Isle of Islay'

One of Donovan's most beautiful and haunting songs, he sings of the 'Isle of Islay', a real island off the coast of Scotland. Islay is the fifth-largest Scottish island and the eighth-largest island of the British Isles. After Donovan's arrest for marijuana and subsequent court hearing, the musician needed a short break, so he and Gypsy Dave took off to Scotland to the Isle of Islay for some peaceful time. Out of that visit came this song.

This minor-key masterpiece features impressions of farm life on the island as well as the setting's natural beauty and just how at peace it makes Donovan feel. There is great depth in its simplicity, a spiritual connection to the natural world. The powerful emotions evoked by the song have resonated with fans through the decades and it remains a favourite amongst Donovan devotees.

After the stress of the bust and the court hearing, Donovan fled the busy, chaotic city life of a pop star in search of a more peaceful, more spiritual approach to a life closer to nature. He seems to have found that on Islay.

'The Mandolin Man and His Secret'

With Donovan singing a lilting melody, accompanied by his fingerpicked acoustic guitar, and punctuated here and there by a plaintive harmonica that is almost flute-like in its sound, this song features another of Donovan's 'wandering minstrel' characters, 'The Mandolin Man'. It tells the story of a wanderer who comes into town playing a mandolin, an instrument often associated with the bards of old, beckoning the townsfolk to gather around him, where he tells them that he wants to hear 'all that's pretty' and 'all that's nice'. Contrarily, the townsfolk merely laugh at him, leaving him on his own. That is until the children of the town hear the call of his mandolin and gather around with sparkling eyes as he tells them his desire to hear 'all that's pretty' and 'all that's nice'. Unlike the adults, the children understand and offer to tell him all that's pretty and nice.

This could very well be a metaphor for Donovan himself and the way some critics ridiculed his music for being soothing and gentle in an age of edgier rock 'n' roll. In dedicating his album to the 'little ones' he's saying that his critics simply just don't understand his music, but if they could find their inner child, they would get it, as the children themselves do, in a way echoing the themes of 'The Land That Doesn't Have to Be'.

The character of 'The Mandolin Man' is a kind of Pied Piper figure, though a more benevolent one than the Pied Piper of German folklore. It comes as no surprise then that Donovan would re-record this song for his 2002 children's album *Pied Piper*.

'Lay of the Last Tinker'

Tinkers appear in various places on the album. The tinker is hinted at in 'The Enchanted Gypsy' and more explicitly referred to in 'The Tinker and the Crab'. In 'Lay of the Last Tinker', it is more implied that the character the narrator meets is a tinker.

A tinker is a usually itinerant mender of such things as pots, pans and kettles, once again, another incarnation of Donovan's wanderer character. The word 'lay' from the title, in this use, means a short narrative, a poem or a song.

Although situated on the children's half of *A Gift from a Flower to a Garden*, the song hints at some darker, more adult themes, as the narrator notices the mark of an old lashing on the tinker and mentions what sights the tinker's tambourine may have seen, including the 'Blazing eyes of dances/Daughters of tinker queens', the vague but implied possibility of sexual dalliances.

This song is unusual in that it has no guitar on it, not even Donovan's acoustic. Set to a percolating calypso rhythm, it features Tony Carr and Candy John Carr on hand drums, Harold McNair on flute and Ken Baldock playing an infectious, syncopated bassline on the double bass.

'The Tinker and the Crab'

Donovan was inspired by the stories of Lewis Carroll to write 'The Tinker and the Crab'. Like many of Donovan's songs, 'The Tinker and the Crab' has themes of wandering, happiness, freedom, loneliness, the sea and nature, and has Donovan's ever-present seagulls. It's another song featuring Donovan's wanderer, possibly the same tinker he invited to share some bread, cheese and wine with him in the song that ended the first side of *For Little Ones*. It's also possible to see the 'tinker' as Donovan himself, roaming free along beaches in St. Ives, his only possession, his beat-up old guitar. Whichever the case, rather than focusing on the past of the tinker, this one narrows in on the here and now, a song about enjoying the beauty of the world around you as you walk through it. 'The Tinker and the Crab' particularly evokes images of the ocean and the seashore in quite imaginative ways: 'White horses riding/On the sea pasture on to the sand'.

While no conversation occurs between the two characters of the story, Donovan still feels a sense of the unusual about it. He said during a *Peel* session on 21 January 1968, 'This meeting to me, it was sort of very magical I felt. It's a strange meeting.'

There's more of a lusher arrangement on this one, with percussion, Donovan's vocals double-tracked on the chorus, and Harold McNair's dancing and pirouetting flute giving it a bit more of a folk-pop vibe. Had a single been released from the *For Little Ones* portion of the album, this would have been a good choice.

'Widow With Shawl (A Portrait)'

Donovan returns to his roots for this breathtakingly beautiful traditional style British folk song. On his 1968 live album *Donovan In Concert*, he introduces the song as such, 'This next song, you must imagine, takes place in the 18th century, in England, somewhere. And this song tells the story of a young lady who is lamenting her lover, who has gone to sea. This is in the days of the sailing ships, and when they went to sea, they went away for … a long time. Twenty-five years, maybe thirty years. Well, this is a widow … She supposes she's a widow, and she's walking along the beach. And this is her song.'

Like 'Lay of the Last Tinker', which hinted at more adult themes, this song as well, dealing with loss and longing, seems to be more directed at adults. Children do have these same feelings, though, so perhaps Donovan intended it as a way to tell children that they were not alone in the way they sometimes felt, that the sad, sorrowful and uncertain feelings were things that adults felt too. Musically, the song definitely fits in more with the stripped-down acoustic vibe of the second album in the set.

This song is such a powerful lament that it can easily bring tears to your eyes, and its deeply poetic beauty shows just how far Donovan has come as a songwriter in only two short years. Donovan's words and voice display the empathetic power of his performance and songwriting. Donovan fan Karen Slawson put it perfectly when she said in a comment under a YouTube video of 'Widow With Shawl', 'I've loved this song for many decades, and just tonight, it occurs to me that the thing that has amazed me all these years is that Donovan not only writes so truly from a woman's perspective, but sings from one'.

'The Lullaby of Spring'

'The Lullaby of Spring' is a beautiful, though rather sombre-sounding song, brimming over with images of the natural world and themes of birth and rebirth. Through verses laden with water, newborn animals and flowers opening their petals to the sun, the song ties together in the chorus with a mother chiffchaff and her clutch of eggs. The chiffchaff is a bird common to Northern Europe and its distinctive song can be heard from a field recording at the very beginning of the song.

Donovan revisited the themes and images of 'The Lullaby of Spring' again in two of the songs on his next album, 'The River Song' and 'A Sunny Day', with the chiffchaff even making an appearance again in the latter.

'The Magpie'

The shortest song on the album is also one of its most memorable, with a melody that sticks in your head and nursery rhyme-like lyrics. In fact, it was inspired by a traditional children's nursery rhyme. The carpenter who had mended the door to Donovan's house gave him the traditional rhyme: 'One brings sorrow, two brings joy, three brings a girl and four brings a boy.'

Exploring the complexities of emotion, feeling joy and sorrow at the same time is symbolised by the dual nature of the magpie. With its feathers of blue, black and white, it is a beautiful and royal bird, but by nature, it can be noisy and mischievous, in European folklore a thief even. But in some cultures, especially East Asian ones, the magpie is a symbol of luck and good fortune. Like the song before it on the album, it also may have been designed to help children to better understand complex feelings.

It begins with a few seconds of bird sounds before the music begins. Donovan sings his haunting melody while accompanying himself with a gently picked acoustic guitar and manages to, in a simple and charming way, capture all these attributes in a celebration of 'a most illustrious bird'.

'Starfish-on-the-Toast'

After another wash of waves comes this, another of Donovan's odes to the sea. Almost certainly drawing once again on imagery remembered from his summer in Cornwall, he conjures up timeless images of men in crabbing boats seen from across the harbour, sandy coves, tide pools in rocky coasts, big clouds in the sky, seagulls and empty beaches.

But unlike his more carefree songs of the sea, this one has a bit more philosophical heft to it. It contemplates the relationship between land and sea and the struggles and joys of those who live by the ocean, those who derive their livelihood from it and those who support them. It sees another side of seagulls, usually symbols of freedom in his songs, this time in a more realistic view. The deeper layers of the song are neatly summed up in one of the verses, a beautiful moment concerning sea snails: 'Holding whelks and periwinkles/Tingling in his hand/Little does he know they hold him too.' It's all about the relationship between man and the sea. What we get from the sea is what the sea gets from us.

'Epistle to Derroll'

This is another of Donovan's 'epistles'. This one was for the banjo player and singer Derroll Adams who had had a profound impact on the young Donovan in his early days.

Derroll Adams was born in 1925. He was a tall and lanky American who played banjo and sang with a rich, deep voice. In the 1950s, he met Ramblin' Jack Elliott and they began playing and recording together. Adams also recorded some of his own music without Elliott, but his recording career was somewhat sporadic. Donovan met Adams in 1965 and the two formed a friendship. Donovan saw the seasoned musician as a direct link to the American Folk Revival, a man who had known Pete Seeger and Woody Guthrie. Adams took the young folk singer under his wing, acting as a mentor and a teacher. Even though Adams played banjo and Donovan played guitar, the older musician taught his student how to play with depth, emotion and thoughtfulness. In fact, Donovan viewed Adams as a kind of Zen Master.

Donovan explained why he wrote 'Epistle to Derroll' on *I Was Born In Portland Town*, a TV tribute to Adams after the banjo player passed away in 2000: 'I remember why I wrote it. Derroll and his wife, Danny, had invited me to visit them in Belgium, but I was becoming famous by then. So I couldn't come. So I wrote a song. So the song goes to Derroll when I couldn't go to Belgium.'

At almost six minutes, 'Epistle to Derroll' is the longest song Donovan had done since 'Legend of a Girl Child Linda', but unlike that one, this was simply Donovan and his acoustic guitar, unadorned save for some waves crashing on the shore at the very beginning. Through ten verses, it tells a magical tale of Donovan imploring some starfish to bring him news of 'a banjo man with a tattoo on his hand' from across the North Sea. After some bargaining and discussion, with the eldest starfish getting involved, Donovan hears news that his friend is doing well and would like him to come to Belgium to visit. Via the starfish, he sends his regrets back that he would love to, but he has too much work ahead of him to be able to.

The song and the album, end with one of the most beautiful, poetic images Donovan has ever written:

I walked along the evening sand
As charcoal clouds did shift
Revealing the moon shining
On the pebble drift
Contemplating every other word
The starfish said
Whistly winds they filled my dreams
In my dreaming bed

A Gift from a Flower to a Garden is an unqualified success. It spent 22 weeks on the *Billboard* Top 200 album charts, peaking at number 19, and 14 weeks on the UK charts, peaking at number 13. But more than that, it was an enormous artistic success for Donovan, a rich and evocative statement of all the things that Donovan was feeling and thinking in those times, distilled into a coherent concept that features memorable song after memorable song, each one making its own mark on the album but also contributing to the overall magical, dream-like power of the album. The adult portion of the album offers up a lot of diverse sounds, yet they all seem to go together perfectly, conveying Donovan's message, the Bohemian Manifesto, throughout, especially in the gorgeous single 'Wear Your Love Like Heaven'. The children's portion of the album (which adults can thoroughly enjoy too!) presents both haunting, magical moments alongside instances of thoughtful and sometimes profound beauty. It doesn't talk down to children, but it speaks to them in their language, one filled with imagination and wonder, but also with cautions and lessons to be learned. I can imagine that these are songs, once heard by young adults and children, now all much older and wiser, are even now rich and powerful songs that still spark the imagination and bring meaning to their lives.

Earlier in 1967, film director Ken Loach approached Donovan to write some songs for his movie *Poor Cow*. Donovan quickly agreed since he always wanted to write film music. John Cameron did the orchestral arrangements for the new track, 'Poor Cow', and also scored the movie, his first of many movie soundtracks. Cameron was surprised that he'd be scoring the film. 'Don had set (to music) a Christopher Logue poem, 'Be Not Too Hard' for Ken Loach's Poor Cow',' he recalls, 'And because I'd been doing … all these arrangements and I'd been on tour and all this kind of thing, he asked me to arrange it for the session. So we went into the recording session and we were playing it back, and I didn't know that Don had been asked or contracted to actually score the movie. It was about the time that it was quite fashionable for people to just sit in front of the movie and improvise. Sonny Rollins did it on *Alfie*. But the (line) producer Teddy Joseph … was more old school. And he said to Don, well, who's actually going to write the music for the score … for the movie? And he (Donovan) said, he is and he pointed to me. And Teddy said, well, this was a Tuesday. We need to dub it a week tomorrow. Can you get it ready for that? So I said, yes.'

Cameron used Donovan's melodies as a cue to score the film, creating orchestral variations on them for the soundtrack. He also arranged Donovan's song 'Poor Cow' for the film, in which Donovan had already played a stripped-down version in live performances. 'Poor Cow' is on the recording of the Anaheim Convention Center concert from 17 November 1967. The concert would be released as Donovan's first live album in 1968 and was titled, simply, *Donovan in Concert*. Oddly though, Donovan introduces it in the live performance as 'Poor Love'. A re-recorded studio version of 'Poor Cow' would later appear as the B-side to the 'Jennifer Juniper' single, again with a lush arrangement by John Cameron.

While the film, released in December 1967, was not a great success, the US tour definitely was. Donovan's father, Donald Leitch, had been very supportive of his son, signing contracts when Donovan was too young to legally do so, and basically helping to manage Donovan's career. He even found the cottage for sale that Donovan bought and moved himself and Enid into. Donovan brought his father along on this tour and had him introduce his son at the beginning of the shows. Donald's voice can be heard at the beginning of *Donovan In Concert* after Rhett Walker from the Los Angeles radio station KRLA does his introduction.

Amidst all the touring, songwriting, recording and spiritual searching that took place in the last third of 1967, Donovan felt that his relationship with Enid was slowly coming apart. 'Here I was on the road and I didn't feel that Enid was part of all this, any more than she was part of my spiritual quest,' Donovan says in his autobiography. Although Jenny Boyd appeared with Donovan in the Karl Ferris promotional video, the musician had actually met her through George Harrison, as she was the sister of Harrison's wife at the time, Pattie Boyd. Donovan admits that he was quite infatuated with the young model and that this made him finally realise that his relationship with Enid was over. Although Jenny and Donovan never ended up having a relationship other than being friends, Jenny inspired Donovan's next single, 'Jennifer Juniper'. The single, recorded in November 1967, was released on 16 February 1968 in the UK, where it rose to number five on the charts, and the following month in the US, where it peaked at number 26.

Donovan's relationship with Enid ended in early 1968, though he vowed to make sure that both she and their son were financially secure. He spent a lot of time in those days at George Harrison's place, discussing Eastern spirituality with the Beatle and his wife and also with Jenny Boyd, all of whom were deeply interested in it. Jenny Boyd, in fact, had quit modelling after she discovered Transcendental Meditation. George gave Donovan a copy of *Autobiography of a Yogi* by the Indian Guru Paramahansa Yogananda. Although originally published in 1946, it had come into popularity once again with the youth of the late 1960s who found it deeply inspirational (for example, it was the book that inspired Jon Anderson to write the lyrics for Yes's 1973 concept album *Tales From Topographic Oceans*). The book deepened Donovan's interest in Eastern spirituality and when Jenny, Pattie and George invited him to come along on a trip to India, he decided to join them, both in pursuit of Jenny Boyd and in pursuit of a deeper spiritual meaning in his life.

Much has been documented and said about the trip to Rishikesh, India, largely due to the presence of The Beatles, but also because of the presence of other celebrities such as Mike Love of The Beach Boys, the actress Jane Asher, Canadian jazz flautist Paul Horn, the actress Mia Farrow and her sister Prudence Farrow (who would inspire the John Lennon-penned Beatles tune 'Dear Prudence', from *The White Album*), as well as, of course, Donovan, along with Gypsy Dave. All of them were at the ashram of the Maharishi, who was going to teach them more about yoga and Transcendental Meditation. For The Beatles, it was one of their most productive periods of songwriting. During their time there, Donovan taught Lennon his fingerpicking style. Lennon would go on to incorporate it in some of The Beatles' songs, most notably 'Julia', from *The White album*. But ultimately, disillusionment set in and The Beatles, along with some of the others, left early to fly back to London. Amidst rumours and conflicting stories, The Beatles announced that they had parted ways with the Maharishi.

Donovan, however, seems to have left on much better terms with the Maharishi. He told the Guru that he also had his own personal mission, to bring his message of peace and love to the world and that, as much as he wanted to stay there, he felt he had to return to his world of music. But the time there had no doubt inspired the young musician as he had continued to write songs. This trip and the Maharishi's influence can be heard all over Donovan's next album, *The Hurdy Gurdy Man*.

Photographer and filmmaker Paul Saltzman, who was in India with them, recounts in one of the stories on his website, *The Beatles In India*, what Donovan said to him about the time spent at the ashram: 'I actually went deeper into my roots in India: my blues roots, my folk roots, Celtic chants, and The Beatles seemed to follow me, because we were playing every day at one point. So I discovered the spiritual sound of my Celtic past. The 'Hurdy Gurdy Man' chant I wrote was really my first solid Celtic rock song. Through going east, I was trying to find my Celtic past. But surely, there's a spiritual path that is the Celtic path. And, sure enough, there is. India centred me. It was what I needed. I needed to centre really deep. It reaffirmed that there is a transcendental world and that it is the most important influence on my life.'

Donovan had left for India in February, having recorded seven of the 12 songs for what would become *The Hurdy Gurdy Man* album. He returned to London in April, apparently spiritually recharged and over his infatuation with Jenny Boyd, even as the song she inspired was peaking on the US charts. Getting together with Mickie Most, Donovan recorded the remaining five songs for the album, including the title track, which would be released as his next single. Mickie Most felt that the song 'Hurdy Gurdy Man' should be different from anything Donovan had done before … something heavier. Most was right, as usual. 'Jennifer Juniper' had not done poorly by any means, peaking at number five on the UK charts, but it only reached number 26 on the US *Billboard* Hot 100. Released in May 1968, 'Hurdy Gurdy Man' rose to number four in the UK and number five in the US on the *Billboard* charts and number three on *Cash Box*.

While the 'Hurdy Gurdy Man' single was ascending the charts, Donovan was back in the studio in May to record new versions of his singles 'Catch the Wind' and 'Colours'. Epic wanted to release a *Greatest Hits* album, but Pye still owned the rights to the original recordings of 'Catch the Wind' and 'Colours'. The solution was to record different versions of them, and quite different they were. Far from the stripped-down acoustic folk of the originals, these versions got a lavish Mickie Most production with a full band. During the same recording sessions, Donovan recorded three of his new songs 'Happiness Runs', 'Where She Is' and 'The Swan (Lord of the Reedy River)'.

Donovan headed to Rome, Italy, in May to perform at the First International Pop Festival held at Palazzo dello Sport dell'Eur. It was to be a huge and extravagant event, intended to be the world's biggest pop music festival ever, consisting of four days of some of the biggest names in popular music of the time. Unfortunately, it didn't go as well as planned. After the date was moved several times, some of the performers, including Jimi Hendrix, had to drop out. To make matters worse, the 'scene' in Rome wasn't quite as big as the promoters expected and only a few hundred people showed up to enjoy the music. And then, disaster happened! On the third day of what was supposed to be a four-day festival, Jeff Lynne's band The Move accidentally set the stage on fire with one of their pyrotechnics effects. The band was arrested and the authorities shut the festival down. Donovan left the festival disillusioned and wanting to get back to something more basic within himself. He asked his father, Donald, if he would scout out some islands off the Scottish coast for him.

During the summer, the two of them went to check out three small islands that Donald found: Isay, Mingay and Clett, near the Isle of Skye. After exploring them with his father, Donovan decided to purchase all three of them. He had an idea in his mind of setting up a sort of commune where artists like himself could live together in peace and love, creating their art for themselves and the rest of the world. He thought a small Scottish island might be the perfect place for such a venture.

Pye issued the single, 'Hurdy Gurdy Man', on 25 May 1968 with a non-album cut, 'Teen Angel' (not to be confused with Dion and the Belmonts' 1958 song of the same name, nor the Mark Dinning 1959 classic, this song was a Donovan original). Donovan's singles had been doing well in the UK and this one was no exception, working its way up to the number four position on the charts. Epic released it in the US the following month, where Donovan's more recent releases had been struggling a bit. Not so with 'Hurdy Gurdy Man'. It peaked at number five on the *Billboard* Hot 100, making it a Top 10 hit on both sides of the Atlantic and it has remained one of Donovan's most recognised songs over the years.

In August 1968, Donovan's first live album, *Donovan In Concert*, was released with a selection of some of the songs performed at the Anaheim Convention Center the previous year. The album captures Donovan at the peak of his powers as he is joined by familiar faces from his recordings, including Harold McNair on flute and sax, Tony Carr on drums and Candy John Carr on bongos and finger cymbals, as well as Loren Newkirk on piano, Andy Troncosco on bass and strings from The Flower Quartet. Despite all the backing musicians, the music does still have a bit of a stripped-down but nicely spacious feel to it. Harold McNair's superb flute playing is essential and is the second star of the show. Just listen to the versions of 'Celeste' or 'The Fat Angel' on the album to experience the true magic of Harold McNair. Donovan has released many live recordings since, but this is the one to get if you want to hear him in his prime, especially if you are able to get the 2006 EMI reissue *Donovan In Concert: The Complete 1967 Anaheim Show*, which includes eight previously unreleased songs from the show. The original *Donovan In Concert* LP peaked at number 18 on the *Billboard* Top 200 album charts.

In September 1968, Donovan was back in the studio again, with Mickie Most and John Cameron, to record another non-album single, the beautiful and haunting 'Laléna'. The song's lyrics were inspired by the actress Lotte Lenya and, specifically, Jenny, the character she played in the 1931 film *The Threepenny Opera*. In a larger sense, it's about the roles that women have thrust upon them in our society; roles they are expected to play without questioning them. The song features Donovan on acoustic guitar along with Danny Thompson on bass, Bobby Orr on drums and Harold McNair on flute. The song features one of John Cameron's best arrangements, with sweeping, cinematic strings played by the Royal Philharmonic, infused with a certain weeping melancholy that perfectly complements Donovan's performance which is one of his most striking. The single was released in October 1968. While it was not as successful as some of his more pop-oriented songs, being a far cry from the heavy psychedelia of 'Hurdy Gurdy Man', it still cracked the Top 40 in the US, peaking at number 33 on the *Billboard* charts. The dispute between Pye and Epic was rearing its ugly head again and 'Laléna' was never released as a single in the UK. It was the last studio collaboration Donovan had with John Cameron in the 1960s.

October also finally saw the release of the album *The Hurdy Gurdy Man* in the US. The continuing contractual dispute with Pye Records prevented the album from being released in the UK, despite the success of the two singles from it in the UK charts.

The Hurdy Gurdy Man

Personnel:
Donovan: vocals, acoustic guitar, tamboura (track 1), harmonium (tracks 2 and 10)
Alan Parker: lead electric guitar (track 1)
John Paul Jones: bass, arrangement and musical direction (track 1)
Clem Cattini: drums (track 1)
Danny Thompson: bass
Tony Carr: drums and percussion
Candy John Carr: bongos and percussion
Harold McNair: flute and saxophone
David Snell: harp (track 8)
Deirdre Dodds: oboe (track 8)
John Cameron: piano and arrangements
Highest chart place: US: 20
Running time: 35:02
Tracklisting:

1. Hurdy Gurdy Man (Leitch); 2. Peregrine (Leitch); 3. The Entertaining of a Shy Girl (Leitch); 4. As I Recall It (Leitch); 5. Get Thy Bearings {Leitch); 6. Hi It's Been a Long Time (Leitch); 7. West Indian Lady (Leitch); 8. Jennifer Juniper (Leitch); 9. The River Song (Leitch/Mills); 10. Tangier (Mills); 11. A Sunny Day (Leitch/Mills); 12. The Sun is a Very Magic Fellow (Leitch/Evans); 13. Teas (Leitch)

Donovan wrote and recorded half of the album in November 1967 ('Peregrine', 'As I Recall It', 'Jennifer Juniper', 'The River Song', 'Tangier', 'A Sunny Day' and 'Teas'). The rest of the songs were recorded on 3 April 1968, after Donovan's visit to Rishikesh, India. The album was only released in the US, but the singles 'Jennifer Juniper' and 'Hurdy Gurdy Man' were released in both the US and the UK, the former on 16 February 1968, the latter on 25 May 1968, both prior to the album's release in the autumn of 1968.

Whereas *A Gift from a Flower to a Garden* had a very cohesive sound to it, possibly because it was just Donovan producing the majority of it, *The Hurdy Gurdy Man* was by far Donovan's most eclectic album to date, with a great diversity in sounds, every song very distinctively different from the rest. Surprisingly though, it all comes together very well with darker and sometimes mysterious songs sitting nicely alongside lighter, more joyous numbers. I love all of Donovan's albums, but *The Hurdy Gurdy Man* is my personal favourite. It really spoke to me, as a young teenager searching for my identity. It stoked the fires of my growing interest in both folk and jazz music. The song 'Hurdy Gurdy Man', especially, profoundly affected me and for a time, I even had plans to head out on the road bringing my own songs of love to a broken world. But the 1980s were a different time from the 1960s and ultimately, that plan fell by the wayside as I pursued other directions in life. But *The Hurdy Gurdy Man* has still always had a special place in my heart.

'Hurdy Gurdy Man'

After the pastoral and peaceful music of a *Gift from a Flower to a Garden*, this single heralding the release of Donovan's next album came as quite a shock to many. With its fragile but strange vibrato vocal opening, the rolling waves of buzzing drones from Donovan's new tamboura, the riotous drum fills from Clem Cattini, and most of all, the acid-drenched heavy electric guitar soloing, it was like nothing Donovan had released before. As Lee Thompson, who had been a young radio DJ at the time, put it, 'Donovan was well known for putting out some unique music. But when 'Hurdy Gurdy Man' came out, it was so weird we didn't really know what to do with it. Then, we came to love it.' And indeed, they did. Fans embraced the new song, propelling it to number five on the *Billboard* Hot 100 in the US and number four on the UK singles chart.

Donovan began writing 'Hurdy Gurdy Man' while on his trip to Rishikesh to learn Transcendental Meditation from the Maharishi. While there, George Harrison gave Donovan a tamboura as a gift. A tamboura is a stringed instrument from India that is used to create harmonic drones. While trying it out, Donovan began to work out the beginnings of the song that would become 'Hurdy Gurdy Man', drawing not just on Indian music but also on his own Celtic roots.

One story says that it was originally intended to be a gift to the Danish psychedelic band Hurdy Gurdy which included an old friend and mentor of Donovan's, Mac MacLeod, but when Donovan heard their version, he was not happy with it and decided instead to record it himself.

But there is another side to it. John Cameron tells an amusing little story about something that happened while he, Mickie Most and Spike Heatley were working out the arrangement for 'Sunshine Superman' at Ashley Kozak's place back in 1966: 'Halfway through the session, Chas Chandler came rushing in very excited. He'd just got off a plane from New York to announce he'd found this amazing guitar player … and it was Jimi Hendrix. Of course, we all went, 'Oh, jolly good,' little realising quite the importance of what had happened.'

While Jimi was in England, Donovan befriended the American guitarist, soon to become a legend in his own right. In his autobiography, Donovan says that he actually wrote 'Hurdy Gurdy Man' for Jimi, hoping the guitarist would record it, but when Donovan played the song for Mickie Most as he had often done, he recognised the song would be a hit and told Donovan he should record it. Most told John Tobler and Stuart Grundy in *The Record Producers* in 1982, 'I felt that Donovan needed something a bit heavier … and out of that came 'Hurdy Gurdy Man' which was a bit weightier, and was what he needed to widen his audience, because America had become a bit heavier … you could see Cream happening and the things which we now know as heavy rock 'n' roll.'

The 'Hurdy Gurdy Man' of the title is yet another incarnation of Donovan's wanderer, one bringing a message of love and peace to a troubled world through his music. This particular incarnation would seem to be the one Donovan himself most closely identifies with as it was not only the name of a song and an album by him but the name of his

2010 autobiography as well. In fact, Donovan told Paul Zollo in his 2003 book *Songwriters on Songwriting,* 'I am the Hurdy Gurdy Man. But also the Hurdy Gurdy Man is all singers who sing songs of love. The hurdy-gurdy is an instrument from the 16th century. The Hurdy Gurdy Man is a chronicler, the Hurdy Gurdy Man is like a bard, and The Hurdy Gurdy Man is any singer-songwriter in any age … Any singer for peace is a Hurdy Gurdy Man.'

The narrator of the song seems to be having a dream where he finds himself standing peacefully on the seashore, when along comes this wandering musician, The Hurdy Gurdy Man, 'singing songs of love'. The Hurdy Gurdy Man is on a mission, it seems. In an unenlightened world cast in shadows where humanity cries, he comes to bring enlightenment through love. This, of course, has been a recurring theme through many of Donovan's songs, an expression of his own personal mission. It's a protest song, but of a different kind. As Donovan says in his autobiography, 'I still felt that my own protest should soothe instead of agitate.' With connections to folklore, Celtic tradition, Eastern spirituality and flower power psychedelia, it is perhaps one of the purest examples among his songs that is everything Donovan was in the 1960s.

Towards the end of the song, another name is introduced, the Roly Poly Man, although it's unclear whether this is actually a new character or just another name or incarnation of the Hurdy Gurdy Man.

Whilst in India and writing the song, George Harrison contributed a verse which was ultimately not used in the final version of the song due to time constraints. At least since the 1980s, when performing the song live, Donovan has often included Harrison's verse, usually telling the story of how it came to be before singing it. George's words add even more depth to the song, reflecting a yearning for enlightenment and tying into Donovan's own amended chorus that talks of an awakening:

> When truth gets very deep
> Beneath a thousand years of sleep
> Time demands a turn around
> And once again the truth is found
> Awakening the Hurdy Gurdy Man
> Who comes singing the songs of love.

George's verse apparently came from one of the Maharishi's teachings about how after being forgotten for long periods of time, transcendental consciousness can be reawakened. This suggests that the Hurdy Gurdy Man is a mythic and mystical figure, not unlike King Arthur, who will come in the times that he is most needed, and bring with him this long-lost knowledge, leading to enlightenment.

'Hurdy Gurdy Man' is also one of Donovan's most unique and creative songs, musically speaking. Produced by Mickie Most, it was arranged by John Paul Jones (who also played bass on the track). Jones had been involved in several of Donovan's most recognisable songs, having played bass on 'Sunshine Superman' and arranged and played bass on 'Mellow Yellow', so it was somewhat fitting that he was brought in for 'Hurdy Gurdy Man' as well, bringing his own unique stamp to this trio of iconic classics.

There has been much speculation over the years as to who played the electric guitar on the song, with several names being thrown about, from Jimmy Page to Allan Holdsworth. In his autobiography, Donovan says he'd wanted Jimi Hendrix to play it, but the American guitar wizard was unavailable at the time. Page includes it on his website as one of his session credits. But it appears that what may have happened is he played on a version of it that was not used and wiped. It's generally recognised now that it was actually session player Alan Parker who played the instantly recognisable guitar lead. John Paul Jones, who booked the session musicians for the recording, has said that it was Parker.

A wide range of performers have covered 'Hurdy Gurdy Man' from vocal group The Four Freshmen on their 1969 album *In a Class By Themselves* to Eartha Kitt on her 1970 album *Sentimental Eartha* (on which she also did a cover version of 'Wear Your Love Like Heaven') to prog and space rocker Steve Hillage, who covered it on his 1976 album *L*. One of the stranger covers came along in 1990 from The Butthole Surfers, a hip alt-rock/avant-garde band from the US. In an interview with *Goldmine* magazine in 2008, Donovan said of the cover, 'It's a completely hilarious version; I love it.' The Butthole Surfers' recording in part prompted the late 1980s/early 1990s reassessment of Donovan, with other modern artists rediscovering his music as well. Even Mac MacLeod finally recorded it in 2002 and it appeared on his anthology album *The Incredible Journey Of The Original Hurdy Gurdy Man*. It has also appeared on a number of modern film and TV soundtracks, most notably David Fincher's 2007 thriller *Zodiac* and as the opening theme music of series one of the historical fantasy TV show *Britannia*.

'Peregrine'

'Peregrine' is the first of two songs on the album to be based around the harmonium and stands in stark contrast to the opening title track.

The harmonium is a variant on the pump organ and is of European origin but has come to be associated with India and Indian classical music. Beginning in the 1960s, it caught on with pop musicians exploring new sounds. John Lennon played one on *Rubber Soul* (1965) as well as *Sgt. Pepper's Lonely Hearts Club Band* (1967) and Pink Floyd utilised it on one song from their *Piper At the Gates of Dawn* album (1967). Donovan uses it as the primary instrument on two tracks on *The Hurdy Gurdy Man* album, the first being 'Peregrine', a drone-based piece with influences from traditional Celtic folk.

The song was written for George Harrison and, like Harrison's verse for 'Hurdy Gurdy Man', was based on one of the Maharishi's teachings. The Maharishi had described people's thoughts as being like boats on the sea of being. Donovan found George Harrison's thoughts, as expressed in his songs, to be quite beautiful and decided to write a song about it. The result was 'Peregrine'.

The peregrine is a type of falcon. Its name comes from the Latin word *peregrinans* which means wanderer or pilgrim, so perhaps this can also be seen as a veiled reference to Donovan's wandering minstrel.

Musically, it's lovely and dreamy, with the harmonium creating a floating feeling while Donovan sings of a falcon floating on the air and boats floating on the sea. Danny Thompson bows his bass creating long, sad notes, with John Carr's hand drums propelling the piece along. Like 'Hurdy Gurdy Man', 'Peregrine' was like nothing else Donovan had recorded before.

'The Entertaining of a Shy Girl'

One of Donovan's shortest songs, 'The Entertaining of a Shy Girl,' returns to his folk roots with some gorgeous fingerpicking on his acoustic guitar, featuring a descending melody that seems almost nostalgic. He tells the humorous little tale of the narrator trying to impress a girl he sees sitting alone in a cafe, but she seems a bit shy and resistant to his charms. As it turns out, though, she's waiting for someone else, a man who shows up at the end of the song. So the narrator cheerfully says goodbye but cutely tries to save face by adding that he has to go anyway because he has a girl waiting for him too. With very few words, Donovan still manages to conjure up a vivid image of the scene. The song has a light arrangement with cello and Harold McNair's flute adding to its whimsical and sometimes wistful nature. Danny Thompson once again plays bass.

'As I Recall It'

'As I Recall It' is most certainly about Donovan's best friend and road companion, Gypsy Dave. Donovan recalls meeting his friend for the first time in a 'Marie Antoinette room', likely a cheeky misdirection as they actually first met in a public urinal in the Old Town Hall nearby, where Donovan was working in a cake stall. The meeting was quite inauspicious for what would become a lifetime friendship as it occurred through a misunderstanding that had angered Gyp. However, they ran into each other again one night at a local jazz club at the Cherry Tree pub in Welwyn Garden City. While listening to New Orleans jazz, they bonded over shared interests and they both heard the call of the road. They were both 16, born less than a month apart.

In the song, Donovan recalls that the sun was high when they met. Well, it was late morning when he left the cake stall to go to the bathroom. Perhaps in memory of the New Orleans jazz they were listening to the second time they met, 'As I Recall It' is a rollicking jazz number with a strutting bassline, exuberant horns and some jaunty barrelhouse piano.

Referring to Gypsy, Donovan sings that he 'used life as a toy', describing the young man's wild and carefree ways. He sums it all up with a chorus of:

Many good times we have had
We been happy, we been sad
But I think we both feel glad
That this life is so mad, mad, mad.

It's a spirited, feel-good song about his best friend and the times they shared together. In a way, it's kind of a sequel to Donovan's earlier song, 'To Try For the Sun', which talked about the hopes, plans and dreams they shared when they were 16-year-olds out on the road together. So perhaps when he sings that 'As I recall it, the sun was high/Yellow in the blue, blue sky', it's not about the time of day at all, but about how high that sun seemed at the time ... and how they ultimately reached it.

Sadly, Gypsy Dave passed away on 18 June 2019, just a few weeks short of his 73rd birthday.

'Get Thy Bearings'

How far ahead of his time was Donovan? In this case, possibly as much as 25 years. 'Get Thy Bearings' is another jazz-based piece though a completely different style of jazz from 'As I Recall It'. This time out, it has a smoky bar, late-night vibe to it. But with Danny Thompson's snaky acoustic bass and Tony Carr on echo-laden drums, a sound is achieved that is uncannily like trip hop or downtempo, a style of electronic music developed in the early 1990s and used by such artists as Massive Attack and Portishead. In fact, the late American rapper Biz Markie sampled the song extensively, using its unique beats as the backdrop of his 1991 song 'I Told You'. In 2013, prominent trip hop artist Bonobo did a cover of it for his mix album *Late Night Tales: Bonobo*, with Szjerdene on vocals.

Jazz is one of the styles that trip hop evolved from and 'Get Thy Bearings' has a great jazz feel to it as well, with Harold McNair, unusually this time on saxophone, chewing up the scenery with his superb soloing. When he repeats Donovan's melody in the middle of the song during his solo, it sends shivers down the spine.

Lyrically, Donovan draws on his world-weary persona that emerged on the *Mellow Yellow* album. He's a soul that is tired of delivering his message of hope to the world and seeing no change happening. It's simplicity, he says. 'Just get together and work it out.' In the chorus, he insists that the whole world knows what he's saying. He seems to be saying that the world has had its answers all along but can't see straight. That they need to get their bearings, figure out where they are and then they can begin to build a better world.

As if to underscore the simplicity of it all, the lyrics are delivered in two five-line quintains and are very brief. Over two-thirds of the song is instrumental.

In the early 1970s, the song was sometimes covered live by progressive rock band King Crimson. They would use the song as a starting point before it evolved into a ten-minute-long jazz rock jam. An example of it can be heard on *The 21st Century Guide To King Crimson Vol. I 1969–1974*, released in 2004.

'Hi It's Been a Long Time'

'Hi It's Been a Long Time' features one of the more complex arrangements John Cameron did for Donovan. It opens with some pretty and melodic piano sounding almost like the beginning of a children's song. It's accompanied by bass and drums. The full orchestra sweeps in during the first chorus. It's a frothy, happy arrangement with the horns and woodwinds bum-bum-bumming along in a joyful way, but the strings add a certain wistfulness, an underlying sadness, appropriate to the song's lyrics.

In the song, the narrator details three meetings with a woman through time. In the first verse, she's proud and pretty, full of life. The narrator himself seems to have found recent success in life, driving a 'flash car', a new and expensive vehicle designed to impress people. But he tells the woman that he hopes she doesn't feel uncomfortable riding with him, suggesting that they knew each other before the narrator's fame and success. The second verse and chorus is repeated twice, as he runs into the woman on a second occasion and acknowledges that both of them have changed quite a bit over time. It's suggested that they were once lovers, and the narrator hopes they could be again. In the third verse, the narrator runs into her again. This time she is no longer proud, she looks tired and dragged, possibly from drug use, or perhaps just disillusionment. It's possible that the woman is also a mirror for the narrator's, in this case, Donovan's life, from the innocence of his initial stardom to the world-wearier Donovan of 'Get Thy Bearings', after being burned by the music industry and seen the coming of hard drugs into the flower power hippy culture.

It's a deceptively simple little song that, when delved into, reveals underlying layers of complex emotional growth through life's changes along with its attendant fears and hopes. It sounds like it could have taken place over a whole lifetime. What's remarkable is that Donovan's rise to fame had only occurred a scant three years earlier and he was only 21 when he recorded the song.

'West Indian Lady'

Like 'The Entertaining of a Shy Girl', 'West Indian Lady' is another love song of sorts, with a twist in the story as well. This one, however, is appropriately set to an effervescent calypso rhythm. Donovan had tried out the calypso style in previous songs like 'Lay of the Last Tinker', and 'There is a Mountain', both of which featured Jamaica-born Harold McNair on flute. Unlike the previous two songs, this one's lyrics fit the music a little bit more as the woman of the narrator's affection is, as the title suggests, from the West Indies. The twist comes, however, when it's revealed that she is actually just a picture on the narrator's wall whom he loves so much that he even loves the printer's name on the picture and even the thumb tacks (drawing pins) holding the picture up! There are hints of romantic and sexual fantasy in the song as well.

There is a final twist, however, as Donovan adds, 'She's the belle of Kilburn, yeah, yeah, yeah,' to the chorus right near the end. Kilburn is a neighbourhood in northwest London known for its large Caribbean community, suggesting that the narrator may know the woman after all, with him living right there in London where she is.

It's Donovan at his playful and humorous storytelling best.

'Jennifer Juniper'

You couldn't ask for a more perfect pop song than 'Jennifer Juniper'. With its spritely arrangement by John Cameron, its light and innocently romantic lyrics and its irresistible melody, Donovan knocked one out of the park with this one. Fans agreed, sending the single up to number five in the UK charts and number 26 on the *Billboard* Hot 100. 'Jennifer Juniper' was the first single released from *The Hurdy Gurdy Man* album but was actually released half a year before the album release.

The song came together quite quickly, as John Cameron tells it, 'He (Mickie Most) phoned me up on a Tuesday and said, "Donovan has got a great song. Will you go and see him?" And he only lived down the road. So I went to see him, talked about it, phoned Mickie up and said we want to use oboe, bassoon, French horn, harp, bass and shaker. And Mickie said, "*Really*?" You know, not exactly a rock and roll line-up. We went into … Kingsway studios on the Friday … it was on Radio Luxembourg on the Sunday. You know, when people talk about deadlines, that's the reason why. Hey, that's how we used to work. You know? "Jennifer Juniper" was a big hit. It was lovely. I really liked that one. I just remember doing it and thinking this is so off the wall, but it works!'

The song was inspired by Jenny Boyd, the sister of George Harrison's then-wife Pattie Boyd. She had been a model, but quit modelling to turn her attention to teaching Transcendental Meditation. She appears in the Karl Ferris promotional video for *A Gift from a Flower to a Garden* as an elf in the secret land Donovan discovers. In July 1968, Jenny, along with her sister, opened a boutique in Chelsea Market, a fashionable district in London. Inspired by Donovan's song, it was named Jennifer Juniper.

'The River Song'

Donovan co-wrote 'The River Song' with Gypsy Dave, one of three tracks on the album that his friend would have a hand in creating. In the vein of 'The Magpie' and 'Isle of Islay', 'The River Song' is a haunting, minor-key meditation on nature, specifically the river and the life that is tied to it. The kingfisher, a bird who first appeared on the *Sunshine Superman* album, makes a reappearance here. Donovan sings the repeated phrase, 'Oh, the rivers flow so old.' The ancient river has been bringing water and life to creatures long before man set foot on its grassy banks. The powerful melody captures the essence of how deep time truly is. Built around a simple fingerpicking pattern, the song features Danny Thompson on acoustic bass and Candy John Carr on hand drums. The percussion is quick but subtle, mimicking the quietly gurgling sounds the river makes as it flows on by. Though never a single, 'The River Song' has remained a fan favourite over the years, even appearing on the TV show *This Is Us*.

'Tangier'

'Tangier' was written by Gypsy Dave Mills. 'Tangier' is similar in ways to 'Peregrine', being based around the droning sound of the harmonium and featuring hand drumming. But this time, the melody and indeed the lyrics are much darker in nature.

Tangier is a city in north-western Morocco and, during the 1960s and 1970s, was part of the so-called 'hippy trail', a route from Europe through the Middle East and on to India and South East Asia that many in the counterculture followed as a sort of 'alternative tourism' journey.

As famed Moroccan writer Mohamed Choukri captured the severe mid-20th century poverty in Tangier so vividly in his controversial 1973 autobiography *For Bread Alone*, so too does Dave Mills in his gut-wrenching lyrics for the song, albeit in a simpler form and from the point of view of an outsider from the West. Donovan sings with reverence and deep sadness at people trying to emerge from their desperate situation, simply happy that they manage to live a little longer than the previous generation.

Bert Jansch plays uncredited guitar on the song in a unique and distinctive style on 'Tangier'. Donovan had no doubt been very excited to get his hero to come into the studio and play on a track, but apparently, Mickie Most didn't recognise Jansch when he strolled in and was quite bewildered by it all!

'A Sunny Day'

Another song that Donovan co-wrote with his friend Gypsy Dave, 'A Sunny Day' is a blissful, summertime reverie set to a gently played jazzy beat.

The song has a lazy, strolling pace and is impressionistic, bringing to life a warm summer day. Donovan's lyrics are quite unique, evoking both the carefree sense of peace the narrator feels while also emphasising the active and busy lives of the wildlife he encounters. He uses short, clipped words in a sort of lyrical onomatopoeia, using the words themselves to imitate the flurry of animal activity surrounding him. Along with Donovan's gently strummed guitar and Harold McNair's twirling, chirping flute, it creates quite a vivid setting, especially when the piece brilliantly speeds the tempo up for a short moment in the middle of the song.

In a sense, this is perhaps, metaphorically speaking, similar to *Mellow Yellow*'s 'The Observation', where the enlightened one walks serenely through the hustle and bustle of the lives around him. Or it could just be Donovan enjoying a nice summer day and the beauty of nature. Or even both, as Donovan's deceptively simple songs, often have so many layers.

Nonetheless, it's a nice break after the sonorous and darker 'Tangier'.

'The Sun is a Very Magic Fellow'

'The Sun is a Very Magic Fellow' is another simple folk song with a loping, bouncy rhythm. It has a very lullaby feel to it. Donovan personifies earthly forces and cosmic entities, the sun, the wind, the rain, the sea, the moon and a star in a mythical way, showing how each one affects him in different but very human ways. In the end, he brings it all right back down to humanity and love, singing 'a girl is a pillow for my sadness', suggesting that although these forces and entities may have an effect on us, it is the comfort we can give to each other that will make our sadness go away and bring us joy.

Donovan co-wrote this song with Mal Evans at the ashram in Rishikesh. Mal Evans was the road manager for and personal assistant to The Beatles up to their break-up in 1970 and made several contributions to their songs as well.

'Teas'

'Teas' is one of the most underrated songs off *The Hurdy Gurdy Man* album and a personal favourite of mine. It is another stunning example of how well Donovan could paint vivid pictures with his words and music. Set in a 'deserted seaside café' in the off-season, Donovan sits and reflects on his life and perhaps his romantic entanglements, the failure of his relationship with Enid, his still ongoing, seemingly unrequited love for Linda. The song could also be referring to Donovan's growing disillusionment with the pop star life and the music industry. In the second verse, he changes the word teas to memories, perhaps those of a more free and innocent time for a younger Donovan.

Built around a slow and wistful chord-based piano phrase played by John Cameron, the song is yet another totally unique song in Donovan's catalogue. In the chorus, Donovan's voice is altered, giving it a very psychedelic vibe. A lovely ending to the original album.

Released in the US in October 1968 by Epic Records, *The Hurdy Gurdy Man* reached number 20 on the *Billboard* Top 200 charts. From heavy rock with sizzling, psychedelic guitar to soft and sometimes mysterious, sometimes light-hearted folk pieces; from jaunty, jazzy numbers to Indian-influenced ragas; from catchy chamber pop to calypso music, *The Hurdy Gurdy Man* is a small masterpiece of eclecticism. It's impossible to say exactly why it works ... it just does. Every odd and eccentric piece contributes to the whole. It's like finding pieces from a bunch of different jigsaw puzzles and discovering that, somehow, they all magically fit together.

It would be the last Donovan album fully produced by Mickie Most until *Cosmic Wheels* in 1973. It was also the last Donovan album on which John Cameron would do arrangements until *Donovan* in 1977.

By late 1968 John Cameron had become busy as the musical director for the weekly TV variety series *Once More with Felix*, featuring folk singer Julie Felix, whom Cameron had done some arrangements for, including several of her Donovan covers. 'Laléna' ended up being the last studio collaboration Donovan had with Cameron in the 1960s. Donovan was also once again having disagreements with the direction Mickie Most thought he should be going with his music and began distancing himself from the producer.

In November 1968, he flew to Los Angeles to work with producer Gabriel Mekler. Mekler had just produced Steppenwolf's first two albums which were both released in 1968. The success of the albums, especially the singles 'Born to Be Wild' and 'Magic Carpet Ride', had made him an in-demand producer. The sessions, recorded at the American Recording Company in North Hollywood, California, produced a selection of wildly eclectic songs with the American producer, from a children's song ('I Love My Shirt') to a song about free love ('The Love Song'), a Vietnam protest song ('To Susan On The West Coast, Waiting') a rowdy ode to a girl

Donovan had met while on tour ('Pamela Jo') and a mystical, mythological piece that had a lengthy spoken-word recitation ('Atlantis').

Pye decided to take a chance with 'Atlantis' as a single, with the B-side being 'I Love My Shirt' and quickly released it on 22 November. By Christmas of 1968, it had peaked at number 23 on the UK charts.

5: End of an Era 1969

Barabajagal

Epic chose to release 'Atlantis' in the US in January of the new year but felt that it was too long to be a single and thought that the spoken word part would not go down well with American audiences, so they made it the B-side of Donovan's next single, another of the Mekler-produced cuts, the anti-Vietnam War protest song 'To Susan On the West Coast Waiting'. Despite the growing protests against the Vietnam War, the song didn't connect with the US audience, only reaching number 35 on the *Billboard* charts. But it turned out that radio DJs were flipping the single over and playing the B-side, 'Atlantis' and the mythological anthem was connecting with listeners becoming, no doubt to the chagrin of execs at Epic, a huge hit worldwide. Not that the execs would have been complaining. 'Atlantis' reached the number seven position on the *Billboard* charts (making it Donovan's last Top 10 single). It hit number 12 in Canada, number four in Austria, number two in South Africa and Germany, and it was a number one hit in Switzerland.

In January, Donovan's *Greatest Hits* was released with newly recorded versions of 'Catch the Wind' and 'Colours'. Besides the two re-recorded tracks, it comprised all the major album and non-album Epic singles up to and including 'Laléna' (by the time of its manufacturing, it was too late to include 'To Susan On the West Coast Waiting' and 'Atlantis'). The version of 'Sunshine Superman' included was the original unedited cut, one minute and 15 seconds longer than the version that had appeared on the album and as the original single. *Greatest Hits* also included 'Season of the Witch' which, despite not having been released as a single, had become one of Donovan's more well-known songs, in part due to some popular covers of it in the late 1960s by the likes of Al Kooper and Stephen Stills, Terry Reid and Brian Auger, Julie Driscoll and The Trinity. *Donovan's Greatest Hits* became Donovan's bestselling album, gaining gold record status by April and reaching number four on the *Billboard* Top 200.

Donovan gave another stab at a song that had been hanging around since the *Sunshine Superman* days and the third time seemed to be the charm. 'Superlungs My Supergirl' (previously known as just 'Superlungs') was recorded in March with John Paul Jones arranging and Big Jim Sullivan brought in to play electric guitar.

In April, the movie *If It's Tuesday, This Must Be Belgium* was released, starring Suzanne Pleshette and Ian McShane. It's a romantic comedy adventure about an amorous tour guide who takes a group of Americans on an 18-day whirlwind tour of Europe. The movie features a plethora of guest appearances, including one by Donovan in which he plays his haunting song 'Lord of the Reedy River' to an enraptured group of young tourists. This is not the version he recorded earlier with Mickie Most, however, which had Donovan accompanied by a band and had a jazzy vibe to it, but a stripped-down solo performance of the song. Ultimately, the earlier version was not used for Donovan's next album either and instead, the song would find its way again in a more stripped-down version onto Donovan's 1971 children's album *HMS Donovan*. Donovan also wrote the title song for the film, but it was performed by J. P. Rags. Donovan does not appear to have recorded the song himself, but the J. P. Rags version was released as a single in 1969.

Despite Donovan starting to distance himself from Mickie Most, the producer had not quite given up on the musician and was cooking up another idea. He wanted Donovan to work with a band instead of a collection of session musicians. Most had just produced 'Beck-Ola' for the Jeff Beck Group in April and thought they would make a great match with Donovan. While much of the work had already been done for the next album, Most managed to coax Donovan into the studio with the Jeff Beck Group for a session in May. Jeff Beck and his bandmates were entirely unrehearsed when they showed up at the studio having not even listened to the songs they were going to record. Nonetheless, they managed to knock off three numbers: 'Goo Goo Barabajagal (Love Is Hot)', 'Trudi' and 'The Stromberg Twins'.

Pye issued 'Goo Goo Barabajagal (Love Is Hot)' as a single in June with 'Trudi' as the B-side. It was exciting and something new for Donovan. It was funky, groove-laden and danceable, but still had that little bit of mystic power to it. And it had the Jeff Beck Group, who were very popular at the time. Yet, it didn't quite catch on with fans and radio DJs as some of Donovan's previous hits had. Still, it did quite respectably in the UK, reaching number 12 on the British music charts. But when released as a single in the US the following month, it only managed to climb to number 36 on the *Billboard* Hot 100. Perhaps it was a sign. Donovan did like to believe in the prophetic nature of music. Indeed, 'Goo Goo Barabajagal (Love Is Hot)' would be the last Top 40 single for Donovan, signalling, in retrospect, the end of an era. Times were changing.

By 1969, after some enormously successful tours, Donovan had pulled back on his touring schedule, but he did make an appearance as one of the opening acts at The Rolling Stones' now legendary free concert in Hyde Park on 5 July. Donovan must have had Linda Lawrence on his mind as this was just two days after the former Rolling Stones guitarist Brian Jones had been found drowned in his swimming pool and The Stones introduced their new guitarist, Mick Taylor, at this concert (he was no relation to the Mick Taylor that had recorded 'London Town' and did artwork for Donovan).

On 11 August 1969, Epic released the album *Barabajagal*. Due to the continuing contractual disputes, it was once again not released in the UK. In the US, despite the lacklustre response to the title track as a single, the album did well, peaking at number 23.

Barabajagal

Personnel:
Donovan: vocals, acoustic guitar
Jeff Beck: electric guitar (tracks 1, 9)
Ron Wood: bass (tracks 1, 9)
Nicky Hopkins: piano (tracks 1, 9)
Tony Newman: drums (tracks 1, 9)
Big Jim Sullivan: electric guitar (track 2)
John Paul Jones: bass and arrangement (track 2)
Danny Thompson: bass (track 3)
Tony Carr: drums (track 3)
Richard 'Ricki' Podolor: electric guitar (track 8)
Bobby Ray: bass (tracks 5, 6, 7, 8 and 10)
Gabriel Mekler: piano (tracks 5, 6, 8 and 10); melodica (track 7); organ (track 8)
Jim Gordon: drums (tracks 5, 6, 7, 8 and 10)
Alan Hawkshaw: piano (track 3)
Harold McNair: flute (track 3)
Graham Nash: backing vocals (track 4)
Mike McCartney: backing vocals (track 4)
Lesley Duncan: backing vocals (tracks 1, 4 and 9)
Madeline Bell: backing vocals (tracks 1 and 9)
Suzi Quatro: backing vocals (tracks 1, 4 and 9)
Produced at Olympic Studios, London, May 1968, March 1969 and May 1969 and at American Recording Company, Los Angeles, November 1968 by Mickie Most
Highest chart place: US: 23
Running time: 33:43

Tracklisting:
1. Barabajagal (Leitch); 2. Superlungs My Supergirl (Leitch); 3. Where Is She (Leitch); 4. Happiness Runs (Leitch); 5. I Love My Shirt (Leitch); 6. The Love Song (Leitch); 7. To Susan on the West Coast Waiting (Leitch); 8. Atlantis (Leitch); 9. Trudi (Leitch); 10. Pamela Jo (Leitch)

The *Hurdy Gurdy Man* was an extremely eclectic album that somehow gelled together perfectly. *Barabajagal* is just as eclectic, but it doesn't work as well. It has some great songs on it, but it's a mixed bag of clashing styles and influences.

It was recorded in a very patchwork manner with 'Where Is She' and 'Happiness Runs' recorded in May 1968 in Olympic Studios in London, during the same sessions with Mickie Most when 'Catch the Wind' and 'Colours' were re-recorded for the Greatest Hits album. 'Atlantis', 'To Susan On The West Coast Waiting', 'I Love My Shirt', 'The Love Song', and 'Pamela Jo' were recorded with Gabriel Mekler producing in November 1968 at the American Recording Company, North Hollywood, California. 'Superlungs My Supergirl' was recorded with Mickie Most in March 1969 and the title track and 'Trudi' in May 1969. Some of the songs were shelved for the time with no exact plans for an album.

When an album finally did come together in the form of *Barabajagal*, it was a very weird mix, with very adult-themed songs like 'The Love Song' sitting uncomfortably alongside children's songs like 'Happiness Runs' and 'I Love My Shirt'. But in a way, it was symbolic of the times and the flower children that flocked to Donovan's concerts caught halfway between the exciting but often harsh realities of adulthood and the innocence and naivety of youth, a place Donovan himself could relate to very well.

Some have said that *Barabajagal* is the last of Donovan's 'classic' albums. I would argue differently. I think albums to come over the next few years, such as *Open Road* and *Cosmic Wheels,* are just as classic. But *Barabajagal* did, for many reasons, mark the end of an era for Donovan.

'Barabajagal'

In April 1969, Mickie Most was in the studio with the Jeff Beck Group. Beck had released the album *Truth* in 1968. Although it featured all the members of what would become the Jeff Beck Group – Jeff Beck on guitar, Ronnie Wood on bass, Nicky Hopkins on piano and keyboards, Micky Waller on drums and of course Rod Stewart on vocals – it was credited to just Jeff Beck. The next album, *Beck-Ola* would be the first album recorded and released under the name the Jeff Beck Group. After producing that album, Most had the idea of a collaboration between the Jeff Beck Group and Donovan. Always searching for new ideas and different sounds, Donovan was excited about the prospect.

On all of his previous albums and tours, he had either played it solo or used session musicians to accompany him. This was something new, something he'd never done before. Mickie Most explained on the BBC radio documentary series *The Record Producers* in 1982: 'One of Donovan's problems was that he never really had a band. He'd go on tour and say, "This is going to be a flute tour," and he'd take a flute player, an upright bass player, and he'd play acoustic guitar himself. And then he'd say he was going to do a rock tour, and he'd pick up some rock musicians, but he never had anybody he could bring into the studio, there was never that sort of working relationship, so I always used to use the people who I'd used on the Herman's Hermits records, the session guys. But when Jeff Beck had his group buzzing away, I thought it might be an idea to put the two things together after Donovan sang me this song called "Barabajagal".'

However, when Beck and his bandmates (minus Rod Stewart) showed up in the studio to record the new songs in May 1969, Donovan assumed they would have heard the demos and worked out their parts and rehearsed them. To Donovan's chagrin, Mickie Most had not given Beck any of the demos that Donovan had recorded, and they were coming in cold to play whatever Donovan had for them. It definitely shows but in a good way. 'Barabajagal', released as the second single from the album, is full of loose, vibrant playing; crackling with unrehearsed and unbridled energy. The Jeff Beck Group were consummate players, so the sessions didn't end up becoming a mess. What resulted was, once again, something totally unique in Donovan's catalogue to date. The folky elements are ditched here in favour of funky grooves based around a two-chord vamp. Donovan's lyrics are electric, sexual and mystical. The addition of female backing singers Madeline Bell, Lesley Duncan and Suzi Quatro adds heat to the already spicy vibe.

The full name of the song is 'Goo Goo Barabajagal (Love Is Hot)'. 'Barabajagal' is a made-up name for a character who is a herbalist. In the song, a woman comes to see him for a cure for her pain and he prepares her a tea. He mentions a celandine in the song, which is a type of poppy, though not the kind that opium is made from. Nonetheless, in herbology, it is believed to have healing properties. In the middle of the song, there is a spoken word part where things get somewhat hallucinogenic and maybe even sexual:

Multi-colour run down over your body
Then the liquid passing all into all (love is hot!)
Love is hot, truth is molten!'

The song reached number 12 on the UK charts and number 36 in the US. It would be the last song of Donovan's to crack the Top 40 in either country.

'Superlungs My Supergirl'

Another upbeat, rock-oriented song, this one once again pushes the boundaries of what you could sing about in a pop song. In 1965, Donovan was one of the first artists to reference marijuana in a popular song, namely 'Sunny Goodge Street' from the album *Fairytale*. It was an oblique reference; one you may not even notice if not listening closely. By 1969, things had changed.

'Superlungs My Supergirl' tells the story of a 14-year-old girl who likes smoking marijuana. Since a significant portion of Donovan's fan base were teenage girls, it was likely the kind of girl he often saw at his concerts, as marijuana had steadily become more of a part of mainstream youth culture over those four years.

The song was originally just titled 'Superlungs' (although Supergirl was still referenced in the lyrics), a reference to the ability of the song's protagonist to inhale the marijuana smoke. The added Supergirl reference in the title may have been related to the Superman reference in *Sunshine Superman* and Donovan's love of comic books as a young boy. When Donovan sings that he loves his Supergirl, he's not talking about a romantic love but more of an admiration of her ability.

Donovan recorded three versions of this song. The first one was done during the *Sunshine Superman* sessions and was a kinetic, garage rock style number full of raw energy with searing, echoey guitar work from Don Brown and a superb organ solo from Lenny Matlin (who did the equally excellent organ solo on 'Season of the Witch'). Possibly it was felt to be too heavy, or possibly there was some concern at the time over the lyrical content, but it did not make the final cut for the *Sunshine Superman* album. Donovan next tried it during the *Mellow Yellow* sessions. Featuring an arrangement by John Cameron, this second version was a much jazzier and pop-oriented version with horns throughout. The final version was a little shorter than the earlier versions mostly due to its faster tempo. The chorus has been changed to emphasise 'Supergirl' instead of 'Superlungs', with some nice psychedelic effects added to Donovan's voice and some acidic guitar work from Big Jim Sullivan. Each version has its own charms. My personal favourite is the blistering psychedelia of the first version, but the final version is definitely the one that fits best with the overall sound of *Barabajagal*. The first version was first heard on the 1992 *Troubadour* anthology and was also included on EMI's 2005 remaster of *Sunshine Superman*. The second version first appeared on the EMI 2005 reissue of *Mellow Yellow*.

'Where Is She'

'Where Is She' is a yearning love song of the sort Donovan did on his earliest albums, but this one is dressed up with a lavish Mickie Most production featuring lush orchestral arrangements and beautiful flute from Harold McNair (McNair's only appearance on *Barabajagal*) as well as some lovely piano work from Alan Hawkshaw. It's a somewhat lesser song in Donovan's catalogue but nonetheless makes a stark and enthralling contrast to the two previous songs on the album.

'Happiness Runs'

'Happiness Runs' was another of the songs Donovan wrote on his trip to India. Just as he'd done in the song 'Peregrine' from his previous album, Donovan used the Maharishi's description of thoughts as boats floating on the sea of being as the starting point for this song:

> Happiness runs in a circular motion
> Thought is like a little boat upon the sea
> Everybody is a part of everything anyway
> You can have everything if you let yourself be.

The song, however, opens with a beautiful little folk-inspired piece that describes an encounter between a naturalist (perhaps the same one from 'Song of the Naturalist's Wife'?) and a pebble on the beach, comparing the size of the pebble to a man and the size of the man to the universe, before breaking into a round featuring the voices of Graham Nash, Mike McCartney and Lesley Duncan. The song describes Donovan's experiences in meditation while studying in India. It became a fan favourite at live shows when Donovan would encourage the audience to sing along, filling in the parts that Nash, McCartney and Duncan sang on the album.

In fact, it first appeared in an earlier version on the live album *Donovan In Concert* under the title 'Pebble and the Man'. The live album was first released in 1968, a couple of months before *The Hurdy Gurdy Man* album.

The song has a playful, child-like innocence to it, no doubt the reason it was chosen as one of the songs Donovan re-recorded for his 2002 children's album *Pied Piper*. It was notably covered by folk singer Mary Hopkin on her 1969 debut album, the Paul McCartney-produced *Post Card*, and more recently by singer-songwriter Lissie in a rock version, as her contribution to the 2015 Donovan tribute album *Gazing With Tranquility*.

'I Love My Shirt'

'I Love My Shirt' is another track that was redone for *Pied Piper*, and it is no surprise. It's a perfect little singalong song that seems tailor-made (see what I did there?) for kids. It's a song about enjoying the simple pleasures in life, in this case, one's clothes. But on a deeper level, Donovan could also be saying that you should feel comfortable in your own clothes, i.e. comfortable being yourself, an important message for both children and adults.

The song is set to a romping beat with jazzy piano from Gabriel Mekler, who also produced the track.

'The Love Song'

'The Love Song' is a joyous paean to free love, a concept that was very much a part of the youth culture conversation in the late 1960s. Donovan continues to push lyrical boundaries, but in his usual playful and poetic way suggesting oral sex:

Take her to the woods and show her what to do
She could see the stars if she's looking up
Drink the sweet juice from a loving cup

and even group sex:

Hey, have you ever seen the lonely ones
Putting down the lovers for having fun?

The very same thing that would set them free
They should catch an evening with my lover and me
Whoopee!

Indeed, part of the charm of the song is Donovan's refusal to be explicit, remaining only suggestive in his words.

The song is an upbeat romp with playful piano from Gabriel Mekler, with Donovan's acoustic guitar keeping the song from straying too far into the more rock territory of songs like 'Barabajagal' and 'Superlungs My Supergirl'. There is, however, a very strange break in the middle of the song featuring Donovan's friend Murray Roman, who was a writer for comedian Tom Smothers, as he does a crazy spoken word call to everyone to join in with the festivities. Apparently, Roman got so into it that he overdid it and Donovan had to gag him with his hand to get him to stop while they were recording. This middle bridge part is backed by not only the music but the sounds of a wild party. Considering the theme of the song, it could even be the sounds of an orgy. The partying sounds return near the end of the song, with female backing singers exulting, 'Hark awhile and listen to the love song.' While it is a fun song, it is a bit of a mess with a bit too much going on in it.

The song was offered to the UK soul band The Foundations as a potential single, but they did not end up recording it.

'To Susan on the West Coast Waiting'

'To Susan on the West Coast Waiting' was another of Donovan's rare protest songs, specifically referencing the Vietnam War, which was still six years away from ending. Framed as a letter from Andy, who is overseas fighting in the war, to Susan, who is waiting for him to come home, it mirrored the experience of countless young women and men in the same position.

In a sense, it's similar in theme to 'Widow With Shawl (A Portrait)' with a woman waiting for her husband to come back from years of sailing, not knowing if he is alive or dead. In this case, though, it's from the man's point of view but still carries the ominous possibility that he may not return.

The song lyrics:

Our fathers have painfully lost their way
That's why, my love, I'm here today

Hear me when I say there will come a day
When kings will know and love can grow

… echo themes in Donovan's earlier song 'Ballad of a Crystal Man' and of the Buffy Sainte-Marie song he covered, 'Universal Soldier', both of which had appeared on the EP of the same name, and the former of which had also appeared on *Fairytale*.

This was one of the songs that Donovan recorded with Gabriel Mekler in Los Angeles and it features Mekler on melodica. There is also a chorus of three female singers. These were actually fans who had been waiting outside for days to meet Donovan, so he invited them in to sing the backing vocals on the song. What an experience that must have been for them!

The song was released as a single in the US on 20 January 1969. It reached number 35 on the *Billboard* charts, but the response was much more enthusiastic to the B-side of the single, which was 'Atlantis'.

'Atlantis'

Despite not being a big hit in Donovan's native UK, 'Atlantis' was a huge hit for him in the rest of the world. While Donovan would see some chart success with the single 'Barabajagal' and a few other releases in the early 1970s, 'Atlantis' was his last true worldwide smash hit.

The first third of the song is a spoken word narrative detailing the story of the lost continent of Atlantis and its ultimate fall, whereas the remaining portion of the song is a glorious, anthemic singalong. Recorded with Gabriel Mekler in Los Angeles in November 1968, it was inspired by a book Donovan was reading at the time, *A Dweller on Two Planets* written by Frederick Spencer Oliver in the late 1800s and first published in 1905. Oliver's book was particularly influential on the 20th century New Age movement, especially in the notion of Atlantis as an advanced, enlightened civilisation that fell due to natural catastrophe but sent out emissaries before the collapse who planted the seeds that gave rise to the great ancient civilisations such as Egypt and India.

Over a chord pattern taught to him by Derroll Adams, Donovan recited his version of the tale, with Gabriel Mekler on piano, accompanying Donovan playing his acoustic guitar. The strange, haunting harp effect was produced by Donovan strumming the piano strings. The latter part of the song brought in Jim Gordon on drums and Bobby Ray on bass. The melodic electric guitar solo break was performed by the studio engineer Ricki Podolor.

The song's mystical legend-telling and uplifting singalong ending resonated with the hippy culture of the time as it had much deeper meaning than simply an ancient tale. As Donovan said in Paul Zollo's 2003 book *Songwriters on Songwriting,* 'Atlantis is actually a state of mind, maybe a perfect society. Inside, humanity is the same. There are different colours, different locations. But inside, there is a constant knowledge that everybody has in every age. And thus, the myths are similar in all ages.'

The song is one of Donovan's best, a transcendent anthem voicing the ideals and hopes of his generation in the context of myth and legend. It was a perfect capper to five years of incredible work from Donovan, a journey told through words and song, a beautiful send-off to the 1960s and all that made up the counterculture of that time. It would have made a perfect final song on the *Barabajagal* album, but oddly, it was decided to sequence it with two tracks following it to end the album.

Donovan revisited the song in 2001. He'd approached Disney to see if they were interested in using his song in the animated film *Atlantis: The Lost Empire* being produced at the time. While they declined, he was asked if he'd like to collaborate with the up-and-coming all-female German vocal group No Angels for an album by artists inspired by the movie *Atlantis: The Lost Empire* intended for the German market. Donovan reprised his poetic telling of the story for the song and joined the group, strumming acoustic guitar and singing in the latter half of the song. He also appeared in the video for the song.

Donovan also did a parody of the song for 'The Deep South', an episode of the animated series *Futurama.* In it, the characters visit the lost, sunken city of Atlanta, Georgia, while Donovan, appearing in the episode in cartoon form, narrates the strange story just as he did in the spoken word portion of the original.

'Trudi'
'Trudi' was another of the songs recorded during the sessions with the Jeff Beck Group in May 1969. In the liner notes of the EMI 2005 reissue of *Barabajagal*, Lorne Murdoch calls it 'a pleasant if unremarkable hoedown' and it's a pretty accurate description, especially in the context of the album where it immediately follows 'Atlantis'.

'Trudi' is actually somewhat of a rewrite of 'Lay of the Last Tinker' from Donovan's *A Gift from a Flower to a Garden* album. More accurately, the lyrics were likely written at the same time as 'Lay of the Last Tinker' but discarded in favour of lyrics that more accurately fit the theme of its album (not to mention the different arrangement). Trudi bounces along to a variation of the famous Bo Diddley beat while Donovan tries to entice a woman to go to bed with him. Moreover, the woman already seems to be with another man, Johnny, but in the narrator's eyes, he doesn't appreciate her. It's not entirely clear if the woman in question is the Trudi of the title, or if Trudi is a wild and carefree friend of the woman. There's even the vaguest hint of a lesbian relationship and that Trudi appreciates the woman far more than her husband does: 'You got a friend called ramblin' Trudi / Oh, Johnny never looked you like that'. Ramblin' Trudi takes off onto the road at the end of the song, a neat gender reversal to Donovan's earlier 'Ramblin' Boy'. This time there's no poetic language or mystical symbolism, no 'coded', covert lyrics; it's pretty straightforward other than the exact identity of the woman. Donovan enticing her to join him in bed is pretty clear. In fact, when 'Trudi' was released as the B-side of the 'Barabajagal' single by Pye Records in the UK, its original title was 'Bed With Me'. Pye executives, however, felt the title was a bit too daring and tried to change it, a little bit too late. An initial run of copies of the 45 were released under the original name before it could be changed to 'Trudi'.

Other than the minor controversy, and a nice turn by Nicky Hopkins playing some boogie-woogie-style piano, there is nothing that really distinguishes 'Trudi'. The third song recorded during the Jeff Beck Group sessions, 'The Stromberg Twins', is a far more interesting track and in my opinion, should have been chosen over 'Trudi' for the album.

'Pamela Jo'

'Pamela Jo' was the last track recorded with Gabriel Mekler in Los Angeles. It was an ode to a young woman Donovan met while on his North American tour in the autumn of 1968. As Donovan himself tells the story:

> Pamela Jo and I met once on a long day off during that hectic tour. A Southern girl, she seemed like a friend from the past – perhaps previous lives. Lying in the shaded hotel suite in the afterglow, she talked softly about her life, and I forgot the massive pressure I was under.

From that, you might expect the song to be a soft, acoustic ballad with thoughtfully romantic lyrics, but you would be far from correct. 'Pamela Jo' begins with a jazzy, music-hall kind of vibe before becoming something of a drunken-sounding pub singalong with Mekler pounding away at barrelhouse piano.

Like Trudi before her, Pamela Jo is framed as a bit of a ramblin' woman, dreaming of far-off lands and wanting to follow the railroad tracks to see where they go, which Donovan encourages her to do. During the song, Donovan sings, 'She looks just a little like a circus child.' This is a reference to Pamela Jo bearing a resemblance to film director Federico Fellini's wife, Giulietta Masina, who played Gelsomina, a circus character in the film *La Strada*.

While it's certainly not a bad song, it's not one of Donovan's best either, a rather inauspicious end to the album, even if the singalong chorus is quite catchy (and as it actually says in the lyrics, 'The words are very easy to follow').

Although *Barabajagal* is far from a weak album and does include some genuine Donovan classics, its patchwork nature perhaps prevents it from achieving quite the same heights as some of Donovan's previous albums. *The Hurdy Gurdy Man* managed to use its eclecticism to its favour, but for *Barabajagal*, eclecticism becomes a weakness as the oddball variety of songs don't quite all come together as a whole. Nonetheless, it still holds a place in the hearts of many Donovan fans and it is still widely considered to be one of the musician's classic albums. While it was not the last of Donovan's albums to chart, it was his last album to produce any Top 40 singles.

Donovan set out on his third major US tour in September to promote *Barabajagal*. But things were a bit different this time; things were frayed around the edges and beginning to unravel. The tour was punctuated by star-studded parties where Donovan participated but didn't feel like he was part of it. 'Some who met me commented that I was so natural, not fazed by it all,' he recalled in his autobiography, 'but deep inside, I was more than fazed. An emotional time bomb was ticking away inside me that year. Gypsy could plainly see it and was seriously worried for me.' At one of the parties, Linda Lawrence showed up hoping to get in to see Donovan. Ashley Kozak encouraged Donovan to let her come in, but the singer said no.

He returned to the UK after the tour, exhausted and quickly retreated to his cottage. He wanted his son to have an education in England, so he asked Enid to move back to the UK with their child. Until they could find a place for Enid to stay, Donovan said she could stay at the cottage.

Donovan had set up his commune on Mingay Island, and in November 1969, along with a few friends, including Donovan's old school chum

Sam, whom he had sung about in Skip-a-long Sam, he and Enid went to stay there. The commune, for many reasons, would not end up working out and Donovan ended up selling the islands off. Despite the fact that he and Enid's relationship was over, their brief stay up there did produce Donovan and Enid's second child, Ione Skye Leitch, who would go on to become a famous actress in the 1980s. Upon return from the island, however, the couple did not get back together. Donovan's final concert of the decade brought him back to the Royal Albert Hall with John Cameron and his Orchestra to perform a selection of songs, both new and old.

Life and the future were left a little bit hanging and uncertain for Donovan at the close of the decade. His love life was in ruins, a half-decade of battles between his labels that had prevented the release of a number of his albums in his own native country had worn on him, and the relentless pace was overwhelming him. It was the end of an era, not just for Donovan but for the youth of the 1960s that had loved him and brought him fame. But in order to finish the story of Donovan in the 1960s, we'll need to take a brief peek into 1970.

6: Legacy

Don has that special honesty and simplicity which is understandable to
all. He will always have this as his greatest strength.
Joan Baez

It had been only ten years since a young teenager living in
Hertfordshire, England, filled with hopes and dreams, first picked up a
guitar and started to learn how to play it. No one could have imagined
the incredible decade that lay ahead for the aspiring musician except
maybe that young musician himself. Donovan wanted to try for the sun
and in so doing, he practically became the sun itself, so brightly would
he shine upon that decade of the 1960s.

As the decade of the 1970s was dawning, Donovan was still a popular
draw at concerts and his *Greatest Hits* album, released in 1969, had been
the biggest seller of all his releases, spending 56 weeks on the *Billboard*
Top 200, peaking at number four.

Perhaps inspired by his sessions with the Jeff Beck Group, Donovan
decided that he wanted to form a band for his next album and brought
together keyboardist Mike O'Neill, bass and guitar player Mike Thomson
and long-time collaborator Candy John Carr on drums. The band was
dubbed Open Road. Donovan had already distanced himself somewhat
from Mickie Most during the *Barabajagal* sessions. He was tired of Most's
elaborate productions and strict work ethic and wanted to get back to
something looser and more basic in nature. He parted ways with the
producer and went into the studio with his band to record their self-titled
album, *Open Road*, with Donovan in the producer's chair.

The result was an album that was a little rougher around the edges,
more organic in nature, perhaps reflecting the more down-to-earth vibe
Donovan wanted. The idea of doing it must have excited Donovan as he
wrote a strong set of tunes more inspired than a lot of *Barabajagal* had
been, including the bouncy 'Riki Tiki Tavi' and the extraordinary 'Roots
of Oak' (the former released as a single with the latter as its B-side).
Donovan drew on some of his Celtic roots in the songwriting, and
although he may not have exactly invented the subgenre of Celtic rock, he
did give it its name from the title of one of the songs on his album. He'd
touched on environmental issues on some of his 1960s albums, but a
large part of the lyrics of *Open Road* dealt with the industrialisation of the
ancient landscape and the loss of a more peaceful, natural world.

The album became his third bestselling album in the US. It looked as if Donovan's success in the 1960s was going to translate well into the new decade. But as the band Open Road embarked on a world tour, Donovan suddenly had a change of heart. Sick of the endless schedules, the gruelling night after night performances and the machinations of the music industry, Donovan cancelled the rest of the tour and returned to England, retreating to the countryside.

It was fortunate timing, for as he did, a certain young woman named Linda Lawrence had also returned to England, tired of the grind of trying to be a model in the US and was also looking for a place to live in the country with her young son, Julian. Julian's father, Brian Jones, had accidentally drowned in a pool during a party in July of the previous year, forever ending any prospects of them coming together as a family. By chance, she ran into Donovan at a small get-together and rekindled her relationship with him. Donovan, never having lost his love for her, asked her to marry him and this time, she said yes. They remain married to this day.

But while that was just beginning, things seemed pretty much over for Open Road with Mike O'Neill also exiting the band. Undeterred, the remaining members recruited Barry Husband and Simon Lanzon to fill out their ranks and returned to the studio to record their own album *Windy Daze*, released in 1971. It would be their only release.

Donovan would never again see the kind of success he had in the 1960s and still continued to forge a career through the 1970s but on his own terms. He tried a number of different ideas from children's albums to glam rock, even briefly reuniting with Mickie Most for the excellent 1973 *Cosmic Wheels* album (his last album to enter the charts) and both Mickie Most and John Cameron for his less successful self-titled 1977 album *Donovan*.

The world was moving on from the 1960s. It was becoming clear that the ideals of peace and love embraced by the hippies would be more difficult to achieve than they had imagined. The Kent State shootings in 1971 had forever altered the perception of protest. The youth of the 1960s were faced with a growing disillusionment in the 1970s and the 'Me Decade', as writer Tom Wolfe dubbed it, brought on a certain cultural narcissism. The rise in popularity of new styles of music like disco, funk and heavy metal reflected new attitudes. Donovan's gentle folk style and mystical songs of peace and love no longer seemed to fit in with the altered cultural landscape. Certainly, Donovan himself had grown up too and made attempts to forge ahead with new more modern sounds, but he'd been an icon of the flower children, a symbol of all they had believed in, and was now forever associated with that innocent time. With the rise of punk that came in the late 1970s, the youth of the time no longer embraced the idealism of the 1960s, further distancing Donovan from the popular mindset.

The 1980s saw Donovan somewhat in retreat though he did continue to record albums without much success, and he did continue to perform to smaller but enthusiastic audiences of old fans and newer young fans who related more to the culture of the 1960s than they did to the culture of the 1980s (this author included).

But the 1990s began to see a turnaround in Donovan's fortunes. Youth culture was shifting once again. The rave generation was enthusiastically embracing psychedelia (albeit in the form of electronic dance music) and younger artists were rediscovering Donovan's music. The Butthole Surfers made a splash with their cover of 'Hurdy Gurdy Man' in 1990. However, 1992 was a pivotal year in the resurgence of interest in Donovan. June of that year saw the release of Canadian alternative music label Nettwerk's Donovan tribute album *Island of Circles*. Featuring an introduction by Donovan himself, other notable artists involved in the project included Sarah McLachlan, with her cover of 'Wear Your Love Like Heaven', Brix E. Smith of The Fall doing 'Hurdy Gurdy Man' and Spirit of the West covering 'Sunshine Superman' among many other intriguing covers. No-Man, the duo of Steven Wilson and Tim Bowness, who had scored a minor hit in 1990 with their cover of Donovan's 'Colours', contributed a cover of 'Turquoise' to the album. Barely a week after the tribute came out, Epic released *Troubadour: The Definitive Collection 1964–1976*, a double CD which not only featured many of Donovan's classics but also included a couple of his 1964 demos and some of the alternative versions of his songs. Both releases were quite successful. Then 1994 finally saw the official release of the original US versions of *Sunshine Superman* and *Mellow Yellow* in the UK as well as the two albums that had not been released at all in the UK, *The Hurdy Gurdy Man* and *Barabajagal*, in a four-CD box set issued by EMI called *Four Donovan Originals*.

With Donovan's name in the musical conversation once again, Donovan was contacted by legendary producer Rick Rubin to record an album. Rubin had produced the Johnny Cash album *American Recordings* in 1994, which had given the country star's career a resurgence in the 1990s, and the producer thought he could possibly do the same for Donovan.

The result was 1996's *Sutras*. Unfortunately, it didn't do as well as expected, but it nonetheless once again established Donovan as an active recording artist and his fan base rallied around it.

In the 2000s, Donovan released albums sporadically, culminating in the 2010 double CD studio album *Ritual Groove,* for which he encouraged fans to make their own videos for the songs. In 2013, he released an album of country-flavoured songs called *Shadows of Blue*. The last few years have seen a flurry of activity from the artist, including several archival releases such as *The Sensual Donovan*, a record he recorded in 1971 with John Phillips of The Mamas and the Papas producing, a tribute album to Harry Belafonte called *Jump In the Line*, and a compilation of his environmental songs called *Eco-Song*. In 2021, the year I started writing this book, Donovan released *Lunarian*, an album of re-interpretations of some of his earlier songs that were inspired by his wife Linda, coupled with a book of her photography. He also released two new singles, 'I Am the Shaman' and 'Gimme Some a That', both produced by avant-garde film director David Lynch who also shot the accompanying videos for the songs.

Throughout a career of over five decades, with twists and turns, ups and downs, Donovan has held on to his core values and never given up his message, the Bohemian Manifesto. His legacy is vast, from his hits of the 1960s when he led a love revolution, to influencing numerous artists from the 1960s to the present and impacting legions of fans worldwide. He is one of the most covered artists in existence, with, according to the website *Second Hand Songs*, 75 artists having covered 'Sunshine Superman', 48 covering 'Season of the Witch', 30 covering 'Hurdy Gurdy Man', 43 covering 'Mellow Yellow', 60 covering 'Colours' and a staggering 91 different artists having covered 'Catch the Wind', among many covers of his other songs.

Donovan's been criticised in recent years for too much self-aggrandising, but it is really hard to blame him? While contemporary 1960s artists like The Beatles, Bob Dylan and The Beach Boys, whom Donovan rubbed shoulders with, are still household names recognised by even many young people, Donovan's name often draws blank stares from those outside his fan base, despite his accomplishments, his influence and impact on music and culture. Why is that?

I think it began in the 1960s at the very beginning of his career, when the press unfairly tried to create a rivalry between Bob Dylan and the teenage Donovan by proclaiming him the UK's answer to Dylan, setting him up for mockery. Then there were the record label disputes that prevented the release of most of his classic 1960s albums in his UK home country or at least delayed their release. *Sunshine Superman* was legitimately one of the very first psychedelic albums ever recorded (The Beach Boys' *Pet Sounds* had come out just a few months earlier), but by the time of its partial release in the UK, the world had already heard subsequently recorded albums such as The Beatles records *Revolver* and *Sgt. Pepper's Lonely Hearts Club Band*, and Pink Floyd's debut, *Piper at the Gates of Dawn*. The UK release of *Sunshine Superman* limped in concurrently with The Incredible String Band's game-changing psychedelic folk album *The 5000 Spirits or the Layers of the Onion*, long after the singles 'Sunshine Superman' and 'Mellow Yellow' had left the UK charts.

But I think, perhaps, mostly, it was that Donovan was of his times. I've referred to him as the troubadour of the Flower Power generation. But Flower Power and psychedelia didn't last very long. The Woodstock Music and Art Fair was 'Three Days of Peace and Music' in August 1969, a cultural touchstone for that generation. But just months later, in December 1969, the Altamont Speedway Free Festival, which was supposed to be the West Coast's answer to Woodstock, ended with the murder of Meredith Hunter and was a collective bummer for that same generation. The cultural landscape was shifting. As the 1970s came on, the youth of the 1960s were becoming the adults of the new decade and with that came the responsibilities and pressures of adulthood. As Canadian singer-songwriter Dan Hill so memorably put it in his 1976 classic 'Hold On':

So you flung your fist high in the air
But the world remained the same
And all the demonstrations
Filtered out through graduation
And the times that were a changing
Never changed

In some ways, Donovan was part of those times that never changed, and he remained indelibly linked to them. As Tim Bowness said in his podcast *The Album Years* on 12 June 2020, 'Maybe the fact that he was sort of so immersed in the imagery of the era, he's been bypassed. Cause you know … this kind of psychedelic image and psychedelic sound seems to be all-encompassing for a very brief moment. It was quite ephemeral, really.' Donovan never saw his generation create that utopia of love and peace that he had envisioned and was sure was coming. The beautiful, bright colours of psychedelia slowly faded and with them, so did Donovan's fame and fortune. Donovan never gave up on his dream to be sure, but the rest of the world sadly did.

And yet, Donovan's music never entirely faded away. He's had a quiet influence on numerous artists and has had an impact on genres as diverse as folk music, trip hop, alt-rock, pop and jazz. His songs may not be heard often on the radio anymore, but they are heard often in advertising campaigns and on TV shows and in movies, often to evoke the past, especially the 1960s.

And isn't it possible that in these troubled times we live in, Donovan's message may be even more relevant than it ever was? It may not have brought about the utopia he envisioned, but it did and does give us something to hope for. And hope is a very powerful thing.

As I sit here at my desk writing these final words of the book, I'm listening to *Donovan's Greatest Hits*, where it all began for me. Something I notice now, though, while listening, is that in doing the research for this book, in delving deep into Donovan's life and his music, it has given me a whole new appreciation for these songs that I have been listening to and enjoying for almost 40 years now. I can listen to them with a new perspective, a kind of insider's insight into them which reveals refreshing new dimensions to me.

I hope that having read this book, it has done the same for you.

Resources

Books

Ferris, K., *The Karl Ferris Psychedelic Experience* (Blurb, 2021)
Harper, C., *Dazzling Stranger* (Bloomsbury Pub Ltd, 2007)
Leech, J., Weeks, G., *Seasons They Change* (Jawbone Press, 2011)
Leitch, D., *The Autobiography of Donovan: The Hurdy Gurdy Man* (St. Martin's Press, 2005)
Roxon, L., *Lillian Roxon's Rock Encyclopedia* (Grosset & Dunlap, 1969)
Tobler, J., Grundy, S., *The Record Producers* (St. Martin's Press, 1983)
Unterberger, R., *Jingle Jangle Morning: Folk-Rock in the 1960s* (Richie Unterberger, 2014)
Vassal, J., *Electric Children: Roots and Branches of Modern Folk Rock* (Taplinger, 1976)
Young, R., *Electric Eden,* (Faber & Faber, 2011)
Zollo, P., *Songwriters on Songwriting* (Da Capo Press, 2003)

Articles, Blogs & Podcasts

Unknown, 'Donovan' (*Goldmine,* Krause Publications, Inc., 13 November 1992, vol. 18, no. 23, issue 321)
Altham, K., 'Donovan: All Things Bright and Beautiful' (*New Musical Express*, 14 January 1967)
Altham, K., 'Donovan: "I Put Myself Into My Music"' (*New Musical Express Summer Special*, 1968)
Carpenter, J., 'Donovan: The Rolling Stone Interview' (*Rolling Stone*, 9 & 23 December 1967)
Cramer, J., 'A Very Candid Conversation with Shawn Phillips' (Stone Cold Crazy, 2018) (http://jeffcramer.blogspot.com/2018/07/a-very-candid-conversation-with-shawn.html)
Harrington, R., 'Donovan, Mellow Fellow' (*Washington Post*, 6 March 1997, https://www.washingtonpost.com/archive/lifestyle/1997/03/06/donovan-mellow-fellow/1b1e6f3b-c247-4fdf-a8d4-f58c736a0590/)
James, D., 'In The Shadow of Dylan' (*Rave*, 1965)
Saltzman, P., 'Donovan. The Beatles in India' (https://thebeatlesinindia.com/stories/donovan/)
Wilson, S., Bowness, T., *The Album Years podcast,* (12 June 2020), (https://anchor.fm/the-album-years/episodes/5-1967-The-Beach-Boys--Leonard-Cohen--Donovan--Love--more-efao6g)

Websites
http://donovan-unofficial.com/
https://donovan.ie/
https://secondhandsongs.com/
https://www.rocksbackpages.com
https://www.rollingstone.com/
https://www.songfacts.com/
https://www.officialcharts.com/
https://www.*Billboard*.com/
https://albumlinernotes.com/

Video/DVD
Pennebaker, D. A. (1967) *Don't Look Back*. Leacock-Pennebaker, Inc.
Rossacher, Hannes (2008) *Sunshine Superman: The Journey of Donovan*.
Ryko Distribution.
Squires, Charlie (1966) *A Boy Called Donovan*. BBC.

Other Resources
Lorne Murdoch's four-part essay 'The Mickie Most Years', spread across
EMI's 2005 deluxe reissues of 'Sunshine Superman', 'Mellow Yellow',
'Hurdy Gurdy Man' and 'Barabajagal'.

Joni Mitchell - *on track*
every album, every song

Peter Kearns
Paperback
160 pages
35 colour photographs
978-1-78951-081-1
£14.99
$21.95

Every album and every song by this legendary Canadian singer-songwriter.

In her long career, Canadian songstress Joni Mitchell has been hailed as everything from a 1960s folk icon to 20th century cultural figure, artistic iconoclast to musical heroine, extreme romantic confessor to both outspoken commentator and lyrical painter. Eschewing commercial considerations, she simply viewed her trajectory as that of any artist serious about the integrity of their work. But whatever musical position she took, she was always one step ahead of the game, making eclectic and innovative music.

Albums like *The Ladies Of The Canyon*, *Blue*, *Hejira* and *Mingus* helped define each era of the 1970s, as she moved from exquisitely pitched singer-songwriter material towards jazz. By the 1980s, her influence was really beginning to show via a host of imitators, many of them big names in their own right. He profound influence continues in popular music to this day.

This book revisits her studio albums in detail from 1968's *Song to a Seagull* to 2007's *Shine*, providing anecdote and insight into the recording sessions. It also includes an in-depth analysis both of her lyrics and the way her music developed stylistically over such a lengthy career, making this the most comprehensive book on this remarkable artist yet written.

Elton John 1969 to 1979 - *on track*
every album, every song

Peter Kearns
Paperback
144 pages
35 color photographs
978-1-78952-034-7
£14.99
USD 21.95

Every track recorded by music legend Elton John during the 1970s, arguably his most creative and most commercial successful period.

In 1970, Elton John, formerly Reginald Kenneth Dwight, stepped from the obscurity of suburban Pinner, Middlesex, England, into a pop culture reeling from post-Beatles fallout, to become one of the biggest-selling recording artists in the world. To date he has sold over 300 million records from a discography of 30 studio albums, four live albums, over 100 singles, and a multitude of compilations, soundtracks and collaborations. He is the recipient of six Grammys and ten Ivor Novello awards, was inducted into the Rock and Roll Hall of Fame in 1994, appointed a Commander of the Order of the British Empire in 1995 and knighted in 1998. In 2018 he embarked on what is intended to be his swansong world tour, *Farewell Yellow Brick Road*.

This book covers the period from Elton's earliest 1960s releases to his final 1970s album, *Victim of Love*. It is a critical overview of every track on the thirteen studio albums released in an era when Elton was at his most successful and that many fans consider to be the musical high-point of his career. Also included are the two live albums *17-11-70* and *Here and There*, and the trove of album-worthy B-sides that augmented the discography along the way.

Aimee Mann - *on track*
every album, every song

Jez Rowden
Paperback
160 pages
39 colour photographs
978-1-78951-036-1
£14.99
$21.95

Every album and every song by the innovative Californian singer-songwriter.

Any consideration of the songwriting craft would be incomplete without the inclusion of American singer/songwriter Aimee Mann. From her first steps as singer and bass player with 1980s synth pop band 'Til Tuesday, who scored a massive MTV hit with 'Voices Carry' in 1985, she has continually produced starkly autobiographical songs, with a sense of melody that cuts through the emotional detail.

With a career now spanning almost forty years, she has built a catalogue of nine studio albums, from debut *Whatever* to 2017's *Mental Illness*, since going solo in the early 1990s. Via a series of record label frustrations, Aimee has developed into a fiercely independent recording artist, flying outside the mainstream. Her critical acclaim has never wavered, however, and while happy to continue working in a niche market, her soundtrack for the film *Magnolia* and the accompanying Oscar nomination raised her profile considerably, adding to her stalwart army of fans.

This book gives an overview of Aimee Mann's career from her earliest days when she 'made it big' with 'Til Tuesday, through her solo career, investigating every recorded track. It is a comprehensive guide for fans and new listeners keen to investigate a double Grammy winner who is also a true original and whose work deserves to be much more widely recognised.

Roy Harper - *on track*
every album, every song

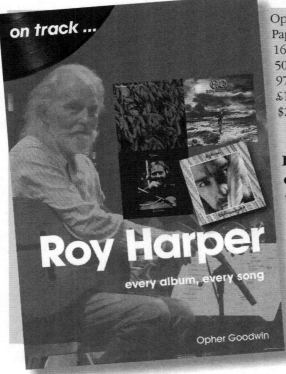

Opher Goodwin
Paperback
160 pages
50 colour photographs
978-1-78951-130-6
£14.99
$21.95

**Every album and
every song by
this legendary
troubadour.**

Roy Harper must be one of Britain's most undervalued rock musicians and songwriters. For over fifty years, he has produced a series of innovative albums of consistently outstanding quality, putting poetry and social commentary to music in a way that extends the boundaries of rock music. His 22 studio albums and 16 live albums, made up of 250 songs, have created a unique body of work.

Roy is a musician's musician. He is lauded by the likes of Dave Gilmour, Ian Anderson, Jimmy Page, Pete Townsend, Joanna Newsom, Fleet Foxes and Kate Bush. Who else could boast that he has had Keith Moon, Jimmy Page, Dave Gilmour, John Paul Jones, Ronnie Lane, Chris Spedding, Bill Bruford and Steve Broughton in his backing band? Notable albums include *Stormcock*, *HQ* and *Bullinamingvase*.

Opher Goodwin, Roy's friend and a fan, guides the reader through every album and song, providing insight into the recording of the songs as well the times in which they were recorded. As his loyal and often fanatical fans will attest, Roy has produced a series of epic songs and he remains a raging, uncompromising individual.

Laura Nyro - *on track*
every album, every song

Philip Ward
Paperback
160 pages
42 colour photographs
978-1-78951-182-5
£15.99
$22.95

Every album and every song by this legendary American singer-songwriter.

Laura Nyro (1947-1997) was one of the most significant figures to emerge from the singer-songwriter boom of the 1960s. She first came to attention when her songs were hits for Barbra Streisand, The Fifth Dimension, Peter, Paul and Mary, and others. But it was on her own recordings that she imprinted her vibrant personality. With albums like Eli and the Thirteenth Confession and New York Tendaberry she mixed the sounds of soul, pop, jazz and Broadway to fashion autobiographical songs that earned her a fanatical following and influenced a generation of music-makers. In later life her preoccupations shifted from the self to embrace public causes such as feminism, animal rights and ecology – the music grew mellower, but her genius was undimmed.

This book examines her entire studio career from 1967's More than a New Discovery to the posthumous Angel in the Dark release of 2001. Also surveyed are the many live albums that preserve her charismatic stage presence. With analysis of her teasing, poetic lyrics and unique vocal and harmonic style, this is the first-ever study to concentrate on Laura Nyro's music and how she created it. Elton John idolised her; Joni Mitchell declared her 'a complete original'. Here's why.

Warren Zevon - *on track*
every album, every song

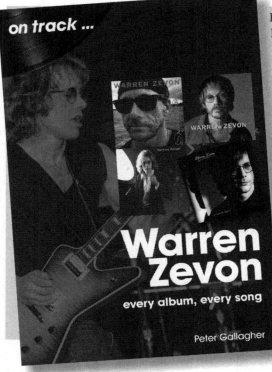

on track ...

Warren Zevon
every album, every song

Peter Gallagher

Peter Gallagher
Paperback
128 pages
40 colour photographs
978-1-78951-170-2
£15.99
$22.95

Every album and every song by this underappreciated American songwriter.

Bruce Springsteen called him 'one of the great, great American songwriters', Jackson Browne hailed him as 'the first and foremost proponent of song noir' and Stephen King once said that if he could write like Zevon, he 'would be a happy guy'. The list of artists that lined up to appear on his records include Springsteen, Neil Young, Bob Dylan, Dave Gilmour and Emmylou Harris. So how is it that most people, if they have heard of Warren Zevon at all, know him only as 'that werewolves guy'?

This book goes beyond that solitary hit single to examine all aspects of Zevon's multifaceted, five-decade career, from his beginnings in the slightly psychedelic folk duo Lyme and Cybelle, through to his commercial breakthrough in the late Seventies with *Excitable Boy*, his critically acclaimed late Eighties comeback *Sentimental Hygiene*, his decline into cult obscurity, and his triumphant if heart-breaking final testament *The Wind* released just prior to his death in 2003.

Along the way, the reader will discover one of rock's consummate balladeers, as well as his cast of characters, which include doomed drug dealers, psychopathic adolescents, outlaws of the Old West, BDSM fetishists, ghostly gunslingers and, yes, lycanthropes unleashed on the streets of London.

On Track series
Alan Parsons Project – Steve Swift 978-1-78952-154-2
Tori Amos – Lisa Torem 978-1-78952-142-9
Asia – Peter Braidis 978-1-78952-099-6
Badfinger – Robert Day-Webb 978-1-878952-176-4
Barclay James Harvest – Keith and Monica Domone 978-1-78952-067-5
The Beatles – Andrew Wild 978-1-78952-009-5
The Beatles Solo 1969-1980 – Andrew Wild 978-1-78952-030-9
Blue Oyster Cult – Jacob Holm-Lupo 978-1-78952-007-1
Blur – Matt Bishop – 978-178952-164-1
Marc Bolan and T.Rex – Peter Gallagher 978-1-78952-124-5
Kate Bush – Bill Thomas 978-1-78952-097-2
Camel – Hamish Kuzminski 978-1-78952-040-8
Caravan – Andy Boot 978-1-78952-127-6
Cardiacs – Eric Benac 978-1-78952-131-3
Eric Clapton Solo – Andrew Wild 978-1-78952-141-2
The Clash – Nick Assirati 978-1-78952-077-4
Crosby, Stills and Nash – Andrew Wild 978-1-78952-039-2
The Damned – Morgan Brown 978-1-78952-136-8
Deep Purple and Rainbow 1968-79 – Steve Pilkington 978-1-78952-002-6
Dire Straits – Andrew Wild 978-1-78952-044-6
The Doors – Tony Thompson 978-1-78952-137-5
Dream Theater – Jordan Blum 978-1-78952-050-7
Electric Light Orchestra – Barry Delve 978-1-78952-152-8
Elvis Costello and The Attractions – Georg Purvis 978-1-78952-129-0
Emerson Lake and Palmer – Mike Goode 978-1-78952-000-2
Fairport Convention – Kevan Furbank 978-1-78952-051-4
Peter Gabriel – Graeme Scarfe 978-1-78952-138-2
Genesis – Stuart MacFarlane 978-1-78952-005-7
Gentle Giant – Gary Steel 978-1-78952-058-3
Gong – Kevan Furbank 978-1-78952-082-8
Hall and Oates – Ian Abrahams 978-1-78952-167-2
Hawkwind – Duncan Harris 978-1-78952-052-1
Peter Hammill – Richard Rees Jones 978-1-78952-163-4
Roy Harper – Opher Goodwin 978-1-78952-130-6
Jimi Hendrix – Emma Stott 978-1-78952-175-7
The Hollies – Andrew Darlington 978-1-78952-159-7
Iron Maiden – Steve Pilkington 978-1-78952-061-3
Jefferson Airplane – Richard Butterworth 978-1-78952-143-6
Jethro Tull – Jordan Blum 978-1-78952-016-3
Elton John in the 1970s – Peter Kearns 978-1-78952-034-7
The Incredible String Band – Tim Moon 978-1-78952-107-8
Iron Maiden – Steve Pilkington 978-1-78952-061-3
Judas Priest – John Tucker 978-1-78952-018-7
Kansas – Kevin Cummings 978-1-78952-057-6

The Kinks – Martin Hutchinson 978-1-78952-172-6
Korn – Matt Karpe 978-1-78952-153-5
Led Zeppelin – Steve Pilkington 978-1-78952-151-1
Level 42 – Matt Philips 978-1-78952-102-3
Little Feat – 978-1-78952-168-9
Aimee Mann – Jez Rowden 978-1-78952-036-1
Joni Mitchell – Peter Kearns 978-1-78952-081-1
The Moody Blues – Geoffrey Feakes 978-1-78952-042-2
Motorhead – Duncan Harris 978-1-78952-173-3
Mike Oldfield – Ryan Yard 978-1-78952-060-6
Opeth – Jordan Blum 978-1-78-952-166-5
Tom Petty – Richard James 978-1-78952-128-3
Porcupine Tree – Nick Holmes 978-1-78952-144-3
Queen – Andrew Wild 978-1-78952-003-3
Radiohead – William Allen 978-1-78952-149-8
Renaissance – David Detmer 978-1-78952-062-0
The Rolling Stones 1963-80 – Steve Pilkington 978-1-78952-017-0
The Smiths and Morrissey – Tommy Gunnarsson 978-1-78952-140-5
Status Quo the Frantic Four Years – Richard James 978-1-78952-160-3
Steely Dan – Jez Rowden 978-1-78952-043-9
Steve Hackett – Geoffrey Feakes 978-1-78952-098-9
Thin Lizzy – Graeme Stroud 978-1-78952-064-4
Toto – Jacob Holm-Lupo 978-1-78952-019-4
U2 – Eoghan Lyng 978-1-78952-078-1
UFO – Richard James 978-1-78952-073-6
The Who – Geoffrey Feakes 978-1-78952-076-7
Roy Wood and the Move – James R Turner 978-1-78952-008-8
Van Der Graaf Generator – Dan Coffey 978-1-78952-031-6
Yes – Stephen Lambe 978-1-78952-001-9
Frank Zappa 1966 to 1979 – Eric Benac 978-1-78952-033-0
Warren Zevon – Peter Gallagher 978-1-78952-170-2
10CC – Peter Kearns 978-1-78952-054-5

Decades Series
The Bee Gees in the 1960s – Andrew Mon Hughes et al 978-1-78952-148-1
The Bee Gees in the 1970s – Andrew Mon Hughes et al 978-1-78952-179-5
Black Sabbath in the 1970s – Chris Sutton 978-1-78952-171-9
Britpop – Peter Richard Adams and Matt Pooler 978-1-78952-169-6
Alice Cooper in the 1970s – Chris Sutton 978-1-78952-104-7
Curved Air in the 1970s – Laura Shenton 978-1-78952-069-9
Bob Dylan in the 1980s – Don Klees 978-1-78952-157-3
Fleetwood Mac in the 1970s – Andrew Wild 978-1-78952-105-4
Focus in the 1970s – Stephen Lambe 978-1-78952-079-8
Free and Bad Company in the 1970s – John Van der Kiste 978-1-78952-178-8
Genesis in the 1970s – Bill Thomas 978178952-146-7
George Harrison in the 1970s – Eoghan Lyng 978-1-78952-174-0

Marillion in the 1980s – Nathaniel Webb 978-1-78952-065-1
Mott the Hoople and Ian Hunter in the 1970s – John Van der Kiste
978-1-78-952-162-7
Pink Floyd In The 1970s – Georg Purvis 978-1-78952-072-9
Tangerine Dream in the 1970s – Stephen Palmer 978-1-78952-161-0
The Sweet in the 1970s – Darren Johnson 978-1-78952-139-9
Uriah Heep in the 1970s – Steve Pilkington 978-1-78952-103-0
Yes in the 1980s – Stephen Lambe with David Watkinson 978-1-78952-125-2

On Screen series
Carry On... – Stephen Lambe 978-1-78952-004-0
David Cronenberg – Patrick Chapman 978-1-78952-071-2
Doctor Who: The David Tennant Years – Jamie Hailstone 978-1-78952-066-8
James Bond – Andrew Wild – 978-1-78952-010-1
Monty Python – Steve Pilkington 978-1-78952-047-7
Seinfeld Seasons 1 to 5 – Stephen Lambe 978-1-78952-012-5

Other Books
1967: A Year In Psychedelic Rock – Kevan Furbank 978-1-78952-155-9
1970: A Year In Rock – John Van der Kiste 978-1-78952-147-4
1973: The Golden Year of Progressive Rock 978-1-78952-165-8
Babysitting A Band On The Rocks – G.D. Praetorius 978-1-78952-106-1
Eric Clapton Sessions – Andrew Wild 978-1-78952-177-1
Derek Taylor: For Your Radioactive Children – Andrew Darlington
978-1-78952-038-5
The Golden Road: The Recording History of The Grateful Dead – John
Kilbride 978-1-78952-156-6
Iggy and The Stooges On Stage 1967-1974 – Per Nilsen 978-1-78952-101-6
Jon Anderson and the Warriors – the road to Yes – David Watkinson
978-1-78952-059-0
Nu Metal: A Definitive Guide – Matt Karpe 978-1-78952-063-7
Tommy Bolin: In and Out of Deep Purple – Laura Shenton 978-1-78952-070-5
Maximum Darkness – Deke Leonard 978-1-78952-048-4
Maybe I Should've Stayed In Bed – Deke Leonard 978-1-78952-053-8
The Twang Dynasty – Deke Leonard 978-1-78952-049-1

and many more to come!

Would you like to write for Sonicbond Publishing?

At Sonicbond Publishing we are always on the look-out for authors, particularly for our two main series:

On Track. Mixing fact with in depth analysis, the On Track series examines the work of a particular musical artist or group. All genres are considered from easy listening and jazz to 60s soul to 90s pop, via rock and metal.

On Screen. This series looks at the world of film and television. Subjects considered include directors, actors and writers, as well as entire television and film series. As with the On Track series, we balance fact with analysis.

While professional writing experience would, of course, be an advantage the most important qualification is to have real enthusiasm and knowledge of your subject. First-time authors are welcomed, but the ability to write well in English is essential.

Sonicbond Publishing has distribution throughout Europe and North America, and all books are also published in E-book form. Authors will be paid a royalty based on sales of their book.

Further details are available from www.sonicbondpublishing. co.uk. To contact us, complete the contact form there or email info@sonicbondpublishing.co.uk